Praise for *Isabella Moon*

"*Isabella Moon* mixes the paranormal, crime, and romance in a plot that exposes the sordid side of a small town . . . the ending holds more than one surprise."
—*The Boston Globe*

"*Isabella Moon* is a tense and creepy hunt for the truth about what lies beneath. . . . Laura Benedict's debut will definitely have readers sleeping with the lights on—if they sleep at all."
—LISA UNGER

"There are plenty of secrets in this thickly atmospheric debut novel. . . . Kate Russell is a complex and captivating character."
—*Alfred Hitchcock Mystery Magazine*

"An engrossing, many-layered story."
—*Mystery News*

"Fast-moving . . . Laura Benedict has written an amazing debut novel. . . . [Her] characters, plot and dialogue are all written on the level of a more experienced author."
—*Daily American News*

"A rich read—deliciously complex."
—LEE K. ABBOTT, author of *Living After Midnight*

"Told with intelligence, precision, and an essential artfulness, Laura Benedict's haunting and sharp *Isabella Moon* is not unlike *The Lovely Bones*, but bigger, faster, and with a much broader scope. You won't forget these characters or the story that fuels them. A joy to read from first to last."
—FRED G. LEEBRON, author of *Out West*

BALLANTINE BOOKS NEW YORK

ISABELLA MOON

A NOVEL

Laura Benedict

2008 Ballantine Books Trade Paperback Edition

Copyright © 2007 by Laura Benedict

Published in the United States by Ballantine Books,
an imprint of The Random House Publishing Group,
a division of Random House, Inc., New York.

BALLANTINE and colophon are registered trademarks of
Random House, Inc.

Originally published in hardcover in the United States by Ballantine Books, an imprint of
The Random House Publishing Group, a division of Random House, Inc., in 2007.

LIBRARY OF CONGRESS CATALOGING-IN-PUBLICATION DATA

Benedict, Laura.
   Isabella Moon : a novel / Laura Benedict.
      p.   cm.
   ISBN 978-0-345-49768-0 (acid-free paper)
   1. Missing children—Fiction.   2. Supernatural—Fiction.   I. Title.
   PS3602.E6627I83   2007
   813'.6—dc22   2007016274

Printed in the United States of America

www.ballantinebooks.com

987654321

Book design by Dana Leigh Blanchette

FOR MY PARENTS,
JUDY AND JERRY PHILPOT

Acknowledgments

A first novel has a lot of history behind it. It would be impossible to thank everyone who contributed to the genesis of this one. But the list would be woefully incomplete without the following people:

Kermit "Pig Helmet" Moore, my favorite sheriff's deputy and true Renaissance man, not only read the novel in its early stages, but was also my consultant for all things law enforcement. Doctors Tom Eldridge and Mark Todd joyfully provided medical and drug information. Debra Cook provided invaluable funereal details. Erin Jones was my consultant for all things hair.

I have found a wonderful, if slightly accidental, home at the David Black Literary Agency. For many years, I was able to give my extraordinary agent, Susan Raihofer, only friendship and the promise of a novel. She took my work seriously long before even I was able to. Her advice, friendship, and encouragement continue to mean the world to me. Leigh Ann Eliseo has also been terribly good to me since those early days. And I'm grateful to David Black, the man himself, for letting me hang around.

Everyone at Random House and Ballantine Books, including and especially, Gina Centrello, Libby McGuire, Kim Hovey, Rachel Kind, Paul Taunton, Beck Stvan, and Shona McCarthy. And, most important, my editor, Mark Tavani, to whom I owe an unparalleled debt of gratitude for, as they say, taking a chance on me.

Many thanks and much affection to Mr. and Mrs. Raymond Smith for their encouragement and the kindest series of rejections a writer could hope for. I'm also grateful to Janet Hutchings of *Ellery Queen Mystery Magazine* and Amanda Cockrell of Hollins University.

Finally, there are those to whom I owe a debt of the heart: Monica Wilmsen and Teresa McGrath, Cleve and Ann Benedict, Barbara Bowe, Andy Beedle, Cindy Foster, Cynthia Todd, Sue Thoms, William and Margaret Tear, Vera Wilson, and especially, Maggie Caldwell. Pinckney, Nora, and Cleveland—you are my reasons for living.

Isabella Moon

KATE WAS SURPRISED when the stern-looking young woman at the duty desk told her to take a seat instead of just asking her name and sending her on her way when she announced, in a voice she could barely keep from shaking, that she knew where they could find the body of Isabella Moon. Maybe it was the hesitant way she spoke, her purse clutched protectively against her stomach. Although there were deep shadows beneath her eyes, with her auburn ponytail and cashmere sweater and tweed slacks, she knew she didn't look like a standard nutcase—she wasn't coffee-splattered or disheveled, she wasn't waving napkins with lipstick maps on them. She looked like a patient mother of young children (she had none), or perhaps a librarian (she was not). She looked trustworthy, she knew. But more than once during the bleak, endless hours of the previous night, as she'd waited by her window for the stubborn sunrise, her resolve to tell what she knew had flagged. If she was so filled with doubt about her own sanity, what right did she have to imagine that the sheriff would think differently?

She settled into one of the molded plastic chairs facing the wire-studded window that separated the waiting area from the sheriff's inner office. Not wanting to look like she was staring, she tried to keep her eyes on the clock on the wall above the sheriff's desk. She'd had no breakfast and her mouth was dry. A water cooler sat on a stand only a few yards away, but she was so nervous that she didn't trust herself to cross the room.

Behind the glass, the deputy leaned over the sheriff's desk, presumably telling him why she was there. For a brief moment Kate's eyes met the sheriff's, but she quickly looked away. She'd seen him on the street before, but not up close. Jessup County was prosperous, but not so wealthy that politicians spent campaign money on billboards bearing their photographs. She had voted for him in the last election not because she liked him or knew anything about him, but because the man running against him had brushed purposefully against her while they waited for their take-out lunches at the crowded counter of the Carousel Café. It wasn't even so much that he touched her but that he had reeked of stale cigarette smoke.

As soon as she looked away from the sheriff—his eyes had been frank and curious, not at all dismissive as she'd feared—she regretted it. People who lie avoid eye contact. And she wasn't lying. At least, not about this.

Most days, Sheriff Bill Delaney really liked his job. Given that Carystown was a county seat, he found himself spending more time than he liked in the courthouse, but it was the rare day that he couldn't make his way home for lunch with his wife, Margaret, who was the director of the Cary-Lowe House, a museum in the historical district that bore her family's name. Back before he'd made detective in Louisville, he worked hellacious hours that kept them apart nights. He would let himself into their apartment after his shift ended at 8:00 A.M. to find breakfast in the oven and a note on his pillow, but there was no substitute for Margaret herself, whose curved, soft body molded itself to his hands with an urgency that never ceased to amaze him. Now, even though he wasn't much more than a tax collector with a sidearm, he couldn't imagine going back to those lonesome, empty days.

The young woman on the other side of the glass seemed to have sharper edges than his Margaret. He'd seen her going in and out of Janet Rourke's insurance agency and in restaurants with a local guy who worked for the timber company. There was a closed-in look about her, but she was a pretty thing, fine-boned and slender in the way of young women from the city and the junior matrons around town. He didn't know for a fact how long she'd been in Carystown, and was only sure she was newer to the area than he was. Twelve years hadn't bought him too much familiarity. He only had his job because the Lowes—Margaret's family—had been among the first settlers in the area and Margaret herself was liked by the local pols.

"She seems all right," Daphne said. "Looks a little stuck-up maybe."

It was a very Daphne sort of judgment. Daphne herself bordered on the homely, but she bore her elegant name with bravado. How many times had he heard various town jokers refer to her as "Deputy Daffy" to her face? She was a quick sort who either gave it right back to them or made sure they knew she wasn't in a mood to play. She was also a mean shot with her .45 Glock. With the exception of Frank Skerrit, an ex-Marine who was his most reliable deputy, he would rather have Daphne at his side in a shoot-out than anyone else. He was particularly leery of the younger ones who only went to the range when their annual qualifications were coming up. Plus, Daphne was built like a truck, and her narrow, hooked nose and seemingly permanent scowl meant that only the drunkest of her charges were distracted by the fact that she was a woman. Margaret liked to say that Daphne's infrequent smiles were like "sudden rays of sunshine in a tornado."

"Go on," Bill said. "Bring her in and get us both some coffee. She looks like she's had a rough one."

But instead of going straight for the coffee, Daphne stood up to her full five-two height and looked to the ceiling and sighed.

"Please, ma'am," Bill added.

The case of the missing girl was still open but had been on the back burner for most of the last year for an almost complete lack of evidence—lack, even, of a body. It was his personal opinion that the child had run away. She had a crazy hippie for a mother and lived in a kind of commune without any other kids around for all of her nine years. But of course the woman on the other side of the glass probably had no idea how things stood. He just hoped that she wasn't going to tell him she was some kind of psychic. He had zero time for that kind of bullshit.

Isabella Moon's disappearance almost two years before had filled the town with satellite trucks and frantic reporters, male and female, trailing grubby young men with shoulder-mounted cameras and racks of bright lights. He had grown weary of their changeable faces and instantly sincere smiles. Far stranger, though, was the small collection of earnest amateur psychics and healers that had shown up in his office. Several of them eventually drifted over to Iris's Whole Foods and Tea Shoppe to congregate after Daphne put them in their places, one after the other. A couple had never left town.

It was a damned shame that the child had never turned up, dead or alive, but he sure didn't miss the circus that had engulfed Carystown for weeks. He wasn't looking for it to return, ever. But he decided there was no reason to give this woman a hard time. She was good-looking, and they did have to live in the same small town.

Finally seated across the desk from the sheriff, Kate accepted the paper cup of coffee from Daphne with a grateful "Thank you." She hadn't even bothered to ask for decaf, as she usually would. Her body felt hollowed out. Anything warm would do. She was sure that she would never sleep again anyway.

As she gingerly sipped the strong brew, the sheriff sat back down in the chair from which he had risen to greet her and motioned to the delinquent tax roll printouts on his desk.

"Funny how no one wants to pay their taxes," he said. "But just let the county miss one garbage pickup and they're lined up from here to Sunday."

Kate thought to say that death and taxes are the only sure things in life, just as she'd often heard her grandmother say. But then she remembered why she was there.

They sat in silence for a long minute. The telephone on Bill Delaney's desk buzzed once, startling them both into brief, nervous smiles, but Daphne was quick to pick it up at her desk. When the sheriff got up to close the door, which Daphne had left open a few inches, Kate relaxed a bit. She'd wondered if the deputy left it open on purpose.

"It's been a long time since anyone's come forward with information about that child," he said. "Several months anyway. Folks have lost interest." He absently crossed a line through a dead woman's name on the tax roll. "I'm guessing we fielded ninety, a hundred calls a day from all over the country when it first happened. A couple came in from England. You can imagine they weren't much help. More of a novelty for Daphne."

"It was strange to see the town on the news every day," Kate said. "But it never actually *looked* like Carystown on television. It was like they were talking about somewhere else."

"We had a couple movie agents and such interested, thinking the story might sell, I guess," Bill said. "In the end, there didn't turn out to be much of a story, did there?"

Kate shook her head. "No. I guess not."

As Bill leaned back in his chair, it made a painful squeak. "How long have you lived in Carystown, Miss Russell?"

Kate took a deep breath. This was more like what she had expected. If he believed her at all, he was sure to look at her as a suspect first.

"A little more than two years," she said. "I have a house south of town near the old candy factory. It's an antique mall now, but everyone still calls it the candy factory."

The wind still sometimes carried the scent of chocolate through her windows. It had been on just such an afternoon that she'd rented the house after living in an inexpensive motel out near the highway for a few weeks. The factory building hadn't yet been converted when she moved in, but was just a cavernous brick fortress with boarded windows, fronted by a long, crumbling porch. Such a vast emptiness so close to her house had overwhelmed her in those first months, but the smell of the chocolate was something of a comfort. And in those early, alone days, she had needed it.

"Best peppermint sticks in the country," Bill said. "Never cared much for their chocolate stuff. Moved the operation down to Mexico about five years ago. Too bad." He shook his head.

"We get a lot of tourists in for the antiques," Kate said.

"Ah, yes, the tourists," Bill said with apparent distaste. "So, have you ever been to Mexico? Is that a travel agency you work for?"

Kate wondered how long he was going to play with her. She was sure he'd want to hear what she had to say.

"Insurance," she said. "Janet Rourke's agency." She looked at her watch. "I should be there now to open up. Janet had a breakfast meeting."

"Good Rotarian, Janet. Assertive," he said. "Gets things done." What Janet Rourke really was was a bitch on skates. But he guessed that his opinion wouldn't be a surprise to this young woman. "You from somewhere south of here, Miss Russell? Alabama, maybe? Georgia?"

Kate straightened in her chair. "I lived in South Carolina for a long time. Around Charleston." It was enough of the truth. Just because he was some kind of policeman didn't mean that she could trust him. "But this isn't about me, Sheriff," she said, knowing she was breaking one of the cardinal rules of southern conversation. One didn't blurt out one's business right off; one was supposed to come around to things gradually, delicately, give everyone involved time to know exactly who stood where on a subject. There was a lot of courtesy involved. Only Yankees came at things straight on.

But it had taken her so long to come to the decision to speak to someone, someone who might be able to help her, that she just wanted to get on with it. The girl was dead, yes, but she was hardly resting in peace. She seemed almost as alive to Kate as in the weeks before she disappeared two winters before, when she'd occasionally walked past the agency in her bright yellow coat and red snow boots. Isabella Moon hadn't been an extraordinarily pretty child, but Kate had noticed her (thanks to the coat, probably) and wondered at her careful, self-possessed way of walking, as though she were much older than she appeared.

The suffering of the girl's mother also caught her attention, and disturbed her. She had seen Hanna Moon on the news and, more frequently, on the streets of Carystown. Hanna Moon looked lost to her, and, somehow, more childlike than her daughter had been. Truth be told, she looked a little crazy. Even in cold weather she wore colorful, loose linen dresses of the sort favored by the women of the area's hippie community and woven sandals. Her thick black hair was often twisted into a braid that hung down to her waist and tied with a ribbon, just as her daughter had worn hers in the photo that had been reproduced and taped onto windows and nailed to telephone poles all over town. Sometimes Hanna Moon appeared to be talking to herself, or, at least, to someone who wasn't there.

It had been that singular photo of the smiling nine-year-old, her eyes wide and serious, that finally prompted Kate to come to the sheriff. Most of the photos had long since been taken down, but a couple days after Isabella Moon came to her in the night, she saw one taped to a coffee can at the drugstore where she'd gone to get some sort of over-the-counter sleeping pill. The can had been pushed back into a corner behind the cash register and was surrounded by rolls of register tape, old coupons, and rags. It seemed to have been forgotten, like the little girl herself. Something about the way the tape had worn off at the edges so that the photo was in danger of curling itself off the can drew her attention. The can was turned so that HELP US was all she could see of the words below the photo. From memory she knew that the whole sentence read: "Help Us Find Our Isabella Moon."

She felt like she was losing her mind, so invaded had she been by the need to reveal what she knew, what Isabella Moon (*It was the child herself, wasn't it? Not some devil or evil spirit that I don't believe in, anyway, right? God, how am I to know?*) apparently wanted her to tell.

"Please," Kate said. "Will you just listen to me?"

Bill Delaney had nothing better he wanted to do that Friday morning, and he was a man who hated to see another human being suffer—particularly a woman. So he listened, even though he wasn't quite sure that he could trust her.

Mary-Katie.

The voice is a whisper, calling a name that doesn't belong to her anymore.

Mary-Katie.

Kate struggles as though she's escaping from a troubled sleep, her movements slow and exaggerated, as in a dream. But if it is a dream, why does she slip some nearby shoes onto her feet as she gets out of bed? Who thinks of shoes in a dream?

The hillside outside her window is bathed in silver light, and there, beneath the hickory tree shading the back porch, is a girl.

Mary-Katie.

The voice doesn't seem to be coming from the girl, but from inside her own head. Her breath fogs the glass as she watches, knowing that the girl wants her to come outside.

Suddenly she is following the girl over the hill and across the open pasture on its other side. Her feet are light as she runs—yes, she is running!—through the brittle stubble of the winter grass. The few lights of the town are ahead of her. She doesn't often go into town this way, usually preferring to stick to the familiar road that runs in front of her own little cottage. But the ground is firm and fast under her, and she wonders why she doesn't come this way every day.

The girl disappears into the dark stand of trees at the edge of the pasture, but she knows the girl is still there, waiting. Even if she has run on ahead, Kate understands that she will find her. She is meant to find her.

There she is, standing in the street beyond the trees, her brilliant yellow coat vibrant as a bale fire in the night.

Kate runs faster, and the girl turns her back and leads her on toward the town, through the grounds of the old medical college, where the buildings stand mute and shuttered, through the backyard of the crumbling president's house, where a single rusting bulldozer sits as testimony to someone's forgotten plans.

As the girl runs out into Main Street without pause, Kate's heart jumps, but there are no vehicles at all, not even a straggling log truck or a sheriff's cruiser. As they pass the glassy storefronts, Kate is racing her own mirror image, but she can't stop, she won't stop, because the girl will not slow now. They cross over to Bridge Street and follow it until it ends in a blinking yellow light. Will the girl go left or right?

When she goes left at the corner and disappears behind a tall hedge, Kate keeps going. As she passes the Methodist parsonage with its stiff wrought-iron fence, she wishes that she had a stick to hit against its spindles and realizes at the same moment that, yes, there is a stick in her left hand. But when she reaches out with it as she runs, there is no satisfying plunkplunkplunk of wood against iron. In fact, there is no sound around her at all except the sound of her feet striking the pavement: no dogs, no sirens, no night birds. She's not afraid. She is certain once again that she is dreaming.

The girl reappears in the light from the street lamp at the next corner.

Isabella!

How does she know the girl's name? She hadn't seemed to know it when she looked out her bedroom window to see the girl standing beneath the hickory tree like someone's lost shadow.

The girl pauses at Kate's voice but doesn't turn around. Kate sees that her dark hair is shot with glimmering strands of silver. But she knows the girl can't be more than ten years old and the silver is just a trick of the light from the street lamp's broad halo.

Isabella!

The girl begins to run again.

Kate drops the stick, thinking it might speed her progress. In the next block there is a rottweiler who growls when she passes on her regular evening walks, and she has often carried a stick as a sort of talisman, thinking she would use it on him if she had to. But still there are no animal sounds, no lights on in any of the houses she passes, no cars slowing down to see why a woman is running through the streets in the middle of the night in her pajamas, wearing a scuffed oxblood loafer on one foot and a tan and white nubuck slip-on on the other. She is safe from the dog, at least.

They approach Birchfield Avenue, where her friend Lillian lives. But instead of going down Lillian's street, the girl enters the first road, one where there are no street lamps. This road—she doesn't know if it even has a name—twists through a set of woods for a distance, to finally end at the town's water processing plant. No one lives back here in this no-man's-land, the unofficial divide between Carystown's small black community and the rest of the town. Amazed that she is not winded, she nearly catches up with the girl, who has finally slowed. Without street lamps, the road is black at their feet and the trees around them are like walls reaching to the sky. But Kate can see well enough: the silver in the girl's hair is its own light, and she follows her easily.

Isabella must want her near. As they slow to a walk, Kate realizes that the girl is as silent as everything else around them. If it weren't for the scuffing of her own feet, she would think she'd gone completely deaf.

Without warning the girl leaves the pavement and heads across the road's shoulder.

Wait!

As Isabella pushes her way through the brush, Kate tries to keep up. But the girl seems unhindered by the brambles and tangle of slender branches that whip against Kate's arms and face. The brambles sting, and Kate laughs to herself that it must be a pretty pitiful dream if she can't even keep from getting scratched up in it.

Now they are in a clearing that Kate can't remember ever seeing before. Part of its ragged circle is an expanse of brick that shines a brilliant white even in the dim moonlight. She has the feeling that if she were to put her hand against the wall and push, ever so lightly, it might disappear. She has that feeling, too, about the tall cedars that rise around them, their uppermost branches drawn together in soft, wavering points against the sky. Beneath her feet the ground is spongy, and she is surprised to realize that the clearing, though silent, has a distinct smell. She covers her mouth with her hand.

She thinks about those times when she wakes herself to use the bathroom in the night, turning on the light, even pinching her thigh as she sits down to urinate to make sure that she is not dreaming, that she is not about to drench herself and her bed. Now, she resists pinching herself because she has begun to suspect that she is not dreaming. She knows that if she rests her fingers against her thigh and squeezes, the pain will be just as real as the smell of decay filling her nostrils.

She calls to Isabella, who stands in the center of the clearing. But the girl only sinks to her knees, her silvered hair falling forward over her yellow coat.

As Kate approaches her, the wind picks up around them and the smell intensifies. Unafraid, Kate reaches out, thinking to touch the girl, to stroke her young head, to reassure her that someone is there, that someone wants to help her. But her fingers touch nothing and she is alone in the clearing.

She stands there for a moment as the sounds of the woods and beyond reveal themselves: a screech owl in some distant barn, a rabbit or raccoon hurrying through the brush, a truck downshifting out on Route 12. Suddenly cold in the pajamas that had been fine for a March night spent beneath a down comforter, Kate wraps her arms around herself as though it will make a difference and begins to think about the long walk home.

FRANCIE CAYLEY AND HER MOTHER, Lillian, were already at their regular table at The Lettuce Leaf when Kate arrived, out of breath from hurrying from the office. She relished the idea of a break from her own thoughts. All morning at her desk she couldn't help but wonder what the sheriff had really thought of her and what she'd had to say.

No matter what her state of mind was, she couldn't help but smile when she saw Francie and Lillian together. Like a pair of carefully altered copies of a single person, they had the same high forehead and finely etched cheekbones. Lillian's clear mahogany skin was almost as unlined as Francie's lighter skin, but Francie's nose and cheeks were dotted with freckles that made her look even younger than thirty-two. The freckles were a constant bone of contention between the two women: Lillian insisted that Francie had brought them on herself by not wearing a hat or sunblock when she went out during the day; Francie said that they were the one permanent thing her father had given her, a part of him that no one could ever take away.

"Will you please tell my daughter that if she doesn't eat something besides burgers she's going to end up with saddlebags on those size six thighs?" Lillian said, looking up at Kate. "Sit down, honey. You all look like something the cat dragged in."

Kate leaned over and brushed Lillian's cheek with a kiss. Lillian smelled of Coco and lavender. Kate slid into the chair across from Francie.

Francie looked up from her menu and rolled her eyes at Kate. "*Soy* burgers, Mother," she said. "No one gets fat from soy burgers."

Lillian touched the bun high at the back of her head. Despite her hair's severe style and her sixty-plus years, she looked stunning and carried herself more like a well-preserved fashion model than the schoolteacher she had been for most of her life.

"Everyone gets fat from eating fried foods," she said. "And those burgers are fried in something nasty."

"Francie's the nurse," Kate said. "She knows what's good for her." She grinned at Francie, who shut her menu and slid it to the edge of the table.

"You should listen to Kate, Mother. She's a smart girl."

Francie took in Kate, who was studying her own menu. Smart girl or no, Kate looked a few beats off, not quite as put together as she usually was. Her skin, always fair, was paler than ever, and the whites of her hazel eyes were red and heavily veined, as though she'd been weeping or staring too long at a computer screen. A worn smear of lipstick covered her lips, which looked rough and bitten. Concerned, Francie reached out and lightly touched Kate's arm.

"You still not sleeping?" she asked. "You *do not,* as my mother says, 'look like something the cat dragged in.' But you do look tired."

Kate smiled. She didn't want to offend Francie, but there were times when Francie seemed to want to get too close to her. She knew that she was a difficult friend to have, and she was grateful that Francie had hung in with her the past couple of years, ever since they'd met in a book group at Carystown's small public library.

And they *were* close, but how could she tell Francie that a little girl who'd been missing for two years and presumed dead had appeared outside her bedroom one night, wanting her to come out, to follow her into the darkened town? How could she tell her about the cloying odor of decay—*and had there been honey as well?*—that had filled her nostrils so that she thought she'd never breathe clear air again?

"Construction at the antique mall," Kate said. "They start those saws at six in the morning, like no one lives around there."

"That porch has been a disgrace as long as I can remember," Lillian said. "I don't know what they're thinking, restoring more of that place. As though it's not already just fine to sell people old junk. It's a firetrap if you ask me."

"Right," Francie said, ignoring her mother. "If you say so, Kate." She had learned not to press Kate too hard, particularly in front of other people. Kate had confided something about her life before Carystown, but not much. Francie knew that Kate was pretty much alone in the world, and she, who'd had the love of both of her parents for at least a time and had been treasured her whole life, felt protective of her.

As they ate, Kate also updated them on the construction of Janet Rourke's new house west of town. With its six chimneys, horse pastures, and iron gates salvaged from the demolition of one of the grandest houses in the area, it was the talk of Carystown. Kate had become the job's unofficial foreman, and as a result, was having a hard time keeping up with the office paperwork. Francie and Lillian were thrilled to have inside information about it, especially Francie, who entertained the other nurses on the second shift with stories of Janet's tantrums.

"The granite for the countertops in the kitchen and the granite for the bar didn't quite match, but I thought they looked fine," Kate said. "Janet was so pissed off that she took one of those huge chisels they use and threw it so hard that a big chunk came out of the bar piece and it's going to cost her an extra two thousand to get another one."

It was a relief to Kate to be able to talk about Janet, even though she knew it was gossip and that she shouldn't gossip about the woman who signed her paycheck. She needed the paycheck more than she cared to admit. The money she'd brought with her to Carystown had covered her rent for a while and the purchase of her car, but there was very little left. But everyone talked about Janet. She was a bitch, and a bit of a joke with her better-than-you attitude toward even the moldering town mothers and fathers. Then again, as the sheriff had said, she knew how to get things done.

A few minutes before one, Kate signaled for the check. She had to get back to the office.

"No, you don't," Lillian said. "It's my turn to treat today. You girls need to save your pennies."

The three of them argued politely for a few moments, but when the check came, it was brought not by the waitress, but by someone else.

Like every other attractive woman who spent more than a few weeks in Carystown, Kate had had a date with Paxton Birkenshaw. They were about the same age, and Paxton had the Birkenshaw name to recommend him. (She'd seen it on Carystown street signs, an office shingle, and on a plaque on the front of the historic Episcopal church building.) She hadn't been much interested in dating at all, but the other woman in the office, Edith, who had worked for Janet for years, was a fellow garden club member of Paxton's mother.

"Old, old family, you know," Edith had said. "And Paxton went east for prep school and some college. I don't know that he actually graduated, mind you. I think he didn't get along well with the dean or some such nonsense." She paused a moment. "There was something about a frozen turkey and a broken television. But I don't think anything was proved."

Kate had wanted to laugh, but covered her mouth so as not to offend Edith, who was kindhearted and seemed not to want to see her lonely. (Lonely was just what she was looking for then. But that was before she'd met Francie, who cheered her, and Caleb, a man whom she was just beginning to trust.) She had imagined Paxton as a giant, spoiled child, perhaps wearing plaid pants and glasses and a shirt with a tiny embroidered figure of a man on a polo pony on it.

But Paxton himself appeared neither to be an eternal frat boy nor a preppy nerd. Paxton Birkenshaw was a damned good-looking, muscular charmer of a man.

Their evening together was pleasant enough, but they hadn't clicked. Kate was still uneasy about her new life and didn't have much to share as far as the details of her past went. But it didn't matter because Paxton contented himself with telling her tales of the county where his family had lived since before the Civil War. Watching him speak, his blue eyes animated with amusement at his own stories, Kate could see that, confident as he appeared, what he really wanted was an audience. He might have been a movie actor, with his shock of blond hair and extraordinarily white teeth that seemed to emanate a subtle glow in the dim restaurant in which they ate. She relaxed, finally, and let him talk on until nearly midnight.

At her door, they shared a friendly handshake (*that* had been a surprise—she thought she rated at least a peck on the cheek), and Kate watched him drive away in his vintage Mercedes coupe. He never called her again after that night, and she never expected him to. Now they exchanged hellos on the street or in restaurants, but that was about it. She had since come to the conclusion that while Paxton Birkenshaw was attractive, he was not particularly bright. With his bounding gait and effusive manner, he reminded her of an overbred Labrador retriever.

"It would be my pleasure to take care of this for you ladies," Paxton said, standing over them. "Particularly you, Mrs. Cayley."

The waitress hovered uncertainly behind him. Francie waved her away.

"I was sitting over there at my little table in the corner and saw the three of you and thought: 'Now, there's a table of goddesses.' It was as if Dido, Oshun, and Ala were chatting about how to wreak havoc in the lives of us mere mortals."

Kate glanced across the table at Francie, who was shaking her head and wearing a look that Kate could only describe as one of disgust. She wasn't sure who Dido, Oshun, and Ala were. These days, though, she wasn't feeling like much of any sort of goddess. *More like god-cursed.*

Lillian, though, seemed willing to play along. At least for the moment. "That's very kind of you, Paxton," she said. "Please give your mother my best."

She turned back to the table as though Paxton might just wander away to the cash register.

Paxton instead took her words as an invitation. As he sat down in the chair beside Kate, he folded the check in half and tucked it into the inside pocket of his sport coat. His skin wore a healthy-looking tan and there were faint, whitish lines at his temples where his sunglasses had been. Kate wondered briefly if he would remember to pay the check.

"Sick as she is, she'll outlive all of us, ma'am," he said. "I just brought her back from Hilton Head—"

Kate had been trying to look interested despite the fact that she was due back in the office right at that moment. But at his words, her arm gave a reflexive jerk and she knocked over her iced tea glass.

Lillian and Francie immediately took to the mess with their napkins. Within seconds the waitress was there with a towel.

"I'm sorry," Kate said. "I'm such a klutz."

As they cleaned up, Paxton continued as though nothing had happened. "She had plenty of time to relax by the water and had us all waiting on her hand and foot."

Abruptly changing the subject, he said, "Kate, I hear you've really taken our favorite insurance agent's new house in hand. Contractors around here aren't much used to taking their orders from a woman, but I guess most of them are down here from Louisville or Cincinnati. Things are different there, I believe." He leaned close to her, as though he would speak confidentially. "Or maybe it's because you're a woman—a darned good-looking woman—that makes them say 'how high' when you say 'jump.' "

Kate blushed, something that aggravated her but that she was prone to do. She went on the defensive. "Actually, they've all been very nice." (This was just a little white lie—some of the men, particularly the subcontractors, had been downright rude and she'd had to have them fired.) "And so far, none of the contractors, not *even* the local ones, have said anything about a penis being required for the job."

"Ha!" Francie said.

Paxton laughed, too, but his had a hint of uncertainty about it.

Kate did not look at Lillian, afraid that she had offended her.

"Now, I don't think we would have heard anything like that kind of language back in Mrs. Cayley's classroom, would we have, Mrs. Cayley?"

Lillian sat up straighter in her chair. "I do believe that I have even said the word 'penis' myself in the classroom, Paxton. I've always taught that we should use the proper words for things."

Kate smiled with relief.

"Paxton, I think the goddesses have wreaked havoc with you today," Francie said.

"Touché, Francie," Paxton said. He turned to Kate. "Mrs. Cayley is all about teaching me lessons. You know, she once smacked my hands so hard with a ruler that I couldn't hold a baseball bat for a week."

"You might have whacked *me* with a baseball bat, Paxton, if you hadn't been kept in line," Lillian said. "You were that mean."

Kate was embarrassed for him, but Paxton just laughed.

"I was a boy with a temper then, ma'am," he said. "I had too much icing on my cupcake and you taught me how to be respectful. I needed that."

"I wonder if that lesson will ever stick with you," Lillian said. "Respecting your elders' opinions."

"Mama," Francie said quietly.

Paxton laughed again, but this time seemed ill at ease.

There was an awkward moment when no one spoke. The waitress noisily bused the table beside them, dropping glasses and plates into her tub as though they were made of something sturdier than glass and porcelain.

"I need to get back to the office," Kate said, pushing her chair back.

"Well, a man's got to respect *that*," Paxton said, flashing her a smile. His teeth were so perfect, Kate wondered if they were capped. "I'll move on," he said. He stood up and gave a curt bow. "Ladies. It's been a distinct pleasure."

"Paxton," Lillian said.

Kate gave him a polite nod.

When he was safely at the waitress station paying the bill, Lillian rapped her knuckle lightly on the tabletop.

"Strangest boy I ever knew to teach," she told Kate. "Generous to a fault one minute—you remember, Francine, when he had his mother bring ice cream for the whole school every day for a week during that heat wave?"

Francie blinked. "I recall," she said. "What a show-off."

"Then there was that time it was said he tried to run over that boy in the Winn-Dixie parking lot over the Christmas holidays."

"That Paxton," Francie said. Kate heard a strong note of sarcasm in her voice. "He's so unpredictable."

"Amen to that," Lillian said. "Best none of us should forget it."

3

BILL DELANEY HAD just zipped up the back of his wife's wool skirt and lifted her hair to lightly kiss the back of her neck as a *thank-you* for obliging his lunch hour whim when his pager buzzed on the nightstand.

"Must be your lucky day," Margaret said with a laugh. "Daphne's timing's way off. She usually catches us before we can even get the window shades down."

"Daphne would be shocked," he said.

Margaret smiled at her husband's naiveté; it was one of the things she treasured about him, his innocence about the ways and knowledge of women. Sometimes it got him into trouble, but her life was maybe a little more amusing because of it.

"Oh, I don't know that she'd be so surprised," she said. "Daphne knows what a woman wants."

"As the kids say, 'I don't think I want to go there,'" he said. He let his hand slide slowly down to his wife's bottom and squeezed. "Um, um," he said. "Now, that's sweet."

Margaret gave her hair a flirtatious toss and stepped way from him and over to the mirror to brush it. He loved to watch her brush her hair. He pretty much loved to watch her do anything: butter toast, read a magazine, scrub the bathtub, balance the checkbook. Eight years before, he nearly lost her to ovarian cancer, but she had beaten the odds and licked it. Sometimes, when they lay together, he would run his finger over the rough scar that crossed her pelvis like a souvenir from a brutal battle. It was a battle that had cost her nearly all of her female insides and hadn't let her get far from the house for almost a year, except to go to the cancer center up in Lexington, but she had won it.

There had been a few guilty moments back then, when he imagined a life without her, during lonely, empty nights when he had to leave her alone at the hospital. He thought of them with shame now. He'd suffered a lack of faith in her, in their marriage, in God. He hadn't had faith in anything. When it was finally over, he decided that it had been Margaret's stubbornness that got them through.

"Guess we can fool around all we want now," she'd said, looking up at him from her hospital bed after the anesthesia from the radical hysterectomy had worn off. Her skin was jaundiced because her liver function was low, and her hair—cut short to hide the fact that the chemo had taken so much of it—rested in dark, damp curls about her face. Still, her eyes were just as bright and blue as the day he'd met her at a U of K alumni barbecue.

"Just try to keep me away," he'd told her. And he was true to his word. Who knew if he was making up for lost time, or trying to reassure her, whatever—at nearly fifty years old, he was hot after her like a teenage boy on a prom queen.

The pager buzzed again.

"They can't live without you," Margaret said over her shoulder. "I need to get back anyway. There's a seniors' bus tour coming in at two."

"My lucky day," Bill said, shutting off the pager.

"Frank says it's one of the kids from the east end of the county, out near Anderson," Daphne said. "You want me to send somebody out to the kid's house?" Bill could hear Daphne's tiny portable television playing her afternoon soap in the background.

"Sounds like Frank's got it all figured out," he said. One of his most conscientious deputies, Frank liked to lay claim to and hold cases as long as he could, reporting to him only when he knew he had to. Bill understood that it was just enthusiasm, but probably had something to do with his long tenure as an enlisted Marine.

"He's over at the medical center talking to the docs," Daphne said. "The kid had a heart attack in the ambulance."

"Tell him I'm on my way," he said. "And Daph, turn off the tube before you get back on the radio. We don't need it going out over everybody's scanners."

"You bet, boss," she said, her voice devoid of repentance.

Slowed by Friday afternoon traffic around the Buyer's Mart store straddling the town/county line, Bill flipped on his blues to get the minivans and pickups out of his way. The medical center was a couple miles outside of town, in what Margaret jokingly referred to as Carystown's suburbs: a rocky expanse of countryside dotted with cheap subdivisions and car dealerships. There was no reason to hurry, and he didn't like to use the siren if he could help it. Daphne hadn't said, but he would have bet a stack of dollars that it was some kind of overdose that had gotten the kid. If it wasn't the occasional hunting accident or severe beating inflicted by their so-called friends, the kids who died in and around Carystown usually did it to themselves—suicide by shotgun or a noose slung over a sturdy tree branch in the family woods. These days, though, drugs were often the cause, sometimes intentional, sometimes not. From the numbers he'd seen, the county stats, percentagewise, weren't so different from those of Louisville or Lexington.

Once he got past the Buyer's Mart, traffic was clear for a mile or so, until he came up fast on a stuttering and ancient VW bus whose driver apparently wasn't checking his rearview mirror. Bill hung back, looking to go around it, but after a steady line of oncoming traffic they came up on a lengthy blind curve and he started to get impatient. He knew the bus, one of three owned by the Chalybeate Springs Co-op Farm, which was just around the curve.

The co-op had actually begun its life as a commune, a place for hippies from up East to get back to nature. They had been there fifteen years by the time he and Margaret had come to Carystown, getting by on a truck-farming scale, selling vegetables in the farmer's market in town, harvesting honey from their bees, and peddling pottery at craft shows. But in the last few years, with the help of a questionable character by the name of Charlie Matter, they'd managed to tap into the Internet for their goods, selling their pottery and honey all over the country. Now, a professionally painted sign had replaced the rotted wooden shingle at the co-op's entrance. At the end of the operation's gravel drive sat two hundred acres of prime farmland with an iron-rich spring that gave it its name. The commune had bought the land cheap from a do-nothing named Glenn who wanted to make the place into a resort but never scared up the money to build anything but a big metal shed over the fifteen-by-twenty pool where he and his buddies drank beer and floated themselves in the sulfurous water for their rheumatism.

And here was one more thing Chalybeate Springs was known for: it had been the home of Isabella Moon.

When the VW bus slowed further, and turned into the farm without benefit of a turn signal, Bill sped past.

Isabella Moon hadn't been far from his mind that day. It wasn't the girl herself so much as the woman who said she knew where the girl's body was buried. He tried to figure what kind of angle the woman might have, coming to him. Her story had been damned strange, if not downright loopy, full of mysterious figures in the night and voices—no, not voices, but *thoughts* that spoke inside her head, which the woman said weren't hers, if he had it right. Certainly she was nuts. She had asked him, *begged* him, really, to follow up on it, to go and see for himself if her information was correct. She had been agitated, but earnest. She didn't seem to understand that he couldn't (or wouldn't) just grab a shovel and go digging. He wondered if he shouldn't check her out with Janet Rourke. Then again, he'd rather put a fork in his eye than ask a favor of Janet Rourke. There was that other woman in the office, Edith, who might be more approachable. He wanted to be careful, though. When law enforcement asked even the most casual questions around town, people got nervous.

Pulling into the hospital's parking lot, Bill noted wryly that two of the town's five cruisers were parked in the fire lane outside the medical center's emergency room. He slid his own into one of the spaces marked POLICE CARS ONLY at the close-in parking lot.

In the E.R. examining area, Frank, a couple of emergency technicians, and another deputy, Clayton Campbell, stood in a grim cluster, giving desultory attention to the boy on the gurney. The heart monitor was shut off. Some other machine clicked in regular intervals, but the boy himself was obviously dead.

"Bill," Frank said. "Come on over." He introduced Bill to the doctor, a woman about his own age wearing improbable red high-heel pumps with her otherwise rather dull doctor's jacket and shapeless gray dress. With her oversprayed hair and flashy jewelry, she looked more like a trashy sort of schoolteacher than a doctor, but Bill reckoned that it took all kinds. Shaking his hand, she looked directly into his eyes, serious.

After the introductions, Bill got down to business. "Any kin available?" he said. "What do we know?"

Frank read from his notes.

"Brad Catlett. Seventeen. Good student, according to the coach. Cross-country runner. Lives out near Anderson," he said. "Collapsed playing basketball during gym period right after lunch."

"Any contact injuries?" Bill asked. "Did anyone see him go down?"

"A gym full of boys and girls," Frank said. "The gym teacher. Looks like a straight-ahead heart attack to me. Maybe some congenital thing." He nodded toward the doctor, who was looking restless. "But what do I know? What do you say, Doc?"

"Let's get him covered up," she said to one of the technicians. "Has someone contacted the boy's parents?"

"No answer at home, the cell phone number on his school emergency card was no good," Clayton offered.

The doctor looked at a sheet on the clipboard in her hands. While she read over the EMT's notes, she tapped the head of a pen against the metal. "We know we're looking at some kind of heart event, but without any history to look at or a look inside, I can't tell you much right now. His blood pressure and body temperature were through the roof. His temp was 105 when they got to him—that's abnormal for an attack brought on by a heart defect. Sounds more like an infection, maybe, but there would have been other symptoms. Had he been ill this week? Do we know if he was sweating a lot or nauseated, vomiting?" She looked at Frank.

"No, ma'am," he said. "But I'll try to find out."

"That's it, then," the doctor said. "We'll get on it, make sure we're not dealing with some sort of contagion. But beyond that, we won't know much until we get the autopsy done. And we'll need the next of kin for that."

Given the kid's tender age, Bill couldn't see sending Frank or one of the other deputies out alone to talk to the parents, though it was a part of the job he really disliked. He walked over to the gurney and lifted the corner of the sheet.

Brad Catlett was a good-looking kid. Probably had a cheerleader girlfriend who liked to bake him chocolate-chip cookies. That was his own fantasy, of course. He knew that just because a kid had neatly cut hair and kept his face shaved, he was not necessarily an angel. Girls, too, at this age (and younger) were also as likely to be into drugs and alcohol, or even home porno movies just for kicks. There had been a scandal at the high school last year when they'd had to arrest the sixteen-year-old daughter of the political science teacher on prostitution charges. The girl had managed to take down a long-haul trucker and a lawyer from the next county, too, who testified that he'd been told she was eighteen. He'd since been disbarred and then divorced by his wife, but he hadn't bought any time. It was still a small state in a lot of ways.

The boy's face was already ashen and empty. One of his eyelids revealed just a sliver of white, as in a lewd wink. His skin still looked taut, only raw around the nostrils—coke, maybe, or just from blowing a hundred times during a cold. Bill didn't recognize him, but saw in him every white or black or Hispanic or Asian kid whose death he'd had to follow up on in the past twenty-five years. They all looked the same in death whether they were shot up, cut up, or overdosed. They looked wronged, often mildly surprised, like it shouldn't have happened to them.

He reached over and closed the boy's eyelid the rest of the way.

"Tox screen, don't you think, Doc?"

"Part of your friendly coroner's package," she said. "As long as you ask."

Outside, Bill got the boy's address from Frank, who looked a little rough around the edges. No one liked to see a kid die. Or perhaps there was trouble at home with his young wife, Rose, who'd developed MS a couple of years ago. Frank worried a lot about Rose.

"Want company, Sheriff?" he asked.

The boy's house was way out in the country, just shy of the next county line. It never ceased to amaze Bill that kids from out here had to ride a bus into town for almost an hour to and from school each day.

The east end of Jessup County was dirt poor. Just at the edge of worn-out coalfields, it had no industry except a small amount of timber to recommend it. Some years before, a congressman had managed to get a textile company to relocate here from the North, but once the tax relief and bonuses it extracted from the county petered out, the jobs started to slowly disappear. Finally, the entire operation had shut down. Most of the folks in the neighborhood were on some kind of disability. For some families, disability—carpal tunnel, Epstein-Barr syndrome, back trouble, whiplash—was the family business.

Bill and his deputies spent a fair amount of time out here, serving notices and enacting foreclosures. He was often asked to tag along with the BATF or the Feds when they went after the pot growers or the rare whiskey still in the area. There was nowhere else to hold the suspects except the county jail, which was his province. No one out here was ever glad to see him, and he wasn't particularly glad to see them.

When Brad Catlett's mother answered the door, Bill knew immediately that someone who knew what happened had reached her. She was a trim woman, athletic, different from the area's usual overweight welfare mavens. Her face was mottled with hives from her weeping. She had the same fine features as her son, the same small bump on the bridge of her nose and prominent cheekbones.

"Our pastor's wife works at the school," she said as he entered with Frank. "I was out in the garden shed earlier. Won't be too long before we can put in some broccoli," she added, as though they needed the explanation.

She offered them coffee, but before they could say no, she said that she forgot she was out. The three of them stood in awkward silence for a moment. Tears slid down her face and her body began to shake with sobs. Frank guided her to sit in a chair.

Photos of Brad Catlett sat on several surfaces of the room: the television cabinet, a shelf above the couch, a side table. The photos spanned his entire short life, from Brad as a drooling infant in a jump seat, to a grinning six-year-old showing off a missing front tooth, and Brad and his father standing proudly beside a restored 1970 GTO. Brad had been the Catletts' only child.

Frank spoke in quiet, comforting tones to the woman. Bill was glad that he'd come along.

"I need to see Brad," the woman said. "Why can't they bring him home? He should be here with his mama. He didn't finish up his breakfast this morning. He's always in such a hurry, that boy. Always wanting to go somewhere."

"They need him at the hospital right now, Mrs. Catlett," Bill said. "Is Brad's father close by? In town?"

"He works at the Toyota plant," she said. "I don't want to tell him over the phone. He'll go crazy."

The plant was an hour's commute from this end of Jessup County; Bill considered that dedication to making a living. It looked like the Catletts were probably good people.

"Somebody will contact him, Mrs. Catlett," he said, making a mental note to put Daphne on it. "Can you tell me if Brad had any heart problems?"

"It's stupid," she said with disgust. "Those stupid doctors. I don't know what happened to Brad or what the people at that school did to him, but he's got nothing whatever wrong with him. He's had a cold for a while, maybe a little allergy with spring and all. But there was nothing wrong with his heart. He was a runner, for God's sake. He would run with me, five, ten miles a day, sometimes."

"Frank, maybe Mrs. Catlett could ride back into town with you," Bill said. "She needs to get to her boy at the hospital."

"Sure thing, Sheriff," Frank said. "Maybe there's somebody you want to call to meet us there?"

As though on cue, the telephone in the kitchen began to ring.

"Do you mind if I take a look around Brad's room, Mrs. Catlett?" Bill said. He hoped that in the confusion of the phone ringing and her desire to get to the hospital, she wouldn't think too hard about it.

She didn't. As she got up to answer the telephone, she waved a hand toward the hallway. "The last bedroom," she said, and disappeared into the kitchen.

"I'd call that permission," Frank said in a low voice. "I'll stay here."

He knew it was probably unnecessary, but Bill pulled on a pair of plastic gloves as he went into the boy's bedroom. It was remarkably tidy for a teenager's room: the bed was made and there were no dirty clothes littering the floor. The dresser, television, and video game console were free of dust and the goo that he knew generally went along with having kids. He suspected that Mrs. Catlett ran a pretty tight ship.

With expert speed he pawed through the boy's clothes-filled drawers and found nothing unusual but a plastic Baggie filled with condoms (*Extra Ribbing for Extra, Wild Pleasure!*) and, in a drawer's corner, a few loose pot seeds that were so old they'd lost their scent.

There were pictures in this room, too. These were unframed, taped to the mirror or stuck on the bulletin board: more shots of the car; a snapshot of the boy, younger, with a famous astronaut (space camp, maybe?); and several of pretty girls smiling shyly for the camera. Maybe he was an okay kid, after all.

On the way out of the room he noticed the Buyer's Mart bag hanging on the back of the door. Inside were five or six boxes of cold medicine, the liquid nighttime stuff, and several boxes of generic cold tablets. He wondered if the mother had bought them herself or if it had been the boy, hiding things in plain sight.

4

FRANCIE LET HERSELF into the apartment a few minutes before two o'clock. She had two hours before her shift at the hospital began, but she would have plenty of time to get there. Closing the door softly behind her, she could hear noise from a television in the apartment below. She had come into the building through a side door that opened onto a sheltered sidewalk, so she was certain that she hadn't been seen.

She dropped her purse into a chair and sat down on the edge of the couch to slip off her shoes. Stretching her legs out in front of her, she surveyed her feet. The night before, she'd given herself a pedicure, scraping her heels and soles with a pumice stone and slathering them with a rose-scented lotion she'd gotten in a Christmas gift exchange. Then she trimmed her toenails and painted them a delicious, golden apricot color. Even in this uncomfortable place, she preferred bare feet.

No one had been in the apartment for several days, and it had a stuffy, shut-in feel to it. She went to the window and turned the casement handle to let in some air. With it came the sounds of Middleboro's afternoon traffic. Only fifteen minutes up the highway from Carystown, Middleboro was less of a town than a suburban accident. From the window, she could see four fast-food restaurants (she'd driven through them all more than once on her way to work), five gas stations, and a single minimall with a grocery store, hair salon, cheap shoe store, and dollar store. The other thing that Middleboro had in abundance was hastily constructed apartment complexes, like the one that held the apartment in which she stood.

The apartment was ugly. But it hadn't been her idea to rent the place, and it certainly wasn't her money. The walls were painted an uninspired yellow, someone's lame attempt at getting beyond the standard beige of most furnished places, and the cushions of the couch were a badly faded puke green and covered in dark stains that spread over them like amorphous blossoms. The two tables in the room were of some kind of veneered plywood, their grains like no wood she'd ever seen. A single chair and floor lamp with a shade whose shape vaguely resembled an elephant's head sat in a corner. When she'd first seen the lamp shade, she laughed, thinking it was a joke, but it had lost its bizarre charm for her now. There was nothing funny about the thing. The two dark spots like eyes on either side of the shade seemed to watch her expectantly from across the room, asking her some question. She didn't know what, but she imagined she wouldn't like what it was.

Thirsty, she went to the kitchen and switched on the dusty radio by the sink. It was tuned to the only AM station that came in fairly well here, one that played obnoxious oldies music that had been old even when she was a little girl: the Chi-Lites, the Four Freshmen, the Supremes, Chuck Berry. But it was company.

With the Coasters cooing on about someone's new love, she opened the cupboard to find a glass. As she reached inside, a cockroach flung itself onto the counter. When she opened her mouth and let out a shrill little shriek, the thing scuttled down the front of the cabinet and into an open drawer.

"What's all the noise about, Buttercup?" Paxton shut the door behind him and slid the chain onto its bar.

Francie hurried out of the kitchen, her skin crawling with goose bumps. "You don't even want to go in there," she said. "This place gets nastier every time we come here."

"What? Our little love nest?" Paxton said, crossing the room, his arms open to her.

"It's nasty," she said, turning her back on him. She hated that he made her feel petulant, hated asking him for things. Even so, there wasn't really so much wrong with the place. Someone could spray for the bugs.

As she knew he would, he wrapped his arms around her and pulled her against his chest. She relaxed against him. There was something about the bulk of his body—he'd played football at prep school and a couple years of intramural at college before he was thrown out—that made her feel wonderfully small and cared for.

But she was sure that he didn't care for her, not deeply anyway, despite his promises to the contrary. It was sex that he wanted from her, and, if she were honest with herself, it was what she wanted from him. Or maybe it was something more than that. At that moment, though, she didn't really give a damn.

Paxton began to gently massage her arms, her shoulders, letting his hands caress her upper back, rubbing circles with the pads of his thumbs on the back of her neck. The sounds of the traffic disappeared for her as he moved his hands down the front of her body, lingering on her breasts, feeling the shape of them with his fingertips and carefully sliding the buttons of her blouse out of their holes. As his fingers worked, he put his lips against her hair, the tips of her ears, and breathed softly on her.

She began to help him with the buttons of the blouse, and the two of them together slid it off her body and it dropped to the floor.

He turned her around to face him and lifted her off her feet so she could wrap her legs around him. She hung her head back and laughed as he carried her to the bedroom.

"You were *such* an asshole at lunch today," she said. "What was all the goddess bullshit?"

"Was I?" he said, sounding just the slightest bit winded from carrying her. "Maybe I meant to be an asshole. We have to keep our secret, right?"

When he dropped her on the bed, she scrambled to pull the spread over herself. The March afternoon was cool and damp, and there'd been no heat on in the apartment overnight. But he reached for her and pulled her back to him.

"No, you don't," he said.

"You are the meanest thing," she said. "I'll freeze to death." And to prove her point, she pretended to shiver, chattering her teeth and giving her shoulders a shimmy.

"You are so fucking sexy," he said. "I want the rest of your clothes off."

"I thought I was a goddess," she said. "Not your screw toy."

"Same difference," he said, roughly unbuttoning her jeans.

~

Everything about Francie made him feel like his prick was going to explode. At lunch he'd had to make an effort to keep from staring at her, from putting his hand right up inside that tight-fitting top she'd been wearing. He'd had to concentrate on being polite to her too-sainted mother and that bitch Kate, who always had a stick up her ass. Ever since Francie and he were fifteen and he came back for the summer after his first year of prep school to find that she was working at the snack bar at the swim club, he'd found it almost impossible to be around her without wanting to fuck her right there and then.

On her breaks at the pool, he would find himself staring at her, then, drawn from the safety of his buddies to crouch down near the lounge chairs where she sat with her friends, he would joke around with her. He pretended nonchalance, but his body frequently betrayed him—he learned quickly to wrap a towel around his waist before he approached her. What he really wanted to do was to coax her back onto the grassy hillock behind the snack bar, throw off the towel, and jerk her bikini bottoms off and give it to her. But he never did.

It was torture, the way she had ignored him.

Francie was the only black girl in the group, but her skin was such a light caramel color that she didn't look much different than the deeply tanned and sunburned girls around her. It wasn't long before those girls, the ones who expected his attention as their due—Molly Bean, Arabella Taylor, the rich girls—caught on, and before the end of June, Francie was spending her breaks alone.

But it didn't help him. She refused to go out with him no matter how many times he asked or how many times he called her house. He knew she wanted to, he could tell by the way she pushed her carefully straightened hair behind her ears when he approached her. Each time she said no, he knew she wanted to say yes.

Once. There had been one small break in her reserve. She'd gotten off early one afternoon and he followed her home, riding his bike in the street beside her as she walked the mile to the East End, not far from the slaughterhouse.

He was silent, inarticulate with desire for her.

She surprised him by stopping dead in the road in front of a vacant lot that was thick with burdock and trash.

"Here," she said, pulling at the sleeve of his T-shirt so that he nearly toppled off the bike. She stepped forward and put her hand behind his neck. He was smaller then, only a few inches taller than she. He hadn't yet had the growth spurt that would put him over six feet.

Her kiss was insistent, surprising, her tongue cool and small and frantic in his mouth. His erection came on quickly, but his mind was too filled with her to give any thought to it.

In a moment it was over. She stepped back and regarded him with serious brown eyes.

"I thought so," she said. Then she turned and ran through the lot, quickly disappearing into the brush at the edge of it, so that by the time it occurred to him to run after her, he saw the flash of a single white tennis shoe in the greenery, and she was gone.

The next day, as though a result of some cruel magic, his mother got wind of it all—he didn't know how. Perhaps from Marlette, the day woman who also lived in the East End.

His mother stopped him as he was on his way out the door to ride his bike into town. She didn't even look at him, but at herself as she stood at the hall mirror to check her makeup before going to garden club. "Paxton, honey, you're making a spectacle of yourself," she said. And that was all.

When he got to the swim club, Francie wasn't there. When he called her house, he was told by Mrs. Cayley that she was "out" and would be for the foreseeable future. As small as Carystown was, he didn't see her the rest of the summer.

They lay beside each other, the sheets beneath them soaked with sweat.

"Are you warm now?" Paxton asked, cuddling against her.

"You really are an asshole," she said. "But, yes, I'm warm enough." She grabbed her watch from the dusty windowsill above her head. "I've got to get to work. You made me late last week."

He put a hand on her breast and dropped his head to bite playfully at the nipple he held between his thumb and forefinger.

"Ouch!" she said.

"You liked it a few minutes ago," he said. "What? Tired of me already?"

"That was an hour ago," she said, pulling away from him and getting out of bed. "I'm grabbing a shower. Did you get new soap?"

Paxton rolled over and watched her walk across the room. He liked how perfectly proportioned her body was from her butt to her well-toned shoulders. If her thighs were the tiniest bit broad at the tops, it only served to make her more interesting.

"You know," he said, "you could quit that stupid job and stay here and be my fuck-bunny forever."

Francie paused in the doorway of the bathroom. It upset her when he talked like this. She knew that he could easily support her in a place like this or one five or six times nicer. And in the back of her mind, wasn't that what she really wanted? To be connected with Paxton in some kind of semipermanent way? Did she dare even think the word *married*? How many times, as a kid, had she daydreamed of being Mrs. Paxton Birkenshaw, replacing his high-hatted mother in the house at Bonterre, that big damned horse farm that the Birkenshaws had owned forever?

But *this* is what she had instead, and, somehow, it suited her for now. Even though she hated herself every time she came in the door of their pathetic "love nest." Even though she hated herself only slightly less when she went out again.

"You wish," she said, closing the bathroom door behind her.

5

THERE WASN'T MUCH TRAFFIC on the road, but Kate stayed at its graveled edge, wary of the occasional car full of teenagers out for a Friday joyride. She had zipped her fleece anorak and pulled on thick gloves against the early evening air, but still, she was almost grateful for the cold. It would keep her going, and she needed the walk to clear her head.

Ironically, living in a small town with little traffic and a lot of countryside around it hadn't been particularly good for her walking habit. No one walked here unless it was to do business or shop in town, where there were sidewalks. And those were limited to seven or eight streets with which she'd become very familiar. Janet had once taken her aside to tell her that people had been asking about her, that she'd become a kind of character, someone known for walking down roads at times when no one had any business walking, as though she couldn't afford a car or was up to something illegal. Janet seemed to take their criticism of her as a personal offense, and Kate understood that the lecture meant she was probably supposed to stop. But that had been more than a year ago, and she was still walking whenever and wherever she felt like it.

She hadn't had a definite route in mind today, but as the Methodist church came into view, she knew that she was being drawn to the East End yet again. Of course, now it was of her own volition, her own choice.

Going back there was like picking at a scab: she couldn't let the damn thing heal—she had tried, she'd gone to the sheriff, hadn't she?—and was driven to worry it, to keep the wound fresh. She couldn't let go of the thought of Isabella Moon.

The streetlights stopped near the beginning of Birchfield Avenue. They had never been extended into the East End. "Darktown" is what she'd heard it called once by Edith in the office. In response to her puzzled look, Edith, who always seemed to be at least functionally educated and enlightened, had shrugged and said, "You know, the East End." Kate understood that the neighborhood's nickname hadn't come from its lack of streetlights.

"Kate, honey, come on over here," Lillian called from her porch. She had been sweeping when Kate approached, and wore a cotton scarf tied at the back of her neck to keep the dust off her hair.

There were evenings when Kate was happy to see Lillian outside when she walked by her house, which was always a landmark for her on this particular route. But at that moment she would've preferred to pass by unnoticed; the small clearing to which Isabella Moon had led her was part of the cemetery not far from Lillian's house.

When she waved but didn't immediately go up to the house, Lillian said, "I've got one of those giant éclairs from the bakery for my dessert, but I can't eat it all myself. Coffee, too."

Kate sighed. *So much for her plans.*

She made her way up the walk through Lillian's tidy yard, with its row of trimmed boxwoods along the porch and heavily mulched islands of azaleas and rhododendrons in the grass. Though the trees in the neighborhood had just begun to show the faintest of buds, a wave of sunny daffodils rose out of the gray dusk to beckon her forward. The stained-glass panels that Lillian's father had made so many years ago as a wedding present for Lillian's mother poured forth a faint, warm light onto the lawn. Lillian's house looked like a home.

Kate followed Lillian around the back of the house. Inside, Lillian took her anorak and gloves, then hung her own sweater on a hook just beside the door. The kitchen was ablaze with light and smelled of lemon potpourri and chicken soup.

"There's nothing on that worthless television tonight," Lillian said. "Why aren't you off on a date with that good-looking Caleb? When he wasn't working, Friday nights were always date nights for Albert and me."

"Work," Kate said. "He's off somewhere in the woods. I don't know when he's coming back." She liked that Caleb, who worked for the timber company, was gone for long stretches at a time. It gave her time to think, to miss him, to appreciate his return. The past few nights, though, she'd wished desperately that he could be beside her in her bed. She worried that the girl might return, and thought that Caleb's presence might keep her away.

"At least the railroad gave Albert a regular schedule," Lillian said. "On one week, then off four days. It breaks my heart that he didn't live to spend the pension he worked so hard for."

Lillian halved the éclair and put the two plates on a tray with the coffee. Kate followed her to the living room, where they sat beside each other on the overstuffed love seat facing the front window. Outside, it had gone full dark. The reflection of the room obscured the street.

Black-and-white photographs of Francie and a few of Francie and her father, all in identical silver frames, covered one wall. Photography was one of Lillian's hobbies, and Francie was her favorite subject. Each time Kate saw the photos, it struck her how truly lovely Francie was and how the camera adored her. Lillian's camera was able to capture that fleeting look of longing in Francie's eyes, the one she was always trying to hide from Kate and the rest of the world. But once, after they'd had a couple of glasses of wine, Francie had told her how she was afraid she'd never have a husband, children, that she couldn't see it happening in Carystown. Ever. She'd lived away for several years but didn't want her mother to live in Carystown without any family to take care of her.

"Who knew I'd die an old maid?" she said. She laughed ruefully. Kate objected, but she didn't know what else to say.

Later, Kate remembered her words and wondered briefly—she hadn't much time then to dwell on the details of Francie's life—if Francie would choose to remain in Carystown permanently.

"Would you like to tell me what's going on, or do I have to sit here all night and wait for you to make up your mind that you can trust me?" Lillian put her hand lightly on Kate's arm, just the way Francie had at lunch.

Kate gave Lillian a nervous smile and fooled with her hair, shaping it into a loose ponytail, letting it go. "It's just work, Lillian," she said. "The invoices are piling up and I can't get Janet to sign change orders or to write very many checks. Then she blames me when things don't get done at the house. It's so close to being finished. I don't know if she's having cash flow problems or what."

Lillian looked at her evenly, expectantly.

"Really," Kate said. "And I haven't been sleeping well. Stress. Really."

"Well, that's an answer," Lillian said. "It's bull, but it's an answer."

Kate felt close to tears. She wanted to trust Lillian. But she hadn't even been able to bring herself to talk to Francie. How could she confide in Francie's mother? A small voice inside her asked if she wouldn't want to tell her own mother if she could.

"Did Francine ever tell you that she used to smoke cigarettes?" Lillian said.

Kate shook her head. She wasn't in the mood for a walk down someone else's Memory Lane.

"She was fifteen and she would smoke them in her bedroom and blow the smoke out the window screen. Now, Albert smoked, too, so I didn't notice at first," Lillian said. "But I would find ashes by her window and burn holes on some of her clothes. And I could smell it on her when she came out of her room."

"Wasn't it just something she had to go through?" Kate said. She herself had smoked for a while, but quickly tired of it when she realized how expensive it was.

"I didn't say anything to her because I knew Francine couldn't bear to live with a lie for very long. It's not in her nature. So I waited her out. But, you know, that child surprised me. She held out for a good six months. I thought I was going to have to speak to her. Or have her father do it."

Kate knew that at the end of the story she was going to be expected to 'fess up, to tell Lillian what was plaguing her. Once the sheriff went to investigate what she'd told him, wouldn't Lillian know anyway?

"In the end I didn't have to because the septic tank backed up, and when the plumber went in he found that the biggest problem was inside the house, in the back bathroom that Francine used. Down in that pipe, he found about two hundred cigarette butts stuck in a great big wad about the size of a baseball." Lillian began to laugh. "You should have seen the look on Francine's face when she saw all those cigarette butts in his bucket. She looked just as surprised as he did."

Kate laughed at the notion of Francie so mortified. It felt good to laugh, too.

"Albert said he would've spanked her, even at that age, but she was so embarrassed that she was in the way of punishing herself."

Kate wiped at the tears that had sprung up in her eyes. Inside, she felt the dam of her detachment from her own fears break. She knew she had nothing to fear from Lillian.

"So," Kate said. "Is it that my toilet's going to back up if I don't tell you what you want to know?"

"I guarantee it," Lillian said. "And it won't be pretty."

"I don't know that there's anything to see," Kate said as they passed through the freestanding stone pillars at the entrance of the cemetery.

Lillian pulled her jacket tightly around her. "Child, if you spend enough time in graveyards in the middle of the night, you're sure going to see something."

"I can't believe that they don't have a fence around it," Kate said. "But then, where we're going is not actually *part* of the cemetery. At least I don't think so."

Lillian swept her flashlight over the modest headstones before them. "This is the colored cemetery," she said. "Nobody wants to come messing around in here, I promise you. Maybe a few kids thinking they're really doing something, turning over stones and tearing up the grass, but that doesn't happen but every few years."

They walked in silence over the rough gravel of the cemetery's central path. Despite the wind and misting rain earlier in the day, the air was calm and the sky clear enough that there was some light from a sliver of moon.

"Did you know the girl?" Lillian asked. "Alive, I mean."

"Not to speak to," Kate said. "But I recognized her when I saw the posters and her picture on television. She would walk down Bridge Street and pass in front of the window at work. Always alone. I never saw her with other little girls. Now, it's her mother. She's in town almost every day."

"Terrible thing to lose a child," Lillian said. "Your heart grieves forever."

Kate didn't respond.

They walked a few moments longer and Kate interrupted the silence.

"You must think this is ridiculous," she said. "I never should have brought you out here. You're cold. And what if nothing happens?"

Lillian put her arm out to stop her. "What was that?"

"What? What did you hear?" Kate said.

Lillian pushed at her lightly and laughed. "It's the sound of your imagination, Kate, working overtime. Now, if you want to do this, stop messing around. I know this cemetery like the back of my hand. I've buried more people here than you've known in your life. This child is telling you something, so you've got to listen, because it's my guess that nobody listened to her before. And with you, she's found a sympathetic ear." She tilted her head, looking at Kate. "I wonder why."

It was a question Kate had asked herself more than once in the past few days, and she still didn't have an answer. She smiled. "I guess I'm just a soft touch," she said. "Even for ghosts."

The squat mausoleum that Kate had come in search of stood at the cemetery's northwest corner. Its peeling white paint and elaborately carved columns topped with cherubs and stone clusters of grapes gave it the look of an aging ruin in the faint moonlight. Lillian shone her flashlight at the name carved over its lintel.

"Josephus Taylor," she said. "Mean old bastard. Claimed kinship with Zachary Taylor on his father's side, but I doubt that they claimed him. Nowdays they'd call somebody like that a loan shark, but back then he was just somebody you went to when you were in trouble. My grandparents never had any truck with him, but he died owning half the houses in the East End."

Kate nodded, not really listening. "It's around back," she said.

"Ah," Lillian said.

The side of the mausoleum was planted with bramble roses that at this time of year were just a tangle of thorn-covered branches lying close to the ground. The branches caught at their pant legs as they passed.

"That Josephus—greedy for anything he can get, even in death," Lillian said, pulling away from the branches. She thwacked the side of the marble building with the flat of her hand. "Shame on you," she said.

Kate giggled in spite of her nervousness.

Behind the mausoleum they found the small clearing ringed by cedar trees. A number of mounds of leaves about five or six feet in diameter spread out over the ground in front of them. The clearing smelled not of cedar, but of decaying leaves. It pricked Kate's memory and she was overcome with sadness.

"Compost," Lillian said. "The town sends a crew out here to the cemetery every fall to clean up the leaves. I thought they were supposed to haul them off, but here they are, dumped like garbage. Wish I could say I'm surprised."

"Last time . . ." Kate said, but her voice trailed off.

"Is she here?" Lillian said. She sounded excited.

"I don't think it works like that," Kate said. "I don't think she *hangs out* here or anything like that."

"She told *you* to come here."

Kate had tried to explain to the sheriff and then to Lillian how the girl communicated with her. But it wasn't something she could verbalize well. It was as though she had been privy to the girl's emotion, an emotion that had taken up residence in her mind, like a memory of her own, but it was not exactly her own. And when she thought of this place, it filled her with a paralyzing dread.

The night she had awakened in her own bed almost three years ago and put her hands to her belly and realized her baby had been taken from her, she had rolled over and vomited onto the floor. She vomited until she was vomiting thin strands of blood, yet her body still felt full and numbed and she retched for an hour. Later, she lay on the cold bathroom floor wanting to escape her own skin because her body had reached the limits of its existence: It felt like a living death. This was the feeling she got from Isabella Moon about the clearing.

Kate sat down in the path of flattened leaves. Lillian crouched beside her.

"What are we supposed to do?" Lillian said. "Does she want us to dig her up? We'll have to go back and get a couple of shovels."

The ground was cold and damp through Kate's sweatpants. She thought about the girl and how, if she was indeed beneath the leaves there in front of them, she would be horribly cold and uncomfortable. But she was dead, Kate knew, and couldn't really feel anything. So the feeling had been left to her.

"I don't know," she said. "I want to, but I don't know that we're the ones to do it."

"That *is* a lot of leaves," Lillian said. "Maybe pitchforks. You know, it wasn't too long ago this used to be kind of a lovers' spot. One of those places kids go. It's a little inhospitable for that now."

Kate was about to suggest that they return to the house when a breeze shifted the branches of the cedars with a soft, rustling sound and circled the clearing, stirring up a few of the drier leaves. It died down, but picked up again quickly, this time catching up more leaves and carrying them, swirling, into the air.

Puzzled that she could not feel the breeze that was so obviously close, she held her arm out into the air in front of her. The air seemed denser, yes, but still.

"We need to go," she said.

She helped the silent Lillian to her feet, but despite her words, neither of them moved.

By now the breeze had stiffened and begun to pulse with form and life. It seemed to suck the rotting leaves from the ground and drive them ahead like some fierce and angry tornado.

"Lord in heaven!" Lillian shouted.

As the leaves rose from the ground, twisting into a tight column that blocked out the moon and stars, a low roar like the sound of an approaching freight train bore down on them. They felt a change in the air pressure. Lillian's grip tightened on Kate's arm.

Lillian's flashlight dropped to the ground.

"Look," she shouted over the wind. "Under the leaves."

Kate followed the narrow beam of the fallen flashlight. The ground beneath the column lay completely exposed, strangely flat and empty. Nothing grew there, there was nothing remarkable to see.

Now Kate felt something pressing against the palm of her hand. She looked at Lillian, but Lillian was still focused on the ground beneath the swirling leaves. Looking down at her hand, she saw that it was empty, but still there was the pressure. Then she felt an insistent tug.

When she tried to shake off whatever it was, it only gripped her tighter and tighter so that she thought it might break the bones in her hand. The breadth of it across her palm wasn't particularly wide—it felt like a child's hand in hers. *Of course it was a child's hand! What else could it be? Hadn't she been waiting, expecting the child?* Its stubborn persistence frightened her. She wanted to scream, to warn Lillian, or to run away herself. But she knew she couldn't leave Lillian there alone. Her only choice was to give in, to let Isabella—surely it was Isabella—lead her.

As Kate was pulled toward the leaves, Lillian touched her shoulder, but Kate shook her off. There was *something* about the empty ground before her that attracted her. Unmindful of Lillian's sudden cry, she let herself be led forward.

The wind clutched at her hair, her clothes, even her skin, pushing and pulling at once. She realized that she had no control here, that she was at the mercy of the wind around her, but the sense of panic she'd experienced a moment earlier had disappeared. Beneath her feet the ground was soft and yielding. The leaves stayed high above her.

When she was at the center of the clearing, she felt the child's hand slip from hers. Around her the wind moaned. She stood there, feeling an odd kind of peace. Looking back, she saw that Lillian's mouth was open, saying something or shouting, but Kate couldn't hear her. She felt as though she might stand there forever.

Just as it had started slowly, the sound of the wind began to recede, and she was overcome with emotions that weren't hers. She felt the spreading, violent pain of the place. It filled her body and tore at her muscles. She had felt pain, cruel pain, but never imagined that *this pain* could exist, could be held in one body. She began to weep because it was the child's pain, and no child should feel *this pain*.

Kate eased herself to the ground and put her wet cheek against it to comfort the girl who was surely there, waiting for her. The dirt was warm, not cold as she'd imagined. Lying there, the wind quieting above her, she closed her eyes.

But here was Lillian trying to pull her to her feet.

"We have to go, baby," Lillian shouted at her. "Come on!"

Lillian half dragged Kate across a few feet of blank dirt until Kate began to come to herself and allowed Lillian to lead her away from the clearing.

Behind them the sound of the wind receded and changed in tone to something less alive, less mournful. When they reached the cemetery's gravel path, Kate looked back. There was nothing to see above the mausoleum but the motionless outlines of the cedars etched against the sky.

They were silent on the drive to Kate's house. When they'd returned to Lillian's from the cemetery, they discovered that it was nearly ten o'clock, a good three hours after they'd set out. In unspoken agreement, Lillian went inside to get her keys, and when she emerged, Kate followed her to the car.

"You want me to come inside?" Lillian asked five minutes later, when they reached Kate's dark cottage.

Lillian had resumed her attitude of relaxed efficiency, but beneath it Kate sensed that Lillian was as unsettled as she. She hoped they could talk about it, but not yet.

"You need to get back home," Kate said. The last thing she wanted was for Lillian to be involved in whatever insane thing was happening to her. "Maybe Francie should stay with *you* tonight," she said. "You want me to call her? You know she would."

Lillian waved her off. "I didn't much like what happened tonight, honey, but I'm not worried that I'm going home to ghosts. Albert's the only ghost I need, and he's much less of a bother than he was in life."

Kate tried to smile. She'd always been a little jealous of Francie's relationship with Lillian. Francie complained a lot about her interfering ways, but Kate felt blessed in some way that Lillian had been with her. She still felt horribly guilty, but grateful just the same. Finally, someone—and it was someone she trusted—knew that she hadn't made up her encounter with Isabella Moon.

"Go in and sleep," Lillian said. "And I bet you'll sleep like a baby."

"If only," Kate said.

When she got inside, she found her answering machine blinking twice. The possibilities of who it was were limited. Only Francie, Caleb, or Janet called her. She pressed the message button and Caleb's deep, reassuring voice filled the cottage's front room.

"It's late," he said. "Sure wish you were home. It's awfully lonesome in this motel room and I miss the sound of your voice." He sighed. "Another fine meal at the motel's diner. I had the fish special tonight—big mistake. But I was thinking about taking you to the ocean this summer, Pumpkin. Get a little sand in your bathing suit."

His voice paused a moment and Kate could hear the sound of the television in the background.

"Hey, I miss you. I'll call you tomorrow, okay?"

While it was true that she missed him as well, she couldn't imagine what she would tell him about what had just happened to her. She hadn't been able to bring herself to tell him anything about the little girl. There were so many secrets she felt she had to keep from him. But she didn't know if she was protecting him or just herself.

The second message was a hang-up. Whoever called had waited to hear the whole announcement, which wasn't her voice, but the electronic one that came with the machine, and then hung up. She found those kinds of calls unsettling. But tonight she wasn't willing to let her imagination go anywhere with it. She had enough going on in that department already.

6

KATE OPENED HER EYES to find the bedroom awash in spring sunlight. But it was a sound, not the sun, that had snapped her out of her sleep. Out in the living room she heard heavy but hesitant footsteps, as though someone were trying not to make any noise as they walked through the room. Kate rolled over to her right side and carefully slid open her nightstand drawer. Without being able to see inside, she felt around for the pistol, the Ruger .22 that had been hers since she was a teenager.

The gun was cold in her hand, but comfortable. Her hands shook some and her heart was racing. It was good, though. She felt ready. One of the thoughts that flew through her head was of the hang-up the night before. She hadn't wanted to think of it as a clue, a precursor to a confrontation, but there she was.

As the intruder came down the hall, the procedures came to her automatically: Get a wall behind her back and distance herself from the kill funnel—the doorway—for a clear shot. Don't shoot to wound. Aim for the head or the heart.

Kate closed her eyes briefly and tried to steady her breathing. The moment seemed to last forever, and indeed lasted too long. When she opened her eyes, she saw Caleb standing in the doorway. If it had been anyone else, anyone who wanted to do her harm, she would be dead.

"Whoa, Kate," he said, putting his hands in the air.

"Oh, my God, Caleb!" she said, lowering the gun. A nervous laugh escaped her before she could stop it.

"Hey, that's not really funny," he said. "You scared the shit out of me."

"Of course it's not funny," she said, composing herself.

Caleb watched her as she carefully slipped the gun into the nightstand. "I knew you had that thing," he said. "But I never expected to be on the receiving end."

Still shaking, Kate went to him and put her arms around his waist. Resting her head on his chest, she heard his heart pounding against the inside of his shirt. "I thought you were going to be gone until the middle of next week," she said. "You should have told me you were coming back today."

He kissed the top of her head and she lifted her face to his. He seemed to be searching her face for an answer to a question that he couldn't bring himself to ask. She wanted him to trust her, but knew there was nothing she could say to make him understand that she had to protect herself from ghosts of the past, transparent or not.

"You know I get nervous sometimes," she said. "It just goes with the territory, living alone. I'm really sorry."

He finally smiled. "Here I was thinking I'd climb into bed and wake you up with kisses and maybe one or two other things," he said.

"And what makes you think you won't get me right back into bed?" she said.

"I didn't say I couldn't do that," he said. He leaned down to kiss her then, working his mouth hungrily against hers. But he suddenly pulled away. "Thing is, I was up at the crack of dawn so I could come and get a gun pointed at me, and I haven't even had breakfast."

Kate gave an exaggerated sigh. "Well, I guess I at least owe you breakfast," she said.

"Oh, that ain't all you owe me, girl," he said, squeezing her backside through her pajamas. "But if you've got all the stuff, I'll cook."

"Oh, you're funny," Kate said. The sparse contents of her refrigerator were a running joke between them. She wasn't a bad cook, as she'd proved to him more than once, but when she knew he wouldn't be hanging around her house, she seldom went to the store. He teased her that she was some kind of witch or fairy, that she didn't actually need food at all.

"Just let me clean up some," Kate said.

"I'm really hungry," Caleb said.

She could tell he was serious, but also that he would probably indulge her. "I'll be fast," she said, running for the bathroom. As she hurried through her ablutions, she felt a small rush of excitement at the prospect of some relaxed time with Caleb. Even though she wasn't sure she could trust him to understand what was happening to her, she did know that he cared deeply about her.

True to her word and relatively clean, she led him out of the house ten minutes later.

"What exactly is a *latte*?"

It had been a little more than a year since Caleb had first settled himself in the armchair beside Kate's in Craddock's on Main Street, Carystown's only coffeehouse. She hadn't even known his name, but had laughed aloud at his lame opening line. Up to a couple of weeks before that, he'd always come into Craddock's with a tall, energetic blonde in sheepskin boots whose minimally made-up face always looked freshly scrubbed. The blonde was striking in her own way, but it was Caleb who drew her attention.

Taller even than the blonde (she later learned that he was six-two in his socks and didn't fit into her bed very well), Caleb walked with an appealing confidence. He wore his wavy brown hair cut close and was bulky about the arms and chest, but not in a way that spoke of vain hours spent at the gym. She had the impression that he worked with his hands.

"What's so funny?" he'd said, looking a little worried.

"You are," she said. "You aren't trying to pick me up at nine in the morning, are you?"

When he'd smiled, she knew she would have a hard time resisting him, even if she wanted to. She'd never seen him smiling with the blonde. It was a good sign.

"I could wait until about nine-thirty," he said, looking at his watch. "But that's about my limit. Then I'll have to move on to someone else."

She'd made a show of looking around the coffeehouse. Two teenage boys sat drinking sodas and poring over a trail map. Mrs. Kraus, the diminutive woman who ran the used bookshop next door, was ordering at the counter. The young woman behind the counter was very sweet, but Kate guessed that her chemically pink hair and dramatic black and white makeup wouldn't appeal to the rather earthy man beside her.

"Hmm. I don't know how Mr. Kraus, that lady's husband, would feel about that," she said, indicating the older woman. "Then, there *is* Jessica behind the counter. Though she might be a little young for you."

"Why do women want to pierce their noses?" he had said, suddenly serious.

"I don't know," she said. "But I've seen Indian women with lovely jewelry on their nostrils."

"Sure," he said. He lowered his voice. "But I think your friend Jessica up there got hold of a nine-penny nail and a watch battery."

Kate had laughed so hard, she almost bathed them both in latte.

Maybe it was the brightness of the morning, or Caleb's unaffected manner, but much of her hesitation to become involved with another man seemed to evaporate when he spoke. Her attraction to him had been so immediate that she was afraid to trust it. But she'd been alone then for well over a year. Friendships with other women were one thing, but a small part of her cried out for intimacy, communication on a more elemental level. It wasn't just that she hadn't had sex in all that time. Even before that, what had sex been to her? Physically pleasing, but Miles, the man with whom she'd spent so many years, so many intimate days and nights, had made it shameful in the end. And that relationship? *Poison.* She was a different person now. Reinvented. She knew it suited her, just as Caleb suited her.

When they got to Gatchel's diner, Kate found that she was hungry, particularly after her dinner of popcorn the previous night. She ordered a scrambled egg, toast, sausage, and juice. Caleb's meal was a marvel to her: a stack of pancakes, two eggs, sausage, biscuits, and grits with gravy.

"Are you sure you're not still hungry?" she teased. "They might have to go to the grocery, but I'm sure they can get you something else."

"You wait," he said. "I'm going to need all that energy later."

"Promises, promises," Kate said.

As it turned out, when they finally made it back to her cottage later that afternoon, he fell sound asleep on the couch minutes after he took his boots off. But before they left the diner, she convinced him to drive out to Janet's house to see if anyone was working and what the progress was.

It was only ten-thirty in the morning, and the temperature on the bank sign already read an unseasonable 65 degrees. When they got into the car,

Kate asked Caleb to help her get the top down on her small blue convertible.

"Pushing it a bit, aren't we?" he said. "It's not even April yet, hotshot."

"Oh, come on," she said. "Live a little."

They headed west out of town into the lush part of the valley, where several of the old families had their farms. Miles of white fence wound up and down the rolling hills alongside the road. A few early foals ran alongside their mothers or chased one another gamely across the pastures, playing hide-and-seek behind the mares and small hillocks.

Driving out to the new house one afternoon in Janet's Range Rover, Janet had hinted that Kate would be welcome to keep a horse in the stables she was building—paying its board, of course—but Kate laughed and told Janet that she couldn't imagine what would've given her the idea that she'd want to do such a thing.

Janet had shrugged it off. "I don't know," she said. "You just seem like the horsey type."

It seemed unlikely to Kate that Janet would have noticed how her eyes moistened a bit as she looked out the passenger window of the Range Rover. She put it down to coincidence and Janet's tendency to stereotype everyone she met. Funny, though, how often she seemed to be right, Kate thought. She'd loved to go horseback riding as a girl. Janet had a strange talent for knowing what people wanted, and it had helped her make a lot of money in insurance and real estate.

"I wouldn't mind living out here if it weren't for snooty types," Caleb said now. "What a pain." He turned in his seat to follow the oncoming car that approached and zipped past them in the southbound lane. "That, honey, was how fast I was driving at dawn to get back to you this morning."

Kate smiled. "Paxton," she said, "I understand that he pretty much always drives like that."

"If the guy weren't such a snake, I'd admire his car," Caleb said.

"I like your truck just fine," Kate said. She reached over and squeezed Caleb's hand, then slid her hand playfully onto his jean-clad inner thigh. He leaned over and kissed her on her neck, which the wind passing through the convertible had exposed by blowing her hair out behind her.

Caleb's kiss and the fast-moving wind cleansed her thoughts of the funk that had settled over her in the past week. She wanted the way she felt this morning to last forever.

Janet's house was set far back from the road atop a small hill so that it seemed to tower over the green pastures around it. Kate drove slowly up the gravel road leading to what would soon be a circular drive; the paving crew wasn't scheduled for another few weeks, when all the heavy equipment and trucks were supposed to be gone. It was Kate's opinion that the house's stucco walls and terra-cotta red tiles on the complicated roof were better suited to the shores of the Mediterranean than central Kentucky, but it was still going to be a beautiful place to live.

"Great," she said. "Janet's here."

She hadn't seen the Range Rover at first, parked as it was between an electrician's truck and a pickup.

"I've got zero need to talk to that woman," Caleb said.

"Just tell me if she tries to put her tongue in your ear," Kate said.

Caleb stretched his arms above his head and yawned. Then he said, "You know, for a good-looking woman, you can be pretty nasty, Kate Russell."

"Kate, come on up here!" Janet had opened one of the front windows to shout down to them. "They've messed up the chandeliers."

"She's seen us now," Kate said.

"I'm going in covered," Caleb said, putting his hands over both ears.

"You want me to have a job, don't you? Those giant breakfasts you eat don't come cheap." She pulled him into the house through one of the open doors of the six-bay garage.

"Hey," he said, sounding hurt. "I offered to pay, but you were all about apologizing for almost blowing my head off."

"Oh, yeah," Kate said. She grinned back at him. "I guess I forgot about that."

"Watch out." Caleb grabbed her arm to keep her from stumbling over a rolled-up Oriental rug. "You're a danger to yourself and others, you know that?"

They found Janet in the master suite berating a man in work blues who stood a good six feet up a ladder in the center of the room. Kate recognized the look on his face—he was just about fed up with Janet and her demands.

"The media cabinet looks great, Janet," Kate said, trying to deflect her attention from the man.

"I wanted it to start six inches off the floor," Janet said. "Seems someone forgot all about that." Her tone and the hard look at Kate made it clear that Kate was the someone of whom she spoke, but Kate ignored it. She'd explained to Janet more than once that the weight of the solid walnut entertainment cabinet precluded it from being free-hanging.

Janet Rourke was a woman who used clothing, jewelry, and, Kate suspected, plastic surgery to play up her best physical features: a voluptuous, perfectly balanced pair of breasts; large, deep blue eyes; a waist that Scarlett O'Hara would envy; and a backside that seemed to laugh at gravity. Even in the tight peach velour jacket and track pants she was wearing, she gave the impression that she had dressed with considerable care. Her jet black hair was intricately styled, curled, and sprayed, and her makeup, down to her generously applied mascara and deep burgundy lipstick, was almost theatrical in its precision.

For all her professional poise, Janet had an aggressively sexual aura about her that puzzled Kate. She wasn't sure if it was natural or simply cultivated from long years of practice. But even though Janet was a frequent subject of town gossip, there was very little that wasn't business-related. The men called her a "ball breaker," but they usually gave her her own way because she had a knack for making herself and her associates money.

"Plus, the place wasn't even locked up when I got here," Janet said. "That damned contractor's not doing his job."

"Ma'am," the man on the ladder said. "You want me to switch out this chandelier with the other one or not?"

Ignoring him, Janet told Kate to deal with it.

When Kate followed the electrician out of the room, Janet's irritated mood suddenly changed. She smiled sweetly at Caleb.

"Our Kate's such a treasure," she said. "I don't know what I'd do without her." She hurried over to the bank of windows at the front of the room, the kitten heels of her sandals clapping brightly against the newly laid wood floors. "What do you think of my view? Isn't it fabulous? You can see almost the whole county from here. You can see almost all the way out to the Quair."

Caleb remained standing near the door, where he'd been since he first entered with Kate. "Looks too expensive to me," he said.

"You're just not used to the best, honey," she said. "It doesn't take long to acquire a taste for the good things in life. You just have to taste them first."

Caleb walked slowly to the window, close to where she stood. "Cut the shit, Janet," he said.

Janet relaxed her smile a degree, but it remained bright.

"I've spent well over two years of my life working on this house. All that time since I lost Richard," she said. "And I think it should be appreciated."

Caleb laughed. He half expected her to stamp one of her pedicured feet. To him, Janet was better than television, she was so damned unpredictable. "I think this house would've been finished a year ago if you hadn't ridden your men so hard. You've made Kate's life hell over this place."

"She can handle it," Janet said, her eyes narrowing. "I don't think you know our Kate as well as you think you do."

"Is that right?"

She leaned forward and gently scraped a long, polished nail across his forearm.

Caleb didn't like her so close. Ridiculous as she was, she was disturbingly sexy. He'd been sucked in by her more than once, and he wasn't about to be sucked in again.

"Oh, she's full of secrets, our Kate. What if I told you," she whispered, "that our Kate knows all about our little conference in the bathroom at the arts fund-raiser?"

"Fuck you, Janet," he said.

The sound of her delicate laugh seemed to echo off the glass and fill the room. "But you've already done *that*," she said.

Caleb had a strong urge to wrap his hands around her skinny throat and make her eyes pop out of their sockets. The idea of this woman telling Kate how he'd almost ripped off her dress in a fit of lust fueled by three or four glasses of George Dickel made him sick to his stomach. Sometimes when he was making love to Kate, Janet invaded his mind: his hands, his mouth on her breasts; the smell of perfume that emanated from her. The way he'd been desperate to fuck her without hesitation filled his mind, so that Kate disappeared beneath him and he couldn't help but do to her what he'd been so driven to do to Janet. It filled him with shame and self-loathing, but he couldn't stop himself. But equally disturbing was Kate's reaction: she didn't object, but only seemed to become dead to him, her eyes empty, her body willing but unresponsive.

He could smell that perfume now as Janet leaned close. He jerked his arm away from her, her nail leaving a jagged scratch on his skin.

"You're just another slut, Janet," he said. "You're nothing special, and this pile of sticks you've built is nothing special either. You think your money buys you class, but everything about you is cheap and always will be. I hope this playpen you've built for yourself burns down around you."

By now Caleb's hands were balled into fists and pressed against his thighs to keep them from grabbing Janet.

A look of shock passed over her face, but she recovered quickly. There were no more smiles. She turned and hurried from the room, shouting for Kate.

Caleb's first thought was to go after her, but now that she was gone, he suspected that she'd been bluffing about saying anything about them to Kate. She wouldn't, at least not until she could use it to some advantage.

When Janet had gone, Kate took a quick walk through the house, making some notes on what was left to be done before the decorators and painters came in. She had a good relationship with the contractor and his subs, and if she could just keep the money flowing from Janet, the house would finally be finished. Her own bank account had improved since she'd been depositing the extra money that Janet paid her for her work on the house. She figured that she could have worse jobs.

She found Caleb standing in front of the house where the landscaper had begun to lay tile and block out where the plantings would be.

"Hey," she said. "I'm sorry that took so long."

"No problem," he said, still looking out over the pastures.

His eyes looked sad to her. There was still so much she didn't know about him.

"Penny for your thoughts," she said.

Caleb looked down at her as though suddenly realizing she was there. He leaned down and swept her off her feet to cradle her in his arms. "You are so damned corny sometimes," he said.

"I can't help it," she said. "Comes with the package."

"Nice package," he said. He kissed her hard and put her down. But he held tight to her hand.

As they walked back to the car, the wind picked up hard enough to blow dirt and small bits of gravel across their path.

Remembering the fierce wind the night before, Kate pulled him gently on.

They got the car doors open and she turned the key. But Caleb bent down and picked something up off the ground.

"I'll be damned," he said. He looked around at the treeless pastures and the bare yard around the house as though he were looking for something in particular. "Wonder where these guys came from."

He held out his open hand for Kate to see. Nine miniature pinecones lay spread across his palms.

"Cedar," he said. "And I sure don't see anything that could've dropped these around here. Must be some wind if it blew these out of the woods."

"Some wind," Kate echoed. She felt like a door had opened inside her and the wind was blowing straight through it.

7

IT WASN'T THAT Bill didn't like going to church. It just seemed to him that, given the projects with which Margaret liked to occupy him on Saturday mornings, he deserved a serious sleep-in at least once a week. Most of the previous day had been spent clearing brush in a sunny corner of the backyard that Margaret decided would be good for a vegetable garden.

"Why now, after all these years, do you want vegetables back there?" he had asked.

She shrugged. "It takes a few years to get asparagus going," she said. "I haven't had a veggie garden since I was a girl. Seems like now or never."

It seemed to Bill that between Carystown's Farmer's Market and the Kroger, they did okay for vegetables, but he got out the scythe, weed killer, and wheelbarrow anyway.

Now, as he lay in bed, he could feel the heavy work of the day before in his back. But he could also smell the coffee and bacon that she'd started in the kitchen. They were his gentle clue that she expected him to accompany her to church. He took her pillow and crushed it to his face to block out the sun streaming in the windows. He felt the sharp edge of frustration rise inside of him, but before it was strong enough to cause him to react, to stomp down to the kitchen to tell her that he didn't want any of her damned bribe of a breakfast or to have anything to do with the stiff-necked crowd at High Street Presbyterian, he got control of it. Better to have her, a woman who loved him enough to bribe him, alive and warm and vibrant, than to be in the house alone, missing her. The idea of losing her was never far from his mind.

Still, as he showered he reckoned it wasn't much of a bribe: the bacon was turkey bacon, given that she'd banished the real stuff in deference to his cholesterol, and the coffee was decaf.

After the church service, Bill followed Margaret down into the under-croft for some real coffee and whatever pastries the blue-haired ladies of the Women's Guild had scared up. He was about to whisper a five-minute warning in her ear when he saw Edith from Janet Rourke's office standing near the piano, the feathers in the purple felt hat she wore trembling vig-orously as she brushed coffee-cake crumbs from the front of her dress. He slipped away from Margaret, who was chatting with the choir director.

Bill quickly poured himself a coffee and casually walked up to Edith.

"Nice service, don't you think?" he said to her. "Good music today."

Edith put a hand to her hat, adjusting it. Now the feathers were crooked, giving her the look of a wan, curious bird.

"Why, Sheriff," she said. "We don't often have the pleasure of your company on a Sunday morning. This is a real treat."

He was familiar enough with the ways of women of a certain age to know that he'd just been chastised.

"Just out making the county safe for ladies like yourself, Miss Edith," he said, leaning ever so slightly closer to her.

Edith blushed beneath her mask of bisque powder.

"We've been after your Margaret to join the Garden Society, Sheriff," she said. "It's her right, you know. Her mother served three terms as presi-dent."

He shook his head. "You know Margaret and her museum work," he said. "I can hardly get her to come home in time to make me supper."

Edith raised her voice a bit, drawing the attention of several nearby women. "I only work because I choose to, Sheriff," she said. "My husband left me very well provided for. He was with the railroad, you know, many years before they shut down their operations here."

"Where do you find time for things like the Garden Society?" Bill said. "Don't they meet for lunch or some-such?"

He'd seen the antique collection of women in the private room at The Lettuce Leaf more than once, dressed in their luncheon suits and sporting clever handbags and curious-looking hats. It pleased him that Margaret chose to decline their annual invitation to join. He didn't like to think of his wife as having anything in common with those old women. First off, she was only forty-nine. He also knew that several of them were seriously behind on the property taxes on their crumbling houses and fully grown gardens. It was only his forbearance that kept their names off the delinquent tax rolls posted at the courthouse every six months. They were illegal, his omissions from the rolls. And there were those who would think the consideration granted to the women was racist or at least discriminatory against less prominent folks, but Bill rationalized that the shame would probably kill at least one of the old girls. Things would only get sticky if the state got around to an audit.

Edith lowered her voice. "Janet isn't very understanding, if you get my meaning," she said, raising her eyebrows for emphasis. "But after Kate came on board, things got a little easier in that department."

"A nice person, is she?" Bill asked.

"Oh, nice as pie," Edith said. "I can get the odd two-hour lunch if I need it. And sometimes our speakers do go on. You should've heard that man from the arboretum down in Nashville. Very, very interesting, but he did go on and on about crepe myrtles, blah, blah, blah . . ." She made a puppet mouth with her hand and opened and closed it with each word, making Bill laugh. "And we just can't grow them all that well around here."

"You know where she's from?" Bill said.

"He was a man, and I said he was from Nashville," Edith said, looking puzzled. "Oh, you mean Kate?"

When Bill nodded, she said, "Nice as pie, that girl is. No personal life that I can tell of. No family calling her at the office, no weddings or funerals to go to or anything like that. Socializes with a colored girl named Francie. She calls sometimes."

Margaret came to stand beside him and slid her arm beneath his sport coat and around his waist.

"What are you all up to here, looking like a couple of sneak thieves?" she said teasingly.

Bill looked at his watch. "Guess we'd best be getting on home," he said. He couldn't very well continue questioning the older woman with Margaret standing there. She would have questions of her own when they left the building, and he wasn't ready to go into the whole Isabella Moon subject right then.

"Your sweet husband was asking me about my work, Margaret," Edith said. "Pretty Kate Russell in the office. Do you know her, Margaret? She's helpful about making sure I get to the Garden Society meetings. The ones *you* should be going to, dear."

Margaret smiled. It was a smile Bill recognized, a smile that offered nothing, not even an argument. "Pretty, is she?" She gave Bill a secret squeeze on one of his small love handles.

"I set her up with Paxton Birkenshaw once, but I don't think it worked out very well," she said.

"A pleasure, Miss Edith," Bill said. "Don't talk to strangers, now. I don't want to hear about you getting into any trouble."

He steered Margaret toward the steps to leave.

"Oh, Sheriff," Edith called after him. "Beaufort, it was, I think she told me. Beaufort, South Carolina."

Bill smiled at her and gave her a friendly salute.

Outside, the morning had turned warmer, and Bill thought he might be able to get in nine holes of golf at the public course out behind the hospital. Margaret interrupted the pleasant thought.

"Are we keeping track of all the pretty girls in town now?" she said.

"Just the ones who might be trouble," Bill told her. He wasn't sure how much trouble Kate Russell was going to be. It bothered him, though, to be thinking about her at all around Margaret.

"Don't you think Edith knew you were patronizing her?" she said. "I just don't know how you get away with it, Bill Delaney. I'd have pinched you."

"You *did* pinch me, woman," he said, reaching behind her to squeeze her bottom. But he only got a handful of silk skirt.

"Please, Bill, we're not even out of the parking lot," she said, looking around to see if anyone had noticed.

"Yeah, you got me. Conduct unbecoming an officer," he said. He held his arms out in front of him. "Better get out the cuffs."

She pushed lightly at his arms. "You," she said. "I don't know what you're up to, chatting up old ladies, but I know it's something."

A few minutes before nine on Monday morning, Bill saw Frank come in and drop a folder of papers on Daphne's desk. Daphne seemed to be treating him with some consideration, but he could hardly call it friendly. He was constantly reminding his deputies to be nice to one another—though he didn't always follow his own advice. With the exception of Daphne, all of his deputies were ex-military and pretty good at taking orders, but they had their difficult days. Frank could be moody, but Bill put that down to Rose's illness. Frank didn't talk about it much, but her illness had put a number of strains on them, financially and emotionally. Daphne couldn't keep her mouth shut about department business, even though she had a handful of warnings in her file. Mitchell Carl was too distractible—particularly by attractive women. It was the reason his wife had left, Bill was certain. Clayton Campbell was just young. The others weren't much trouble, and in the end, everyone seemed to get the job done. Fugitives from the law, robberies, and suspicious deaths were pretty rare in the neighborhood, murder even rarer. Most Carystown miscreants were drunk and disorderly, welfare and tax cheats, or deadbeat dads.

Bill picked up his coffee and wandered out to Daphne's desk.

"What's the good news, Frank?" he said.

"I worked overtime talking to the kids this Saturday," Frank said. "Rose about had my head. She's wanting the yard cleaned up for spring. You *know* I was sorry to miss that."

"You bet," Bill said. "I had my share of outdoor chores this weekend myself."

"You two are lucky you have homes at all, the way you talk," Daphne said. "You act all helpless inside the house, then complain when you have to help keep the outside nice. Both your wives ought to put you out with the cats."

When Frank protested that he was the better cook in the house, Daphne just shook her head. "Excuses, excuses," she said.

Bill wasn't in a mood for one of Daphne's man-bashing rants. "So, any bites?"

Frank indicated the folder containing the reports on Daphne's desk. "Depends on what you call bites. The girlfriend's a mess, could barely speak, and his buddies swear up and down there were no fights and no drugs. Maybe it's a straightforward heart thing after all."

Bill took a sip of his coffee. "Keep me posted."

Frank looked for a moment like he wanted to add something, but instead he said that it was no problem and left the office.

Daphne picked up the reports. "You want me to pass these on to Mitch?"

Mitchell Carl was his chief deputy. The lights in Mitch's office were dark. He spent the better part of his day on Monday in court. Bill was always surprised that he made it in early after his weekends in the city. A part of him envied Mitch his freedom, but he knew it was an expensive sort of freedom. He owed a pile of child support and always had at least one or two other women to help him spend what was left.

Bill took the folder from her. "I think I'll just thumb through them before I pass them on," he said, heading back to his office.

Daphne watched him. "Why the personal touch, boss?"

Bill shrugged. "Hey, sometimes it's good to shake things up a bit," he said.

The reports were dutiful. Brad Catlett had been a campus favorite. His grades had been slipping some in the previous months. At least two of his teachers had attributed it to the rites of spring and his preoccupation with his girlfriend. The track coach reported that he thought the boy had been under the weather lately, but said he'd been turning in great times and was poised to make the team serious competition in the state meets. Bill wondered whether it was true or just the coach's wishful thinking. There was nothing there that was particularly helpful—and it didn't really matter anyway until he got the coroner's report.

He was glad that he'd had somewhat more success with his research on Kate Russell. Edith had been helpful.

Beaufort, South Carolina, was not Charleston, South Carolina. He'd found in his line of work that when people lied, their lies were often very close to the truth, as though that made their lies more acceptable. She probably wasn't from Beaufort either. He pulled a map of South Carolina up on the Internet and saw that they were both near the eastern shore of the state. He figured that if she hadn't lived in either place, she hadn't been far away. Maybe somewhere in between.

When he pulled up Kate Russell's DMV records, he found that she didn't have so much as a parking ticket. There were no previous addresses listed for her in any of the online phone listings. He made a note of her Social Security number so he could check her out in the national databases the state subscribed to.

Later, on his way home for lunch, he cruised past Janet Rourke's office on Bridge Street. A light mist fell on the cruiser, and the sidewalks were emptier than usual. While he waited in line at the long traffic light at Bridge and High, he saw the woman he'd been thinking about all morning step outside the agency office and shut the door behind her. She seemed okay, but criminals were criminals, and if she was thinking that she was going to make some kind of profit on her bullshit notion about the lost girl, then she was a criminal, plain and simple.

Today she moved with an easy grace that had been absent when she came into his office. Her hair framed her face, pointing up the delicacy of her features. She looked much younger than the thirty-two years listed on her driver's license. Still, she had the confident look of a tomboy tamed. He wasn't surprised that she'd attracted the attention of the guy he'd seen her out with. As he felt the blood rush to his groin, he was blind-sided by the realization that she reminded him of a young Margaret.

As he watched, she approached a woman who leaned dejectedly against the agency's front picture window. When she reached the woman, she tilted her umbrella in the direction of the mist to keep them both dry.

Carystown was small enough that there wasn't a homeless problem. He and the Social Services people quickly swept most of the mentally ill into the state system and the transients were briskly moved along. This bare-legged woman, with her loose, lavender dress and skin that spoke of too many hours in the sun, was familiar to him, but in the confusion of the moment, he couldn't think of who it was.

As Kate Russell gently took the woman's arm, she chanced to glance up and, he thought, caught him watching. He quickly looked away to see that the cars in front of him had already cleared the intersection. As he crossed High Street, it came to him that the woman Kate Russell had been speaking to was Hanna Moon, Isabella's mother.

8

Mary-Katie carefully sipped the coffee that one of the other volunteers had brought her from the hospitality table. A fine November mist was falling, obscuring the sunrise, but the mood of the runners arriving for the Children's Hospital Half-Marathon was light. She almost wished that she had trained for the race, but she was no runner and had never fooled herself about the fact. Running gave her a headache. What she really liked was walking, miles and miles of walking for the pleasure of it. It seemed to her that when she ran, she missed too much.

In years past, her grandmother, Katherine, after whom she'd been partially named, had walked with her. Together, they knew every inch of Beaufort and the surrounding countryside. Sometimes they went all the way to the beaches, but mostly they stuck to the flats, finding odd little roads that dead-ended after miles at someone's truck farm or piney woods. Now Mary-Katie took her walks alone, always coming home to tell her grandmother what she'd seen, what new houses were going in nearby, who had been outside gardening, and who had asked her to stop and chat. But more and more often, her grandmother was asleep in her comfortable chair by the front window, where she'd be waiting for her to return. She'd made great progress from a stroke, but not enough to allow her to walk more than the distance from her chair to her bedroom or the kitchen without stopping to rest a few moments.

One of the runners dropped his registration card on the table, startling Mary-Katie, who had been watching the crowd.

"Got anything in the forties?" he said. He glanced at her name tag. "Forty-two, if you have it, Mary-Katie." He smiled.

The name written on his card in compact block letters read, MILES CHENO-WETH.

Miles Chenoweth was neat, like his handwriting. Not tall; she guessed he was no more than a couple of inches taller than her own height of five feet six inches. In fact, when she later looked at his card, she saw that he was five-seven. Overall, he had the look and bearing of a wrestler: squarish shoulders, tapered waist, and muscular arms (that were, she noted, on the hairy side). He was, in fact, a rather hairy man, with small, tight curls peeking around the edges of his runner's jersey. But the hair on his head, which was the same deep brown color, was close-cropped to keep it from unruliness.

"We have to give the numbers out in the order that people come up," she said. "I'm sorry. The best I can do is 138."

He gave a low whistle and looked at his watch. "I can't be that late," he said.

Mary-Katie laughed. "They started at one hundred," she said.

"Why aren't you on this side of the table?" he said. "You look pretty fit to me."

"Running's not my thing," Mary-Katie said. "But I love the Children's Hospital. I was a candy striper there in high school."

"One of those little red and white uniforms?" Miles asked. "And a pointy cap?"

"T-shirts," she said. "But they were red and white."

When he smiled, his arctic blue eyes narrowed with amusement. Mary-Katie envied his thick eyelashes. Her own were rather thin and lighter than her hair. She hadn't thought to put on makeup that morning. The sun hadn't even been up at all when she'd had her breakfast.

"Will you be at the finish?" Miles said. "Or are you only registering people?"

"Will you be at the finish?" Mary-Katie said. She felt herself responding to this very forward man in a way that she knew her grandmother wouldn't approve. But she told herself that she was twenty-four years old, not fourteen, and she was old enough to make a sensible judgment about what a man was like.

"I'll be the first one across the line," he said. He said it so matter-of-factly that it didn't sound like a boast.

~

At exactly one o'clock, Miles walked into the café where Mary-Katie had agreed to meet him for lunch. It was crowded for a Saturday afternoon, and most of the well-dressed diners looked like tourists in to start their Thanksgiving Day holiday a few days early.

When she saw him come in the door, Mary-Katie lifted her hand to wave, but dropped it again quickly into her lap. She didn't want to seem too eager.

Miles scanned the crowd as though he were looking for something important. He looked so serious, in fact, that his forehead was creased. Mary-Katie imagined that this would be how he looked when he was angry. She decided then and there that it would be a terrible thing to see him in a rage. Finally, he spotted her sitting against the back wall that glinted with the shards of pottery and fake gems plastered and painted onto its surface. When they made eye contact, his face lighted up with pleasure. Mary-Katie relaxed. He was glad to see her.

"They could have put us at a better table," he said, brushing her shoulder with his fingertips as he sat down. "A woman like you should be right out front, not hidden back here in no-man's-land."

Mary-Katie blushed. Of course, sometimes when she was alone, she would look in the mirror and tentatively admire what she saw there: the slender, straight nose, the spray of freckles across her cheeks that she had so hated when she was in high school, the almost auburn hair and the hazel eyes that were just like her father's. She knew she wasn't homely, but she certainly had never thought of herself as beautiful.

"I was afraid you wouldn't find me back here," she said. "But it's close to the kitchen, so we should get served quickly."

Miles looked at her, wondering if she was sincere. When he saw that she was, he said, "Of course."

They drank wine at lunch, something Mary-Katie rarely did. When she told Miles that the chardonnay put her in mind of apricots and wood smoke, he agreed and poured her another glass.

Through the wine, Mary-Katie talked more than she ever thought she could, or should. Miles listened to her describe growing up under the watchful eye of her grandmother after her father had left when she was five. He laughed in all the right places when she told him about her teller's job at the bank, and about the characters who sometimes wandered in off the street trying to convince her that they had money there waiting for them even though they had no *identification and there was no record of them in the computer. He frowned when she told him of the woman who had hit her child so hard for misbehaving in line that the child fell backward and hit her head and went unconscious. As she talked, he leaned forward, listening intently, as though what she was saying was critical information, as though she were the most important person in the world.*

Much later, thinking about that day, it wasn't the lunch that she remembered so clearly, but the early part of the day and the end of the race. Miles had come in second, not first, as he'd told her he would.

Only a few seconds behind the winner, he hadn't seemed so much exhausted when he crossed the line as he did irritated. Mary-Katie didn't think second was a bad finish. She even found herself a little relieved that he hadn't won. If he had, he would've been the center of attention and she would've felt too awkward about approaching him. Still, she hung back until the early finishers had toweled themselves off before she broke off from the crowd to stand a few feet behind Miles, waiting to congratulate him.

Miles and the winner were standing close to each other when the winner suddenly turned to Miles and slapped him on the back.

"I thought you had me there, man," he said. "That last quarter was rough."

He offered his hand to Miles, who seemed taken aback. Just when his hesitation might have appeared rude, Miles grabbed the winner's hand and shook it heartily.

"Next time," he said, smiling. "What's your name?"

"Lev," the winner said. "My name's Lev Kaplan. But, you know, I'm just out here for the practice. These half-marathons are just to keep me sharp for the real thing, you know?"

Miles dropped the man's hand and turned away abruptly, leaving him standing there open-mouthed.

As he started past her, looking down, Mary-Katie said Miles's name quickly. On seeing her, his smile returned.

"You're still here," he said.

"I told you I would be," she said. She was a little embarrassed for him, knowing that he had been certain he would win.

"Did you see the finish?" he said.

There was something about the way he asked that told her he hadn't really wanted her to see.

"I'm sorry," she said. "I had to run back to my car for just a minute and I didn't hear them announce that you all were coming in." She didn't like to lie, but there were times when it had to be done.

When she saw the relief on his face, she knew she'd said the right thing.

"That guy came out of nowhere. Didn't even look winded," he said. "Some of these people cheat and don't think anything of it."

After lunch, Miles wouldn't let her go home in her own car.

"What would your grandmother say, you coming home from our first date tipsy?" he said. "And you shouldn't be driving. You might hurt yourself."

Mary-Katie thought she was fine to drive, but she didn't argue. When he'd paid the bill, he guided her out of the restaurant, his hand resting proprietarily at the small of her back.

Somehow she'd known that his car would be black. She sank into the fragrant leather interior of the BMW and put her head back against the headrest. As the engine purred to life, music came through the speakers—bright, lively music, all violins.

"Do you like Vivaldi?" he asked. "I've got several other choices in the changer. Some Dvorak, I think some Chopin as well."

"This is fine," she said, closing her eyes. She didn't know Vivaldi from spaghetti, but she didn't want him to know how ignorant she was. It wasn't until after they were married that she discovered that the manager of a small music store down in Savannah selected his music for him and sent CDs to him in the mail every month or so.

They drove out to the beach at the state park and got out of the car. The misty rain from the morning had long disappeared, and the wind coming off the Atlantic was brisk enough that she accepted the offer of Miles's navy sport coat gratefully.

The beach was deserted. It was too windy and late in the day for fishermen, much too cool for sunbathing. As they walked, Mary-Katie felt the effects of the wine ebb with the receding waves. She marveled at the fact that Miles had known just what she'd needed.

Miles didn't touch her as they walked. They spoke little, as though they were old friends who didn't need casual conversation. When they reached the rotted husk of a boat half buried in the sand since a hurricane had put it there in the 1960s, they took shelter from the wind for a few minutes beside it. Mary-Katie *laughed as she tried to run her fingers through her tangled hair, but Miles took her hand gently.*

"Leave it," he said. "It looks beautiful."

He was looking into her eyes and she thought that he might kiss her then. She wanted him to kiss her. But the moment passed. Miles stood and she followed, a little puzzled, a little embarrassed, back to the car.

"I'll take you home," he said. "We'll go back tomorrow for your car."

That was how it was decided: She would see him the next day and the next and the next.

When they pulled up in front of the house she shared with her grandmother, she asked him to come in.

"Not today," he said. "Soon. It's important that I meet her. But not today."

"Okay," Mary-Katie said. *She was disappointed. She wanted her grandmother to meet this strange, interesting man. She thought that maybe her grandmother could tell her what she was feeling. Right now, she knew only that she was drawn to him, but she wasn't sure why. It was sexual, certainly. But there was something else, something that was at once comforting and darkly thrilling.*

Miles kissed her tenderly on the cheek before she got out of the car.

"I'll call you in the morning," he said.

As he drove away, she stood at the door and waved. She knew that he would call. She knew that she would be waiting by the telephone.

9

WHEN THE PORTABLE PHONE RANG in her gardening apron pocket, Lillian pulled it out immediately, certain it was Francie answering her page.

"What is it, Mama?" Francie sounded annoyed. Lillian knew she disliked being called at work. "Is something wrong?"

In the background Lillian could hear the other nurses laughing and talking. By now all the patients had had their dinner and first evening round of medications, so the nurses could hang around the station and update their charts until the shift change. She hadn't wanted to call Francie early in the day because she knew she'd be asleep. Except for church, Lillian had been alone at the house all weekend, a mistake, she knew, after Friday night's adventures. She told herself that she should have known better. It wasn't that she was afraid—no, maybe *disturbed* was a better word. The notion that there were bodies buried in the cemetery not far from her house had never bothered her. But it did bother her, deeply, that the little girl might be there.

"You'd be the first person I'd tell, honey, if there were something wrong, and there's just not," Lillian said. "I was thinking that you should come by here for a late supper. I made a quiche and you know how the crust goes all soggy if you don't eat it the first day."

Francie sighed. "At nine I'm going to go home and get a shower, then I'm going straight to bed," she said. "I'm whipped. Plus, I'm pulling a double tomorrow because Sarah's starting her maternity leave."

As Francie spoke, Lillian stood on tiptoe to hang a set of pottery wind chimes that she'd taken down for the winter. Francie had made the chimes in Girl Scouts, and their sound was nothing special, but Francie had etched each of their names on the three chimes: Francine, Lillian, Albert.

"You sound tired," she said. "Should you be taking on extra hours? You would tell me if you needed the money?"

"Mama, we're just short-staffed," she said.

"Did you pick up the dry cleaning we dropped off on Friday?" Lillian asked. "It's not right to make those folks wait for their money."

Lillian could tell that Francie was getting impatient. Even when Francie was silent, Lillian could read her daughter loud and clear.

"I'm going to go now," Francie said. "I'll come by on Wednesday, okay? I've got to go check on a patient. Good-bye, Mama."

Lillian waited for the disconnecting click, but there was none. She could still hear the nurses in the background.

"I love you," Francie said. "I really will be there Wednesday. Okay?"

"You have a good rest tonight, baby," Lillian said. "I'll see you."

Lillian slipped the telephone back into her apron pocket, a little sorry that she'd even brought it outside. Her Francie hadn't been herself for a while now. She'd always been independent, but now her behavior was just plain manic.

When she was at the house, she was all nervous, worried about every little thing. Did Lillian have enough groceries? Were all her bills current? Was the yard work too much for her? Treating her like she was eighty years old, for goodness sake. Then, on the phone, she was distant, as she was tonight. She had no time for anyone, especially her mother. Lillian knew the symptoms well: Francie was involved with a man, a man she had no business being with. *If she had seen him, just days earlier, hurrying from a local widow's house at seven in the morning, carrying his necktie, what could she say?* She would have done what she could about it, but her daughter was a grown woman. She would just have to wait it out and be there to help Francie put herself back together when things got bad.

In the trees, the few birds that had come back for the early spring were settling noisily for the evening. Out of the corner of her eye she saw her favorite late feeders, a ruby-colored cardinal and his dowdy mate. She watched as the male swept down from a chestnut tree at the edge of the woods to perch on the feeder. As he ate his fill, he looked about every so often to check for competitors. Finally, the female began her approach, one branch, one bush at a time, until she reached the ground just beneath the feeder. She pecked at the empty sunflower hulls scattered there while she waited for the male to finish. When he was safely away, she flew to the perch and ate a bite or two before darting back to the chestnut where the male waited. Lillian wondered how she sustained herself, eating so little.

Lillian had spent so much of her own life waiting, some of it in this house, some of it long before Francie was born, in rough apartments around the South, Georgia, Virginia, North Carolina, waiting for Albert to get home from whatever work he'd found, waiting to get on to teach at a school wherever they were. She was a good teacher, and even though school segregation was still struggling to hold on in many of the places they had lived, she never had a problem finding a job. But she had always wanted to come back home. And she'd had to wait a long time for that.

She carried her gardening trug, filled with weeding tools and trimmers, around to the back of the house. The light had faded considerably since she'd come out, but there was enough that she could see to pull a few brown, wintered-over weeds from the annual bed in the center of the backyard. For years Albert had teased her about being a midnight gardener, never satisfied with the daylight the Lord gave her.

She stepped carefully around the wheelbarrow and pitchfork that the Evans boy had left out when he went home to supper. Time was when she would've mulched the perennial beds herself, even helping the man from the garden center fork it off the trailer under Francie's disapproving gaze. But the arthritis in her hands and wrists had put a stop to that.

The annual bed was rich with humus and manure she'd tilled in over the years, and, even though it was far too early for putting out the geraniums, heliotrope, and petunias that would give the bed its magnificent color, she liked to get a start on the weeds, the young dandelions and chickweed that had snuck in before they began to multiply. Reaching far into the center, she paid special attention to the space around the stubs of the bed's single bush, a white hydrangea that, in the summer, dressed itself in a hundred puffballs made up of tiny, heart-shaped bracts that fell like snowflakes at the slightest touch.

~

Lillian and Albert had been careful for so many years, not wanting to have a baby when they were living like gypsies, staying in one place for no more than a year at a time. Now they were finally in their own house, built with the money left by her father, a man who never thought Albert good enough for his Lillian: too poor, too stupid, and, worse, with a mother who was white. But now that her father was dead, they were back in Carystown, where Lillian had wanted to be all her life.

It was deep summer and the peepers called from the woods. There were not yet houses on either side of them, and the only light to see by came from their kitchen window. Still, the yard was filled with the sparks of too many fireflies to count, and the night was clear, so that the stars shone with startling brilliance above them.

After dinner they sat eating their pie on the wedding-ring quilt she'd spread in the center of the yard that afternoon. Another quilt, also made by her mother for her hope chest, lay at their feet. When they finished eating, Lillian put their plates aside and they lay on their backs looking at the sky.

"So, it's time," Albert said, reaching for her hand.

She hadn't known it would happen, but she began to cry.

Albert laughed softly. "Here, baby," he crooned. He took her into his arms and kissed her tears and made love to her.

Later, as they lay wrapped up together in one of the quilts, Lillian felt herself slipping into a dream in which she gave birth to a hundred children who, like the fireflies, flew off into the night.

In the distance Lillian heard the sound of a lawn mower start up. It was too early in the season for grass cutting—someone was surely mulching late-falling oak leaves. She smiled to herself, thinking that she wasn't the only midnight gardener in the neighborhood. Actually, it was only 7:45, and full dark had just come. An automatic light she'd had installed on the side of the house came on as the neighbor's tabby passed beneath her kitchen window.

" 'Evening, Pudding," she called, but the cat merely stiffened her raised tail and continued across the patio.

Sitting back on her feet, Lillian stretched her arms above her head. The cool air from the woods had begun to move through the yard, and the last thing she needed was to be out in the damp. As she gathered up her garden tools, her mind rushed forward to her evening routine: shine up her sink, take the garbage out, wash her face, and clean her teeth. She rose, stiffly, and headed to the back door of the garage.

She was about to reach for the doorknob when she saw a movement behind the garbage cans.

"Pudding!" she said. "Scat!" The cat, which belonged to her neighbor, Aletha, had a taste for trash and was damned clever about getting into it. No doubt the salmon fillet she'd had the night before had attracted it.

When no cat dashed out, she looked more closely. Again, the movement. She put her hand to her chest when she saw a small girl rise up from behind the can's lid. Her face was pale, paler than one could ever imagine a person's skin being. Lillian felt that if she looked hard enough, she would be able to see through her skin and into the inner flesh of the girl. Her hair was black, almost invisible in the shadows. A thin hand rested on the edge of the can.

When Lillian's breath returned, she said, "Child," but couldn't force any other words from her throat.

There was a sound behind her, a swishing sound like a wave of silk sweeping across the lawn, and the girl, not even looking toward the sound, turned away.

Lillian reached out to her, but before she could take a step, she felt the presence of someone behind her and started to turn. Something hard hit her in her right temple, then hit her again and again as she fell to the ground, the curve of the trug's handle beneath her, digging into her stomach.

Stunned but still able to move, she tried to raise herself up, to find out what had hit her, and who. But something jabbed at her, hard, in the back. This time she lay with her eyes closed, but her strength wouldn't return. The whisper of a prayer escaped her lips.

A small hand that was neither warm nor cold slipped over her open palm and squeezed. Lillian opened her eyes and blinked several times, trying to clear the blood from them. The little girl knelt beside her, looking at her impassively.

Lillian wasn't sure if the girl was speaking. Her mouth didn't appear to be moving, but inside her head Lillian heard the words, *It's all right all right all right all right,* over and over, like a mother's lullaby. So absorbed was she, so transformed by the pain and the little girl's words, that she barely moved when the pitchfork pierced her, puncturing a lung and snapping her spinal cord in two.

10

FRANCIE LAY WITH HER HEAD on Paxton's chest. His shirt, which he hadn't bothered to take off, was soaked. Her own legs and butt were exposed, but the interior of the car was still warm.

Only twenty minutes earlier she had hurried out of the hospital, exhausted and anxious to get home. But before she could pull out of her parking space, Paxton rapped on the driver's-side window, nearly scaring her to death. Now, they were both in the passenger seat of her car, still breathing hard from the sex they'd just had.

"That nursey uniform is so fucking hot," Paxton said. "I can't believe all those old men in there aren't trying to drag you into their beds and fuck themselves into heart attacks."

Francie laughed and raised her head to bite playfully at his lower lip. "You're so full of shit," she said. Her uniform was a baggy pair of white pants and an oversize smock.

"No, I'm serious," he said. "You don't know what a fine piece of ass you are. That's what I love about you."

"Well, the guy driving around in the security truck is going to know if we don't get out of here," Francie said, trying to pull away. But Paxton pulled her closer and began to stroke her hair.

"Come on up to Keeneland with me when they start running in a couple of weeks," he said.

Francie didn't move, waited to answer. Lexington wasn't that far away, and the track was a fairly public place. Paxton never talked about people he knew up there, but the rumor mill was rife every spring with his horse-circuit partying.

"Hey. Are you asleep?" he said, nudging her.

"We really are living on the edge today, aren't we?" she said. She twisted around to pull up her panties and pants and climbed awkwardly back over to the driver's side. It confused and irritated her when Paxton brought up the subject of their being seen together. One day he said he didn't give a damn, other times she wouldn't see him for weeks when he thought that they might have been seen in Middleboro or in a restaurant an hour from Carystown.

"I hate to bring it up," she said. "But what about your mother? Isn't it always about your mother?"

Pax buckled up his pants and reset his seat. "Come on, baby," he said. "My mama's so out of her head these days with whatever bullshit the doctor's got her on, she doesn't know her ass from her elbow."

That much she knew about Freida Birkenshaw. The woman had been ill for almost a year. Francie often saw her in the hallways of the medical center on her way to her doctors' appointments, leaning on Paxton or her housekeeper.

"What about *my* mother, then?" Francie said. "Don't you care what she thinks?" She was feeling guilty about not going by her mother's house, and now she would be on her way to bed. On the phone, her mother had sounded the slightest bit sad.

"We can play that game all fucking night if you want, Francie. But then I guess we both got ours, didn't we?"

"Where the hell did that come from?" she said. Paxton had turned suddenly nasty. It was a side of him she didn't like. She thought it might be the coke talking. When he'd shown up at her car, his eyes had been glassy, his smile just a bit too wide.

"Someday you're going to be all out of excuses, sweet cakes," he said. "And you're going to be fucking all alone. Because we both know that even if I bought you a fucking gold ring and let you put it through my nose so you could lead me down fucking Main Street, it wouldn't make any difference to you. Would it?"

Francie shook her head, but she was trembling inside. "Whatever. You're just stoned," she said. "You don't know what you're talking about."

She looked around for her purse as though getting ready to get out of the car. She didn't know what to do. She just wanted to be away from him.

"You don't fool me, Francie," he said. "I've known you too well for too long."

"You don't know shit," she said. "You don't know anything about my life. What would you know, living in that big fucking house with your four fucking cars and your old black Bonterre servants to wipe your ass for you? What the hell do you know about real life?"

The look in Paxton's eyes was hurt, angry. So many times they'd played games where they got close to the edge of pain, but they were only games. Would he hurt her? Here, in the car? It scared her more, though, to realize that at that moment she felt something deeper for him than the lust she had been experiencing for months.

"You're a snob, Francie. You have been all your life. You can't see your way out of your precious family circle," he said. "You're fucking pathetic if you think it's some kind of crime to have money. And in about five minutes you're going to be fucking sorry you blew me off, because you're going to need me, sweet cakes."

He sat for just another moment in the car, staring at her, his breath coming heavily. Then he got out.

A minute later Francie heard the Mercedes start up a few rows over. She looked up as he gunned it down the parking lot aisle and bounced out onto the highway.

11

AFTER A LONG MORNING OUT at Janet's new house, Kate sat at her office desk picking at the salad she'd had delivered from The Lettuce Leaf. She'd already eaten the sunflower and walnut roll that had come with it, butter and all, and had dabbed at the crumbs before brushing them into her trash can. The salad displeased her. For once, she was truly hungry, and the deep green romaine leaves and crisp veggies seemed offensive. What she really wanted was comfort food: peanut butter, macaroni and cheese, caramel popcorn with nuts, cookies, cookies, cookies, and then, perhaps, some ice cream. But she knew better than to go down that road. Once she started, it would be too hard to stop.

For the first time in more than a week, she had slept through the night. There had been no sudden awakening, no sickening worry that she was being watched. Saturday night had been peaceful too, with Caleb breathing evenly beside her in the dark, though she'd awakened herself several times waiting, wondering if the girl would come again.

Self-conscious about their lovemaking, Kate had insisted, to Caleb's amusement, that they make love in the living room on a blanket on the floor. She'd had him light a fire in the fireplace and they used up the last of the wood she'd had delivered for the winter. By the time they finished around midnight, they were both dripping with sweat, so warm was the room.

"Let's get a shower," he had said. "Then maybe we can start all over again in bed." He ran the tip of his tongue lightly from the hollow of her throat to the tender skin on the underside of her jaw. "Mmm. Salty girl."

But what if she's there, watching? What if she's at the window?

Kate wriggled out from beneath him and wrapped herself in the throw from the couch. She glanced down the hallway to the bedroom.

"What is it?" Caleb asked.

She gave him what she hoped was a reassuring smile. "Let's get dressed first. Or maybe you could just put these on." She picked up the plaid boxers that lay near a leg of the couch and tossed them so that they landed at his feet.

He looked at the shorts but made no move to pick them up. "What the hell? The shades are pulled down."

"Well, maybe they aren't in the bedroom," she said.

In the waning firelight, Caleb's skin gave off a warm, bronze glow. She knew how lucky she was to have him in her life. He had never done a single thing to hurt or worry her. She knew she didn't deserve to be treated so well. Someday he would know the truth about her and he would probably leave. Pushing him away was the furthest thing from her mind, but right then the little girl seemed more important.

"Pretty please?" she said, giving him a playful pout.

When he stood up, towering over her with the firelight behind him, he was like a dark shadow come to life. Naked, he walked past her to the bedroom and the bathroom beyond.

"You may be one of the best-looking women I've ever known, Kate Russell, but sometimes I think you're a little nuts," he called back to her.

She heard the bathroom door close behind him and the shower start up. Later in bed, though their bodies were spooned comfortably together, they spoke little before they fell asleep. As he prepared to leave Sunday, Caleb had kissed her passionately, but she felt like there was a new distance between them.

In her heart she knew she'd been a little ridiculous about the whole thing. *Paranoid* really was the word. The girl could go anywhere she wanted, obviously—to a cemetery, out to Janet's house (Kate was sure that the pinecones had been brought there by the girl, or she had caused them to be there). The absurdity of the situation was starting to get to her. The notion that she was making choices in her life based on what she thought were the concerns of something or someone that didn't even exist put her off balance. She was worried that maybe her mind was playing tricks on her, that her conscience was catching up with her. She had thought she'd left the worst part of herself and her fears behind her when she fled South Carolina. But maybe she was wrong. Still, hadn't Lillian seen? Hadn't she understood that the girl was asking for her help?

"That woman's back again," Edith said, startling her out of her thoughts. "Janet's going to have a fit."

Kate sighed. "I told her yesterday that she was going to have to stop hanging around out there."

Hanna Moon leaned with her back against the window, her broad shoulders and tangle of dark hair spread against the glass. She was looking up as though watching the sky for something.

"It's so sad about her daughter," Edith said. "I think I'd go a little crazy, too. But I don't think I'd actually become a *street* person. Maybe I should get someone at the church involved. Or maybe we should just call the police even if Janet said not to. She's going to have a fit, just a fit. What do you think, Kate?" Edith stood with her hands on her hips, watching the woman at the window with mild perplexity, as though she were trying to decide which hat to wear.

Kate closed the lid on her uneaten salad and dropped the container into the trash.

"She thinks her daughter's *here*, Edith," she said. "I mean, she thinks she's seen her on the street." The day before, Kate had stopped just short of telling Hanna Moon that she knew where her dead daughter was hanging out, and it wasn't in front of an insurance agency on Bridge Street.

"Honestly," Edith said, walking back to her desk. "Some people take advantage, don't they? Remember how Janet donated all that reward money to find the child? That woman probably just wants more."

Kate spun around in her chair to face Edith. "You can't mean that, Edith," she said, genuinely shocked. "That's so cruel."

Edith shrugged. "We'll see," she said.

Certain that Edith was wrong, Kate went back to work and tried to ignore the woman's dark presence at the window. She'd been in cities where people like Hanna Moon, people who had mental problems, would claim bits of sidewalks for themselves so that they became part of the landscape, so that people who passed them would have to go out of their way to avoid making contact with them. She tried to put Hanna Moon out of her mind, to accept her for the time being, as she'd decided to accept the presence of her daughter.

At a quarter past two, Janet let herself in through the agency's back door, which led from their private parking area.

"I'm back," she called as she went into her office.

Within a minute Edith had gathered Janet's messages and mail and followed her inside. But one of the first updates Edith gave her must have been about Hanna Moon.

Kate cringed ever so slightly when she heard Janet's door open and her clipped footsteps on the hardwood floor. Janet came straight to her desk, as Kate had known she would.

"You were supposed to get rid of that woman, Kate. What the hell do I pay you for?" she said. She was in what Kate's grandmother would have called "high dudgeon," her chest puffed out in indignation, her nose in the air. Kate wanted to laugh. The last thing Janet needed to do was stick out her breasts to get them noticed. She wore an equestrian-themed scarf-print silk blouse today, with only the first two buttons undone. Kate guessed that her morning's appointments must have been predominantly female.

"She's not doing any harm," Kate said. "I asked her not to come back and she said she wouldn't."

"Big clue, Kate," Janet said. "She *lied*. Who's going to want to come here and do business with that"—she pointed to the large form in the window—"purple elephant standing guard?"

Kate stood up, taller than Janet, even though Janet wore her usual three-inch heels.

"I've done all I can think to do, Janet, except call the police," she said quietly. She remembered how the sheriff had watched her the day before from his car. She hadn't heard back from him after their meeting on Friday and was beginning to suspect that he wouldn't get back to her at all. "Or you could talk to her yourself."

Janet glanced in the direction of the window and seemed to consider. Kate thought she saw a look of, what—apprehension? fear?—cross her face. Perhaps it was Hanna Moon's closeness to tragedy that scared her. Janet was a shiny and new, upbeat kind of person. She didn't like drama or highly emotional situations. She was all business—even though her business frequently depended on exploiting the emotions and needs of others.

"Just talk to her again," she said, and went back into her office, slamming the door.

Hanna Moon was waving one arm in a slow arc back and forth in front of her. It occurred to Kate from time to time that she should switch jobs, maybe get a job selling clothes in one of Carystown's numerous pricey boutiques. She knew enough people in town now, even if she wasn't close to anyone besides Francie. The woman who owned Petals, up the hill, thought she had great taste and would pay her a good commission. But the thought of filling out paperwork that might expose her to more scrutiny worried her. Two years before, Janet had been so anxious to get someone both literate and presentable in the office that she'd been rather lackadaisical when hiring her. Still, Kate had worried all through the process.

When the phone rang, Edith was still in Janet's office. Kate picked it up. A woman identified herself as Daphne Poteet from the sheriff's office. Kate recalled the deputy's homely face and efficient manner.

"I'm calling for Kate Russell," she said.

"This is Kate. How may I help you?" Kate was suddenly both hopeful and a little afraid that she was going to get to speak to the sheriff again, that he'd either decided to believe her or would tell her to take a hike with her nutty ideas about Isabella Moon.

"The sheriff would appreciate it if you would proceed over to the home of Lillian Cayley, 112 Birchfield Avenue," she said. "Right away."

"What is it?" Kate said. "Is something wrong?"

The deputy hesitated a moment before telling her that there had been an incident there.

"What kind of incident?" Kate said.

"A death, ma'am. According to the sheriff, you probably want to go right away," she said.

As she hurried past Janet's office door, Kate said, "There's an emergency. I have to go." And she was out the back door before Janet or Edith could respond.

Her hands trembled as she tried to fit the key into the car's ignition. If something had happened to Lillian, it was surely her fault, having dragged her into the business with the dead girl the way she had. Lillian would be yet another person to pay with her life for something she had done or said or wanted. Only this time, Kate was afraid that the murderer was not flesh and blood, but something harder to control, harder to fight—and impossible to punish.

12

WHEN THE DAUGHTER of the murdered woman asked him to send for Kate Russell, Bill had found it more than a little startling. He didn't like the way she had been showing up in his business, seemingly out of nowhere, over the past few days. Her name was now connected to a murder and the disappearance of the Moon girl, and he still knew very little about her. He had a line on some information down in South Carolina, but was waiting for a call back. His database searches had been inconclusive.

He handed off Mrs. Cooper, the woman from next door who had found the body, to Mitch when he saw the Russell woman park her car in front of a neighbor's house. Watching her approach, he saw that she looked shaken, distressed, just as she had the previous Friday morning.

"Where's Lillian?" she asked. "Is she here? What's wrong, Sheriff?"

She took off her sunglasses. With their odd, dark green lenses, they reminded him of glasses his mother would've worn. He hadn't noticed until now that Kate Russell had hazel eyes.

"Mrs. Cayley's daughter asked for you," he said. "You a friend of hers?"

"I'm a friend of Francie *and* Lillian," she said. "Where's Lillian? Why won't you tell me what's happened?"

She didn't wait for an answer, but tried to push past him. Bill reached out and caught her by the arm.

"Mrs. Cayley is dead," he said. "And I'd like to know what you know about it."

She looked up at him in disbelief, then flushed when she realized that they both knew why he was asking. Lillian's house was only a few hundred yards from the cemetery where she'd told him he should look for the body of Isabella Moon.

But when she spoke, she didn't sound confused or afraid, as he'd expected. She was just plain angry.

"If Lillian's already dead, then you might as well let me go see Francie," she said. "I can't kill Lillian twice, can I?"

"Don't screw around with me, Miss Russell," he said. "Being a smartass is going to land you in a place you won't like very much. And you haven't exactly presented yourself as very stable up to this point."

Kate stared at him for a moment, obviously considering whether to push him. She backed down.

"May I please, *please*, just go see Francie?" she said. "I promise I'll tell you anything you want later. Please let me go."

Bill realized that he was still gripping her arm tightly. He let go, and she ran toward the front door.

It was an ugly murder scene. He'd been downright embarrassed that the daughter had shown up before they removed the pitchfork from the body. But he'd had to send someone back to the office to get the camera they used for crime scenes.

"What's the word, Doc?" he asked the coroner, Porter Jessup, who sat back on his haunches studying the woman's head wound.

"Nasty," he said. "Almost as good as the old lady gored by that buck. But not quite."

"That's damned helpful," Bill said.

"I'm thinking the whacks upside the head probably killed her," he said. "Sometime between six o'clock and midnight's my first guess. She's stone cold. Body temp's in the toilet."

"Tell me the daughter was in the house when you performed that little deed," Bill said.

"Hey, you know I'm Mr. Sensitivity, Bill," the coroner said, indicating the plastic sheet he'd spread over the body. "She wasn't anywhere near here that I could see."

"Good," Bill said. "You finished here?" he asked the two deputies standing by.

When they nodded, he sent them off to question more of the neighbors. Then he signaled the EMTs to take the body to the morgue. The technicians handled the woman gently. They made a good team and were the two he liked to see when he showed up at a car wreck, where things could get really messy. When she was bundled into the body bag and secured onto the stretcher, he told the technicians to load her up, but to take their time.

Before he let himself in the back door of the house, Bill took off his hat and ran his hand over the top of his head as though he had hair up there to smooth. He followed the sound of quiet sobs to the living room, noting that lights and lamps were turned on all through the house.

Kate Russell sat with her arms around the daughter, Francie, who was still weeping, though not as loudly as before. He waited a moment, giving them time to notice him. He also saw that the deputy he'd assigned to stay in the house appeared to have wandered off. Murders didn't happen every day around Carystown, and his people were bound to be sloppy, but that didn't mean he had to put up with it.

"The sheriff's here," Kate whispered to Francie.

Francie pulled away from her and looked up at the sheriff from the couch. She looked hopeful, like it might have all been some kind of mistake.

As he spoke, he held the rim of his hat tight in his fingertips. The grieving were always unpredictable.

"We've got your mother in the ambulance," he said. "The coroner's going to take a look at her and see what he can find out about her death."

He stopped a moment as Kate picked up on what he was about to say.

"Do you want to go outside, Francie?" she said. "Do you want to see your mother go?" Her voice broke with the realization that Lillian would be leaving her house for the last time.

Francie could only nod.

Outside, a small crowd of people, mostly older black women, some of whom held small children close to their sides, had gathered near the rear of the ambulance. Bill walked a few steps behind the daughter and Kate Russell, who seemed to be speaking quietly to the daughter to keep her going.

The crowd parted as the women approached and the daughter broke away and scrambled up into the ambulance to throw herself over her mother's body. Behind her, the crowd closed ranks, and for a long few minutes the only sound in the clear spring air was Francine Cayley's high and heartbreaking voice keening for her mother.

When the ambulance was finally able to drive away, the coroner's red pickup following close behind it, Bill suggested that Kate take Francie home or to Kate's own place.

"I'm sorry to bother you with this," he said to Francie. He held out a consent-to-search form. "You're your mother's next of kin?"

"Yes," she said. "My dad's been dead a long time."

"We need to collect evidence inside the house as well as outside."

He glanced at Kate, wondering if she realized that he'd be looking for evidence of her there, too. She just looked steadily back at him, as though waiting for him to challenge her in some way.

When Francie had finished signing, he spoke to Kate in a low voice. "You'll want to stop by," he said. "Tomorrow, if not sooner."

"Of course," she said. Bill would've liked to forgive the faint note of sarcasm in her voice, but he found he couldn't. She was still an unknown quantity, even if she did seem to be a caring sort.

Kate put her arm around Francie and led her outside.

When everyone but Mitch and Clayton Campbell, who was interviewing neighbors, had gone, Bill went around the back of the garage. He took a few more pictures himself, concentrating on the fine mist of blood splattered on the garage's back door. It took Mitch and him almost another hour, but they bagged and tagged the garden tools and basket she'd fallen onto and wrapped the pitchfork—which had been carelessly balanced on the garbage cans—in plastic. It was, in the words of the coroner, a nasty way to go. He hoped the doc had been right, that she'd been dead or near dead already when the pitchfork went in.

When he was finished, he felt like he'd done some real work. This death, and the high school kid's, had reminded him why he'd become a cop in the first place—not because he was an altruistic sort or gave much of a damn for his fellow humans like so many cops pretended. No, this kind of work gave his brain something to chew on, a reason to go to work every morning.

Looking at the scene, it seemed probable to him that unless the daughter discovered there were things missing, they weren't going to find much inside. Lillian Cayley had been on her way out to garden or was just going into the house, he guessed, when the killer surprised her.

In the woods at the back of the yard, the trees had just begun to bud and the new brush hadn't yet sprung up. Bill could just see out to the county service road that cut through the woods, half circling the East End before turning off to the town reservoir. If he had his geography right, the road also ran past the back of the East End's cemetery.

13

Mary-Katie laughed when she saw the enormous size of the sanctuary of the Episcopal church where Miles had arranged for them to be married.

"We'll get lost in here," she said, taking in the vast height of the room's paneled white ceiling and the tall stained-glass windows lining the walls. She wasn't sure who the people pictured in the windows were meant to be: several of them looked like angels, but then there was a bleeding man in a pointed hat who had a sword stuck through his head, a woman who seemed to be carrying her eyeballs on a plate, and another man whose severed head lay at his feet. A chill ran up her spine, and she didn't think it was because of the air-conditioning.

The woman showing them around assured her that the sanctuary was appropriate. "We've had weddings here, large and small, for more than seventy-five years," she said. "It's a special, special place."

"But we're having only about thirty people," Mary-Katie said. "Are you sure, Miles? This is what you want?" She reached for his hand. When his fingers wrapped around hers, they felt warm and she relaxed some.

"It's for you," he said. "How beautiful are you going to look standing up there in your dress?"

"This is a rare opportunity," the woman said. "We allow only a certain number of weddings each year."

Mary-Katie bit at the inside of her lip as she looked up at the gold crucifix above the altar. This church was nothing like the simple Methodist chapel back home in which she'd always thought she would be married. And her *grandmother had been disappointed that the wedding would take place in Charleston, so far away from home.*

"You know you want to, Mary-Katie," Miles said, pulling her closer to him. "Indulge yourself. Or at least let me indulge you."

It wasn't at all what she wanted, but she could tell by the hopeful way he was looking at her, urging her on, that it was definitely what he wanted. Why, she didn't know. His guests were all business associates. He didn't even have any family coming, and that made her feel a little sorry for him. But then, her grandmother was her only family to speak of. No one knew where her father was, or if he was even alive.

And so six weeks later she found herself standing at the altar rail of Holy Saints Episcopal Church wearing the most expensive dress she'd ever owned, Miles holding her right hand in his as she pledged to love and honor him for the rest of her life. She knew without looking behind her that her grandmother was quietly weeping with what Mary-Katie hoped was happiness. The collection of saints looked down from their windows with mute indifference.

Even much later, when any thoughts of Miles were tinged with hate and fear, she couldn't look back on their wedding and honeymoon without a degree of grudging appreciation. They had been perfect. No, perfect wasn't quite the word. They had been surreal in their measured beauty.

As Mary-Katie walked slowly down the aisle, her arm linked with her grandmother's, the church was filled with mellow sunlight and the scent of two hundred white lilies. Miles stood at the front of the church, waiting for her, wearing a smile of absolute certainty and pleasure. She felt beloved. Treasured.

The reception was a seated dinner in an intimate room at a downtown club to which Miles belonged. Champagne sparkled in the crystal flutes that Miles's friends (she had thought them friends then, and didn't know them to be interested parties, associates who would've just as soon killed Miles as dined with him) raised to toast her beauty and cleverness at capturing Miles's heart.

Hawaii, too, was like a dream. They stayed for several days at a ranch in the mountains, taking long hikes, riding horses (Miles surprised her with how firmly he seemed to take charge of his horse, even though he'd had little riding experience), and eating amazing gourmet meals made with foods she'd never even known existed. There was another week at the beach, where she was shy in the revealing bikinis that Miles had purchased and hidden in her suitcase as a surprise. They took picture after picture, of the sunset, of the beach, of each other. At night they made love with the doors and windows of their bungalow open to the dark and the soothing, constant waves. She couldn't have made up a more perfect two weeks spent with the man she loved.

If she was annoyed with the way Miles insisted on ordering for her at lunch, or suggested what bathing suit or dress would look best on her that day, or told her how to hold her tennis racquet even though she'd been playing regularly since she was ten, she didn't tell him. In truth, she was more amused than anything else. Still dazed by the beauty of her wedding, the beauty of the islands, the devotion he showed to her, she let it go. Then there was the glittering diamond on her left hand with its matching diamond-encircled band. She was almost used to wearing it, though at first she'd felt like she was brandishing a doorknob. Yes, adjustments had to be made.

Off and on during the flight home she caught Miles smiling to himself.

"What is it?" she asked him. "Do I look funny or something?" She smoothed her hair, took out a compact and checked the mirror, looking critically at what she saw there.

"You're perfect," he said. "When you get out of bed in the morning, you're perfect."

"Then you have to tell me," she said.

"No," he said. "I can't. But you're going to love it. I promise."

The next day, Sunday, she left their condo to drive out to her grandmother's house in Beaufort. Inside the tote bag she'd purchased at the hotel were presents for her grandmother—some hand-painted jewelry, a new woven handbag, and a black caftan trimmed with delicate, hand-embroidered shells—and thick packets of the photos she'd just picked up at the one-hour photo place. Miles had stayed behind to get caught up on some work and sent his love.

Mary-Katie had been surprised at the easy rapport between her grandmother and Miles. He flirted with her, but she took it graciously, as a compliment. They both had a fondness for college basketball, which bored Mary-Katie to tears. He was also helpful around the house, tacking up a loose gutter, power washing the back fence, finding a good contractor to repave the driveway.

He hadn't seemed the type to Mary-Katie to get out and do things like that for himself. He wore fine Italian shoes and hand-tailored sport coats (only lawyers and the occasional bankers wore suits on the island). The palms of his hands and fingers were smooth. Her grandmother had tweaked him about his fondness for jewelry, his wardrobe of watches, his gold pinky ring, the heavy gold bracelet he wore on his right wrist. But he was good-natured about it and even bought her a bracelet similar to his for her birthday.

On letting herself into the house, Mary-Katie found her grandmother in bed, too weak to get herself breakfast or lunch.

"Why didn't you call me?" she asked, setting a tray with a quickly assembled omelet, toast, and a glass of juice on it on the bed. "I would've come back in an instant."

"Don't fuss," Katherine said. "There's nothing wrong with me that a couple days' rest won't cure. I wasn't about to interrupt your honeymoon. Marriage is hard enough without old ladies butting in."

Mary-Katie scolded her again. But Katherine soon got her talking about Hawaii. Mary-Katie got out the pictures and they spent the next few minutes looking over them.

"I probably should have given you that birds and bees talk one more time," Katherine said playfully. "But it looks like you two got to know each other pretty well."

Mary-Katie laughed, blushing a little. Sex with Miles was incredible. He pushed her to do things she had never done before. Some of them had made her a little uncomfortable, but she had to admit that they thrilled her. "We did okay," she said.

Katherine took Mary-Katie's hand in her own slender and wrinkled one. "I want you to tell me if he's ever not good to you, child. Anything you need from me, you tell me," she said.

As she drove home, Mary-Katie wondered if her grandmother knew or suspected something about Miles that she hadn't, if he'd given her some hint of darkness inside him that she herself had missed. But no other mention of it passed between them, and she decided that it was just something a grandmother was supposed to say.

She found Miles in the small bedroom he used as a second office. He was concentrating so deeply on the papers in front of him that he didn't hear her when she first came in. Miles's focus could be intense, as though he imagined that by focusing all of his energy on one thing, he could control it. She wasn't sure what it was that he did to earn his living, but she knew that he dealt with a lot of real estate and that all the energy he put into it paid off. Their condo, which was just a few blocks from the beach, wasn't one of the hastily constructed ones that had been built for snowbirds or time-shares. And he was already talking about a new house for the two of them.

"Hey," she said quietly.

Miles shifted his gaze to her in the doorway, his eyes blank, as though he were thinking hard about something. But after a moment he smiled.

"Hey, yourself," he said. "How's Katherine? What's wrong?"

Mary-Katie told him about finding her in bed. "I don't think she's well," she said. "And she's alone all the time now."

Miles came around the desk. "Listen," he said. "I was going to wait until tonight when we go to dinner, but I think it's better if I tell you now."

He took both of her hands in his.

"What is it?" she asked. She'd forgotten about the surprise, and even though his timing was peculiar, she was still curious.

"You can have all the time you need with her," Miles said. "You're not going back to work tomorrow."

"Of course I have to go back to work, Miles," she said. "I've used up all my vacation for the year. I barely have any sick days left."

"No. You don't need any more sick days or vacation days," he said. "I called the bank two days after we got to Hawaii and told them you weren't coming back. It was a shit job, and you don't need to be there anymore."

Mary-Katie was speechless, a hundred thoughts crowding her head at once. Sure, being a bank teller wasn't much of a career, particularly for someone with a college degree, but she would have been promoted soon enough. Unlike most of the young women she worked with, she'd never dreamed of marrying a wealthy man and hanging around the house, maybe raising a couple of kids. (Though she did want a child. Miles had been noncommittal so far, but she was sure she could change his mind.) She had always had a job, since she turned sixteen and wanted money for a car. But most of all she was shocked at his audacity at making the decision for her.

"That can't even be legal, Miles," she said. "They just let you quit my job for me?"

He wasn't smiling now as broadly as he had been. "Your boss sounded happy for you, Mary-Katie. She knows you're much better off not working there."

"I can't believe this," she said. She sat down on the edge of a nearby chair, careful not to dislodge the piles of paper there.

"I tell you that you have all the time in the world to spend with your sick grandmother and you're pissed off?" he said, suddenly loud. "You can sit home on your ass and eat fucking bon-bons all day and that's okay with me because I want you to be happy and you're pissed off?" He stared down at her, and she felt the full force of his anger and disappointment in her. But she was un-moved.

"It was my job, Miles. It wasn't yours to quit."

"You're fucking unbelievable," he said.

"Don't curse at me," she said.

"Don't worry," he said. He left the room.

Mary-Katie's heart was pounding. She had seen Miles angry, but never so angry with her. It just didn't make sense. She was the one who had been wronged. She was the one who'd had her job taken from her.

She spent the rest of the day in the silent condo. When Miles didn't come back at dinnertime, she made herself a grilled cheese sandwich with some stale bread she found in the refrigerator. At midnight she went to bed alone.

When the alarm shattered the sleep she'd finally found a couple of hours before dawn, Mary-Katie reached across the bed and fumbled for the Off button. Knowing it was Monday, her mind immediately went to her routine, and she started to think about what she would wear to work. Then the reality of the day before washed over her. She looked over to Miles's unwrinkled pillow to see that he had never come to bed. She lay there several minutes, desperately want-ing not to get out of bed, to face the day.

The idea of walking into the bank and having everyone stare at her, won-dering what she was doing there, mortified her. How could she explain? She would have to tell everyone that her handsome new husband had made a mis-take, that he'd told them—against her wishes—that she wanted to quit her job. How stupid would that make her look? She knew she couldn't bear their questions, their assumption that Miles was maybe a little crazy. It was bad enough that she was beginning to suspect that he was a far different man than the one she had thought she married.

As the day wore on, she tried to push that thought away, to soften her heart toward Miles, telling herself that he had meant well. He was such a man's man. Of course he had wanted to give her everything he thought she would want. But she couldn't quite convince herself. He had never asked her what she wanted.

She kept waiting for the phone to ring, expecting that someone from the bank would call, wondering where she was. When twelve o'clock came and went, she knew it wasn't going to happen.

Her hand shook slightly as she picked up the phone and dialed Nancy, the branch manager.

"Mary-Katie," she said. "I was hoping you'd just come in this morning. What's going on?"

"I should have called you," Mary-Katie said. "I'm sorry."

"Is this what you want? Did you ask your husband to call me? I have to say I was a little surprised."

Mary-Katie wanted to say that no one had been more surprised than she, but the truth was, she was too embarrassed. But was she so embarrassed that she would let it keep her from going back to her job? She didn't know what she was going to say until the words came out of her mouth.

"I did tell Miles to call," she said. "It's my grandmother. You know how sick she is, and I need to spend more time with her. But I should have told you myself."

From the brief silence, she could tell that Nancy was taken aback.

"I thought we knew each other better than that, Mary-Katie," Nancy said. "I certainly would've understood. And the other girls, they'll miss you."

"Please tell them I'm sorry." She got off the phone just as quickly as she could after Nancy had put her through to Human Resources to close out her records.

She moved slowly through the rest of the day, still surprised at herself, half regretting what she'd done. At one point she tried to watch daytime television for a few minutes, but turned it off, disgusted. What the hell was she going to do with herself for the rest of her life?

When Miles came home late that afternoon carrying a couple of bags of groceries, he was wearing different clothes. She hadn't thought about it before, but she guessed that he'd probably slept at his office, where he had a shower and a closet for extra clothes.

He looked mildly surprised to see her there. She stood silently by as he started unloading the bags in the kitchen. He talked animatedly of the grocery store, of their need to start keeping a running list of things they were out of. She supposed that she would be expected to keep the cupboards full, now that she wasn't working.

"The fresh spinach pasta looked good," he said. "And I picked up some shrimp. I've got a few papers to go through, but then I'll get dinner started." He kissed her on the cheek as he passed by her on the way to the bedroom office.

When he was gone, Mary-Katie poured herself a glass of chardonnay and went to sit out on the deck. There was only a small view of the ocean between their building and the next one over, but she could hear the ocean, its roar sounding empty and hollow, as though she were listening to it inside a large conch shell. Tomorrow she would go and check on her grandmother. Then she would write a check for the entire amount she had in the bank where she'd worked and take it to another bank and open a new account.

14

EVEN THOUGH IT WAS DARK, Paxton drove a mile past the entrance to Chalybeate Springs, turned around in a shuttered gas station's parking lot, and headed back toward town. The co-op didn't have a light on its sign, and he almost missed it coming back, but at the last second he swerved the Mercedes onto the farm's gravel road and switched to running lights. Truth be told, he loved this cloak-and-dagger shit.

Banging Francie was good, though the novelty of their secret rendezvous at the Middleboro apartment was wearing thin. Francie belonged in a nicer place. There were even times when he imagined her coming down the stairs of his mother's house, her hair swept up in some regal 'do and wearing nothing but heels and maybe some diamond earrings for decoration. But things would have to change in a big way for that to be more than a fantasy. And for the immediate future, poor Francie would be distracted with the death of her mother—in fact, he hadn't been able to reach her all afternoon, which bothered him. But that would pass.

He parked the Mercedes well away from the house and store, but in view of the barn where he was headed. In the past few years the hippies had added a couple of greenhouses and some outbuildings to the old man's original property, which had included the ramshackle clapboard farmhouse, barn, and curious bathhouse. Opening the door of the car, he heard birds in the distance, crows, he thought they were, their raucous cries breaking the peace of the night. What the hell crows were doing out in the dark, he didn't know.

He hurried past the vine-covered bathhouse that gave him the creeps even in daylight. One late night, Charlie Matter, the guy he was now on his way to meet, had convinced him to go inside. By the harsh light of a single bare bulb suspended from the ceiling they had stripped down and gone for a float in the spring-fed pool the old man had built.

The quintessential hippie, Charlie wore his salt-and-pepper hair down to the middle of his back. Before undressing he had shaken it loose from the rubber thong he kept tied around it so that it swung behind his shoulders like a girl's. Not that there was anything else feminine about him. Seen in his clothes, he was a pretty standard character, loping about Chalybeate Springs wearing an easy manner, straight-leg jeans, dollar store cotton T-shirts, and steel-toed farmer boots. But without the bucolic disguise, Paxton could see the hardness of the man. As he moved, the ropy muscles of his upper body seemed to strain at the surface of his fifty-something-year-old skin with an angry energy.

The shaggy ends of Charlie's enormous Zapata mustache brushed at the sides of his chin (which was always well-shaved, Paxton had noticed), and his back and chest were covered in short, wiry hairs that had gone completely gray. The nest of hair surrounding his flaccid penis was gray, too, and the penis itself was nearly as long as a man's hand. Charlie's balls weren't shriveled and cold, as Paxton's own were, but looked firm, like solid rounds of rubber. As he lowered himself into the water, Charlie's biceps flexed, but his movement was effortless, as though his body weighed nothing at all. When he caught Paxton staring, he gave Paxton a wry smile that made Paxton erupt in a nervous laugh and look away, red-faced.

But it was Charlie Matter's eyes that long ago had told Paxton he wasn't someone to be fucked around with. They were the stark blue of a sky reflecting off an icy snowpack. Paxton was just a little bit afraid of Charlie, and he was sure that Charlie knew it.

At the back of the barn, Paxton moved aside an old oil barrel sitting by the rusted root cellar door and tugged on the strip of rope there. Below the ground he heard the ring of a small bell that Charlie had rigged up. Paxton looked around. The barn was at the back of the property—behind him stretched the hillside that held the farm's small blueberry orchard. It was from there that the sound of the birds came.

After a minute or two the door pushed open with a noisy squeal, and

Paxton jumped back to give it room. He put his hand to his mouth to block the acrid fug of ammonia drifting up the cellar stairs. The top half of Charlie Matter emerged from the cellar, an abbreviated silhouette against the dim light.

"Man, you sure took your sweet-ass time," Charlie said, letting Paxton grab hold of the door. He backed down the step and turned to disappear through the ragged black shower curtain that blocked off the entrance to the lab.

As Paxton began his descent, he held back the weight of the door while it closed so it wouldn't bang shut. He didn't much like it when Charlie talked trash to him. He was used to a certain amount of respect. It was a constant misunderstanding between them, Paxton believed. Once upon a time he'd only been Charlie's customer, but he had since become more of an employer, bankrolling Charlie's growing meth business. But sometimes, he thought, Charlie's memory seemed to fail him.

One thing Paxton could never get used to about Charlie's lab was the horrible smell. There was only one small vent in the storm cellar, and it didn't do much to clear out the place. Whenever he left here, he made it a point to change his clothes before going anywhere else.

He nodded to Delmar Johnston, the young man at the small electric stove in the corner. Delmar worked in the stables for Paxton at Bonterre most days and lived in one of the tenant houses.

"What've you got?" Paxton said to Charlie.

"Hey," Charlie said. "I heard about your old lady's mother. Fucking drag."

Paxton stiffened. He didn't like the idea of Charlie bringing up Francie with Delmar in the room. It had been a mistake to mention her to Charlie, period.

Charlie sneered. "Come on, Birkenshaw. Everyone knows you're doing that little nurse," he said. "She's a fine piece of ass. You really shouldn't keep her all to yourself."

Inwardly, Paxton cringed at the thought of sharing Francie with this filthy pig of a man. But he smiled genially. "I like you, Charlie. I like your friends, and I like doing business with you. Let's keep it at the business level."

Charlie looked up from the joint he was rolling and considered Paxton. He shook his head. "You're a cold fish, Birkenshaw," he said. "Coldest fucking fish I know." But he grinned back at Paxton, showing a snaggled mouthful of teeth. When he finished rolling the joint, he gestured to the curtain.

"Why don't we go back outside?" he said. "This here is a *no smoking* area."

They sat on an old water trough outside of the barn. Paxton wasn't a big fan of pot—he felt like it blurred his edges, made him too soft, too easy. He preferred coke—the fluffy white kind, not the crack bullshit—and he certainly never touched the meth that he was so heavily invested in. It made him jittery. It was lucky that Charlie was adept at getting him all the coke he wanted. Going out of town for it was a hassle.

"What's with the birds?" Paxton said after he'd expelled his first drag of the joint. Around them the coarse, sporadic calls of the crows sounding off to one another filled the air. But when Paxton looked up into the sky, he saw only a single bat swoop into the trees.

"Hanna forgot to turn them off out in the orchard," Charlie said. "We were testing them this afternoon. Damn birds nearly cleaned out our blueberries last year." He paused, took another hit, and passed the joint to Paxton.

"Listen," he said. "We've got a problem and I need some cash."

"There's that new store out in Middleboro that just opened up. They'll cash a check for you and hold it until payday," Paxton said, finding himself very funny.

But Charlie ignored his joke. "It's a law enforcement problem. Here and now."

"Ah," Paxton said. "I see."

"No, I don't think you see," Charlie said. "Some pissant kid, one of the regulars out here, keeled over from a heart attack last week. And our friend says that it doesn't look good, that the sheriff's thinking it's an unnatural occurrence."

"So what?" Paxton said. "Maybe he was sniffing airplane glue."

"Sure," Charlie said. "And I'm the good fucking fairy. You, of anyone, Birkenshaw, should know what a small town this is. You can play it any way you want, but our friend thinks that some cash would ease things, help keep the bright, shining light of inquiry off of our enterprise."

"And what if we say no?" Paxton said.

"Suit yourself," Charlie said. "I can stand the heat, make everything disappear. Good times don't last forever, do they?"

Paxton thought for a minute. The meth wasn't making him much money, and he'd never trusted Charlie's methods for getting some of his ingredients—the stuff that was in cold medicine, allergy pills—from the very people he was selling to. But Paxton didn't think they were quite done with the whole thing yet, especially since Charlie had been bragging to him just the week before that they were picking up business two, three counties away, maybe even down into Tennessee. Now, Charlie was getting more and more of his supplies from a buddy in Canada and was dropping the cold medicine angle. Paxton was starting to visualize the power—like he was some kind of serious drug lord. *Suits me to a fucking T,* he thought. If only his old man had lived to see just how powerful he was going to become. It wouldn't have been to his old man's taste—Paxton was just supposed to look after the farm's business—but it meant something all the same.

"Let's give him two large," Paxton said.

"What?" Charlie said. "Do you mean two thousand? You think you're in a *Baretta* episode or something? And he wants five."

"Twenty-five hundred," Paxton said, but he decided he wanted to push Charlie some. "And you've got to put in a thousand of your own."

"Go fuck yourself," Charlie said.

When he thought back on it later, Paxton considered that it had been more reflex than intention that had made him push the cherry of the joint into the back of Charlie's hand, crushing it so that it dug into the flesh so deeply that it seemed to stand there of its own accord for a few seconds before Charlie flung it off with a monstrous groan.

Paxton followed the bright arc of the tiny light and saw it land in the weed-shot gravel a few feet away.

"You sick fuck!" Charlie shouted at him as he stumbled around like a drunk, gripping the wrist of his burned hand.

Even in the darkness, Paxton could see that Charlie was fighting back tears. But Charlie had to be put in his place. He shouldn't have to take crap from two-bit operators like Charlie. He remembered using words like *partners* and *good faith* with Charlie, but the circumstances were distant and unclear to him now, like a movie he'd watched long ago.

Charlie continued to scream at him, but Paxton wasn't listening to what he was saying. As he headed to his car, Charlie's voice was just more noise filling his head, like the constant caw of the imaginary crows out in the blueberry orchard. Were they ever real? he wondered. Where were those birds now? Dead? Their cries trapped forever in the speaker wires running along the orchard fence?

"I'll bring some money by tomorrow," Paxton shouted cheerfully over his shoulder. He didn't know if Charlie heard him, but figured it didn't matter. Business was business and they would carry on. He had the Browning .380 that had belonged to his father in the glove box if Charlie were to come after him, but from the way Charlie was doubled over, he thought it was unlikely.

When he started up the Mercedes, he could hear nothing more of Charlie. Steely Dan flowed out of the CD player, and to Paxton it was music like fine old wine. Those two guys who were Steely Dan would understand what he had to deal with. He felt as though he were living one of their songs. They obviously knew the pleasures of wine and women and good cocaine. Surely they would even be a little proud of him. He suspected that even as rich and sophisticated as they were now, they probably weren't above taking care of business directly, as he'd needed to. *They would definitely understand.*

As he pulled onto the ill-defined gravel road leading out to the highway, Paxton saw Hanna Moon, Charlie's—what was she, wife, girlfriend, concubine?—whatever, throw open the kitchen door of the old house and hurry down the steps. But instead of staying at the edge of the road in the grass, she stumbled blindly into the sweep of the Mercedes's lights and onto the gravel.

Paxton had never run over a person before. Dogs, yes, and all manner of opossums, raccoons, squirrels, and cats. But the *bump* they made under his tires was never quite satisfying and usually resulted only in globs of crap and fur that he had to wash off the underside of his car. He found himself drifting toward the woman, who was waving her long, pale arms in front of her as though she would stop him.

Later, after the haze of the joint he'd smoked with Charlie cleared out of his head, he knew that what had happened next was the result of some hallucination brought on by the weed. He didn't believe in ghosts, and he sure as hell knew he wasn't crazy.

He was only thirty or so feet away and headed right for Hanna Moon, smiling to think that he would at least give her a good scare. But when he realized that he wasn't alone in the car, that there was a young girl with long black hair knitted into a braid that hung over her left shoulder star-ing solemnly at him from the front passenger seat, he swerved away from Hanna Moon and into the sparse grass at the road's edge.

15

"I'm sorry, Mrs. Chenoweth." The funeral director in whose office Mary-Katie sat held out the telephone to her. *"There seems to be some problem with your credit card. I'm sure it's a misunderstanding. But they would like to speak with you."*

Mary-Katie closed her eyes for just a moment. This couldn't be happening. She opened her eyes and smiled at the ever-patient man, whose name was Ralph. When she took the phone from him, he slipped out of the room, his footsteps silenced by the deep-pile gold carpeting.

As Mary-Katie studied the fleur-de-lis pattern of the hideous mauve-and-gold-flocked wallpaper, the woman on the other end explained that she was very sorry, particularly given the nature of her purchase, but that the account would have to be made current before they could cover the three-thousand-dollar deposit for funeral expenses. The account was ninety days overdue, and there was no arguing with her. Mortified, Mary-Katie hung up and called Miles, who told her to write a check.

"Will it be covered?" she whispered into the phone.

"It will be before it gets to the bank," he said. *"I'll call the credit card people and get them straightened out. There's nothing to get all freaked out about."*

Ralph came back into the office a decorous minute after she'd hung up.

"I'll write you a check," Mary-Katie said, pulling her checkbook out of her purse. As she wrote it, she could feel him watching her. She was nervous and had to void the first check because she wrote it out for three hundred instead of

three thousand. Flustered, she felt herself getting warmer and more agitated under his gaze. As she handed the check to him, she wondered if he spent a lot of time wondering how people would look when they were dead.

It wasn't the first time Mary-Katie had been embarrassed by having a credit card declined. Every six months or so since she'd married Miles, she found herself standing red-faced at the counter of some boutique or another as a shop girl told her in the most sympathetic of tones that there was "a problem with the card." As though the piece of plastic were responsible and had managed some neat trick in her billfold to make itself useless. Worse than the sympathetic tone was the knowing smile that seemed to play at the glossy lips of the bearers of the bad news.

When she got home that afternoon, she turned off the car's engine and rested her head against the steering wheel. What would she do without her grandmother? She already missed her grandmother's gentle gossip about the neighbors she had known all her life and her yearly plans for her garden. Mary-Katie's own yard was filled with familiar plants from her grandmother's yard. She tried to imagine making new friends, replacing her grandmother's companionship with that of the wives or lovers (sometimes she had trouble remembering who was the wife and who was the lover, when it came to certain men) of Miles's business associates, loud, brittle women who made only small talk, and that only about fashion and traveling to Atlanta or New York to shop.

Even after several years of marriage, Mary-Katie had never been able to bring herself to tell her grandmother how strange and stressful it was to live with a man like Miles, so compulsive and quickly irritated. She hadn't told her about the volatile money situation or the people who would call—men and women—and ask for Miles at odd times of the day and night, how Miles would tell her he would be going away on business, but she would see him, at a distance, on the island, with people she didn't know. She hadn't told her about Miles's truly disturbing associates, like the man Miles called "Fitz," the thickly muscled, redheaded man with a trilling laugh and a cauliflower ear, who came to the house occasionally for drinks. One evening, Fitz's ill-fitting sport coat had fallen open as he leaned forward to take a scotch and water from Miles, to reveal a hidden shoulder holster with a gun sticking out of it.

There had been times, though, when her grandmother seemed to sense that things weren't quite right and would hold her close, as she had when she was a child. In her grandmother's arms, Mary-Katie knew she could cry and cry, and that she would never be pressed for details.

Above the garage was the small apartment that should have been her grandmother's. But Miles had put Mary-Katie off about it, unwilling (or unable) to spend the money to update the plumbing and have the leaking roof fixed in order to make it habitable. As many buildings as (she thought) he owned, she didn't understand why he couldn't take care of the place her grandmother belonged. If he had, she thought, her grandmother might have been at their house when she'd had her last stroke, instead of in her kitchen, where she died and lay undiscovered by Mary-Katie for at least twenty-four hours. But as much as she wanted to blame it on Miles, she knew it was her own fault for not insisting that her grandmother move directly into their guest room. She should have at least arranged for her to have live-in help. Whatever the cause, she knew she would have to live with the guilt for the rest of her life.

Mary-Katie knew that she should go over to her grandmother's house and start looking through her papers to see what needed to be handled, but the thought of going back there alone paralyzed her with sadness. Once, when she was in college, she'd stayed at the house by herself while her grandmother went on a bus tour to Cape Cod with some of her friends. It had been a kind of adventure, a time to temporarily be an adult and pretend the house was hers. Now it would just seem empty.

After going through the day's mail, Mary-Katie drew herself a bath. The sunken marble tub with its waterfall spigot had made her laugh with wonder when they first looked at the house, but now she treasured it as her own personal retreat. When the water was a few inches from the tub's edge, she unzipped her dress and let it fall onto the floor. She stepped out of her panties and down into the frothy, lavender-scented water.

There were a hundred things to attend to before the visitation at the funeral home that evening, but she did her best to put them out of her head. Sufficient unto the day is the evil thereof.

When Miles woke her, the water had turned tepid and she shivered at his touch.

"Hey, beauty," he said.

As she stepped out of the tub, he wrapped a warm bath sheet around her.

With a slow, tender motion, he pushed aside a wet tendril of hair clinging to her neck and kissed her there. Even in her sorrow, she felt herself responding to the touch of his lips on her skin. But she wasn't in any sort of mood for sex.

"I brought us some lunch," he said. "Go in and get dressed and come downstairs."

She nodded, not ready to speak.

Downstairs, she found a fresh arrangement of flowers on the breakfast nook table and two plates carefully arranged with their favorite assortment of sushi: California maki, spicy tuna, and plenty of yellowtail and salmon. Miles poured her an iced tea and set it on the table.

"Sushi Joe sends his love," he said.

"That Sushi Joe," she said wryly. "He knows the way to my heart."

"I know you're probably not too hungry, but you need to eat something."

Miles was in one of his gentle moods, sorry, no doubt, for the trouble she'd had at the funeral home. She was inclined to let him run with it. It was rare enough.

As they ate, he told her again how disappointed he had been that he wasn't able to come to the funeral home.

"I would've straightened out that bastard about the credit card right then," he said. "He was just being an asshole."

She had her own idea about who the real asshole was, but she didn't say. She kept eating the sushi, which was more restorative than she had thought it would be.

"The closing went pretty quickly this morning," he said. "Really, it was more of a foreclosure. You should've seen the look on that sorry bastard's face. Priceless." He grinned, then popped a piece of spicy tuna into his mouth.

"Who?" Katie said. She felt as though she'd been dropped into an ongoing conversation about which she knew nothing.

"That guy. Lev Kaplan. You know," he said with his mouth full.

The name sounded familiar to her, but only vaguely.

"I can't keep track of all the people you do business with, Miles," she said, bristling with irritation. Of all the times to be focused on work. Her grandmother was dead. She didn't know if she could pay for next week's groceries. Miles's selfishness knew no bounds. "It doesn't matter."

"Hell yes, it matters," he said, tossing his chopsticks onto the table. "Lev Kaplan stole that race from me, Mary-Katie. You were there. You know that guy was shady. He just came up out of nowhere looking like he never even broke a sweat."

"The hospital race?" she said.

"I knew you wouldn't forget it either," he said. "He was riding pretty fucking high that day, wasn't he? Now he's going to have a hard time finding a pot to piss in."

"That was years ago, Miles," she said, incredulous. "And you didn't even know him."

"I know everything I need to know, now," he said. "His wife's left him. She's a looker, too. His T-shirt business is about a hundred thousand in debt. His car's been repossessed. The guy's a loser. Always has been."

She didn't like to know the details of Miles's business dealings. But today she felt so raw, so devoid of anything worthwhile in her life, she felt like she had nothing to lose. She rested her chopsticks across her plate and watched him. He had a spot of soy sauce on his chin, but otherwise he was the picture of a conqueror. He looked smug and, as always, neatly pressed.

"You did that to him," she said. "You ruined his life."

He smiled. "I could have. But he did most of it for me," he said. "The sale was just the icing on the cake, sweetheart."

"That's one of the cruelest, most selfish things I've ever heard," she said. "You're acting like you're some kind of animal."

Miles shrugged. "Animals run only on instinct. They don't do anything because they choose to. It's not the natural order of things."

"Do you call what you did instinct?" she said.

"It's called justice, babe," he said. "Sometimes you have to make your own. Here I thought you'd be happy for me. I can't believe you're defending that sad sack."

"You can't play with people like that, Miles," she said. "What if he commits suicide or something? You would be responsible."

"Everyone's responsible for his own life experience," he said. He got up from the table. "I have to get back to work if I'm going to make it to the funeral home tonight."

When he bent down to kiss her on the top of the head, she recoiled. She half expected him to get angry, to grab her arm, or to at least tell her not to be ridiculous, as he usually did when she (so rarely) criticized something he'd done. But his face merely wore a sympathetic look akin to the one she'd gotten from the funeral director.

After a few minutes she watched his car turn around and head out down the long driveway. She wasn't shocked by what he'd done because it fit so well with his character. She just hadn't realized that his memory was so long. Worse, she didn't know whom she pitied more at that moment: Lev Kaplan or Mary-Katie Chenoweth.

16

IT WAS WITH a twinge of jealousy that Bill Delaney had sent Mitch off to interview the daughter and close friends of the Cayley woman. He'd thought that it wouldn't be too tough a case to solve, but Lillian Cayley had turned out to be as unlikely a murder victim as she could be: no abusive spouse, no son hooked into the local drug scene, no obvious pile of cash that was drawing the interest of greedy relatives. The rumor in town was that she'd been surprised by some drifter to whom she'd shown some kindness, but it was still cold enough that drifters were sparse, and Bill's people hadn't recently had to run anyone off.

The phone at the office had barely stopped ringing since the word got out. Little old ladies all over the county were crying for extra patrols in their neighborhoods. Daphne had even jokingly suggested that they set up a recording on the phone telling them to take their medication and calm down.

Outside his office, Bill could see Joshua Klein, the only full-time reporter for the *Carystown Ledger,* drinking coffee with Daphne. Josh was a likable enough kid, but coming as he did from another small Kentucky town, he always imagined that the news should be bigger, more interesting than it actually was, particularly news about crime. Every lost dog, every high school kid's joyride through someone's front pasture had to have some seriously criminal cause, some plot behind it that would implicate the mayor, a local preacher, or a drug ring. Josh's theories never seemed to pan out for him, but the paper kept him on anyway. Bill figured it didn't hurt that it was owned by the kid's uncle.

He wanted another cup of coffee, but knew that if he emerged, Josh would be pestering him instead of Daphne. Josh hadn't been at the paper when the Moon girl disappeared, so with the Catlett boy's sudden death and now this murder, he looked to be in hog heaven.

Frank was still working on the Catlett death. They wouldn't have the tox screen on the kid's hair and blood or the coroner's report until at least Friday, and now that the coroner had another corpse on his table to deal with, things would be slow.

The other thing Bill was waiting for was the call from South Carolina that might tell him something more about Kate Russell, who was due in his office at any time.

When his private phone line rang, he gestured to Daphne that he would get it himself.

"No lunch today, honey," Margaret said when he answered.

"Got another offer?" he said. "Somebody better looking?"

Margaret laughed. "Someday I will get a better offer, and won't you be sorry? But it's only the mayor wanting a little chat. I think she's trying to pump me for information, seeing as I'm sleeping with the sheriff."

"Is she buying?" Bill said.

"You bet," Margaret said. "But you'll get dinner. I won't let you starve." Margaret, being from one of the old families, was part of an elite Carystown group, but she remained at the edges of it as much as she could. In Bill's opinion, most of them were a pitiful lot, spending way too much time worrying about what historic colors old buildings should be painted, who should be in what garden club, and complaining about what the Chamber of Commerce was up to.

"You're too good for that crowd," Bill said. He looked up to see Kate Russell standing at Daphne's desk, signing in. "Hey, I've got to go, Sunshine. See you at home?"

As he and Margaret said their good-byes, he watched Kate Russell sit down on the bench to wait. It amused him to think that Josh Klein would piss himself with excitement if he knew what was going on with the attractive, neatly dressed woman seated so close by. When he was off the phone, he used the intercom to tell Daphne to send her in.

This man doesn't like me, Kate thought, settling into the hard chair beside the sheriff's desk. She felt like a schoolgirl called to the principal's office.

Bill Delaney was only barely old enough to be her father, but he had a seriousness about him that she found intimidating. It seemed to her that he considered Carystown to be his personal property and that she was an outsider who had brought it trouble. She wanted to tell him that it was Isabella Moon who had brought the town's trouble to *her*, but knew that she was already sounding like a lunatic.

"How's your friend Francie Cayley this morning?" he said.

Kate noted that he hadn't even bothered to offer her coffee. He was hard for her to read, sitting so coolly behind his desk. But from the way he had spoken to her at Lillian's house, she knew he probably wouldn't believe anything she was about to say.

"I took her back to her apartment this morning," she said. "I think she's still in shock. I would be, too, if I'd seen my mother like that." If she looked accusingly at him, could she be blamed?

The sheriff didn't even blink.

"I wasn't too happy to hear Miss Cayley ask for you, Miss Russell," he said. "I don't believe in coincidences. Do you?"

"I think they're possible enough," she said.

He watched her for a moment, but his attention was drawn away by something in the outer office. Kate turned around in time to see the man who had been in the waiting area when she arrived quickly turn his face away from them. The deputy, too, suddenly looked busy.

"Excuse me," the sheriff said, getting up. In a couple of long strides he was across the room, lowering the blinds on the office's picture window.

When he sat down again to take up their conversation, Kate decided she had nothing to lose by speaking out.

"Listen, Sheriff," she said, leaning forward, her voice earnest. She was tired from being up with Francie, holding her as she cried, listening to her talk about Lillian. Every muscle in her body felt weak, but a wave of energy swelled inside her. "Lillian was my *friend*," she said. "I'm not going to let you paint me as some kind of killer, Sheriff. Just like you, I think it's possible—no, probable—that the awful thing that happened to her had something to do with that little girl. And I know I look like the only link between them, but maybe I really am just a coincidence. I'll tell you right now that I have no kind of alibi. I went home after work and ate dinner and went for my walk, which wasn't anywhere near Lillian's—I suppose I said hello to somebody but I couldn't tell you a name—and then I came home and went to bed."

Kate Russell was standing now, her face flush with emotion. Bill was distracted by the fact that she was so lovely. It made him feel guilty at first, then foolish because he knew that even smart, attractive women could be criminals. His discomfort made him speak harshly to her.

"See any ghosts last night? What does the Moon girl tell you about Lillian Cayley?" he asked. "Or aren't they acquainted?"

"As a matter of fact, Lillian and I went together to the cemetery a couple of nights ago," she said, sitting down. "Do you want to hear about it?"

"I wouldn't dream of stopping you," he said.

"She's getting to be a regular around here," Daphne said when Kate left the office. "What do the ghosts have to say about it?"

"I'm headed to the Carousel to get some lunch," Bill said. "You want anything? You must have a real appetite from all that getting up and down to listen at keyholes." He put on the wide-brimmed gray hat that was standard issue for everyone in the department.

"Nothing for me, boss," Daphne said. "Some of us got work to do."

She gave him a smile, but Bill knew he'd gotten under her skin. He trusted her one hundred percent in a standoff situation, and her extraordinarily calm demeanor meant that she was a rock when they were dealing with some drunken foster mother or domestic dispute. But she had a taste for gossip that sometimes got her into trouble.

"Have you heard from Frank?" he said.

"Rose had some problems last night and he had to take her to the emergency room. Said he'd get in this afternoon. You want him to call you?"

"No. We'll talk later. What happened to your playmate?" Josh Klein had left right after the door closed behind Kate Russell.

"Some moron up the road couldn't wait until four o'clock to start burning last fall's leaves in his yard," she said. "I think Josh is chasing after the fire truck. He's kind of enthusiastic that way."

"I hadn't noticed," Bill said.

The Carousel was two streets over and up the hill from the department. Bill had enough work to do that he knew he should just have a sandwich at his desk. But the day was fair, and Margaret would give him a hard time if he didn't get out and get himself some lunch. It didn't hurt that Janet Rourke's office was on the way, and the woman, Kate, wouldn't be in to see him walk by. She'd done a lot of talking, most of it even less believable than what he'd heard during her first visit. The most sense she had made came when she told him that she was planning to spend the rest of the day and the evening as well with Francie Cayley. She hadn't convinced him that she wasn't guilty of something—perhaps fraud, maybe murder (there had been less likely killers than she)—but he didn't doubt that she cared about her friend more than she did her job.

When he reached the block on which the agency sat, he was disappointed to see that the Moon woman wasn't standing beneath Janet Rourke's green-and-white-striped awning. He hadn't talked to her in months. Mitch had been the lead on her daughter's case. It was Kate Russell who said she'd gone off the deep end, and he had a strong curiosity about her.

He put his head in at Pulliam's barbershop and nodded to the duffers lounging in the peeling vinyl chairs lined against the wall. It didn't do for him to linger in his uniform, so he paused in the doorway. Today, Ernst's wife Carmella was at the number one chair giving a balding man Bill didn't recognize a straight-razor shave.

"Where's Ernst?" Bill said.

"Down with the gout," Carmella said, turning to flick shaving cream off the blade and into the basin behind her. "If he doesn't watch himself, he'll miss out on the races and turkey season, both."

"That's a real shame. The boys will make it out, I guess?" Bill said, inquiring about her two high-school-age sons.

Before she could answer, a retired doc who lived out in the west end of the county spoke from his chair beside the rattling RC Cola cooler. "I still got those dump trucks tearing up my cattle guards," he said. "When are you going to send someone out, Sheriff? I'll be dead and they'll be running down my hearse."

A low grumble seemed to move through the line of old men, and Bill knew that he was in for a litany of trespassing and other misdemeanor woes if he didn't get out quick.

"You can call down at the courthouse and see what's holding up that paperwork, Keifer. Then let Daphne know," Bill said. "You all have a good day." He started back out the door, but another, more insistent voice stopped him.

"What do you know about Ms. Cayley, Sheriff? We going to have another one of these murders go unsolved? I ain't looking forward to seeing us look like prime assholes on television again."

The barbershop was quiet and Carmella made a *tsk* sound in the direction of the man.

"The poor woman's only been dead two days," she said. "She was a fine teacher, too. I liked to never got through history if it weren't for her."

"We're on it," Bill said. He knew the man who had spoken as the king of prime assholes. He'd been a union agitator at the textile company before it closed and had developed a medical condition that kept him from working but not from warming the chairs in the barbershop and the OTB parlor down the road.

"Give Ernst my best, Car," he said, and shut the door behind him.

As far as Bill was concerned, there was no proof that the little girl had been murdered. Hanna Moon had sent her off to school that morning, bundled in her yellow coat and scarf and boots, and never saw her again. (At least, not *alive*. Kate Russell had said that Hanna Moon told her she'd seen the apparition of her daughter several times in the past few weeks.) The bus driver and the children on the bus remembered dropping her off at the co-op's entrance, but Hanna Moon hadn't called 911 until after seven that evening. It was a sad comment on the state of things at Chalybeate Springs, Bill thought, that the child's absence hadn't excited any interest until then.

When word got out, television stations as far away as Louisville and Knoxville had taken a brief, intense interest. Disappearances of children were not so rare, but he figured it was probably because she was such an unusual-looking child, pretty in her own way, with long, black hair and wide eyes that held a look of calm trust in every one of the pictures her mother and school came up with. If she'd been two hundred pounds and nearsighted, he imagined that the newspeople wouldn't have thought twice about coming all the way to Carystown to try to find out what had happened to her. But after a while they'd gone away. The child had become just another one of the hundreds who disappeared without a trace every year.

The crew at the barbershop had ruined his appetite. He should have known better than to go in there with not one, but two suspicious death cases so fresh on the town's mind. The crowd at the Carousel would be even more curious. So when he came to Craddock's, the town's coffee-house, he went inside. The crowd was younger here, not liable to speak to him. Most of them were paranoid that he was out prowling for the dime bags of pot stashed in their expensive backpacks.

As the nose- and eyebrow-ring–bedecked young woman behind the counter packed up his coffee and one of the crisp, butter-laden spanako-pitas from the case, another person came into the shop, causing the hand-ful of pot metal bells on the door to jangle brightly. When Bill saw who had entered, he knew it was something more than annoyance with the barbershop crowd that had brought him here.

Deep worry lines creased Hanna Moon's sun-worn face, as though she were concentrating hard on some distant sound or an idea she couldn't quite grasp. Although Bill believed her to be only in her mid-thirties, her hair was streaked with fine strands of gray. Her body beneath her linen dress was what he would call fully fleshed, but even so, the skin at her neck was loose and wrinkled. She'd aged ten years since he had spoken with her at any length.

He quickly paid for his food, trying to keep an eye on where Hanna Moon was going. She'd taken a seat at one of the tall tables in the window, letting her feet swing free from the stool. Bill walked in her direction, ready to make eye contact with her to get her attention. But when he looked directly at her, her eyes widened in recognition.

"Sheriff," she said excitedly, "I've been looking for you!"

"Is that a fact?" Bill said. "We'd like to have news for you Ms. Moon. I'm sure Mitch has told you we're still exploring everything that comes in."

But Hanna Moon wasn't listening to him. She tilted her head like a cu-rious child and waited politely until he was finished.

"She told me to look out for you," she said. "Not you, really, but more for your wife. What's her name?" Hanna Moon glanced at the floor, then looked up at the ceiling as though for an answer written on the ceiling tiles. "Marjory? Mamie?"

"Margaret," Bill said.

"That's it," she said, and gave him an expansive smile full of yellowing teeth. "She said you'll need her help. You need to listen to your wife."

"I don't understand," Bill said, not liking this conversation. He'd wanted to ask her about the Russell woman, to find out if she'd been followed or harassed by her. He also wanted to know if they'd met before Isabella disappeared. But her words began to sink in and he felt the dull ache of worry in the back of his mind.

"Why, your wife. Margaret," she said. Then she spoke to someone else over Bill's shoulder. "I found the sheriff, and I didn't even have to go looking at his office."

"That so?"

Bill turned to see Charlie Matter standing as close as a shadow behind him.

"Sheriff," Charlie said, nodding. He wore a scuffed canvas outback hat that had seen better days. The hand in which he held his cup of coffee had a thick gauze bandage on its back. Even though it was only late March, he, like Hanna, was ruddy from the sun.

"Mr. Matter," Bill said.

"Time to go, Hanna," Charlie said.

Hannah responded to his authoritative voice with a pout. "But I haven't had my coffee yet," she said.

"Go on and get it to go," Charlie said. "Quit bothering the sheriff."

Still in a sulk, Hanna slid from the stool. Bill felt her fingers light on his arm as she passed by. "Wait for me," she whispered.

"How's the police business, Sheriff?" Charlie said. "You catching the bad guys?"

Small talk with the locals was a big part of his job, but he found some citizens harder to stomach than others. Charlie Matter had shown up at Chalybeate Springs about five years before to take the place in hand. He had no priors that Bill could find. He supposed it was probably, technically, against some civil rights lawyer's opinion to investigate someone's background just because he rubbed a man the wrong way, but Bill didn't personally see anything wrong with it. And Charlie Matter had been investigated more thoroughly after Isabella's disappearance, only to come up clean. His alibi for the window of time in which she'd disappeared was tight. But the man was often just a little too eager to please for Bill's taste. He kept himself on the radar mostly, even showed up at the occasional Rotary meeting wearing a collared shirt with his blue jeans. Bill knew that's the way he would do it if he had anything to hide. Plain sight was always best.

"I've been wondering that nobody out your way has been in the office looking for updates on the child," Bill said. "I want to assure you that the case is still open, if anyone's interested."

Charlie bristled visibly, but he managed to sound civil. "We're a law and order bunch, Sheriff," he said. "We know that if there's any information, you'd let us know. Then again, Hanna's convinced Issy's dead and comes to visit her every now and again. She's got her back in that way, and I think that's all she wants."

They both watched as Hanna chatted to the girl behind the counter.

"You ever think about treatment for her?"

"Treatment, hell," Charlie said. "She's happy. And she's not exactly a danger to anyone."

"Maybe herself," Bill said. "You might want to think about that. If the child does turn up someday, a mother who's deep in mental illness isn't going to do her much good."

Charlie laughed, drawing the attention of people at nearby tables. "Don't shit a shitter, Sheriff," he said. "Hey, Hanna. Let's go."

Hanna brought her coffee over to them. "I've told her to tell you herself, Sheriff," she said, shaking her head. "But you know how kids are, especially at that age." She looked puzzled for a moment, as though remembering something. "Of course she's older now. Almost eleven. She should be over that kind of fooling around."

Charlie put his hand on Hanna's shoulder to guide her to the door. "Let's let the sheriff get to his lunch," he said.

Hanna resisted, shrugging him off. She reached up and touched Bill's face, holding her cool fingers against his jaw. Looking into his eyes, she said, "You take care, you hear?"

Then they were gone out the door in another jingling of bells, Charlie Matter guiding her gently and with more kindness than Bill would have imagined him capable of. As they passed out of view of the coffeehouse's large front window, Bill felt an intense sadness come over him, coupled with a desperate need to feel Margaret in his arms.

17

The afternoon Miles asked her to sleep with one of his investors, Mary-Katie thought he was joking. They'd just come in from playing tennis, and her white polo shirt was soaked and the hair around her face was stringy with sweat. She stood by the refrigerator, her back to him as she filled a glass full of cold, filtered water.

"He's really impressed with you, baby," he said. "He says you're smart, funny, beautiful—everything I already know you are."

She was all too familiar with Miles's often appalling sense of humor: The last Fourth of July party they'd had, he employed a pair of little people and had them costumed only in red, white, and blue top hats and tiny swim briefs convincingly stuffed so the men looked like they were hung like horses (Miles's guests—his clients and their dates—thought them riotous). But however varied his tastes were in the bedroom, they had yet to include other people.

"I don't quite get it, honey," she said, not wanting to believe what she'd just heard. But a part of her knew he wasn't joking. She didn't want to turn around to look at him. What kind of man loans out his wife? What kind of wife lets him?

Miles came to put his arms around her waist. Although he wasn't much taller than she, he was still as muscular—maybe even more so—as the day she'd met him. Almost fifteen years older than she, he still beat her at tennis every time they played. But his chest felt cool and dry against her back.

"One night or afternoon, here, or anyplace you want." His voice was a whisper, as though he were telling her something sweet and confidential. "You're in control. Nothing happens that you don't want to happen. I promise."

She pulled away from him and swung around to fling the remainder of the glass of water in his face.

Miles reached over to the counter and tore off a handful of paper towels from the roll. As he patted his face dry, he looked solemn, but not angry.

"I suppose I deserved that," he said. "I knew it was a long shot."

Mary-Katie was shaking, inside and out. She'd never attacked Miles, or anyone else for that matter. She had been gently raised, as her grandmother used to say. Her way was almost always to back down in an argument. Arguing seemed a waste of time to her, particularly with Miles. So many times she had just gone ahead and lied for him or signed whatever papers he asked her to. He didn't respond well to probing questions or challenges.

"I don't suppose it would make any difference to you that it means the difference between—"

"Don't even say life and death, Miles, because I know you better than that," she said.

"Don't be naive, Mary-Katie," he said. "This is the life we're set to lose." He swept out his arm to take in their granite and marble kitchen, with its commercial-grade appliances and hand-planed cherry cabinets. She had fallen in love with the house the minute Miles had brought her through the door. She'd never imagined that she might live in such a place. But Miles had told her she could have any house she wanted if it was under three-quarters of a million dollars, and this was the one she had chosen. It wasn't on the beach, but she could sit on the deck with her coffee and listen to the ocean's distant roar and the shorebirds rejoicing in their breakfasts of a morning.

"Everything's on the line," he said. His shoulders dropped and he suddenly looked older to her, defeated somehow. "It's my fault. I wanted to give you everything, but I got in over my head, and this guy, this Richardson guy, he just stepped in and he's got the cash."

She stood silently as he went on to explain about an office park way up in Charlotte and several other deals that hadn't gone quite the way he'd expected them to. There were other men involved besides this Richardson character— men, Miles hinted, who were looking for money instead of offering it, and wouldn't be so creative in their manner of getting it out of him.

She watched him carefully, looking for any clue that he was playing some kind of game with her. Living with Miles was like living on the edge of a canyon: the view was always spectacular, but one never knew when there was *going to be a landslide. He'd hurt her often enough, turning on her unexpect-edly and denigrating her intelligence, mocking her compassion. But in the end he seemed to treasure her above all other things. When he took on a new proj-ect, he would ask for a kiss for luck. It was all for her, he said. It had become her habit to believe him.*

As he spoke, the shadow of responsibility for their situation crept over her. He had never, ever talked to her about finance problems. It was just something that he handled. Even those periods when the credit cards became a problem were brief. Painful, but brief. Money was just something that was almost al-ways there with Miles, like the series of BMWs, the extensive wine cellar, and the discreet diamond pinky ring he wore on his right hand. When they were first married, he had told her that she would never need to think about money as long as they were together. That had been the first lie, she guessed. And the easiest to swallow. This story she swallowed, too, eventually, not seeing it for a lie until it was way too late.

"This can't be the only answer, Miles," she said.

"I wish it wasn't, baby," he said. "I've done everything I know how to do. I feel like an idiot getting so far out on this limb. It was mistake after mistake."

Were those tears in his eyes?

"We could sell the house," she said. "I don't need a house like this. We have the house in Beaufort. We could live there."

He shook his head. "This house with the Beaufort house wouldn't come close to covering it. And we've got squat for equity."

Mary-Katie had never pretended to understand the deals that Miles was involved in. It wasn't a question of not being able to, but not wanting to know. There was always a tainted air about them. His partners were never quite be-lievable as legitimate businessmen.

She tried one last time. "There are banks, Miles. There are police, the FBI, people who deal with criminals."

"You think I won't go down with them?" Miles's voice was almost a whisper.

Out in the front hallway, the antique Swiss grandfather clock that Miles had once told her belonged to his grandparents rang four o'clock, its chimes as deep and rich and warm as music. She had found out later, from one of Miles's more frequent associates, that he had won it off a man who'd gambled away everything in the house his parents had left to him and then hanged himself in the closet of his suite at an Atlanta hotel. But even knowing that, it was still one of the few things she was later sad to leave behind.

For the next couple of days, Mary-Katie couldn't bring herself to speak to Miles beyond exchanging information about where she would be or the status of the dry cleaning or where they would go to eat their silent, awkward meals. She couldn't lie beside him in bed if she were awake, and moved to sleep on the sofa in the media room with its giant projection television turned on, muted, so that she slept—or didn't sleep—bathed in the shifting light of the screen.

She never thought specifically about Kyle Richardson, or what Miles had begged her to do to save them both. (That was the word for it, wasn't it? Begged? *With the tears and the pronouncement of their ruin.) She didn't really think, except to choose the massage oil the masseuse at the spa used on her, or the color the pedicurist was to paint her toes. She immediately erased the cheery message from the secretary of the women's tennis group she sometimes played in. The last thing she wanted was to have to wear a false smile for a bunch of women she didn't know well and didn't particularly like.*

Five minutes after she arrived at the suite Kyle Richardson had booked at one of the bigger resorts on the island, Mary-Katie was in the marble-walled bathroom throwing up. As she'd walked through the lobby with its smattering of early season tourists, she imagined that they were all staring at her and knew exactly why she was there. Miles had helped her pick the light blue silk twin set and slender skirt from her closet. The sweater set's shell was a low V-neck and sexy, but subtle, so she certainly didn't look out of place among the casually but well-dressed fall tourists. She might have been on her way to meet a friend for lunch. In fact, a woman she knew only by sight from the country club caught her eye from where she sat in the café that bordered the lobby, but Mary-Katie pretended not to see her. She'd continued on to the elevator wearing a tenuous smile that felt frozen to her face. But her stomach and intestines were in an uproar. She had made it to the hotel, but she was afraid that it was all she'd be able to do.

Kyle Richardson knocked timidly on the bathroom door, asking if she needed anything.

Sure. Help getting my head out of the toilet, *was the first thing that came to her mind. She told him, "No, thank you," instead. But as she went to stand up, she noticed a slender curl of pubic hair on the seat, its bulbous root still attached, and began to retch again.*

When she looked in the mirror a few minutes later, she saw that she still looked like herself, a little blotched maybe, but not much different from how she had looked that morning or even the week before, when Miles first told her what he wanted her to do. In the back of her mind she had come to imagine that playing the role of prostitute would make her look like a slattern, perhaps a little more knowing, that her clothes would fit her differently, more provocatively, or maybe she would develop a cynical sneer.

Fortunately, the Valium Miles had given her half an hour before was starting to kick in. (She hadn't known about the prescription, but then again, maybe he'd gotten it just for her. It seemed that there was so much she didn't know about her husband.)

He had told her again and again to be herself, that Richardson was not going to make her do anything she didn't want to do.

"Except fuck him," she said sarcastically.

A shadow of irritation had passed over his face, and he said, "Please don't talk like that with him. It's beneath you."

After swishing Kyle Richardson's orange-flavored mouthwash around in her mouth and spitting it into the sink, she could only think that there wasn't much that was beneath her now.

Kyle Richardson apologized four times (she counted) for the pitifully small size of his penis. If he had been one of the few young men she'd had casual sexual relationships with in college (men about whom Miles had never inquired, and whom she, vaguely embarrassed, hadn't mentioned), she might not have responded, but finished perfunctorily and ended the relationship. Kyle Richardson, though, seemed to want reassurance, and she tried to imagine how a professional would respond.

"You're great," she told him, every time he said it. "You're just fine."

He didn't seem like a bad man. As he sweated over her, his eyes squeezed closed and his fingers digging painfully into her shoulders, she thought that he probably had teenage kids and a wife whose picture he carried in his wallet. She wondered where his wife was, if she minded about the size of his penis that was just barely inside her own vagina at that moment, what kind of car she drove, and if she knew that her husband accepted sex for cash in his business dealings.

When they were finished and Kyle Richardson was putting on his socks and telling her how wonderful she had been, it occurred to Mary-Katie that she should have maybe faked an orgasm.

That evening, Miles took her to the yacht club for dinner. She considered it a kind of victory that she felt nauseated only once, leaving the table briefly to stand, not quite retching, over a toilet in the women's bathroom.

They shared a bottle of wine over dinner. Miles's mood was much lighter than it had been over the past few weeks. He suggested that once he was through with this latest round of business deals, they might go somewhere she'd never been, like Bermuda or somewhere off the coast of South America. Mary-Katie knew that it was just talk. But she wanted to believe him. She wanted to believe him when he said he would never ask her to do what she'd done with Kyle Richardson again.

Later, sated with food and wine, they made love in their own bed, and it was like she'd never been with anybody else. Unlike Kyle Richardson, Miles was a perfect fit for her, and she'd never once in their marriage had to even think of faking an orgasm. But it was a while before she could bring herself to wear the new pair of diamond solitaire earrings she found under her pillow when she was making the bed the next morning.

18

"DON'T YOU THINK we ought to cut the lights?" Margaret said quietly. They were in the closed cab of the pickup truck, but something about the night around them and the emptiness of the county service road made her lower her voice.

Bill shut off the headlights, leaving only the yellow fogs to glow mutely ahead of them. School would be in session tomorrow, so he knew that—unlike any given Friday or Saturday—they were unlikely to come upon any lovers parking along the road. They passed behind what he thought was the line of houses that included Lillian Cayley's; each had a number of back porch lights on, so that their yards were illuminated. There was a single pitch-black gap that he was sure was the Cayley property. No one would be there. He doubted that the daughter would ever want to live in the house again, but she would sure have a hard time selling it.

He slowed the truck to look for the curve that announced the back of the cemetery property.

"There," Margaret said, pointing. "The light at the front gate's there. Right through the trees."

"Yeah, I see," Bill said. He drove across the opposite lane and pulled onto the shoulder. The truck idled for a moment as he tried to figure how far he could go into the brush, which was thicker than he'd hoped. There was little room for the truck, and only just enough for them to get through with the full-size wheelbarrow they'd brought. He pulled the truck as close to the brush as he dared and shut down the engine.

Once they wrestled the wheelbarrow out of the back of the truck, Bill rested the pitchforks, shovels, and the spade inside it.

"Bring the lights," he said to Margaret. She got the backpack she'd brought with her. He had laughed in the light of the kitchen when she packed bottles of water and a can of nuts to snack on, but now that they were at the cemetery, he realized that they might be there the better part of the night.

Only an hour before, they'd been getting ready for bed when he told Margaret both about Kate Russell's insistence that the little girl was buried behind the cemetery's mausoleum and his encounter with Charlie Matter and Hanna Moon at the coffeehouse. He'd been light on details about Hanna Moon's ominous words because he didn't want to scare her. But it had been Margaret's suggestion that they head out to the cemetery that very night. *You need to listen to your wife.*

As he watched Margaret a few feet away, pushing her way through the brush ahead of him, the thought came clearly to him that taking her digging in a cemetery in the earliest hours of the morning not a few hundred yards from where a woman had been murdered two days before was a stupid, fate-tempting thing to do. Still, as absurd as it was, he didn't think their project could hurt anything. It was unlikely they would find the child, and there were few times when he didn't take pleasure in just being around his wife.

When they reached the clearing, he shined a flashlight over the mounds of leaves in its center.

"Didn't look like so much this afternoon," he said doubtfully. "Real equipment would be easier."

"Let's get to it," Margaret said, pulling on the leather gloves she used for heavy garden work. "I've got a lot to do tomorrow."

"Are you sure you want to be here? I never should have even told you about this crap," Bill said. "It's liable to be a big waste of our time."

"Honey, how much longer are you going to let this little girl weigh on your mind? I don't know what has led you to set so much store by what this Russell woman says, but if we do this and don't find anything, you can move on. You'll know you've done the best you can." Margaret picked up a pitchfork. "I don't think it's a perfectly logical thing to do, no. But people who murder other people aren't logical either, are they?"

Uncertainty was a feeling he wasn't used to, but he went ahead and unloaded the rest of the tools and navigated the wheelbarrow between the mounds of leaves the best he could. The ground was spongy beneath his feet, and with every step, the moist, rotten smell of the leaves seemed to intensify. The smell took him back many years to the days when he would hunt with his father, tramping behind him in the sodden woods, desperate to show that he could keep up with the other hunters.

"I knew there was a reason I never liked composting," he said. "This is some nasty stuff." He positioned the wheelbarrow near the middle of the clearing. "She said she thought it was right around here," he said.

"It's earth, honey," Margaret said, handing him a pitchfork. "It's the way it's supposed to smell."

Kate lay on Francie's sofa in her apartment, an old carriage house in the historic part of town, and listened to the sound of Francie's sobs from behind the single bedroom's door.

She thought about going inside, but it was late and Francie had shut herself in the bedroom an hour before, ostensibly to go to sleep. She guessed that Francie needed some time alone. They'd watched television with desultory interest most of the evening and ate a few bites of one of the six casseroles that had shown up that day, the offerings of the Martha Guild at Lillian's church, First Avenue AME.

Kate burrowed into the pillow and wound herself in the cotton blanket she'd brought from home. Francie was notorious for her lack of housekeeping skills and she was not set up for guests, even though Lillian had continually tried to train her to some notion of hospitality. Kate missed her own bed and the relative spaciousness of her own small house. But being there at Francie's place made her feel closer to Lillian, and with Francie in her own room, she gave in to her own tears. She couldn't shake the feeling that she was responsible for Lillian's death, that if she'd never gotten Lillian involved in her problem with Isabella Moon, Lillian would still be alive.

Above the couch, a breeze through the open window brought in the scent of a mock orange tree, reminding her that even with all the death surrounding her, spring was arriving. There were voices, too, of people coming out of The Right Note, a few blocks away. Life was going on.

Hearing them, she thought of Caleb, who liked to go there when a rocka-billy band came through town. He would be home Friday, Saturday at the latest. What she would tell him about everything that had happened, she didn't know.

Finally, long after Francie's sobs abated, Kate fell into a restless sleep.

As though by some unspoken agreement, Margaret and Bill made their way, exhausted, to a fallen log at the edge of the clearing, far away from the ragged circle of earth they had exposed in the course of the last two hours. Most of the mounds of leaves were gone, hauled to one side and dumped from the wheelbarrow.

"It's not as muddy as I thought it would be," Margaret said. "But Lord, I'm filthy."

Bill leaned close to her and kissed her cheek. "Even in the dark you're the best looking woman in town," he said.

They passed the can of nuts back and forth and shared a single bottle of water.

"Careful," Margaret said. "Those things have about fifteen grams of fat in a serving."

Bill took a handful, putting much of it in his mouth. "We've worked it off," he said with his mouth full. "Or we will."

"Doesn't matter," Margaret said. "There'll just be more of you to love."

Bill grunted, put the lid back on the can, and pitched it on the ground near the backpack. They might have been out for a lover's adventure, pic-nicking in the dark. One of their first dates had been a picnic, and he'd found out what a good cook Margaret was. When he'd tasted her fried chicken and German potato salad, he knew that if he didn't fall in love with her, he was an idiot.

With the leaves cleared, they started digging. Their eyes were well-adjusted to the dark, and they used their flashlights only infrequently to illuminate the occasional large rock. Around them the cedars were still and quiet, with the exception of the topmost branches, which seemed to whis-per restlessly against the sky.

When a single high-pitched cry broke the quiet, they both looked in the direction of the sound.

"Screech owl," Margaret said. "How appropriate."

Again they avoided the exact center of the clearing, the place where Kate had said she'd put her face close to the ground, where she was certain that Isabella was buried. They worked their way toward it, digging small trenches only about twenty inches deep. They were both tiring, but the dirt was soft and yielded easily to their shovels. They talked in low voices as they worked, about the museum and the board members that were driving Margaret crazy, about the next election. Finally, while he was still talking, Bill moved to the clearing's center, the place where, if one looked up in the sky, the treetops enclosed a circle of stars and wispy clouds. Margaret joined him, as she often did when he was concentrating on something particularly difficult to do.

They'd dug down about a foot when Bill stopped digging and looked out toward the road.

"Shit," he said. Headlights from a slowly moving car flashed intermittently through the trees. He'd considered it a calculated risk to park so close to where they were digging, and even brought his own truck, thinking it wouldn't draw the attention that his cruiser would.

"Maybe you better get out of sight," he said to Margaret. "It could be anybody."

"I don't think so," Margaret said, flinging a shovelful of dirt to the side. "In for a penny, in for a pound."

It exasperated the hell out of him how stubborn she could be. But given that he'd put her in this ridiculous position, he figured it was no time to give her an argument. His stainless steel .45 Wilson Protector rested snugly in its holster at his side. There wouldn't be any trouble that he couldn't handle.

The car out on the road slowed as it approached the truck. He thought he recognized the erratic *tick-tick-tick* of the engine of the newest patrol car, a Crown Vic, but the car sped off before he could be sure.

"They'll be back," Bill said. "Everyone knows the road dead-ends at the waterworks."

"They'll just think we're in the truck doing the nasty," Margaret said. "Let's get this over with. I've had about as much fun as I can handle tonight."

Recognizing the tired edge in her voice, and knowing that she meant what she said, he attacked the hole they were working on with renewed effort. The brisk night air and the cloying smell of the leaves were getting to him as well. So far they'd come up with only beer cans, weathered candy bar wrappers, a chipped china saucer, and three well-chewed rubber dog toys. They dug in silence, with Bill looking frequently over his shoulder for the car, until Margaret suddenly spoke.

"I'll be damned," she said, lifting her shovel. "Get a light on, Bill."

He dropped his own shovel and shined the flashlight he had clipped to his gun belt down into the hole. A patch of bright yellow stared up at them from the ground, and Bill knew immediately that it was the girl's yellow coat. He squatted down and brushed dirt away from it with a gloved hand.

"Maybe we shouldn't," Margaret said.

Bill knew at that moment that she was afraid. This was no longer just a midnight adventure. This was something real. "It's probably nothing," he said.

"Right," Margaret said. "Someone's idea of a joke. Maybe that Russell woman. Maybe she's some kind of psychopath who plays tricks on people. You always were a sucker for a pretty girl, Bill Delaney." She laughed nervously.

So intent were they on the hole that neither of them noticed that the car had returned until it parked so its headlights shone through the brush.

"Got to be one of mine," Bill said. "I don't know who's on duty tonight, but I guess we'll soon find out."

"What do we do?" Margaret said.

"Wait," Bill said.

They didn't have to wait long. They heard a car door shut. Another light came on, this one a bright police spot. It swept the trees, resting here and there until finally it was close enough to light on them.

"Sheriff's Department!" a voice shouted. "Drop!"

"Go on, get down," Bill whispered to Margaret, who sank quickly to her knees beside the hole.

Bill dropped to one knee and called out, "Mitch, it's Bill. Get that damn light off me."

The light shifted, but Bill and Margaret had already been nearly blinded by it and couldn't make out the shape of the deputy behind it.

"Sheriff?" Mitch said from the edge of the brush. "What the hell?"

~

In her current state of sleepiness and grief, it seemed to Kate to be the most natural thing in the world to see, in the doorway to Francie's bedroom, a young woman whose image seemed to tremble and fade in and out like a bad television signal. Her experience with Isabella Moon had blunted her fear of the bizarre. For a moment she thought she was looking at Francie playing dress-up, her hair swept into a beehive hairdo high on her head, wearing a peach-colored sundress that was incandescence itself.

The young woman was looking around the room as though she'd never seen it before. Standing on tiptoe on her bare, slender feet, she gently swung a small, trunk-shaped purse by its bamboo handle and clutched a brilliantly white pair of gloves in one hand.

"Lillian," Kate said, her voice just above a whisper. "Lillian." Her heart was glad that Lillian had come. She hadn't realized how much she had missed her. She hadn't realized how fully Lillian had come to fill the empty space created inside her when her own mother had died so young. There was so much she wanted to say to her, to apologize for. But beneath all the emotion, only one question was in her mind.

"What should I do, Lillian?" she said.

Then, as though she were looking at a film, there was a tear in the young Lillian's image and it split into two parts that seemed to stretch and then fold into themselves, twisting the young Lillian's anguished face, her torso. Her slim legs and arms bent in agonizing angles that stretched toward Kate so that she could almost touch them.

Kate shrank away, now terrified. And then all vestiges of Lillian were gone. The vibrant light that had seemed to come from inside her dress, from beneath her silken dark skin, was gone. But in Lillian's place stood Francie—the real Francie.

"Francie," Kate said. "Your mother—"

Francie was motionless, and Kate said her name again. Outside, the red lights from a silent ambulance blinked into the room, freezing Francie's expressionless face into a picture from which Kate could not look away.

"Please, Francie," Kate said, getting up to go to her. She dropped the blanket on the floor and held out her hand. "Say something, Francie."

Suddenly Francie *was* looking at her, but her eyes were the empty eyes of a sleepwalker. When she spoke, her mouth moved, but it wasn't her voice.

"There's trials to come, honey," she said slowly. A bit of drool escaped the left corner of her lips and crept down to her chin. "Look out for my Francie. Look out for yourself, Mary-Katie."

Francie's face relaxed and her eyes closed. Before Kate could catch her, she fell to the floor, one forearm across her eyes, as though to shield them from some unwelcome sight.

Bill squatted beside the hole with Mitch standing by. He could feel Margaret behind him, still nervous.

"It's county land," Mitch said. "We don't need any kind of warrant, do we? I say we go ahead and dig in."

Bill was inclined to agree. But he knew they were going to need the coroner if the body was indeed there, and he had no equipment for night photographs, so those would have to wait until morning. And if they were looking at a crime scene, then Margaret shouldn't be there at all. There was a hell of a lot to consider, and they couldn't stand around there all night. He had to be sure that what they were looking at was concealing a body and wasn't just somebody's car blanket left behind by a couple of horny teenagers.

"You got another lamp in the cruiser?" he asked Mitch.

"Sure thing," Mitch said. He stood up and started off to the car.

"Evidence bags, too, Mitch," Bill called after him.

"This is so exciting," Margaret said. "Horrible. But exciting."

Bill got to his feet and put an arm around her. "Why don't you go on home and get some sleep," he said. "If we're right, than it's an all-nighter, plus."

She put a hand against his chest and gave him a gentle push. "You don't get to drag me out here in the middle of the night, then when we find what we're looking for, send me to bed. Forget that, cowboy," she said. "You owe me."

"Consider yourself warned, Margaret," he said. "It could be gruesome as hell."

"Of course," she said. Then her voice was contrite. "But I do hope we're wrong. It makes me sick to think the child has been right here the whole time."

As they stood waiting for Mitch to return, the breeze picked up in the clearing, enveloping them in the scent of earth and decay.

The dirt came away easily from the yellow coat. However many months it had been there hadn't stained it too badly; it was still vibrant in the glare of the lamp Mitch had set up by the hole. Dawn was only an hour or so away, and the occasional bird called from the trees around them. Bill, at least, wasn't particularly anxious to expose what was beneath the coat, which seemed to be front down in the hole. They were nearly to the collar when Bill put his hand out to stop Mitch from taking more dirt.

"Wait," he said. He tossed his own shovel aside and plunged his arm down into the hole. His fingers moved deftly through the dirt that still hid whatever was just above the coat's collar. He seemed to stroke the dirt, and after a moment Margaret gasped above him.

"Oh, Bill," she said.

As the dirt fell away, they could all see that mixed in with it were thick strands of black hair. Bill couldn't feel the hair through his gloves, but he didn't need to. The woods had nearly taken this prize, this small, innocent being, but in the end they had freed her from her shoddy grave.

"Time to make some phone calls," he said, trying to hide the emotion in his voice. "Wake some folks up."

19

KATE WORKED as quietly as she could in the kitchen, assembling breakfast from the groceries she'd brought by Francie's apartment the previous afternoon. Her brain felt fogged and slow. She knew that she must have slept, but couldn't remember. She could recall getting Francie back to bed and sitting on the couch anxious that something else would happen, that Lillian might return, or perhaps even Isabella. But there had been nothing. She thought that maybe she'd fallen asleep as dawn began to break, but she wasn't sure.

On the way to Francie's room to check to see if she was awake, she passed the elaborately framed mirror that Lillian had bought Francie on their European vacation the year before. She wasn't going to stop to look in it, but a single glance pulled her up short: the face that stared back at her seemed unfamiliar. Aside from the deep circles beneath her eyes, she saw new wrinkles around her mouth and eyelids. It jarred her. Even after all the trouble she'd had in her life, she'd never felt like her face paid for it. She considered it one of the reasons she'd been able to get away with living such a normal life in Carystown. Being able to roll out of bed, wash her face, dab on a little mascara, and look good had its advantages. She had the kind of face that could be trusted. But her face looked worn to her now, like it belonged to someone ten years older.

Francie's bedroom door opened, startling her.

"God bless you for making coffee," Francie said. She inhaled deeply, almost comically, as she emerged from the room. She was dressed in blue jeans and a fresh white blouse; her hair was pulled back from her face with a wide paisley headband, and a pair of bright copper discs hung from her earlobes. She looked to Kate as though she were off for a day's shopping instead of the funeral home, which is where, the night before, she told Kate she'd be going. She gave Kate a quick kiss on the cheek. *Breezy* was the word that came to Kate's mind for the way Francie was acting, hardly the way she'd been expecting her to be.

"Francie?" she said. "Are you okay?" She followed her into the kitchen, where Francie began to spoon scrambled eggs from the skillet onto her plate.

"You bought bagels, too?" Francie said. "You are the best, Kate. Just the best."

Kate watched, dumbfounded, as Francie put a bagel in the toaster and poured herself some coffee. She could see that the morning wasn't going to go quite as she'd thought it would. It was pretty obvious that Francie had no memory of coming into the living room the night before, or of passing out on the floor. *Was passing out even the right phrase? Surely she'd never actually been awake.* As Kate had made breakfast, she struggled with whether to ask Francie about it. She knew, too, that she should tell her about taking Lillian to the cemetery. Francie would probably find out eventually. But now Kate didn't know what to say.

"Did work call while I was in the shower?" Francie said. "With Sarah taking off, things are already going to be tight."

Kate poured herself a cup of coffee and sat at the table across from Francie. She spoke gently, unsure how to approach this Francie who was suddenly, alarmingly, so much like her old self.

"Didn't you say that they told you to take as much time as you need?" Kate said. "What about the funeral?"

Francie wouldn't meet her eyes. She chewed steadily, watching her plate. Finally, she waved her hand dismissively. "The autopsy," she said. "The coroner said it wouldn't even be finished until the end of this week at the earliest. Those guys in the basement are slower than death." When she realized what she'd said, she gave a little "Ha!"

But Kate couldn't laugh. The mental image of Lillian's delicate body exposed, naked on a gurney in a cold examining room, her flesh cut and breastbone broken, made her want to weep again, as she had on and off since Lillian's murder. She wished that Lillian might have been spared the indignity of it all. But, of course, it had to be. The autopsy was critical to finding out who had killed her.

Francie, though, didn't seem to be particularly disturbed by the notion. Maybe, Kate thought, it's because she's in shock.

"Are you sure you want to be there, Francie?" Kate said. "So close?"

"She's not *there,* Kate," Francie said, looking her in the eye. "Mama's with Jesus, right? Isn't that what she believed? Why shouldn't I believe that, too?"

"That's not what I meant," Kate said. "I know that's not really her. I just thought it might be hard for you to be at the hospital."

Francie sighed. "You've been awfully sweet, Kate," she said. "But I think it's time for you to get back to your house. Your life. You don't need to babysit me anymore. I'm not going to do anything drastic, honey."

It was more than Kate could take. She knew that there was something wrong with Francie, that something had happened to change her, but she didn't have the inner reserves at that moment to stand up to her, to take care of Francie the way Lillian had asked her to. She'd let Lillian down in so many ways. She felt her throat close up. Unexpected tears fell onto her cheeks.

"Kate!" Francie said, getting up from the table. "Stop it! She wasn't even your mother, for pity's sake." She dropped her dishes in the sink with a clatter. "I don't know what you want from me."

"And I don't know what's wrong with you!" Kate said, almost shouting.

Francie shut off the coffeemaker and the light over the sink before pushing past the table where Kate sat. Out in the hallway, she paused at the bedroom door.

"Quit acting like a baby and get your own life," she called before shutting the door firmly behind her.

Kate sat for several minutes, trying to get herself together. She had already felt like she was losing her mind. Now, her feeling that she was somehow responsible for Lillian's death added to the pressure. For the briefest of moments she thought about leaving Carystown. Running away had served her well in the past. She rarely even thought about Miles and Hilton Head now that they were several years behind her and would, she prayed, keep getting farther away. But there was Caleb to think about. And Isabella Moon. Somehow she knew that leaving town wouldn't stop

Isabella from reaching her. *But hadn't she done what the child had wanted her to do?* Worse, Bill Delaney already suspected her of something, and he didn't seem like the kind of man who would let her go easily. She thought of how kind his eyes had been when she'd come to his office the week before. *Had it been only a week?* How fast her life, so carefully crafted, now seemed to be flying apart.

It took only a few minutes to toss her belongings into her duffel bag. She glanced over the kitchen and the breakfast dishes that cluttered the sink and countertop. She'd come to the conclusion that Francie had just skipped some of the grief process, that because Lillian's death had been so sudden and violent, Francie couldn't be expected to react normally.

She was set to walk out the door, but not hearing any sounds from Francie's bedroom, she decided to give the office a quick call to let Edith know that she'd be in after she stopped at home to get cleaned up.

Edith sounded breathless when she answered the phone.

"Edith," Kate said. "It's me."

"Kate," she said. "You'll never guess. They've found that little girl's body. They've found Isabella Moon."

"No," Kate said. "What do you mean?"

"Everybody's talking about it," Edith said. "Where are you? Are you still at home?"

"No," Kate said. *Why hadn't she known?* She felt a moment's loss. Somehow she'd thought she would be there when the little girl's body was found.

"Where did they find her, Edith? Did they say?" Kate heard the burble of one of the office's other lines in the background.

"I have to go," Edith said. "Janet's called in sick and that might be her. Are you coming in?"

"Where, Edith? Where did they find her?" Kate said.

"In the colored cemetery, of all places," Edith said. "Who'd have thought of looking in a cemetery?"

There was silence on the line, and Kate realized that Edith had hung up. She felt a small amount of weight lift from her chest. Maybe she wasn't insane after all. Maybe she was as sane as homely, dull Edith.

As she closed Francie's front door behind her, she felt better than she had in days. She hurried down the stairs and almost ran straight into Paxton Birkenshaw at their foot.

"Paxton," she said. "Hello."

"Kate," he said. "Good to see you." He gave her a quick smile and stepped around her to take the stairs up by twos.

She looked back after him until he turned at the landing in front of Francie's door. She'd been startled by his sudden appearance, but she knew that he and Francie had known each other a long time. By the time she reached her car, he was out of her thoughts and she had decided that she would not go straight to work, but to talk to Hanna Moon.

20

IF PAXTON HAD SHOWN UP at her door a week ago, Francie would have been unnerved. But seeing him there now, she was completely calm. She was beyond caring about what happened to her, or what might happen to the two of them. Now that her mother was dead, there was no reason to keep Paxton away from her, here or in public. There would be no lectures about how rich folk and middle-class folk didn't really mix, no raised eyebrows at Paxton's goofy behavior, his "unpredictability." If her mother was beyond caring now, then she would be, too.

"Hey, come to Daddy," Paxton said, holding open his arms. "I took the whole day off to be with you."

"You sure took your time about it," Francie said. "Where have you been?"

"Hush. That's just your broken heart talking," he said, coming over to the couch, where she had retreated after letting him in. "Look." He took his stash box from his pocket and laid it in her lap. "I brought feel-better treats and everything."

"You're such a jerk," Francie said. "You didn't even like Mama, so don't pretend you feel all bad." She knew it wasn't quite true. She knew he had maintained a grudging kind of respect for Lillian, but she felt like hurting him anyway. Nothing bad ever happened to Paxton. He was some kind of Golden Boy. Every kind of trouble he'd ever been in, he'd gotten out of in five minutes, no problem. When she started to get up from the couch, he restrained her gently, pulling her back down by her upper arm.

"Quit, you," she said. *Where had this feeling of abandon come from?*

Pouty, angry, foolish—she could be anything she wanted! "I've got to go to the funeral parlor to make arrangements for my mother."

"Let me go with you, Francie," Paxton said. "We'll go to Obermeyer's together and then we'll go somewhere quiet for lunch. Anywhere. Out of town if you want." She could tell by the look in his eyes that he was sincere. He didn't even look high. But then, it was only ten o'clock in the morning.

She laughed. "Obermeyer's? Paxton, honey, even in this enlightened age, black folk still go to their own undertakers." She put a hand to his cheek. "You're such a baby sometimes."

His naiveté had touched her, and she felt her brittle mood break just a bit. What she really wanted to do was lie back in his arms and forget about the stupid funeral parlor and the way her mother had died. *Had that stiffened doll once been her mother? That thing with the pitchfork jutting from her back like some freakish handle?*

"Now you're going to have to let me take care of you," he said.

Francie sighed. She knew that she was going to have to go to the funeral parlor, with or without Paxton—and she thought that *without* would probably be the better idea. But just at that moment, as she watched him lay out the coke on her coffee table, she was grateful for the rest from her grief, from Kate and her intense sadness. It bugged her how upset Kate was. There was something unseemly about her worn appearance, her immersion in sadness over the death of someone to whom she wasn't even related.

They did the lines. When Paxton came close to her face, he told her to hold still, and he tenderly licked some loose grains of coke from the edge of her nostril.

Then, suddenly, he was on top of her, kissing her neck, her earlobes, her forehead. Francie knew it was wrong, with her mother lying in the morgue just up the highway. She knew that her life from this day would be forever different. When Paxton entered her—she was ready for him, always she was ready for him when he was close enough that she could feel his breath on her—she cried out, not from pain, but from relief of the pain she'd been feeling for days now. Finally—*finally*—the image of her mother's empty and mutilated body was pushed from her mind.

21

WHAT SHE'D EXPECTED from Hanna Moon, Kate wasn't sure. She'd gone to the farm with the intention of comforting her, to let her know that she wasn't alone in her grief for her daughter. Hanna had told her on the street days before that she knew Isabella had come to her, but Kate hadn't wanted to admit that she was right. She just wanted to deal with the rescue—*of course, rescue was not quite the word, was it?*—of Isabella's body so it would not have to lie, undiscovered and uncherished, in that grim little clearing behind the mausoleum.

Now, back at her desk, trying to concentrate on purging Janet's client files of nonpayers, she wished that she hadn't bothered with Hanna Moon. The woman was too far gone for help. Kate shuddered to think of Charlie Matter and the way he had stood behind Hanna's chair, insisting on remaining in the room while they talked. He gave her the creeps with his long, theatrical mustache and his tattooed arms wound around with blue and gray snakes devouring each other. He had come to the door without a shirt and didn't bother to put one on after she came inside. Kate decided that his single redeeming quality was the fact that he didn't laugh at the two of them right off or try to patronize them, telling them that *sure* they'd seen Isabella's ghost, *sure* she had led Kate to her grave. Charlie Matter reminded her of several of the men who had worked for Miles: she hadn't known they were dangerous when she first met them, but something about their easy, accommodating manners—most, like Charlie Matter, were passable salesmen—made her afraid to trust them.

Hanna Moon wasn't any different from when she'd seen her on the street: distracted and probably stoned, prone to going on about how Isabella would come to her at odd times, while she was working in the greenhouse, or even in the bathroom.

Kate had blushed at the thought. *Earthy* was the word her grandmother would've used for a woman like Hanna Moon. She would not have meant it as a compliment.

"Issy had no idea of privacy," Hanna had said, laughing. "She would even come barging in when I was on the toilet! Usually, it would be after she'd been working with the honey. That honey. It was like a tonic to her or something. Like it would make her high. She smelled of honey, too. She always smelled of honey, my Issy did."

Perhaps it was for her own reassurance that she had gone to Hanna, Kate thought, an act against the hope that it was the last she would see of Isabella Moon. After the previous night at Francie's, she was beginning to feel as though she'd become some kind of magnet for the dead. Nothing in her past had prepared her for this freakish turn in her perception of the world. And she was starting to think that maybe it was all perception, that the dead were around her all the time, only she couldn't always see them, hear them. It was as if some button had been pushed inside her, or she'd crossed some kind of line that made her a safe bet for them to contact her. All the same, she desperately wanted to be back on the other side of the line.

"Kate!" Edith called to her. "Did you hear me? Janet's on line two." She shook her head at Kate's apparent wool-gathering. Edith didn't approve of wool-gathering.

A split second after Kate rang the doorbell, Bitty Bit, Janet's Maltese, began barking hysterically on the other side of the door. Remembering that Janet had told her to let herself in, Kate opened the door, only to have the dog rush at her feet to get outside.

"No, you don't," Kate said, sweeping the dog into her arms before it could get over the threshold. She closed the door. More than once she'd had to chase Bitty Bit through the yard while the dog ran ahead. Kate felt sorry for the dog. Janet was too busy to play with her much.

Bitty Bit struggled at first, then began to lick Kate's face and earlobe.

"What a beast you are," Kate said. "Where's your mommy?" She cuddled the dog for a minute, loving the warmth of its wriggling body. She'd almost forgotten that she was capable of enjoying such a simple pleasure.

"Scoot," she said, giving the dog a playful push as she set it down on the polished marble floor.

Janet called down from upstairs, "Bitty, go to your bed."

The dog looked in the direction of her voice, then trotted promptly off to the back of the house.

"Come upstairs," Janet said.

Kate knew she was now addressing her, but the fact that Janet had used the exact same tone with the dog was not lost on her.

"You should have let me bring you some lunch," Kate said as she made her way slowly up the steps, trying not to be distracted by the forbidding collection of oil portraits lining the stairwell. It still amazed her that Janet was building a house more fabulous than this one, which had been built by a banker at the turn of the twentieth century and was on the National Historic Register. Janet's husband had spent a small fortune restoring the stately Victorian for his first wife, who died quite young. Janet had told Kate that the narrow, formal rooms and ancient furniture made the place feel more like a museum than a house. She needed space, she said, somewhere that she could breathe.

Janet had disappeared into the master bedroom at the top of the stairs. Kate could hear shouting from the television. She'd never known Janet to watch television in the daytime.

"I brought the chocolate you wanted," Kate said, pushing the door open.

The room was a mess. The bedclothes lay in various piles on and around the four-poster, and several of Janet's silk robes and yesterday's clothes lay on the floor. Janet had climbed onto the middle of the bed and was pulling a pink down comforter around her shoulders. As she struggled with the comforter, she balanced between her knees a large crystal brandy snifter half full of a dark, thick liquid. Her movements were exaggerated and slow.

"About fucking time," she said, glancing at Kate. "Open it."

Kate had dealt with some of Janet's stranger moods, but never with a Janet who was drunk when she was supposed to be working. Glancing around the room for some scissors or something sharp to open one of the bags of M&Ms, she came across a translucent blue dildo lying atop its leather case on a bedside table. Far from being shocked by its presence, she was disgusted only by the memory that it was very like one of Miles's favorite sex toys, given that he occasionally had a difficult time keeping an erection. *Though he'd been hard enough the night she'd conceived. And although he'd denied that the child was his, she'd known in her heart that he was wrong.*

Seeing nothing that might be useful, she made a tiny cut in the edge of the bag with her teeth and used her fingers to tear off the rest of the top. She waited for Janet to make a fuss, but Janet just held out her hand and told her to hurry up. She shook a handful into Janet's hand.

Janet took a large swallow of whatever was in the snifter (from the smell of it, Kate figured Kahlua) and followed it with the candy.

"These stupid girls," Janet said, her mouth full. She pointed to the television. "Not one of them knows who their babies' daddies are. How dumb do you think you have to be to get on one of these shows?"

"Did you want me for something else?" Kate said. "Or just the chocolate?" A sudden weariness had come over her. She'd had enough weirdness in the last twenty-four hours to last her the rest of her life. It was bad enough that she had to deal with Janet when she was sober; she wasn't prepared to handle a drunk-in-the-middle-of-the-day Janet.

"Why are women generally so stupid, Kate?" Janet said. "Men are the simplest creatures on earth. They think with their pricks and their pricks only. If you can remember that, you can have anything you want in this life." She looked levelly at Kate. "But you should have better hair," she said. "You should let me give you a makeover sometime."

"*What* is wrong with you, Janet?" Kate said. "Did you even hear about what's going on in town? Did you know they found that little girl?"

Janet started up from the bed, spilling a broken rainbow of candy across the sheets. "I hear about things in this town before people even fucking *think* them," she said. "And I don't *want* to hear any more about it from you, thank you."

She hurried into the bathroom, dropping the comforter on the floor behind her. Kate could hear her peeing a long time, then flushing the toilet. Janet came back into the room without stopping to wash her hands.

"You know, what you could get me is a pizza," Janet said, climbing back onto the bed. "I think I'm hungry now. I wasn't earlier."

"Fine," Kate said. "Then I need to get back to the office if you want me to take your afternoon appointments."

Janet nodded and proceeded to use the remote to scan television channels.

The sounds from the television followed Kate for a moment down the stairs, but faded by the time she reached the foyer. Bitty Bit clicked down the hallway and stood looking hopefully up at her.

"I'm guessing you haven't been outside for a while, poor thing," Kate said.

The dog followed behind her to the kitchen, where Kate let her out into the fenced yard with its bricked paths and formal flower and herb gardens. She had often written the check to the landscaping company herself for their maintenance services. Bitty Bit had only a small square at the back of the yard where she was allowed to do her business.

While the dog sniffed around the yard, Kate went to the phone to call for a pizza. Janet almost certainly expected her to go and get it herself, but in her present state, Janet wouldn't remember it long.

Finding the county's small phone book in a drawer where she knew it would be (everything in Janet's house, like her office, was placed for maximum utility and accessibility), Kate dialed the number for the nearest pizza place. When they answered, only to put her on hold before she could order, she briefly considered that she should just drive over there, order the pizza, and bring it back. She idly pressed the backward button on Janet's caller ID. The last call had been from the office. But early in the morning there had been a call from *Birkenshaw*, which she guessed was from the house where Paxton lived with his mother. She knew that they were acquainted and moved in the same social circles, but it didn't interest her much. Knowing how Janet was with men—her philosophy appeared to be the same whether she was drunk or sober—it wouldn't have surprised her if she kept Paxton around only for sex. He was rich, but she had plenty of money of her own.

She pressed the button a few more times, and the numbers of contractors, charities, the day spa, the dry cleaners went by. But just as the girl on the other end of the line began to babble, she saw another name she recognized: that of the small motel where Caleb was staying.

It struck her so that she forgot why the phone was in her hand: "Hello?" the girl said. "Hello?"

"Never mind," Kate said. She hung up.

The call could have come from anyone else staying at that motel, but she told herself not to be stupid.

At the back door, Bitty Bit yipped to be let in. Not wanting to think, Kate opened the door and the dog came in to sniff at her shoes. She followed Kate through the house and up the stairs to Janet's bedroom.

Janet still sat on the bed, a small amused smile on her parted lips. Kate didn't have to look at the television to recognize the sounds. Janet had found a satellite porno channel.

"You ever do it with another woman?" Janet said, without looking at her.

Kate was taken off guard. She hadn't known what she would say when she got upstairs. Now she was both disgusted and confused.

"What is Caleb calling you for?" she said. "Why?"

"It feels good," Janet said. "Some women give better cunny than a man." A woman on the television started a protracted moan that seemed to get louder and louder in the room. "Don't worry, though," she said, finally looking at Kate. "I'd never want to do it with you. I bet you're fishy."

"I asked you about Caleb," Kate said.

"Caleb gives the best, don't you think?" Janet said.

Kate stepped over to the bed and slapped Janet, hard, just to get the smile off her face. Then she turned and ran from the room and down the stairs, chased by a yapping Bitty Bit, who seemed to think it a fabulous game.

Even with her car windows closed, Kate could hear and feel the *thud thud thud* of the music coming from the car in front of her. The pounding made her angry, and she had a strong urge to accelerate into the car's back end, pushing it into the intersection where they waited for the light to change. *How dare Caleb—* She couldn't even articulate in her mind what

Caleb had done with Janet. *How dare he!* Shaming her without a second thought. Pretending that he loved her.

In a moment she would have to move her car forward. *Where was she to go?*

On the opposite corner was the sign pointing the way to Route 12, the road that led out to the interstate. And for a moment she knew that she could turn right and leave Carystown behind and start her life over again—and again and again if she needed to.

Then she saw Isabella.

The child walked between two women who were just starting across the street. Her black hair hung loose about her shoulders and her yellow coat gaped open so that Kate could see the bulky orange sweater she wore underneath. The women chatted as they walked, unaware of the unsmiling apparition between them. Isabella looked so alive to Kate, so real, that it seemed she could take one of the women's hands or erupt into laughter at any moment. But she only stared back at Kate, her pale features set in an expression of concern, or possibly fear.

Behind Kate there came two angry blasts from a horn. Startled, she looked in her rearview mirror to see a woman in a minivan gesturing for her to go on. When she looked again for Isabella, she saw that the two women had already reached the corner, just outside Kate's passenger door. Isabella was gone.

22

A FINE DRIZZLE began to fall as Bill drove out to Chalybeate Springs. He radioed Mitch to make sure they got some sort of shelter over the crime scene. Noting how tired Bill looked when he was leaving the cemetery, Mitch had volunteered to go out and speak to Hanna Moon. But Bill wanted to do it himself. He'd waited a long time for this day, even though he wasn't bringing the news that he'd always hoped to bring.

"Shelter's up," Mitch radioed back. "But we're starting to draw a crowd."

"Go ahead and shut down the access road," Bill told him. "Keep everyone out but the guys who work up at the water facility." Nothing was going to screw up this investigation if he could help it, especially given how unorthodox it had already become.

Knowing how quickly gossip spread in town—particularly among the early rising old-timers—he figured that word of his find at the cemetery had spread before he'd even been able to get Margaret home, shower, and get into his uniform. He'd called Daphne at home to tell her to get to the office well before 9:00 A.M., but her phone was picked up by a sleepy, vaguely familiar male voice. While he considered Daphne's personal life none of his business, he felt sorry for the poor bastard, whoever he was. Daphne was not particularly kind to the few men she got involved with, and her relationships tended to be very short-lived.

She hadn't sounded surprised at the news. "So that Russell chick was right? Go figure."

"We're not offering anyone details, Daphne," he told her. "We'll release a statement later today."

But despite her barely subordinate attitude, she'd hustled right into the office and was now riding herd over the constantly ringing phones. He wasn't at all sorry not to be hanging around there himself.

There weren't many places left close to Carystown that were as undeveloped as the farm at Chalybeate Springs. Margaret liked to come out and buy honey and pick blueberries in season. One December she'd even dragged him there to buy one of their live Christmas trees and pine garlands. The farm sat in its own small valley whose sides eased gently into the hills. With its greenhouses and old outbuildings, the place was rustic in the extreme and enjoyed a reputation among the tourists and junior matrons in town as a quaint place to shop.

Bill parked in front of the house, near the farm's odd collection of pickups and vans, and made his way up the steps to the sagging porch, which was furnished with an old sofa covered with quilts of various designs and several unmatched wicker chairs that had seen better days. Among the earthenware pots of still-small plants scattered about, there were garden tools, a beekeeper's shroud, and a large box of new mason jars beneath several rolls of cellophane-wrapped duct tape. When he knocked on the metal frame of the screen door, a large-breasted woman moved in silhouette across the hallway, but she didn't acknowledge him or come to the door. The smell of harsh, cheap coffee and a hint of marijuana smoke did come at him through the mesh.

A shirtless Charlie Matter appeared wearing some kind of ballooning silky pants that Bill could only think must have come from a clown's costume.

"Thanks for coming out, but we've already heard, Sheriff," Charlie said. "I'd ask you in, but not everyone's presentable at the moment."

"I'm looking for Hanna," Bill said. "Maybe you could ask her to come outside."

When Hanna Moon came to the door, he saw that it was she and not the bright-eyed Matter who had been smoking weed. Her eyes were bloodshot, her face puffy.

"That nice girl came out to tell me herself, Sheriff," Hanna said, leaning against the door frame. She spoke dreamily, like she was telling him a story. "You should have listened to her when she first came to you. But it doesn't really matter anyway. That's not Isabella in that dirty grave."

Before Bill could disagree, Charlie interrupted. He pushed a lock of Hanna's loose dark hair out of her face. Again Bill was surprised by the gentleness of the action, the sensitivity he seemed to be showing. He didn't think a hard case like Charlie had it in him. But, of course, Charlie had been in the house since Isabella was six.

"What she means is what she told you yesterday," Charlie said. "Isabella's free of that body. Or what's left of it."

"I can't tell you how sorry I am," Bill said. "I sure wish it hadn't ended this way. And I guarantee you that we're going to do everything we can to apprehend the person or persons who did this to your daughter."

Hanna gave a small laugh. "That's what *she* said, too, Sheriff. And I told her, as I'm telling you. My Issy's going to tell me herself who did it. I just have to wait."

Crazy as a shit-house rat, he thought. Her reference to "that nice girl" bothered him. Somebody else was involved, somebody who shouldn't be talking to Hanna Moon.

"You need to give me any information you might have," Bill said. "It doesn't matter where it came from."

"You want her to come down there to your office?" Charlie said. "You know, for identification and stuff?"

Bill hesitated. The little girl's flesh had been so efficiently dispatched by the bugs in the dirt and the rich humus layered over the grave that the skeleton was as bare as a high school science model. He'd wanted to vomit when the coroner carefully lifted the long black hair to expose the skull lying sideways in the soil.

"There are some clothes that it would be helpful for you all to take a look at," he said. He had asked Mitch to pull the original file and compare what Hanna Moon had told them with the clothes in the grave. Two years ago, when she'd first gone missing, he'd gotten a vivid picture in his head: coat, boots, scarf, blue jeans, orange sweater. Margaret had asked him what sort of mother would send her little girl out to school in the winter without gloves and a hat.

"And she'll want to stop by the lab at the hospital so we can get some blood for DNA identification."

"Sure thing," Charlie said.

They stood in uncomfortable silence for a moment. It wasn't often he had to perform this part of the job, and here he'd had to do it twice in a week. The difference between Hanna Moon's reaction and that of Brad Catlett's mother couldn't have been more different. Poor drugged-out Hanna Moon, with her pronouncements about talking to her dead daughter, was starting to give him the creeps.

"Just call the office when you're ready to come in," he said. "Later today would be good, but it can wait until tomorrow or Monday, if you like. And I'd expect some press bothering you all. But you've been through that already."

Outside the porch, the rain was falling harder. Bill put his hat back on, and Hanna and Charlie started to go back into the house.

"Thanks for coming out, Sheriff," Charlie said. "We'll be in touch." He waved and closed the door behind him.

Getting back into the cruiser, Bill shook the rain off of his hat brim and turned the key in the ignition. The image of Kate Russell huddled with Hanna Moon on the sidewalk in front of Janet Rourke's office came into his mind. *Someone he should have listened to.* So she'd rushed out to the co-op to tell Hanna Moon the news even before he could get out there himself. Everything that woman did seemed geared to make him look like an incompetent asshole, and it was starting to piss him off.

The front office had fewer curiosity seekers than he'd expected, but it was still early. On the way back into town he'd seen a van from Channel 12, a regional television station that was known for putting on the most sensational stories it could find. Their people had hung around the longest after Isabella Moon's disappearance, giving up only when there'd been a grisly murder-suicide involving six people on a farm an hour away from Carystown.

One of the loafers from the barbershop was leaning over the duty desk, pumping Daphne for information that he could take back to the shop like some kind of prize. A toddler played on the floor at the feet of a woman who, Bill saw at a glance, was wearing a fresh bruise just below her right eye. The deputy mayor, Lucy, was thumbing through a magazine, which she dropped onto the adjacent chair when she saw him come in.

"Bill, I can't believe it," she said, following him into his office. "When the mayor told me, I swear I couldn't believe it. And she adored Lillian Cayley."

"So, why the second string this morning?" Bill said. "Is Madame Mayor too busy to walk across the street and browbeat me herself?"

Lucy shut the door behind them. "She had to show some land this morning to a pair of docs. But now that we've got a bona fide crime wave here, I imagine they'll have second thoughts. This kind of thing isn't supposed to happen here."

Bill rummaged around on his desk until he laid his hand on a pen. "Thanks, Lucy," he said. "I'll make a note of that."

"Ha-ha. She said you'd be defensive about it."

"Listen, Lucy," Bill said, trying to fake a patience he didn't feel. He wasn't a big fan of the mayor or her overlipsticked deputy, but he liked to keep things cordial. "Defensive, sarcastic, whatever. My sitting here chatting with you about this isn't going to help find Lillian Cayley's killer, that little girl's killer, process the liquored-up bozo that Clayton brought in last night who shot up his wife's boyfriend's dog and trailer, or help the young woman out there get a restraining order on her asshole of a husband."

"Don't forget that high school boy," Lucy said, and gave him a smug grin.

She had baited him, and he let his temper get the best of him. "Screw you," he said.

Instead of looking shocked, as he'd thought she would, Lucy just took a step back from him, looking uncomfortable.

"Everybody wants the same outcome here, Bill," she said. "The mayor's getting a lot of questions, too. She needs to be able to tell people something."

"When there's something to know, I'll give her a call," Bill said. He didn't like to lose his temper.

"At least tell me who sent you out to that cemetery last night," she said.

Here it was, the beginning of the hard questions. There was no doubt that Kate Russell's name was going to come out eventually, or at least the information that he had followed up on some nut job's hokum hunch. But this wasn't the time.

"That's not something I can offer you right now," Bill said. "Tell the mayor that the investigation is ongoing and that I'll get back to her."

With all of his deputies out, Bill walked the young woman over to the courthouse to swear out yet another warrant against her husband. The boy with her jabbered on the whole time they walked, asking questions about the road, the buildings they passed, Bill's uniform. His energy was a relief to Bill, and he even caught himself smiling once or twice. The woman answered the boy's questions patiently, clearly. Bill wondered why a woman who sounded so sensible and reasonable talking with her child would let herself get beaten up—more than once—by any man.

Later he went back to the scene where they were wrapping up. He brushed by the Channel 12 people, telling them there would be a statement later in the day. The coroner had already packed up what was left of the body and loaded it into the ambulance. Bill noted wryly to himself that the ambulance was about two years too late. While he stood talking to Mitch, who looked tired but intensely motivated, his cell phone rang.

"Delaney here," he said.

When he heard the name, he recognized it as belonging to the woman he'd spoken to in the Beaufort, South Carolina, Sheriff's Department when he called looking for information on Kate Russell. After the pleasantries, the woman got right to the point. She reminded him of Daphne, only with a deep and melodic southern accent.

"The Social belongs to a woman name Katherine Russell. Lived in a house down here for fifty-some years. At least she did until she died four years ago," she said. "The house is in the name of someone named Miles Chenoweth and his wife, Mary-Katherine. Sounds like she could be a connection."

Bill was silent on his end of the phone, thinking.

"It's either a big mistake or someone's trying to get away with something up your all's way," the woman said.

"Four years ago, you say?"

"Looks like it," she said. "Right before she died, the house went into the name of this Chenoweth guy and his wife."

"Any mention of how old the wife is? Around thirty, maybe?" He heard the rustle of paper on the other end of the phone.

"Nothing that I can see right off," she said. "I could send someone out to ask around. But it might take a couple days to get to it."

Bill thanked her, telling her it wouldn't be necessary. Before they hung up, he jotted down the address and phone number of Miles Chenoweth.

A while later he sat in the cruiser and called the Hilton Head number the Beaufort Sheriff's Department had given him.

A man answered. "Miles Chenoweth."

After hearing what Bill had to say, Miles confirmed that his wife's grandmother had left them the property in Beaufort. But when told that someone might be using the woman's identity, he laughed.

"She's been dead for several years," Miles said. "I doubt if she'll mind all that much."

Bill didn't know how to respond to the man's casual attitude. "This could be serious, Mr. Chenoweth," he said. "Maybe I should talk to your wife about it."

He laughed again. "My wife wouldn't have the slightest idea what you're talking about, Sheriff. She's a very beautiful and intelligent woman, but she leaves business to those of us who are actually interested. Now, if you're talking carat size or manicures, she's your girl."

"Does your wife have any female relatives? How old is your wife?" Bill asked.

"Thirty-two on her last birthday, but don't tell her I said so," Miles said. "Where in Kentucky did you say you were calling from?"

When he hung up a few minutes later, Bill was no more enlightened than when he'd picked up the phone. Miles Chenoweth had left him with a vague promise to have his lawyer look into the deceased woman's affairs.

He generally liked to be right, especially about people he suspected were hiding things. But for some reason he felt a sense of disappointment instead of justification at finding out that Kate Russell—or whatever her name was—was not who she said she was. What he couldn't figure, though, was what she was hiding, and why. And what, exactly, did she have to do with the death of the little girl they'd just extracted from a dirt grave? It had been Margaret, really, who convinced him that they go to the cemetery and start digging. *She* had never suggested that Kate Russell might have been involved in the little girl's death and disappearance, but then, neither had he. His interest had been piqued, certainly, when she turned out also to be a friend of Lillian Cayley's, but it worried him that he had never considered her a serious suspect in the woman's death. Somewhere along the line with Kate Russell, he'd lost his objectivity.

23

WHEN SHE HEARD Caleb's voice on her answering machine, Kate felt a brief and unexpected desire for him, the kind of desire that only an hour before would have made her all the more lonesome for him. But after he whispered a quiet "Love you" at the end, she erased the recording quickly, pressing the button so hard that it hurt her finger.

Before she could move away from the phone, it rang and she picked it up with an irritated "Hello."

"Ms. Russell?" It was the voice of a young man. "Joshua Klein from the *Carystown Ledger*."

In her anger, it took Kate a moment to understand exactly who he'd said he was.

"Hello?" the young man said.

"I already subscribe," Kate said, ready to hang up.

"That's great," Joshua said. "But I'm calling to ask you some questions. You've heard about the discovery of that little girl's remains this morning? Out at the East End city cemetery?"

Kate sank into the chair beside the phone, suddenly wanting to make herself very small. *Invisible.* Something about Bill Delaney—his calm, steady manner, the serious way he spoke, the sturdy *presence* of the man— had made her want to trust him. She was certain that he wouldn't involve her, but knew now that she'd been wrong. He didn't trust her at all. Even if—possibly especially because—she'd been right.

"How did you get my name?" she said. "Who told you to call me?"

Joshua's voice was earnest. "I just need to confirm a couple of things with you, Ms. Russell. I'm not far away from your house. I'd like to come over and get a couple of details straightened out."

"There's nothing I can tell you," Kate said. "Leave me alone." She started to put down the phone.

"Wait!" he said. "I've been told that the little girl *spoke* to you, Ms. Russell. That—tell me if I have this right—her ghost led you to where she was buried. Is that right? Can you confirm that?"

Kate hung up the phone. She'd had her chance at the stoplight, but Isabella Moon was there, keeping her in Carystown, interrupting her life once again. Not just interrupting, but ruining! Even though she didn't believe in curses, she was beginning to think that her very existence was cursed. Nothing good would ever happen to her again. It had been only a week ago that the girl drew her outside, with her not knowing if she was awake or asleep, awake or dreaming. Now, her good friend was dead, her best friend despised her, she'd had to walk away from her job, and she'd discovered that her lover was unfaithful. Too stunned to even cry, Kate went to the kitchen, filled the kettle, and turned the gas burner on beneath it.

No sooner had the kettle whistled and she poured the water over the tea bag than she heard a car pull into the driveway and knew it was the reporter, come to try again. She took her tea into the bedroom to listen as he knocked at the front door for a good ten minutes until he eventually went away.

Later, when the telephone rang again, Kate let the machine pick it up. No one spoke, but they didn't hang up either, and she could hear the sound of people laughing in the background. Finally, the machine timed out and cut off the call.

With an irritated tug, Kate unplugged the machine from the wall so the telephone wouldn't ring. Then she slid the dead bolt across the front door and went to her nightstand to see that the gun was still in the drawer. And though it wasn't even three o'clock in the afternoon, she pulled down the bedroom window shades, took off her clothes, and got beneath the covers. The fresh sheets she'd put on a couple days before but hadn't yet slept on smelled of lavender and felt pleasantly rough against her skin. The lavender made her ache for her grandmother, who had loved her without question or hesitation, even when she made a hash of things. She balled the pillow beneath her head and folded her legs protectively against her chest. Her single despairing thought before passing out was, *Who will love me now?*

When she awoke in darkness, Kate rolled over to see that the clock read a little after eight in the evening. Her mouth felt dry and unpleasant, but she was hungry. She thought of the M&Ms she'd brought to Janet, and the memory of the whole horrible afternoon came back to her.

"Shit," she said to the empty room.

Uneasy in the darkness, she wandered through the house turning on lights. She couldn't help but think of Caleb. He had been here, in her living room, wanting her, touching her in the glow from the fire. But the memory soured and she could only picture him with Janet, her fingers with their perfectly manicured nails clutching his arm, pulling him close to kiss him. To devour him. The two of them had surely been in the very bed on which Janet had lounged so decadently, in the room where her own husband had died, no doubt already betrayed by Janet with some other man. Or woman.

Kate closed the living room blinds, although there was no one on the street that she could see. The antique mall had closed at six, and the few people who worked there were always gone by six-thirty. She expected to find the reporter camped out in her driveway, but he wasn't there.

Between the living room's two side windows sat an old, half-size rolltop desk that she'd bought at one of the less prestigious antiques shops in town right after she moved into the house. Small and beat-up as it was, the thing she had liked best about it was that it retained its original key, even after eighty or ninety years. As far back as her childhood, she had liked to have a box or a trunk, something she could lock and know that no one had access to but her.

Now, the rolltop stood open. The cubbies of the desk's interior had been emptied of their paper contents—everything was in a pile in the center of the desk. Unpaid bills lay mixed with coupons and store receipts. Several of the letters her grandmother had sent her at college lay open, as though someone had been reading them. But there didn't seem to be malice in the way the pile was made. It didn't look as though it had been made in a hurry, but casually, as though its maker were merely curious.

Unnerved, Kate looked around the room as though expecting to see someone there with her whom she hadn't noticed before, someone who had come in while she was sleeping. Turning on the desk lamp, she examined the lock. It didn't look forced or broken. She looked around the desk for the key. Not finding it, she took the blue and white Chinese vase from the shelf above the desk. The key was still inside where she'd left it.

Kate quickly sorted through the pile, her hands shaking. She didn't keep anything important in the desk; her real birth certificate and passport were in a safe-deposit box in town. She separated the papers, throwing away some and putting the rest in their appropriate cubbies. When she was done, she locked the desk again and replaced the key. Looking at the closed desk, she could almost imagine that it had never been disturbed. But it was small comfort.

Desperate for normalcy, she turned on the television. Its cheerful noise followed her as she made a quick tour of the house, checking each window and door lock.

Leaning across the kitchen table to lower a shade, she saw the photograph. She recognized it instantly. It was a candid portrait of Miles on their wedding day, one that one of the photographers had taken on the steps of the church before the ceremony. It had been an accident that the picture had come from Hilton Head with her. She'd locked it in the desk, having discovered it pressed between the pages of her confirmation Bible. *Why hadn't she thrown it away?*

The photographer had caught Miles looking into the distance, dark and pensive and unapproachable in his gray morning coat and striped ascot. She shuddered to see his face again. She knew she should tear the photo in two and toss it into the garbage, but couldn't bring herself to do it. It needed to be back in the desk, where she could see it every so often and remember every horrible thing that he'd done to her.

She went back into the living room and opened the desk. As she slid the photograph into one of the cubbies, she noticed something different about the air around her: it bore the faint but unmistakable scent of honey.

24

"LIKE THE MAN SAYS, BILL," Porter Jessup said, "I'm going to go ahead and make your day."

"I expect you can't make it any worse," Bill said, settling into a chair on the other side of the coroner's desk. He was glad to be out of the office. He'd done a press conference—brief as it was—earlier in the afternoon where he'd announced that the remains of a child had been found in a county cemetery and that, from the evidence so far, they appeared to be those of Isabella Moon. Two television stations had been there with reporters, and a couple more newspaper people. Joshua Klein had been front and center, but was oddly quiet, letting the outsiders ask the questions. When they asked how he'd come to look in the cemetery, Bill told them he couldn't provide that information as yet. How he was going to deal with that, he didn't yet know. He figured something would come to him.

Porter laughed. "I bet you can't wait to see your ugly mug back on the tube tonight," he said. "Did you do it on the steps of the courthouse, or did you go the humble, hardworking route and stick with the office?"

"And how many bad chicken dinners did you have to show up at to get your ass elected to this freak show?" Bill asked, indicating Porter's bulletin board with its photographic collection of expressionless corpse faces crammed cheek-by-jowl over the cork surface.

Porter looked over the bulletin board like a man admiring so many pictures of his beloved children, a smile spreading across his face.

"Damn, I love my job," he said. "I say, God bless the poor slobs who put me here. And the way you've got things going these days, this could get to be a full-time gig. No more farmers tipped over on their tractors for me. I'm anticipating some real drug lords soon. Streets awash with blood and bullets, yes, sir. Picturesque. Like the movies."

"So I was right about the kid," Bill said. "Meth?"

"Not using more than a year, I expect," Porter said. "He was a snorter. Slight septum damage, but nothing too nasty. No heart defects that I could see. Healthy all around. Blood work won't be back for a week or two, but, yes, I'd say you were right."

"Mama won't be happy," Bill said. "Seemed like a nice kid."

"What my mama didn't know liked to have killed me, too," Porter said.

The next thing Porter had for him were photos. Bill saw their edges peeking out from beneath a small pile of papers and hoped they weren't more of the boy. He'd seen enough dead kids for the day.

"Lots of people liked this Cayley woman," Porter said, sliding out the pictures. "One of the nurses fell over and concussed herself when she heard. Ironic, given what these pics show. The daughter's a looker, too."

Bill grunted an assent. Francie Cayley was a pretty thing and seemed the type to be on the ball. He'd been surprised that she hadn't called the station wanting to know what was going on with the investigation. She might not yet have recovered from the initial shock, which had been one of the worst a person could get.

"Look here," Porter said, flipping on the desk lamp and sliding one of the photos into the light. "We could go down and look at her in person if you want, but you can actually see a little better in the photo."

The eight-by-ten was of the right side of Lillian's head. Most of the hair had been shaved away from the temple and forehead areas to expose the carefully cleaned wound.

"This is what got her, right here," Porter said, using an index finger to outline one obvious L-shaped indentation running from her cheekbone to her temple. "No splinters in the wounds, so I'm thinking metal. Maybe a gardening tool. I've seen the stuff from the site, but nothing looks good to me. Did she have any plumbing tools around?"

"Damned unlikely," Bill said.

"Automotive, then? Maybe a tire iron?" Porter said. "If it was, it wasn't a real big one. Look at the width of this area here."

"Could be," Bill said. "So, what was the pitchfork for?"

"That's what I call gratuitous," Porter said, shaking his head. "Stabbings are personal. Whoever used the pitchfork on her was expressing himself in a most inappropriate way. Should've said it with flowers."

"Are you ready to turn loose of one of them? Both?" Bill said. The boy's father had been calling every day to get his son back and buried.

"They're all yours, as far as I'm concerned," Porter said. "Now that you've brought me that bag full of bones, I've got plenty to keep me busy."

"Anyone ever point out you're kind of a ghoul, Jessup?" Bill said, getting up.

"Not everyone who spends his childhood dissecting barn cats turns out to be a serial killer," Porter said. "Anatomy is important, you know." He looked at his watch. "It's getting late. You want to go get a beer?"

"I got someone a damned sight better looking than you at home to drink with," Bill said. "But I'll take a rain check."

"Suit yourself," Porter said. "Did I mention that you need to be looking at someone with good upper body strength? I'm thinking that it must have been a man to get that pitchfork to go all the way through. Could be a big woman, but I seriously doubt it."

"Sure," Bill said. "You give me a shout the minute you get a look at the Moon girl."

"Just keep 'em comin', Sheriff," Porter said. "I'm your man."

Both of the boy's parents were at the house when Bill got there. The mother, Doreen, looked like she'd aged about ten years since he'd been to the house the previous Friday. Joe, her husband, shook his hand at the door and stepped aside so he could come into the house. The front room was still neat as a pin. A number of clean and empty casserole dishes sat stacked on the table by the front door. The local church ladies had obviously been busy, but Bill suspected that the food was probably at the bottom of a garbage bag somewhere. Neither Catlett looked as though they'd been eating much, or sleeping, for that matter.

When they were all seated, Bill got right to business, knowing what was uppermost in their minds.

"The funeral home can come and get your son's body," he said. "You can call them tonight, if you like."

Doreen Catlett cried out as though she'd been hit. She reached for her husband, who pulled her close and began to stroke her hair. "It's okay," he said over and over.

No matter how many times Bill saw this scene, it always felt new and horrible to him. Even when it was a bad kid who had died, he was always somebody's son or nephew or grandchild who had started out as a funny or solemn or beautiful boy who, in the eyes of the people who loved him, might someday have been a priest or a president. It kept him aware of how one's life could change in an instant: that first joint, the wrong choice of friends, the harsh word that caused the initial turning away from the path to a life that might be worth a damn.

When things calmed down, he asked them about the boy's behavior, if anything had changed about him in the previous few months. It took them a couple of puzzled minutes to tumble to what he was asking. When Joe Catlett caught on and jumped up from the sofa to come toward him, Bill's hand started to go to his sidearm, but he caught himself.

"You're asking if my boy was on drugs," he said.

"Yes, sir," Bill said. "That's what I'm asking."

His response seemed to take the air out of the man and he backed away.

"Teenage bullshit," Joe Catlett said. "I thought Doreen and I would be the ones not to make it through."

"I won't have cursing in this house," his wife said. "Not over our boy, Joe." She looked directly at Bill for the first time since he'd come into the house. "I thought it was a problem with his girlfriend, Heather. She hadn't been coming out here and she hadn't been calling him as often. But I won't believe he was doing drugs. He knew better than that."

"Yes, ma'am," Bill said. He hadn't expected more from either of them. Parents never did want to hear it, and he didn't blame them. In their place—well, he would never be in their place. He had never wanted to be at the mercy of someone utterly dependent on him, but he could imagine how they felt.

Later, after they'd moved on to the sad details of obtaining the body, Bill was about to take his leave when Doreen Catlett suddenly spoke out, interrupting her husband.

"There was a name I heard a couple of times when Brad was on the phone. I don't think he knew I heard him," she said. "It was somebody named Delmar. I'd never heard of anyone by that name. He wasn't from school, I don't think."

Bill made a note to ask Frank if the name had come up in interviews with any of the other high school kids.

"I just want us to be able to bury our boy in peace," Joe Catlett said.

"I hope you can," Bill said, thinking, *I just don't want us to have to bury any more.*

Margaret had supper ready when he walked in, and Bill, feeling more grateful than he could say, hugged her wordlessly there in the kitchen. They'd planned to go out, but she'd somehow intuited that after the long night they'd had and the press conference, he wouldn't feel like sitting in a restaurant. It was one of the things he didn't like about being the sheriff in such a small town: even people who didn't know him very well considered it their personal privilege to interrupt his meal whenever they cared to for whatever stupid reason. It gave him a good picture of how important some people considered themselves to be.

"It's only pork chops," Margaret said, putting the plate down in front of him. "Baked, not fried. Sorry. We could use a little comfort food, I know. But I mashed some potatoes."

"You're a miracle," he said.

"I got a nap today," she said. "But I had to unplug the phone. Seems like everybody in town heard what you had me out doing at all hours." She shook her head. "I still can't get the image of that little girl out of my head, Bill. Those bones sticking out of her coat. Lying there like she was somebody's Halloween joke."

"I never should've taken you out there," he said. "I should've asked Mitch or Frank. Daphne could've stood it."

"It was my idea, remember?"

"How the hell did I know she'd be there?" Bill said.

Margaret leaned forward, her chin resting on the heel of her hand.

"Yes," she said. "How *did* you know? You're going to have to answer that question. Folks are already asking."

"Just say someone stepped forward with the information," he said. "It won't get to be an issue until we get the evidence together. Charge somebody."

"Then what?"

"Hey, did you make any gravy for these?" he said, digging into the potatoes. "These are great, but they need gravy."

"You think someone's just going to come forward voluntarily?"

"I don't know. Salt and pepper? Butter?"

Margaret sighed. "I don't know why you're protecting that woman," she said.

"Who?" Bill said. Of course he knew damned good and well who she meant.

"Maybe she *is* connected to the girl's murder. Maybe it was her guilty conscience that made her tell you where to find the body. She just couldn't stand it anymore."

"I don't think so," Bill said.

"You trust her?" Margaret said.

"I never said that I trusted her," he said, cutting into a chop as he spoke. "I get enough crap about this out there. I don't need it at home."

"Since when don't we talk about a case like this?" Margaret said. "Why is it so different this time?"

Bill pushed his plate away hard enough that it knocked over his water glass.

"Give it a rest, Margaret," he said. He left the kitchen, his heart beating hard in his chest. He heard her chair scrape back on the floor, but she didn't follow him.

On the porch, he stood looking out on their quiet street. He hated that things were so screwed up. He hated that he could speak so harshly to Margaret. He hated it when things weren't crystal clear, when he didn't know what was going on in his own head.

Later, as he sat alone in his den watching the DVD of an old Charles Bronson film she'd gotten him for Christmas, the phone rang. He ignored it, letting Margaret pick it up in the kitchen. After a minute she brought the handset to him and left the room without saying a word. It looked like their fight wasn't going to be over anytime soon.

"Delaney," he said.

"I just got a call at home from the Catlett boy's girlfriend," Frank said. "She sounded a little drunk, but she was crying and I couldn't really tell what-all she was saying. Then her grandmother grabbed the phone and said the girl wants to come in to talk to us. She said they didn't want to wait until tomorrow."

"I'm on my way," Bill said.

"You stay home," Frank said. "You've had a hell of a day. I can handle it."

"I'll be there in ten minutes," Bill said. He hung up the phone and shut down the DVD.

25

Mary-Katie unwrapped the stiff foil package of the second pregnancy test with trembling hands. The first lay on the bathroom vanity, its vivid pink line stark in contrast to the white, urine-soaked pad behind it. She'd drunk three large cups of water in the past twenty minutes so she could do the second test right away, and her stomach felt full and achy. Worse, though, was the painful tenderness of her breasts, which she'd at first attributed to the onset of her period. But when it didn't come, then was two, three days late, she'd made a special trip to the drugstore, tossing random items—a box of tissues, paper plates, rug cleaner, a bag of cherry sour balls—into her basket because the pregnancy test had looked so strange and significant alone there. Now, all those things lay in a pile on the kitchen counter, forgotten.

The several mirrors in the bathroom reflected a limitless number of Mary-Katies back to her. She was embarrassed to see her own involuntary smile, the naked emotion that seemed to have transformed her from a calm, sensible twenty-nine-year-old into a sheepishly grinning fool.

She wasn't supposed to be pregnant. She'd been religious about taking her birth control pills for years, never missing a single one by more than an hour or two. Miles was finally at least open to talking about having children, but they were supposed to come much later. He treasured her body the way it was now, lithe and fresh, almost boyish in its athleticism. He wouldn't even allow her to sleep with pajamas on. Sometimes she would awaken, chilled, because he had pulled back the sheet to watch her body as she slept. Pregnancy would change all that. Certainly a child would.

The thought that Miles might react badly stole the smile from her face.

Finally, she couldn't wait any longer and did the second test. When she finished, she nervously set it on a pile of toilet tissue. With her eyes on her watch, she washed her hands and tried to calm herself.

She was realistic about Miles's selfishness. He would be unhappy—for a while—and that's all. There were some facts of life that a person just had to deal with.

Mary-Katie checked the temperature of the pinot grigio she had set in the wine cooler beside the hot tub. She had brought two glasses from the kitchen, then realized she wouldn't need one for herself. So many things were going to change. She poured herself an iced tea and sat, waiting, wearing only the gauzy silk robe that Miles had brought back for her on his last trip to Atlanta.

She rested her hands on her lower abdomen, imagining she could feel a slight rounding there. Looking in the mirror as she'd changed out of her clothes, she inspected her profile carefully, but her stomach was as taut and flat as ever. Her clothes hadn't even gotten tighter. When her mind began to race ahead to where she might shop for maternity clothes, she stopped herself, laughing out loud. Soon she'd have the baby already born and on its way to college!

When she heard Miles calling her from inside the house, she went to him, loosening the belt of the robe so he could see that it was all she was wearing.

In the living room, she found him standing in the fading light, his briefcase still in hand, conversing with a man she'd never met before. It was like Miles not to warn her that he was bringing a client home with him.

The evening was not going to go the way she'd planned.

Once Mary-Katie had gotten dressed, she went to the freezer to take out another filet for Miles to put on the grill. He had poured a substantial amount of the pinot grigio she'd opened into a glass for the client.

The client, a Dutchman named Jules, looked at her with—what? Perhaps a shade of disappointment as she came into the room wearing a tissue-thin, black V-neck sweater and a pair of tan silk pants instead of the nearly transparent robe she'd been wearing when he arrived. At first she wanted to snap at him, telling him that the show was over. Instead, she found herself flattered by his attention. Something about having a secret made her feel more comfortable, less reluctant to talk with this man, this stranger.

"Here, baby," Miles said, holding out a glass of wine to her.

She hesitated, but then took it, knowing that she didn't have to actually drink it. No one would notice if she poured it, little by little, into the sink when she was alone in the kitchen.

Jules was a good six inches taller than Miles and better looking, with his ash-blond hair, broad forehead, and chiseled jaw. He'd taken off his sport coat, and Miles had encouraged him to relax and loosen his tie. Unlike Miles, he wore no jewelry. Mary-Katie found him refreshing.

When, at dinner, Miles guided her to the chair closest to Jules's, she felt a flutter of panic, remembering Kyle Richardson and his soft, pleading eyes, his desperate need to please her, despite the fact that she'd been sold to him for the afternoon. But after a moment she was surprised to find that her panic had dissolved completely. No way would she let Miles use her that way again. She had a child to protect! The thought made her bold. She could act as she pleased!

"You should visit St. Maarten," Jules told her. "We have fantastic beaches. Sand the color of snow on the right days."

"You know, I don't really like to fly over that much water," she said. "It's too far."

"What?" Miles said. "You've never told me that before."

"I thought Miles said you were from Holland," she said, ignoring Miles.

"I have a villa in St. Maarten. I never do business when I'm there."

"What about Hawaii?" Miles said. "We flew for six or seven hours over the water. We live by the beach, for Christ's sake."

"Maybe I've just decided," she said, turning to Miles. "Can't people change?" She felt a small thrill in defying him. Throughout the evening she took pleasure in addressing Jules directly, leaving Miles out of the conversation. She knew that she was playing with a kind of fire. But she wasn't alone anymore. There was someone else to think of, another person who would make life with Miles—always unpredictable—slightly more bearable. She was hopeful, too, that the baby would soften him. She knew that he was capable of incredible gentleness. How could he be anything but gentle with his own child?

By the time Jules left with a chaste kiss on her cheek and promises to return to their house when he was again in the area, Miles was as sullen as Mary-Katie had ever seen him. As they carried the dishes into the kitchen from the patio, he was silent.

"What a nice guy," Mary-Katie said. "Is he really from Holland?"

Miles noisily dropped a plate and a salad bowl into the sink, where she would have to retrieve them for the dishwasher.

"What the hell was that all about?" he said.

"I don't know," Mary-Katie said, deciding not to pretend ignorance. She laughed. "I was just feeling kind of loopy. Sometimes I get that way."

"Bullshit," Miles said. "You would've screwed him right there on the fucking table if you'd had five minutes alone with him."

"That's silly, Miles," she said, shaking her head. "You know better than that."

"Fuck me," he said. "I bet you liked doing it with Kyle Richardson, too. Here I thought you were doing it for us. Because I needed you to."

Mary-Katie started back to the patio, but Miles grabbed her arm.

"Tell me," he said. "Tell me you liked it."

"Don't be stupid," she said, pulling away. Until this evening, she'd finally been able to put Kyle Richardson and what she'd done out of her mind for hours at a time. Now, with the child inside her, what she'd done seemed even dirtier to her. She prayed that she hadn't been pregnant at the time.

"Don't even think I'm going to have you sleep with Jules," he said. "You'd want it too much."

"I wouldn't want it at all, Miles," she said, trying to regain her patience. Stress wasn't good for the baby. "You know I don't want to be with anyone else. I did it because I had to. For us."

"I don't believe you," Miles said. "Prove it."

"You're just going to have to believe me," she said. "I can't do any more."

"What if I asked you to do it again? What if I asked you to do it to prove that you're mine and not someone else's?"

"That doesn't make any sense," Mary-Katie said. "Can we just go to bed? I love you and only you. I promise. I promise I don't want anyone else."

"Come on. You could do it again. Just once," he said. "You can make this whole Jules thing up to me. You owe me that."

Finally, Mary-Katie realized that he was serious. He had it in mind for her to have sex with yet another man. He may have even had Jules in mind until she'd tried to make him jealous. He'd lied to her about Kyle Richardson. Of course.

"I'm not sleeping with anyone else, Miles," she said, looking into his eyes. She stood up and straightened her shoulders. He had to know that she was serious. "I'm pregnant," she said.

Later, Mary-Katie told herself she'd been a fool and an idiot to expect any kind of response but the one she got. In the hours since she'd done the pregnancy test, she'd had a hundred daydreams about Miles telling her that he couldn't imagine a better time to have a baby. Of course, she had imagined that he might take a little convincing, but that in the end all would be well and they would be happy.

Miles's initial look of surprise was quickly replaced by the cruel sneer he reserved for people he truly despised. People like the runner, Lev Kaplan.

"Get rid of it," he said. "Make the appointment tomorrow."

"I don't understand," Mary-Katie said.

"You're not stupid."

"What are you saying? I can't believe what you're saying!" Mary-Katie felt her throat tighten. "This is our child, Miles."

"I've been shooting blanks for years," he said. "I told you I wasn't interested. Ever. It must be your buddy Kyle's bastard."

"I don't believe you," Mary-Katie said.

"Believe whatever the fuck you like," Miles said. "Just get rid of it."

"I don't believe you!" This time Mary-Katie screamed at him.

He was going to leave her with nothing.

26

WHEN PAXTON turned on his cell phone and it started ringing immediately, he knew it was Janet before he looked at the caller ID. She was as persistent when she was trying to get hold of him on the phone as she was in bed: the woman never, ever gave up. He wondered where in the hell she got the energy. How much did he prefer his Francie, who was energetic as hell but knew when to relax?

"Where have you been?" Janet said. "I've been all by myself all night. You promised you'd help me."

"I'm right here," he said. "But I've got some business to take care of. I'll be over later."

Janet made a sound that he could only describe as a snort. "Pussy business, I bet," she said. "Your nursey-nurse needs some comfort, does she? Maybe I should call her and we could compare notes on that busy prick of yours."

"Do you kiss your mama with that mouth?" Paxton said.

"Or maybe I'll just drive out to the new house, then drop by on my new neighbor," Janet said. "Mother Birkenshaw and I could spend some quality time together."

Paxton didn't want to go into it with her on the phone, but he knew he had to keep Janet under some kind of control.

"We had a call from the sheriff's office this morning," he said. "Let me call you later."

There was a stunned silence. "Shit, Paxton. Why didn't you tell me? What the hell are we going to do?"

"*You* don't need to do anything, Princess," he said. "This stuff is my problem, and nothing you need to worry about. I'll let you know."

It took several minutes to calm her down and get her off the phone. She was wanting details and, frankly, he didn't have too many.

He *did* know that the call from the sheriff was strictly one of those little courtesies that got exercised in a place as small as Carystown. The sheriff had called to speak to his mother, Freida, who wasn't technically taking calls. But when the housekeeper heard it was the sheriff, she had put her on the phone.

Delmar Johnston, the man they wanted to come out and question, was only a name to his mother. She rarely left the four acres of yard and garden surrounding the house itself. The farm manager did the hiring and usually got the okay from Paxton, so she was never bothered.

The housekeeper had wakened Paxton to tell him what was going on.

"The strangest thing," the housekeeper had said. "The sheriff's on the phone with your mama, but it doesn't sound like he's selling tickets to anything. He sounds like business."

After dismissing her, Paxton picked up the phone in time to hear the sheriff say Delmar Johnston's name. Delmar Johnston was the man who both collected the local ingredients for the meth and distributed the meth that he and Charlie Matter made. He himself was just the money guy.

A quiet young man from east Tennessee, Delmar had been hired on to the farm the previous summer. When Paxton happened on him smoking a joint out near the stables one evening and he hadn't even tried to hide it, Paxton knew they'd get along just fine. It was only a matter of weeks before Delmar was working both on the farm and for Charlie.

The one problem Paxton could see with Delmar, the problem that was sending him out to see Charlie as fast as he dared, was that Delmar Johnston wasn't the sort of man who took personal loyalty too seriously.

"I've got about ten reasons already why I should kick your ass," Charlie said. He raised his bandaged hand. "You've got to be the biggest asshole in town, showing up here, Birkenshaw."

Paxton glanced around at the few cars in the parking area. "Let's go somewhere we can talk," he said.

"We're open for business now," Charlie said. "Make it fucking quick."

Paxton followed him into the house and back into a badly paneled den that seemed to serve as both an office and a bedroom. The futon on the floor was heaped with blankets, atop which lay a fat Dalmatian that raised its head at their entrance but quickly put its nose back down on its paws, uninterested. Charlie Matter shut the door behind them.

"They're questioning Delmar," Paxton said.

"You think you've got all the information, don't you?" Charlie said. "I already heard."

"So what do we do?" Paxton said. "We have to get rid of everything. Shut it down. Right now."

Charlie lit a cigarette, gingerly holding the lighter with the fingers of his bandaged hand. He regarded Paxton.

"Shut what down?"

"The barn," Paxton said. "Everything."

"You wanted to stay local," Charlie said. "Like we were some kind of fucking hometown pharmacy. If you'd have let me bring in my Canadian friends sooner, we wouldn't have been dealing with these pissant kids, and Delmar Johnston would be spending both his days *and* nights playing nursemaid to those wind-up dolls you call horses out there. *You* made this mess, Birkenshaw. And you have to clean it up."

Somehow Paxton had known that it was all going to come down to money. *His* money. Only Francie seemed immune to his money. She didn't care what he had. In fact, the way she talked, he suspected that she hated his money. Charlie, though, seemed to think that he was made of it. While he had plenty to live on and a little more to spend, he didn't know if he could buy his way out of what Charlie had called his "mess." He thought Charlie was mistaken, thinking that it wasn't his mess to clean up. *He* had all the supplies to deal with, the paraphernalia. Those were the things that prosecutors liked to have for evidence.

"If you'd brought me the money yourself a couple of days ago, like I asked you to, we might not have to be concerned with this little problem," Charlie said. "It might have disappeared before it even got to us."

"You say that," Paxton said. "But we never had any kind of guarantee. And why is it you don't have the funds to take care of it, anyway?"

Charlie dropped his cigarette into the ashtray on the desk and twisted the open neck of Paxton's shirt, to pull him close. "Look, shithead," he said. "You've got your dick stuck so far up various and sundry women in this town that it's started to affect your eyesight. This isn't a game, and this isn't a hobby. This is a *business,* and you, sir, have played lord of the fucking manor long enough." He pushed Paxton away.

Paxton took a step back, looking around for something with which to knock the hell out of Charlie Matter. His eye fell on a nubby shillelagh leaning in a corner, but there was no way he could get past Charlie to lay his hand on it.

"Don't be thinking too hard," Charlie said. "Just start peeling off bills, because it's your turn. They're going to bring him in for questioning, and we want it to go well. You need to get your hands on about ten thousand to make this go away. And I need another five to get rid of all our playthings." He picked up his cigarette again and pointed it at Paxton.

"And if we're lucky, really lucky, my friends from Canada will be generous about discontinuing our relationship," he said. "It might go well since we're not in too deep yet, but I don't know about that."

Paxton felt an itch that was only going to be satisfied by wrapping his hand around that shillelagh. Unfortunately, there were too many people who might have seen him come into the house. It occurred to him that there could be newspeople coming around as well, now that the girl had been found. Fortunately, the newspeople apparently weren't early risers. Still and all, he needed to get out of there.

"I've got three thousand with me," he said. "That's all I can get until next week. But it's going to look pretty damn strange if I stroll into the bank looking for that kind of money come Monday morning."

Charlie held out his hand for the fold of cash that Paxton took out of his pants pocket.

"Just get it," he said.

Weary of debasing himself, Paxton turned and went out of the room, leaving the door open behind him. If there was one thing he was certain of, it was that Charlie Matter wasn't getting another dime out of him.

As he drove the Mercedes down the long gravel road to the highway, he glanced at his passenger seat. The last time he'd been on this road, that little girl, that Isabella Moon, had startled him so that he'd almost driven off the road. But he had known then that she was dead, and he even knew how she'd gotten that way. He put down that image of her beside him to the play of his own mind, a reminder from deep inside himself that she was unfinished business. Now that her bones had been found, though, that business was probably also going to have to be concluded.

Then, as though he'd produced them out of thin air, a news van turned into Chalybeate Springs just as he pulled out onto the highway.

27

LATE FRIDAY MORNING Francie pushed open the door of her mother's house to find it filled with still air and silence.

"Mama?" she said. Of course, there was no answer. Her mother was lying on a slab in the basement of the hospital, her internal organs in dull stainless pans, no doubt, and much of her beautiful black hair in a plastic bag.

When the call had come from the coroner's office early that morning to tell her that they were releasing "the body," she had been asleep, alone for the first time since learning of her mother's murder. The idea of going to the house by herself filled her with dread. She'd thought to ask Kate to help pick out clothes for Lillian to be buried in, but she was still angry with Kate. Nothing so concrete as an accusation had formed in her mind, but she couldn't shake the feeling that Kate had had something to do with her mother's death, whether directly or just because Kate was a part of her mother's life. Sometime in the past few days she had decided that Kate was bad news. When she'd said as much to Paxton, he'd said a loud "Hallelujah!" and told her that it was about time.

Inside the house there was evidence of the police search everywhere: drawers in the kitchen and bedrooms were slightly ajar, cabinets stood open, books and magazines were scattered about. Dirt had been tracked over the pale blue carpeting that Lillian installed only six months before. Francie imagined her mother scolding the deputies as they trooped through, reminding them to wipe their feet. She'd had several of them in her classes at the high school, and they would've obeyed quickly.

Francie walked from room to room, straightening things, putting them just as her mother had liked them. Her own apartment was always a mess, but she had lived with her mother for most of her life and knew how things were supposed to be. It didn't occur to her that her mother would never be there to see it, to appreciate her work. Or that she would soon have to sell or store every last item. Or even that the house was now hers to do with as she pleased. She just knew she had to make it right.

Outside, the yellow crime scene tape that had been hung around the back of the house where her mother was found was finally gone.

Someone had killed her. And that someone had had a reason. Francie didn't buy the theory that the neighbors espoused that first day—that some drifter had come up on Lillian working in her yard and killed her for whatever they could find in the house. Francie hadn't noticed anything missing.

She knew every inch of the house and had never felt afraid here, even when she'd stayed, alone, when her mother was away. She felt safer being alone here, even knowing that her mother had been killed just outside, than she did in her tiny apartment with its single entrance on the second floor.

Just after noon, Francie spent a difficult hour with Aletha Cooper in Lillian's bedroom, selecting the clothes she would be buried in. Aletha, with her tender heart and ready tears, wore Francie out. By the time she shut the door behind Aletha and saw that she was safely across the yard, Francie felt desperately in need of some relief. But even with Lillian gone, she was uncomfortable doing drugs in her mother's house. She closed herself in the bathroom and drew the shade.

For years she had tried to get her mother to remodel the pink-tiled bathroom. In junior high she'd loved to visit her friends who lived in the new housing developments just outside the city limits, loved spending time in their shiny, vinyl-floored kitchens and wallpapered bathrooms with their double sinks and fixtures that weren't corroded with mineral deposits and didn't squeak when they were turned on.

"What do we have to live in this old house for?" she'd asked Lillian after an overnight in Bluegrass Estates.

"You don't leave behind a house and your friends just because you can afford different," Lillian had told her. "You don't want to be around peo-ple who live like that. There're people on this very street who could afford to live anywhere they wanted to. But they choose to live here."

It plagued Francie. She suspected that it was more than loyalty that kept them in the East End.

"Maybe we wouldn't be allowed to buy a house in Bluegrass Estates," she said. "Maybe they wouldn't let us."

"Is that what you think?" Lillian said.

Francie didn't answer, but looked away. Lillian took hold of her chin and made her look forward.

"I don't ever want to hear you talk like that," she said. "We live where we choose to live because that's what we choose to do. We don't measure ourselves by where we live, what we have, or whom we choose to associate with. God made us every one His children, and anyone who puts himself above another is asking for trouble. And that includes you, Francine Lil-lian Cayley."

But she knew her mother had strong ideas about with whom she should spend her time. Lillian had made that clear long ago, particularly on the afternoon Francie told her about Paxton following her home. There had been another boy in college, another wealthy white boy she'd dated for a few weeks, but she could never bring herself to tell Lillian about him. They'd broken up—she dumped him, actually—a few weeks before Christ-mas break. She didn't like to think that she'd done it because she knew Lil-lian would disapprove. If someone were to ask her, she'd say with utter conviction that it was because he'd been a sloppy kisser.

Francie opened the coke vial and put the miniature spoon inside to take out some of the fine-grained powder. Holding the spoon to her nose, she found her hand was shaking. When she put the vial on the edge of the sink, it fell, clattering against the porcelain and spilling its contents all over the bowl. Cursing quietly, she tried to brush the coke back into the vial, but much of it had fallen into drops of water and was fast melting away.

She glanced up to catch herself in the mirror. Would her mother even recognize the woman she saw there? She didn't want to recognize *herself* trying to rescue a few dollars' worth of cocaine from flowing into the sewer. Illegal drugs had never been a part of her life before she'd taken up with Paxton. The way she felt now, that might have been a hundred years ago.

~

The modicum of nervous courage she'd gotten from the coke helped her face the other chore she'd been dreading: the thick pile of forgotten mail Aletha had brought in from the mailbox. She was relieved to see that most of it was made up of clothing and gardening catalogs. But along with the catalogs and a couple bills, there was a statement from a brokerage firm. Francie held on to the envelope and just looked at it for a moment. When you died, nothing belonged to you anymore.

She opened the envelope and spread out the several sheets it contained on the table. She knew that her mother had long ago arranged for life insurance to cover her burial. But what was printed on the paper in front of Francie would've covered fifty expensive funerals. Money would never be an issue for her again. She knew that she should've felt happy, grateful. Instead, she just felt empty inside and regretted all over again the coke that had melted away in the sink.

When the doorbell rang, startling her, she stuffed the broker's statement into the envelope as though it were something she had to hide.

She opened the door to find Mitch Carl looking slightly embarrassed to be there. His cruiser sat in the driveway. *God, she was tired of seeing those cars.*

"Mitch," she said. "Haven't you all finished here yet?"

"Just a couple minutes, Francie," Mitch said. "Can I come in?"

She showed him to an armchair and took her place on the couch. They'd known each other since elementary school, but she didn't hold a very high opinion of him. Good-looking, but not a particularly good student and an only so-so jock, he'd never impressed her as a serious person. He'd been too concerned about the girls he went out with, what kind of car he drove. It had been rumored that his mother had taken a job just so she could pay for him to have a car and insurance. Francie couldn't respect someone like that, always taking the easy way at someone else's expense.

"So you made Miss Lillian's funeral arrangements?" he said.

"Did you really come here to ask about that?" Francie said. "It'll be in the paper."

He pulled out his notebook. "I just need to ask you about that night. Monday night."

Monday night felt like a lifetime ago. Lying in her own bed while her mother lay bleeding, dying in her own backyard.

"Your shift ended at nine?"

"Yes."

"You went home?"

"Yes."

"Right away?"

Francie hesitated.

"Come on, Francie," Mitch said. "You can tell me."

"It doesn't matter," Francie said. "It doesn't have anything to do with Mama."

"Try me," Mitch said.

Did it really matter if anyone knew? Hadn't she felt, just that morning, that she didn't give a damn what people thought of her? Paxton wouldn't care. He'd been pressuring her for a long time to be seen with him, not to hide anymore.

"I was with somebody," Francie said. "Not for very long."

"Did you go somewhere? Out where someone would've seen you?"

"It's not really any of your business," Francie said, though she knew she was wrong. It couldn't be more of the Sheriff's Department's business.

"I was in my car," she said. "Paxton Birkenshaw met me at my car."

She watched as a shadow of surprise crossed Mitch's face.

"You went somewhere?"

"No."

"How long were you in the car?"

"As long as it took," she said evenly.

She wanted to laugh at him. She wondered if a woman had ever made Mitch Carl blush the way he was blushing now.

Later, she wished that she hadn't brought Paxton into it. A part of her wanted to pretend they had never been together. A part of her didn't ever want to see him again, as though her mother's death had made their relationship irrelevant. The implications of that thought made her sick to her stomach.

28

A pall of dust lay over the furniture in the Beaufort house. Mary-Katie had been paying a woman to come in once every couple of weeks to check on the house, to dust and run water through the pipes, but she had obviously missed a visit or two. As she crossed the musty kitchen, Mary-Katie caught sight of the tail of a mouse as it slipped beneath the pantry door. When she'd lived here with her grandmother, the mice were annual visitors, seeking shelter when the cool breezes of fall made their way south. But she didn't open the pantry. The mice could have whatever was there.

In the living room, she sat down heavily in the wing chair beside the fireplace. She remembered sitting with her grandmother in front of a Christmas morning fire, sometime after her father had gone, and wondering aloud if he had a fireplace where he was. Sad as they both were, Mary-Katie was the only one who had cried. Her grandmother had told her that only God knew where he was and that Mary-Katie should pray for him to be safe.

This sudden advent of her own child had made Mary-Katie think of him again and again. Soon, even if he came back looking for her, he wouldn't find her. But she herself had grown up with only her grandmother as her family and she'd done all right. The child would have its mother. She told herself that she was all he or she would need.

Mary-Katie knew she had only another week, maybe two at the outside, before Miles started to seriously press her about the abortion. He was predictable that way, always giving her time to come around to his way of thinking before pushing her. Usually, it worked. She found it easier just to ac-

commodate him. But there was no question that this time was going to be different. She wouldn't be around that long.

At home, she kept to her routines—her tennis, her spa appointments. The refrigerator was never allowed to be empty, and she ran Miles's errands with her usual efficiency. As for Miles himself, he was often absent, to her relief. She felt like an actor, playing the role of the woman she'd been for the last five years.

Mary-Katie found it laughable that he had demanded that she get rid of the child. It didn't matter to her who the father was, though she was certain that Miles had lied to her. He was too vain to have given up his shot at immortality so early in his life, no matter what he'd told her. She considered the child inside her to be completely hers and not liable to the whims of anyone but herself. It was as though the line on the pregnancy test had divided her life into two parts: the past, which mattered not at all, and the future, which meant everything. Miles was the past. The child was her future.

There wasn't much that she wanted from her grandmother's house. All of the valuables had long ago made their way into her own jewelry box or the safe-deposit box at the bank. She'd donated most of the silver to charity, knowing she and Miles would never use it.

Up in her old sun-faded bedroom, which looked out over the backyard, she went through her desk drawers a last time, riffling through the piles of school papers and photographs that were stuffed inside. In one album she had collected tiny, two-by-three-inch school photographs of herself from every year since kindergarten. She flicked through them, watching herself grow taller, seeing how she wore bangs one year, barrettes the next. For the briefest of moments she thought of taking them home as a sort of funny prize to share with Miles. When she realized that she would never again share anything with Miles (except, perhaps briefly, a bed), she felt a spot of cold develop in her stomach.

She started to close the drawer quickly, but it caught on a piece of stiff paper that thwacked against the inside of the desktop. Sliding her hand to the back of the drawer, she inched the paper out and saw that it was a gold-bordered certificate. IN RECOGNITION OF SERVICE TO THE SATTLER HIGH GUN CLUB it read in bright red letters.

Her grandmother had laughed when she told her she wanted to join the gun club. "Just like your father," she said. "He thought he was some kind of cowboy." It was then that she had given Mary-Katie his Ruger .22. "He accidentally killed the neighbor's cat, but he couldn't hit the broad side of a barn when he meant to. Let's hope you're a better shot."

Now Mary-Katie thought that it probably hadn't been such a bad thing that her father wasn't more comfortable with the gun. As depressed as he must have been while her mother was dying, he might have used it on himself. Or her grandmother. Or her.

Mary-Katie knew she'd just been competent at the range. But it had been fun, and she gained a certain notoriety for being one of only two girls in the club.

She stuffed the certificate back into the drawer and shut it. For a moment she couldn't think of what she'd done with the gun all those years ago. Then she remembered.

She moved the desk chair to her closet and stood on the seat. Pushing aside piles of moth-eaten sweaters and old purses, she found, shoved in a corner, a fabric-covered hat box that her grandmother had given her when she got rid of all her hats. The Ruger lay wrapped in a soft gray flannel cloth. Beside it, in a flimsy cardboard box, was a small tray of ammo. She hadn't yet decided where she was going when she left Miles, but it made sense to her to take the Ruger with her now that she was responsible for someone besides herself.

She put the gun and the ammo in a denim hobo purse she found on the shelf and quickly set the room to rights.

As Mary-Katie left the house, pulling the door shut and locking it behind her, she had a sense that her grandmother would approve of her leaving Miles. She knew that most likely she would never see the Beaufort house again. Miles would no doubt sell it soon after she was gone; she'd be lucky if she even saw a dime from the sale of it. But it didn't matter. Her grandmother's love was the most important thing she'd ever taken away from the house. And Miles couldn't ever take that away from her.

Mary-Katie drove to the small savings bank where she'd kept her rainy day account since her grandmother helped her open it when she turned eight years old. For a long time it had bothered her that she never told Miles about it. She'd felt deceitful and untrusting of him. But the longer they were married, the more necessary she felt it was to keep something of herself to herself. Besides, she reasoned, he would've laughed at her measly eight thousand dollars if she'd offered it to him.

She knew the money wouldn't get her far. But she could work, she knew, at just about anything. She would clean houses or haul trash to take care of herself and her baby if she had to. A part of her looked forward to living like a normal person again, one who didn't have weekly manicures and pedicures and who didn't have boutique saleswomen falling all over themselves to get her into their latest, most fashionable clothes.

"You want that in cash, honey?"

The teller was a woman who had known her grandmother. Mary-Katie had wanted to avoid her, but she was the only teller available.

"Please," she said. And please don't ask me any questions. *At the bank where she'd worked, they were trained not to be nosy about customers' requests. But this woman obviously felt entitled because of their acquaintance.*

"That will only leave you with ninety-eight dollars and twenty-two cents," she said. "You'll be charged a four dollar a month service charge if it's not at least three hundred dollars."

Mary-Katie imagined the money dribbling away, disappearing into the bank, just as she would disappear. Eventually, they would both be gone.

"Nothing bigger than fifties," she said.

The woman regarded her over the top of her bright red reading glasses, her unsatisfied curiosity obvious in the pursing of her lips.

"Certainly," she said stiffly.

Unused to carrying so much cash, Mary-Katie glanced around the parking lot before heading to her car. Once inside, she put it into the purse with the gun and ammunition. She felt a vague thrill seeing them all together, as though she were about to commit some crime.

It wasn't a crime, was it? To disappear out of one's life? It was her business and her business only. The child wasn't born yet, and Miles had already decided that he wasn't the father, so there was no custody issue. But she owned the car she was driving outright. Her grandmother's small legacy had paid for it, at Miles's insistence. "She'd want you to have something nice," he told her. There was debt, of course: the house and whatever instruments Miles had her sign over the years. Somehow she thought he wouldn't be thinking about that when she left. It would be his pride that was most injured. That was the one thing that worried her. Miles didn't like to be crossed when it came to his pride.

~

Mary-Katie was thinking about dinner when she pressed the button to open the garage door and eased the car inside. She was hungrier than she could ever remember being. She suspected that it was psychological. Weren't pregnant women always supposed to be hungry?

At the grocery store she'd purchased nearly a cartful of produce: strawberries, avocados, grapes, apples, bananas, even a mango. Her diet was already pretty healthy, but she wanted to make sure. Eventually, she'd have to see a doctor. It can wait, she told herself. Getting away and getting settled was the important thing now.

She tucked the purse with the gun and cash beneath the seat, thinking that she had plenty of time to retrieve it before Miles would be home. She wanted to make sure she had a good hiding place, one she could access quickly.

Before getting out of the car, she pressed the button on the remote to shut the garage door. A fixture with a single bulb remained on above her, giving her just enough light in the windowless garage to get around to the trunk to get a few bags of groceries out. The timer on the fixture was brief, and she often found herself fumbling for the light switch at the door to turn it on so she could punch in the alarm code. Today, though, she made it to the step in time and put in the code before the light went out.

For one confused moment she thought the weight of the grocery bags had tipped her backward on the step, but then she felt an arm around her throat, and suddenly she was on the garage floor on her back, staring up at someone standing over her. There was just enough light from under the laundry room door to make out the shape of a large man.

"Please—" she started to say. He must have followed her from the bank. But how had he gotten here ahead of her? She wanted to tell him that she had money, that he could take anything in the house. But before she could get out another word, he kicked her in the side.

He kicked her a second, a third, a fourth time as she cried out. When she tried to roll away from him, to wedge herself beneath the front of her car, he quickly pulled her back and fell on top of her.

As she gasped for air, she inhaled the smell of him: cigarettes and sweat and, faintly, garlic. He was breathing hard, too, and as one of his hands fumbled at her waist, she was certain he was going to rape her. But he only rose up on his knees and began to pummel her abdomen with his fists.

Her breath came out in agonized bursts as he hit her. The pain exploded inside her with each contact, and she squeezed her eyes shut to ward it off. Still, she tried to scoot away on the floor, but before she could move an inch, he pinned her shoulder to the concrete. But her other arm was free and she flailed at him, grabbing at his head and feeling for his eyes. She knew enough to go for his eyes, even in her pain.

She thought of the gun in the car. But there was no way for her to get to it. Still, she grabbed at him, distracting him enough that it was all he could do to keep her pressed to the ground. He was wearing some kind of hat or balaclava, which she pulled off him, but she couldn't see more than an impression of his face: a wide, flat nose, a broad jaw. Under her hand, his beard was scruffy. At last she was able to get hold of his ear and squeeze.

This time it was his turn to cry out in pain. But the surprise was more hers. The ear was thick and deformed, lumpy; it felt more like a small fist than an ear.

His cry was the only sound he made. As he ripped himself away from her, she felt the ear slip out of her fingers. The pain in her stomach and rib cage was bright and violent, but she seemed to feel the grease from his head and the absence of the misshapen ear on her fingertips more keenly.

Again he kicked her. She lost count of how many times. Finally, she lost consciousness, sinking into a place inside herself where, with her child, she felt nothing at all.

29

"HERE COMES TROUBLE," Frank said.

Freida Birkenshaw was out of her car with a speed that seemed unnatural for a woman who spent the better part of every day leashed to an oxygen tank. With her cloud-white hair floating in wisps behind her and her patrician face set in an angry scowl, looking for all the world to Bill like an avenging fury, she made her way up to the tenant house where they were serving a search warrant. Leaning on a sturdy cane that thumped onto the porch steps as she approached, Freida looked at neither Bill nor Frank, but went straight to Delmar Johnston's door.

Bill motioned for Frank to step forward to keep her from assaulting the Johnston character if he should be the one to answer.

"You shouldn't be here, ma'am," Frank said. "We don't know . . . he might be armed."

The look she gave Frank said that she didn't really care. She pounded on the door with the head of her cane.

"Mr. Johnston," she said. "You need to come out here right now."

The clapboard house, its windows still taped up with plastic to keep out the late winter winds, was tiny enough that anyone inside would certainly have heard her voice. Bill saw a movement at the window, a shade pushed aside just a hair. He was certain that what he saw at the edge of the curtain was the barrel of a shotgun.

He shouted for the others to get down.

Frank pushed the old lady to the floor of the porch, covering her body with his so she lay flat against the splintering boards. Beneath him she made a startled warbling noise.

When Bill motioned for them to move away, Frank helped her crawl to the side of the porch and get down onto the grass.

Bill dropped below the lip of the front of the porch and called into the house.

"Sheriff's Department," he shouted. "Delmar Johnston, come out." As he spoke, he unholstered his sidearm and took aim at the window. There was no movement. He waited, suddenly doubtful.

On the other side of the porch the old woman was cursing Frank, telling him, "Get your filthy paws off my neck."

The battered front door of the house opened a few inches and Bill prepared himself to exchange fire with whoever was behind the door.

"You want to just come out," he said. "We don't need any excitement this morning." It had been a hell of a long time since he'd had to shoot at anyone, and he prayed that the Johnston character would not make things difficult.

As Bill called out a second time, Delmar Johnston—a boy, really—eased the door open. His extended hands showed that he had no weapon. Shirtless, he wore blue jeans that he'd apparently had no time to button up. With his dark, tousled hair and sleepy eyes, he was the picture of innocence. Still, Bill didn't trust what he was seeing.

"You got company in there?" Bill said.

"No, sir," Delmar said. "You can see I got no weapon neither."

"Step on down here," Bill said.

Delmar came slowly down the steps. "I was just coming to the door," he said. "I heard Ms. Birkenshaw."

Bill didn't want to be wrong about what he'd seen, but it was looking more and more like he had been. He was glad that Frank was with him rather than Mitch or Daphne—those two wouldn't have let him forget his momentary panic. Panic was never good. He blamed it on his lack of sleep. Still, there was Freida Birkenshaw. It would be a bitch if she'd gotten so much as a scratch from Frank's tackle.

"We're just looking to get a few questions answered," Bill said. "Maybe you can help us out."

"Mind if I do up my pants?" Delmar gave him a Hollywood smile. For a farmhand, he had improbably white teeth. A pretty boy. But his skin was ruddy and his hands rough. Bill guessed that whatever the boy was into, he also managed some work on the operation.

Freida hurried over to the steps. "If you had anything to do with that boy's death, Mr. Johnston," she said, "you can pack up and get out now. I don't run that kind of farm."

When the boy didn't ask who she was talking about, Bill knew they would eventually get some information out of him.

"Frank," he said. "Why don't you and Mr. Johnston go inside so he can get his things on to come down to the office for a chat? Then Mrs. Birkenshaw and I will just take this warrant I've got in my pocket inside and see what we can see."

But the only reaction from the boy was a disinterested shrug. He turned and went into the house with Frank following him.

Bill stood awkwardly with Freida on the thin, wintry grass in the yard. He didn't quite know what to say to the woman. While Margaret was certainly her social equal, it wasn't like they all ever got together for dinner. About the time it began to seem to him that Frank was taking longer than should have been necessary, the door opened.

Delmar Johnston came out first, wearing a dusty, wide-brimmed Stetson that was as improbable as his smile. Behind him, Frank carried a sawed-off Mossberg with a black pistol grip.

"Look here what I found, Sheriff," he said. "Right by the door."

"Hell, Sheriff," Delmar said. "A man's got a right to defend his property. I didn't know what was going on out here."

"So you thought it proper to lie about the shotgun, Mr. Johnston?"

"No lie, Sheriff," he said. "I didn't answer the door with a weapon. Did I?"

"One, it's not strictly your property," Bill said. "Two, it's not the kind of greeting we like to get when we pay folks a visit."

"I didn't do nothing wrong."

"Wait," Bill said. "I didn't get to number three." He took the gun from Frank. "You should know that when you cut your Mossberg down to these unusual proportions, you were breaking the law. You just got a first-class upgrade on your ticket into town."

As Frank led him to the cruiser, Delmar looked back at Bill. "I ain't never been in the back of a police car before. Maybe Ms. Birkenshaw should take a picture." He laughed and winked at the old lady as Frank put him inside.

Somehow Bill didn't think the boy was telling the truth about the cruiser. As they drove away, Bill watched the old woman. He expected her to be angry at the boy's words, but instead she looked like she was thinking about something else. He wondered if she'd even heard him.

"My great-grandfather was a chandler," she said. "I used to think about how he brought a kind of light to this place. But the devil, too, spreads his own kind of ugly light wherever he goes."

Inside, the house was tidier than Bill would have expected the home of a man Delmar Johnston's age—twenty or twenty-one, maybe—could ever be. There were no pizza boxes or empty beer cans anywhere, no random piles of laundry. In the bedroom, the double bed was made so that the spread held no wrinkles. The only personal item in sight was a black plastic comb that seemed to have been carefully laid, horizontally, on top of the dresser. Throughout the house the furniture was shabby, like in most tenant houses, but in the living room it was arranged around a forty-two-inch plasma television that had an Xbox tucked into a floor stand.

"Give your tenants cable, do you?" Bill asked.

"It's not as easy as you'd think to get people to work a farm," Freida said. "Now we have to compete with Buyer's Mart and the Toyota plant. But that's not my television. This is quite a bit nicer even than Paxton keeps at the house."

Bill didn't say that it was also quite a bit nicer than his own television.

"Maybe he's thrifty," he said. "Or your wages are generous."

She waited in the living room while he searched the boy's closet and the rest of the bedroom. He'd been able to get the warrant for weapons, drugs, and drug paraphernalia. When he found one of the dressers stuffed full of porn of the sort one couldn't buy from behind the counter at the local quick-stop, he thumbed through it quickly to make sure there was no kiddy or snuff material. But it was mostly skanky young women busily sticking things into one another and playing with themselves. Not his cup of tea.

Other than a sheathed hunting knife of questionable legality, Bill found nothing of any interest in the house's single bedroom. The same was true for the kitchen, living room, and bathroom. No equipment, tubing, burners. Nothing.

Freida stood in the front doorway, looking out onto the morning. "I never have liked this house," she said, turning to Bill when he came into the room. "The first tenant killed his wife in that bedroom, using one of her own silk stockings. What a woman like that was doing with silk stockings, I'll never know. But this house has seemed like bad luck ever since. I should probably tear it down."

"I didn't see a door to any basement. Is there an attic?"

"The only storage is the crawl space beneath the porch," she said. "There's a kind of lean-to shed attached to the back of the kitchen."

She followed Bill out of the house and down the porch steps.

"We've had enough disruption here today, don't you think, Sheriff?" she said. She was sounding breathless, and Bill began to worry that he might end up with a medical emergency to top things off.

When they reached the other side of the house, they found that the door to the lean-to was padlocked shut.

"You keep anything in here, ma'am?" he asked.

"You're joking," she said.

After getting her permission to bust the lock, he grabbed a hammer from the toolbox he kept in the trunk of the cruiser. He figured that it probably would've been just as simple to take the screws out of the plate screwed to the jamb, but it was more fun to put on a show for the old woman.

"Step back, please, ma'am," he said.

It took three (very satisfying) whacks to get the lock off. As he pulled open the door, Freida was again right there beside him.

"Good Lord," she said. "What is wrong with that young man? We've got Dumpsters all over this farm."

Bill tossed the hammer aside and took out his pocketknife to slash one of the fifty or so plastic garbage bags of various colors that were stuffed into the lean-to's tiny space. The deep green bag gaped wide with an awkward smile and dozens of empty cold and allergy medicine packages fell at their feet. Bill tried to hold the bag back, but it disgorged small boxes and plastic bottles onto the ground until it sagged, nearly empty, beneath his hand.

It took him several minutes to explain to Freida that she was looking at the makings of a substantial amount of methamphetamine, and when he finished, he wasn't certain that she fully understood. At face value, of course, there was nothing wrong with a person hoarding thousands of empty over-the-counter drug boxes. But it certainly didn't look good for Delmar Johnston. He was getting a clearer picture of the dead kid's connection to Mr. Johnston, who, besides lying about the gun, looked to be a cagey bastard. Definitely not smart, hiding all this packaging in his own house, but cagey.

"I'll be sending someone out to take pictures," he said. "I've got no idea where we're going to store this much garbage, even if it is evidence."

30

LATE SATURDAY MORNING, when most of Carystown was lingering over coffee or doing weekend chores, Kate had already walked several miles out Shelbytown Road and was on her way back home. She kept to the fields and fence lines, striding through the still dormant March grass as though she were the most confident woman in the world, as though she weren't plagued with uncertainty. After spending all day Friday at home with the telephone unplugged, she felt the need to get out, to walk as many miles as she could. She wanted to leave Carystown behind for a while, if only for a couple of hours. Walking cleared her head, and, just then, her mind needed some serious clearing out.

The sun was warm on her face and the fresh morning air was cool but not unpleasant as she headed south of town, toward where the Quair River left the valley. At home she'd felt suffocated in the closed-up cottage, afraid as she was to throw open the windows lest the reporter show up again. In the woods not far off the road, the trees had not yet leafed, but the birds were active and noisy. She felt their anticipation of full spring and was jealous of their enthusiasm. How much did she wish that she had something to look forward to besides hard questions and accusations and confronting the man she loved (she thought) about his betrayal?

How could she have been so wrong about Caleb? Even as she had nursed her anger through the previous day and night, she had hoped (it was a tiny hope, a tiny, unwished-for hope) that he would show up unannounced, as he had the previous week. The phone had been unplugged, but he had his key. Was he worried that he couldn't reach her? Certainly Janet had called him, triumphant, as soon as she'd left her house. He had to know how hurt she was. It sickened her to think of Janet with him, Janet touching him, tasting him, pleasing him. For a while, as she walked, she cried.

Was it some wicked, tragic flaw in her character that led her to fall for men like Caleb? Like Miles? There had been a boy in high school, too, a rich boy with a convertible 1957 Thunderbird and the easy manner of someone who knew the world was his for the taking. He was, as they say, far out of her league, usually seen only with golden, pearl-earringed girls who were confident and relaxed in their own right, simply biding their time until they were old enough to snag a med student or full-blown specialist so they could continue their lives of privilege. But one inexplicable evening he had turned his attention to her at a keg party, and she found herself, drunk, with his erection pressing against her stomach, and then, astonishingly, her lips. She was too overwhelmed with awe at his sudden apparent affection for her to refuse to take him in her mouth. But half an hour later they were back at the party and he deposited her with her friends, who hadn't even known that she'd been away. She was speechless with shame as she overheard him tell the other boys gathered around the keg that she gave great head. She ran away into the dark, her friends calling after her. Finally, she came to a small barn and leaned against it and vomited, the smell of hay and manure all around her. Even now she colored with embarrassment to think of it.

It seemed to her that she was safe only when she wasn't involved with a man. But then, her friendships hadn't been working out so well lately either. She thought of Kelly, her sometimes tennis partner back in Hilton Head. She wondered if Kelly had thought of *her* in the past few years.

Lillian was dead. No one had known that Lillian went to the cemetery with her, not even Francie. There was no one who could tie Lillian to the little girl. Except, she thought, Isabella herself. But the idea that the ghost of a nine-year-old child would or could hit a woman on the head and then stick a pitchfork in her seemed too absurd for words even to her, a woman who seemed to have taken up believing in ghosts.

Lillian had told her to look after Francie, but so far she'd done a terrible job of it. Seeing the roof of the antiques mall come up over the rise ahead of her, she quickened her step, thinking that she would go to Francie and try to make amends with her.

The road had been mostly empty all morning, with only a few cars carrying people into town to shop or to have breakfast. As she looked off in the direction of her house, she saw a white truck or van—her long-distance eyesight wasn't great these days—pass in front of the antiques mall and turn onto Shelbytown Road.

Kate shaded her eyes with a hand. Without the glare, there was no mistaking that the car was Janet's Range Rover, with its silly black grille that Caleb called a cowcatcher stuck to the front of it. As it shot past her, stirring up wind and dust, she saw Janet—her hair covered by a scarf, her eyes hidden behind enormous tortoiseshell sunglasses—hunched over the wheel. But Janet didn't turn to look at her.

For the briefest of moments, she thought about their exchange in Janet's bedroom and wished she had done some violence to her, broken one of Janet's expensive, unimaginative objets d'art over her head or at least thrown it in her direction. (Given her own violent thoughts, she should have been more alive to Janet's, she told herself when she was at home later, ice packs placed strategically on the bruises that covered much of her body.)

As she stood looking after the Rover, it abruptly stopped a few hundred yards down the road as Janet slammed on the brakes. It idled like some quiet beast.

Janet *had* seen her. Kate turned away, stumbling as she turned her attention back to getting home. She felt her heart beat harder in her chest when she heard the gravel crunch beneath the Rover's tires as Janet turned the car around.

Surely Janet didn't want to talk to her! She had rehearsed again and again what she would say to Caleb, but hadn't even thought about confronting Janet. It had been foolish of her, of course. Carystown was too small for her not to ever run into a highly visible woman like Janet Rourke.

Kate quickened her step. She thought that Janet had either stopped or was driving so slowly that she couldn't hear her.

But when she heard the Range Rover accelerate, she instinctively looked back. Janet's face was hidden behind the solid mask of gold the sun had laid across the Rover's windshield. But Kate knew Janet. If she was wearing one of her Hermès scarves over her hair, and sunglasses, then she was wearing little or no makeup. Janet wasn't pretty without her makeup;

she created herself each morning when she got out of bed. It gave Kate a small amount of much needed pleasure to know that she had caused Janet to let her facade slip.

The pleasure was too brief. *She would face Janet, the bitch. She didn't owe Janet a moment's politeness.* She stopped on the road's berm to wait for Janet to pull up beside her. But it only took her a fraction of a second to realize that Janet wasn't going to slow down.

Kate began to run, realizing that Janet meant to run her down there in broad daylight.

Losing her footing on the berm's loose gravel, she fell, her arm sliding out beneath her, and felt the skin scrape away onto the pavement. She got up and ran then, knowing that if she didn't, Janet would drive over her, crushing every bone in her body. Janet wasn't a woman who did things by halves.

In the second the Range Rover would have hit her, Kate spread her arms as though she would fly and dove into the weed-and-rock-choked ditch, landing on one shoulder and hip. Janet steered the Rover into the ditch after her, missing her outstretched arm only by inches, and Kate was overcome by the smell of the Rover's tires and the acrid odor and heat from the exhaust. With a grunt of acceleration, the Rover climbed out of the ditch. But no sooner was it out than Kate heard it crash through the pasture fence a dozen feet away from the edge of the ditch. She pressed herself flat against the ground, praying that Janet wouldn't come back for her, that the broken fence would have awakened Janet to the insanity of what she'd just done.

She could hear the Rover above her, but the sound was receding. A moment later she heard another crash, again the sound of breaking boards. Trapped in the pasture, Janet had made her own exit farther up the hill.

Wake up.

The voice was a whisper in her ear.

Kate opened her eyes, confused. A blue-tailed lizard about five inches long regarded her from a small pile of rocks not far from her head. Its tongue tasted the air and disappeared into its mouth.

Kate tried to roll away from it, but her body felt leaden and weak. *Screw you, Janet, you crazy bitch.* As she slowly sat up, the lizard remained still. She brushed her hands together to get the gravel off and wiped her palms across her cheeks. Her left hand came away with streaks of blood.

"Just great," she said, addressing the lizard. "I hope you got the license plate of that truck." She gave a grim *ha-ha.*

Finally, the lizard crouched and slipped soundlessly into a crevice in the rock pile.

The sound of the whisper remained in her head, a child's voice, urgent. Part of her wished that she could choose to believe that the lizard had wakened her.

Her body felt so stiff that she wanted to lie back down, but the rocks and beer cans and skeletons of last year's bull thistles at the bottom of the ditch were hardly inviting. She groaned as she reached for the bank of the ditch and pulled herself up. After a couple of tries, she was able to get purchase on one of the larger rocks and climb out. Looking down at herself, she took stock: ripped sweater sleeve pushed up above her elbow, revealing an impressive array of bloody scratches; a knee torn out of her jeans, the skin beneath also red and inflamed; and the bloody face she already knew about. And as she tried to walk, she felt a sharp pain in her right ankle. *No, Janet didn't do things by halves.*

At the thought of Janet, she looked anxiously around, but the only sign of the Rover was the twice-splintered fence. Some farmer was going to be pissed off. Kate hoped that someone from the farm had seen Janet's little rampage. The sun was a little higher in the sky than when she'd gone into the ditch, so she knew she'd been out for more than a couple of minutes. She figured that someone would've shown up by now if they'd seen.

When she saw a Buick coming toward her, she thought about flagging it down, but she just nodded and gave the old couple inside a brief wave. Questions, more questions, she didn't need. The Buick slowed down some, and the woman inside pointed at the fence and covered her mouth in surprise. *Just keep going. Nothing to see here, folks.*

The car sped away. The people obviously didn't want to get involved, and she could hardly blame them. *She* sure didn't want to be involved. But when her ankle started to burn even more, she almost regretted that she hadn't flagged them down. No telling what sort of damage she was causing herself. And she'd never been the self-punishing sort. Apparently, she let the men in her life do the punishing.

She walked on, realizing only after it was too late to go back that she'd lost her sunglasses. By the time she reached the stop sign where Shelbytown Road ended, she wanted to weep. Her own street was quiet. The antiques mall had been open less than an hour, and its gravel parking lot with its faux hitching posts held only a couple of cars. From the corner, she could see the yellow and purple pansies she'd planted along her front porch to chase away the gray winter a few weeks before, and her heart lifted. But when she saw the back end of Caleb's pickup truck peeking from the driveway on the other side of the cottage, she froze. She knew she wasn't in any kind of shape for a confrontation. *Janet's mouth on his. Janet, naked, lying beneath him. Janet laughing at her.* No, even if she were on her deathbed, she would face Caleb and his betrayal, and all the other people in her life—Francie, Sheriff Bill Delaney, even Isabella Moon, whatever she was—be damned.

The look on Caleb's face when she opened her front door took away her words. He stood in the middle of her living room holding a copy of the *Carystown Ledger.*

"Have you seen this? About that little girl?" he said, holding the paper out to her. Then, noticing how disheveled and bloody she was, "My God, what happened to you?"

He tossed the paper onto the coffee table and hurried over to her, to lead her to a chair. She shrugged his hand away.

"Don't *even* talk to me, you son of a bitch," she said.

He stepped back. These were her new terms, and she was in charge, if only for as long as it took to get him out of her house.

"One time," he said. "One time, Kate. And it was a horrible mistake. She's fucking crazy, she is. I was drunk, Kate."

"You need to leave," she said.

"Jesus, Kate, you're in trouble," he said. "Why didn't you tell me what was going on? What do you have to do with that child?"

"Nothing concerning me is any of your business anymore," she said.

Then, wanting to hurt him, "Maybe if I'd thought I could trust you, I would've told you what was happening to me."

The words stung him. If anyone else had caused him to look as broken as he did at that moment, she would've been after them in a heartbeat.

"I deserved that."

They stood in the silent room, the place she'd designed as a haven for herself, the sunny yellow floral couch, the gilt-framed antique photographs of children culled from local shops, the Depression-era vases (not expensive, signed ones, but pretty enough), the scattering of handwoven rugs, the pillows she'd needlepointed herself in those first lonesome months after her arrival. It was a woman's room. Caleb always looked a little out of place here, unless the room's only light was firelight. *Don't go there or you'll give in!*

"I'm going to call the sheriff about your girlfriend," she said.

"Janet did this?"

"She doesn't get to go around trying to kill people," Kate said. But when she started toward the telephone, the pain in her ankle caused her to cry out and almost fall.

Caleb was there to catch her. She couldn't help but lean on him as he led her to the couch. Even in the midst of the pain, she told herself that she wasn't going to let his tender attitude toward her soften her resolve. He didn't deserve her forgiveness, and she didn't deserve to be treated as though she were some kind of doormat.

"Stay here," Caleb said after settling her on the couch.

They didn't speak as he cleaned her wounds with a wet washcloth. She had no antibiotic ointment or bandages in the cottage. When he finished, he gave her some painkillers and tucked ice-filled plastic bags wrapped in towels around her ankle and the elbow on which she'd fallen.

"I'm going to the drugstore to get a wrap bandage for your ankle," he said, taking his keys from the coffee table and jingling them on his index finger as he often did when he was nervous. "Don't do anything, call anybody, or answer the phone until I get back. Please?"

"Why would I promise you anything?" she said. But she knew that she would do as he asked because she was too exhausted to do otherwise. She also decided that if he came back with flowers, she would have to kill him.

Caleb still had a half-pitying look on his face, but she saw an unguarded spark of alarm in his eyes. *Yes, be afraid! You don't know what Mary-Katie's capable of!*

When he'd closed the front door and locked it behind him, Kate realized she'd been holding her breath. She sighed deeply and closed her eyes as she leaned her head against the couch's plump pillows. The newspaper lay on the coffee table. She didn't need to look at it to know that the whole town now thought that she was either a murderer or a certifiable lunatic.

31

"Come on, baby," Miles said, holding the spoon near her face. "This is great soup. It's from the Fresh Market."

Mary-Katie slowly turned her head away from the spoon. Jagged streams of rain coursed down the outside of the window. It had been raining for two days, something not uncommon on the island in October. She'd been able to get out of bed without Miles's help that morning, but the effort had left her exhausted.

"Maybe later." Miles put the spoon and bowl on the bed tray. "Time for a pill." He took an unlabeled medicine bottle from his sweater pocket and shook out a single tablet into his hand.

Mary-Katie took it with the glass of water he offered. Anything to keep the numbness of her body from turning into something more real.

"The remote's right here," he said, gesturing toward the tray. "Do you want anything else before I go downstairs?"

It seemed useless to her to be unpleasant to Miles. She shook her head, but turned again to stare out of the window. She'd come to think that he wouldn't even understand it if she were rude to him or demonstrably angry. There was something wrong with Miles, she knew now, something neither of them could ever change.

The doctor—if he was a doctor—had told Miles in his thick Pakistani accent that at least one of Mary-Katie's ribs was broken. Dazed by the injection he'd given her as soon as he arrived at the house, she had hardly been able to sit upright as he wrapped her torso in what seemed to be yards of bandages and thick white tape.

There had been kindness in his brown eyes, but as drugged as she was,

Mary-Katie knew better than to ask him for help. Miles hovered nearby, and the only help she would get would be from him.

The first couple of days after the attack were a blur of endless trips to the bathroom, always supported by Miles, who used warm water to cleanse her of the blood that came from her uterus, first trickling, then coming in thick clots. He worked quietly, occasionally murmuring words of encouragement as she moved from the toilet to the shallow water in the tub.

Who would have imagined that he could be such a thoughtful nurse? His soft hands tenderly adjusted her bandages and cooled her brow with damp washcloths. Every couple of hours he would check her temperature as the doctor had instructed him to, watchful for signs of internal injuries.

So thoughtful, so able.

Mary-Katie had stared after him each time he took away one of her soiled maxi pads. He was a man who could, without comment, toss the clump of flesh that was his child into a trash bag and, later, wheel the full garbage can down to the end of the driveway so the waste company could haul it away to be buried in a graveyard of trash somewhere on the mainland.

Watching the rain, she let the knowledge that she would kill Miles comfort her. There was a tightness in her chest made up of tears she couldn't yet shed for her child, for herself. The haze of the drugs kept her from letting them out. But she was patient. The ribs would heal. The bruises on her body would heal, and she would no longer need the drugs. In truth, a very small part of her felt a little sorry for Miles because he would soon be dead and didn't yet realize it.

32

THE GIRLFRIEND of the Catlett boy had given Bill another name: Charlie Matter. He and Frank were the only ones privy to that information, though, and he wanted to keep it that way. He had enough on his plate right now and wasn't quite ready to do a full-scale search at Chalybeate Springs. If it turned out that the recipient of all the over-the-counter stuff in Delmar Johnston's lean-to had been that raggedy-assed hippie, and right under his nose, he was going to have to give himself a good swift kick. The scope of the problem was starting to worry him, too. Carystown was small enough that he should've heard something about the operation before now, and as much as he hated to think so, he couldn't deny that Matter might have some connection within the department.

Like a family of troubled children, his deputies all had their problems. Daphne couldn't seem to keep a civil attitude with anyone, and she certainly had a big mouth. She was probably sleeping with the kid from the newspaper—*God help him*—and maybe had talked too much about the Moon girl's case. But he couldn't see her mixed up with Charlie Matter. She had no respect for the hippies. Mitch was worrisome. There had been a couple of times when the department kitty had come up fifty or sixty bucks short, and rumors that he'd let several of the town bigwigs out of speeding raps for the occasional favor. And Frank—well, Frank was solid to the point that he pissed a lot of people off. He wouldn't let Mother Mary herself get away with stiffing a parking meter. Still, as flawed as they were, they were his best, and he had a hard time imagining any of them going seriously bad.

It burned him that while the Catlett boy was being prepped for burial at the funeral home, Delmar Johnston was probably enjoying the turkey and gravy dinner that Smithy, the jail's "nutrition consultant," had fixed for the weekend prisoners. That is, if Delmar Johnston hadn't declared himself a vegan or vegetarian or lacto-ovum whatchamacallit and demanded a special meal, which, of course, they would have to provide for him. Air-conditioning and cable television weren't enough. The law was soft and yielding these days, and Bill felt like the criminals knew it. Why shouldn't they break the law? It was ripe for the breaking.

The office was quiet. Mitch was the only other person in the building. There never seemed to be enough for Mitch: enough time in the day, enough money, enough latitude in enforcing the law, and definitely not enough pretty, available women in Carystown. Mitch liked to schedule his days off consecutively and get out of town. He didn't confide much in anyone, but the scuttlebutt was that he had at least two girlfriends—one up in Lexington and one way out in Harlan County—who didn't know about each other. It wasn't how Bill would've conducted his life, but he had to admit to himself that he envied Mitch his apparent callousness, his willingness to take risks in order to live his life *large,* as some called it.

He emptied the sludge at the bottom of the coffeepot into his mug and rescued it with some real half-and-half and a couple packets of sugar before stopping in Mitch's doorway.

"Margaret says you're welcome for dinner later," he said. "She's been on a salmon kick lately. Gets it up at the warehouse club in the city. Pretty good for farm-raised."

"Thanks," Mitch said. "She's a heck of a cook."

"Yeah, she is. But she's starving me," Bill said. "I'll be lucky if I get butter on my rice." He didn't go on to mention that things were still pretty silent at home. He knew Margaret was looking for some kind of apology or explanation, but what could he say to her? He'd been completely unprepared for her questions—her suspicions—about the Russell woman. But it wasn't as though he'd actually *done* anything, or even thought about doing anything. To his mind, Margaret was being unreasonable.

Mitch laughed. "I don't think you're supposed to put butter on rice. I heard that once."

"Butter goes on everything," Bill said.

Once Bill sat down, they eventually got around to Lillian Cayley.

"I've got a whole lot of nothing," Mitch said. "Anyone who didn't like her—and there are damn few of them—says they respected her. Even the ones she failed in school. No debts to speak of. No long-lost relatives after her money. Francie's taking it pretty hard."

"You know her?"

"We went to school together," he said. "She was younger, of course. We didn't run with the same crowd."

No, Bill didn't see Mitch hanging around with black girls from the East End, no matter how pretty they were. He had played some football, but kept a pretty low profile with everyone except the ladies. There were still certain Carystown women, now lawyers' and landlords' wives, who blushed when they ran into Mitch. Margaret liked him well enough to have him over for dinner, but she'd told Bill more than once that she found Mitch a little too smooth, too confident. Not even thirty-three, he'd already been divorced twice. He kept a picture of his two kids behind a pile of papers on the file cabinet, but he never talked about them. The skinny, gap-toothed girl, a serious, bespectacled sort who resembled her mother, and the boy, who already had his father's winning smile, lived in North Carolina. No one in Carystown had seen them since they were babies.

"Listen," Mitch said. "I might as well tell you now, Bill. I screwed up the casting of that tire track behind the Cayley place."

"How bad?" Bill said.

"It didn't set right. Crumbled like it was made of sugar."

It would be much too late to get a new one. The curiosity seekers had been all over that shoulder in the past few days trying to get a look at the Cayley backyard, as though they might see the murder happen there all over again. They were stuck as far as evidence went. It was as though the killer had appeared out of thin air just to murder the woman and then vanished again.

"Too bad," Bill said. Sometimes he missed being a part of a real department. Louisville was no big city, but the force had been as professional as any. He felt like a father who'd neglected his duty.

"Photos?"

"Daphne's got them," Mitch said. "Not great. Looked like maybe a truck tire to me."

"Might have been the road maintenance people. Or kids parking," Bill said. "No guarantee it was anything. But let's do a backup next time."

Mitch nodded. "Sure thing," he said. "So, what time do you want me to come by later? I don't want to be late to Margaret's table."

"Early. I'm playing hooky from church to interview Mr. Delmar Johnston with Frank in the morning and I need my beauty sleep."

Mitch snorted. "You're already pretty enough for that asshole," he said. "Hell's even too good for somebody who sells to kids."

"I won't take that as a comment on my looks," Bill said. "We'll see you at five-thirty."

Wanting badly to get home to have some kind of Saturday afternoon nap in front of the television before Mitch showed up, Bill found himself instead standing on the shoulder of Shelbytown Road with Tom Kaptis, a fellow Rotarian who had asked him to come out and look at some vandalized fence.

"I had two calls about it this morning before I could even get down and see this mess," Tom said. "I'm damned glad I didn't have any stock out here. They'd be halfway across the county by now."

"Nobody saw or heard anything?" Bill asked as he took in the ruined fence, the deep tire tracks leading out of the ditch and into the pasture. "You think it happened last night?"

"I can deal with a few slugs through the mailbox or my tractor-crossing sign, but this is more than a person should have to put up with. What the hell's happening to this town, Bill? It's like living in the Wild West around here these days. Where's the law and order?"

It was more of an accusation than a question, and Bill let it go.

"No skid marks," he said, looking on the road. "Must have been something built for off-road to make it up the other side of this ditch so handily." He thought back on his conversation with Mitch, who had said that the tracks behind the Cayley house belonged to a truck. But that was a serious long shot. There were probably a couple thousand trucks or SUVs registered in Jessup County alone. And he figured that murderers who liked to creep around under cover of darkness didn't generally go in for four-wheeling and taking out fences.

"They must have been drunker than hell," Tom Kaptis said.

Bill, who was out of uniform and wearing jeans and hiking boots, made his way down into the ditch near where it looked like the vehicle might have left the road. There was the usual collection of crap—candy wrappers, a plastic bag, a faded beer can. Browned thistles scraped against his jeans as he looked around the rocks and weeds for evidence of an animal or maybe some piece of the vehicle. Anything.

"You can bet I'm going to press charges against whoever did this," Tom Kaptis said above him. "I can't see these two breaks being fenced for under a couple thousand bucks."

Tom Kaptis wasn't hurting for money, Bill knew. And he'd be sure to check it out with his insurance company before spending a dime of his own. He went on talking, but Bill tuned him out. There was something here. But he didn't know what he was looking for until he found it.

"Here we go," he said quietly to himself. Reaching over a flat, saucer-shaped rock, he picked up a pair of sunglasses jutting out of the weeds and held them up against the sky for a better look. They were twisted some, not much, but enough that it looked like they'd been fallen on. It took him a minute to recognize them as belonging to Kate Russell, but when he did, something clicked into place in his mind.

Everything, *everything*, pointed to her. But he still didn't know why.

Bill parked the cruiser in Kate Russell's driveway behind a late model Dodge pickup. It was after five o'clock and Margaret would be wondering where he was, particularly if Mitch showed up before he did. On the way up to the door he walked between the pickup and Kate Russell's small convertible, casually glancing at the front of the pickup to see if it bore recent scratches or other body damage. Only a moron would park his truck in a driveway less than a half mile from the fence he'd just destroyed, but you never knew.

The bumper and grille looked clean except for a few bugs and some tar splashes from road construction. It had been worth a shot.

Kate Russell looked like a child to him. She was huddled on the couch beneath an enormous blanket that covered her body except for her left foot and ankle, which rested on a pillow. Scratches on her face blazed red beneath a sheen of antibiotic ointment that covered her cheek and reached almost to her chin. She watched him warily. It saddened him to see her hurt, but he kept a close check on his reaction.

"What can we do for you, Sheriff?" Caleb said after the introductions. Bill found him defensive: the way he rocked back and forth on his feet told Bill that the man was nervous. But he knew that innocent people, too, got nervous around the law sometimes, and there had been nothing so far to link him to any of the crimes.

"I see you folks got the paper today," Bill said.

Kate glanced down at the paper, her face a blank. Neither she nor Caleb responded.

"I'd like you to know that the paper did not get that information from me, Miss Russell. It's not the sort of thing that I wanted to see in print either."

Caleb stopped rocking. His eyebrows knitted together as he frowned. "I don't know if that's some kind of joke, or what, Sheriff. It's insane, if you ask me. Libelous. Who would make up something like that?"

Bill and Kate exchanged glances.

"What?" Caleb said.

"Is this someone you want involved in all this?" Bill said.

Kate looked up at Caleb. "Two days ago I would have said yes," she said. "I don't know about now."

"Kate, please," Caleb said. "This doesn't have anything to do with what happened. *This* is serious."

"And the other's just fun and games. Is that it?"

Bill realized that there was more going on here than he was privy to. If he hadn't been certain that she'd gotten her injuries from a vehicle chasing her into a ditch, he might have assumed she'd gotten them from the man standing a few feet away. She had that vulnerable quality about her, that wavering confidence he'd seen so many times in women who were prone to be victimized by men. He wondered for the briefest of seconds if that wasn't what attracted him to her, that cruel streak inside him that he believed lived deep inside of every man. Most men kept it buried. Some never even had a clue that it was there.

"I can handle it," she said, turning her attention to Bill. "It's not going to make sense to anybody I explain it to, so I'm just not going to explain. I've already answered your questions, haven't I, Sheriff?"

"Most of them," Bill said. "We still need to talk about a couple of things, though."

"Wait," Caleb said. "You mean this whole ghost thing is true? The ghost of this kid *led you to her body*?"

The way he looked at Kate told Bill that any hope for the relationship between her and Caleb Boyd had probably died at that moment. A woman needed her man to trust her, and vice versa. He felt a little sorry for the guy. He'd been extremely skeptical himself, right up to the moment he'd uncovered that bright yellow coat in the dirt behind the cemetery. Still, he didn't know quite what he believed. All he knew was that she'd been right and had no motive that he could find to have killed and put the girl there herself.

"You probably want to stay away from the press that's sniffing around town," Bill said. "Maybe take a couple of days away from work."

He was surprised when Kate laughed. She pushed away some hair that had fallen into her face. "That won't be a problem," she said. "I don't think I'm expected back there. But you, Sheriff. You're looking just as wacky as I am here. What are *you* going to say to this?" She gestured toward the paper.

It was Bill's turn to smile. "I rarely comment on ongoing investigations. We don't even have confirmation that the child we found is the Moon girl. We should have dental records first thing Monday."

He turned to Caleb. "So, yes, Mr. Boyd. I'd say the gist of the story is true. For whatever reason, Miss Russell here was made aware of—by some currently inexplicable means—the location of the missing child's body. And, for reasons equally inexplicable, I followed up on that information. The body was found during the early hours of Thursday morning. I'd like to say that's the end of the story, but I don't think that it is. We still don't know how the child got there. That's my focus now."

As Bill talked, Caleb looked from one to the other in disbelief.

"Why couldn't you tell me about this, Kate?" he said.

"So you could look at me the way you did a minute ago?" she asked.

Bill thought that it was a good time for him to go. He took the ruined sunglasses from his shirt pocket and placed them on the newspaper.

"I found these down the road and thought you might want them back," he said. "Maybe you want to come by the office in a day or two and clear up a few things?" In his mind he added, *Like who you really are and why you're here.*

This time Kate exchanged looks with Caleb. Bill observed that hers held a good deal of contempt or anger, possibly both. Caleb pressed his lips together as though he had something to say but didn't want to let the words out.

More secrets. Bill wished them both a good evening and saw himself out. He stood on the porch a moment, savoring the view. From here he could see to the southern end of the valley and almost to the Quair. The distant hillsides seemed to be melting into the long shadows rising from the valley's floor. He loved it here in Carystown. It troubled him that it seemed to be falling apart on his watch. But for just that one moment he felt like he could forget it all.

33

PAXTON SAT ON THE HOOD of the Mercedes watching the sun drop behind the hills far on the other side of the river, almost fifteen miles in the distance. From here, the highest point on Bonterre, he could see not only the surrounding farms, but the edge of the national forest that started at the southern end of the valley. He couldn't wait for the day when he could bring Francie up here. They would take a picnic and a couple of horses and wander the farm. He wanted to show her everything—from the stables to the waterfall on the creek to the patch of woods where he'd seen two black bear cubs tumbling in the leaves when he was nine years old. It occurred to him that maybe she didn't ride, being from in town. Funny that he'd never asked her. But there would be time enough for that.

He'd tried to reach Francie over the past twenty-four hours but hadn't had any luck. There were other things that had his attention, true, but he worried that he hadn't tried hard enough. Perhaps her grief embarrassed her and she was afraid to call. But there was a shadow in his mind, a dark and ugly shadow that hinted that she didn't really need him. He pushed it away. *She needed him.*

Before he and Francie had finally gotten together, he'd seen his own future as a lonesome one. His mother was dying and seemed to have lost interest in anything but her magazines, the gardens in which she could no longer work, the television in her bedroom. At least she'd stopped harassing him about getting married, probably tired of coming up with names when he asked her whom he was supposed to marry. He knew for damn sure it wasn't going to be one of the overbred and underfed local horse princesses that had long been paraded in front of him. Sure, they could talk horse breeding, horse trading, horse shows, and Jack Russell terriers, but most of them looked like horses to boot. The parade had, thankfully, trickled to a stop in the past year or two. He figured that the local matriarchs had given up in the face of his disinterest. Marriage—given the evidence of his parents' strained years together—had always looked to him like a giant cage. He'd long ago decided that it was better to be alone (with the exception of frequent entertainments like Janet or reliable acquaintances from out of town) than to live in a hell of confinement.

But Francie inspired the domestic in him. She was so solidly middle class, so dedicated to her work and to making her way in the world—something he'd never had to think about doing. Surely it was something that should be rewarded. With each day he spent with Francie, he felt like he was becoming a better person. Each time they made love, he absorbed a bit of her, and she—he was sure—a bit of him. Eventually they would become one person. Indistinguishable.

He almost missed the sound of the dinner bell ringing outside the kitchen of the main house. Years ago it had called his father in from wherever he was on the farm, its clear, mellow tone rolling over the farm's pastures to tell him to end his day.

It wasn't until he was in his teens that Paxton realized that the bell wasn't just some idyllic tradition: it was actually a warning to his father that he should come in and get showered and dressed in time to fix a scotch and soda for Paxton's mother and himself in the library before dinner was served.

Paxton slid off the hood of the car and got behind the wheel. He didn't want to have to hear about the visit from the sheriff, but he knew he was going to have to soon enough. The icon on his cell phone blinked with message after message from his mother. The farm was still technically hers, and he was supposed to be looking out for it. There was always the chance that Delmar Johnston would be talking already, pointing the sheriff in his direction. But then, who was going to believe some witless horse wrangler/handyman over the son of the late Millar Paxton Birkenshaw and his wife, Freida? It couldn't happen in Jessup County or he'd never have gotten involved in the whole meth deal in the first place. He could handle it if it came up. Francie would stand by him, his mother would stand by him. More important, there were plenty of lawyers who would stand by him, if need be. But he didn't think it would come to that.

Sufficient unto the day is the evil thereof, he'd often heard his mother say. Today's evil was Charlie Matter, and it was looking like that situation could get out of hand very quickly. He started up the car, telling himself that he would think of something. He always did.

He slipped up the back kitchen stairs and went to the private bathroom off his bedroom to splash some water on his face and freshen up with cologne. Before leaving the room, he did a quick line to help him keep his edge with his mother. Even ill she could be tricky to deal with.

When he came downstairs to find the library empty, he was pleased. It took him no time at all to mix her Glenfiddich and soda, something he'd learned to do under her watchful eye when he was old enough to hold the bottle steady.

Might as well tell the boy to piss in it, Freida, his father had said. *Polluting a decent whiskey like that.*

But she had ignored him just as she had in so many things right up until the day he collapsed.

While he waited for her, Paxton made his own drink. He preferred a neat glass of Maker's Mark in the fall and winter. Later, after Derby Day, he'd switch to gin and tonic. He stood at the window thinking of Francie as he watched a pair of Canadian geese glide down from the sky and land out on the glistening pond.

"Where have you been all day?" his mother said from the doorway. She sounded cross, but much stronger than she had in the past few weeks. The oxygen was obviously making a difference for her.

"Mother, let me help you," he said, crossing the room. She held on to his arm as she descended the two stairs into the library. He picked up the portable oxygen cart and set it down on the rug. "That blouse is fetching," he said. "You haven't worn it in a while."

"I'm not in the mood, Paxton," she said, settling onto a chair. "Just tell me why I was the one who had to go through that charade with Bill Delaney down at the tenant house Delmar Johnston's living in."

There had been times in his life when he could talk his way out of things: the sledgehammer dents on the trunk of her Volvo when he was in high school, the situation with the drunken twit from Boston who'd come down for a local wedding and cried "Rape!" five minutes after she'd ripped her own blouse off in front of him, the sock full of dead baby mice in the housekeeper's dresser drawer. But he could tell by the aggravated tone of her voice that she wasn't budging on this one.

"That Delaney," Paxton said. "I don't trust him. If he weren't married to a Lowe, he'd still be in a squad car up in Louisville. He's never liked me and I don't like him. No telling what he would've accused me of if I'd been there. What was it he wanted, anyway? He went to Delmar's?"

"That boy aimed a sawed-off shotgun at my head," she said. "Have you ever had a shotgun aimed at you?"

Angry as she was, Paxton heard a note of panic in her voice. She reached for the oxygen mask and took a long, deep draught.

"Good God, Mother. Delmar Johnston? Were you hurt? Was anyone hurt?"

"It's drugs, Paxton," she said. "Sheriff Delaney told me Delmar Johnston is involved in some kind of drug ring. Here in Carystown. Maybe on this very farm! Do you know what that's going to look like? A gun aimed at my head. Police all over the place. And there are more coming. State troopers."

"Breathe, Mother," Paxton said, standing over her. "Don't let this upset you. It's all going to come to nothing."

Her face was ashen. He spoke soothingly to her while she breathed. The doctors had taken out part of one cancer-riddled lung, and she'd had two serious cases of pneumonia in the past six months. The cancer hadn't spread as yet, but the doctors said it could show up at any time. He wondered idly how much longer she could live.

"Delmar Johnston's obviously some kind of criminal, Mother, and you never have to hear of him again," he said. "I'll send someone over to pack up his things and take them over to the jail. He doesn't need to come back here."

"Our farm is a 'crime scene,' " she said. "The sheriff's not letting anyone near that house."

"I said I'd take care of it, Mother," he said. "I let you down by not being here today. But I won't let it happen again."

She gestured toward her drink and he handed it to her, knowing that the doctor had told her she shouldn't. She drank, grimacing as the scotch hit her tongue. When she handed the glass back to him, it was half empty. She watched him until he started to get uncomfortable. He wished he knew what she was thinking.

"You were with the Cayley girl today?" she said, looking into his eyes. "Is that why no one could find you?"

But he could look right back at her and tell her no.

"Her mother's going to be buried soon, I hope," she said. "I don't know why they haven't done it already."

"It was the coroner. The autopsy," Paxton said. "The funeral's Monday."

"I don't want you going there and making an ass of yourself," she said, sounding suddenly like the same woman she had been more than fifteen years before, when she first told him to stay away from Francie.

He marveled at the way things hadn't changed one bit in all those years. To her, he was the same wayward boy with a forbidden crush on a black girl from in town. But he'd spent too much time dreaming about a life with Francie, making her his wife, his partner, his permanent lover. They would continue to play their lovers' games even after the wedding, he'd decided, maybe even keep the tawdry little apartment over in Middleboro, laughing about it as a lark, an escape from the luxury of his mother's house. Thinking about Francie—naked, spread over the bed in the tiny bedroom, her pelvis arched in the air to receive him, the sound of the water-filled radiators ticking on in the background, the way her nipples responded immediately when he touched them with his tongue—gave him a sudden hard-on that he hoped his mother wouldn't notice.

He dropped to his knees in front of her, startling her so that she moved back in her chair.

"You have to know I love Francie," he said. "I'm going to marry her, Mother. She doesn't know it yet, but I am."

Freida laughed in his face. "Don't be ridiculous, Paxton," she said. "You're not going to marry Francie Cayley even if she would have you."

Stunned, Paxton stood up, his erection quickly fading. He stepped back away from his mother's chair. The time had come for him to fight for Francie, to show his mother that he was serious.

"I don't want to talk about this anymore," she said. "I want to go in to dinner."

She started to rise from her chair, but Paxton put a hand on her shoulder to keep her from getting up.

"Take your hand off of me," she said.

"You have to listen to me, Mother," he said. He spoke slowly, distinctly, as though she just hadn't heard him the first time. "I'm going to make Francie my wife. We're going to get married."

"Over my dead body," she said. Her cane was in her hand and she banged it on the floor. The small *thump* on the thickly padded rug was probably not the effect she was looking for. "You will not bring that girl into this house."

"Why do you have to be such a racist? This is Francie we're talking about. It doesn't matter what she looks like. You have to understand that."

She looked at him again in disbelief, then laughed again. He wondered if she wasn't going crazy. Although crazy would actually be easier in some ways. He would have control of things sooner.

"Lillian Cayley told me you had marriage on your mind," she said. "Did she tell you that you couldn't marry Francie because you're not black? What *did* she tell you?"

What Lillian Cayley had told him was that Francie was too good for him, that she would do everything she could to keep Francie from ruining her life with him. She'd known, somehow, about Janet. She'd told him that he was worse than any low-class player she'd ever seen, and she'd seen plenty in her life's travels.

You will not break Francie's heart! she told him.

"She didn't understand," Paxton said. "She was cruel. She didn't have any idea how much Francie loves me."

"Don't you think a daughter would tell her mother something like that?"

"She wouldn't have listened. She'd made up her mind a long time ago. She never even gave me a chance."

Freida looked at him pityingly. Her lost son. Her only son. What had she done to him to make him so blindly selfish? He was like his father in many ways, only less sure of himself. She'd made a mistake trying to marry him off to all those girls and was thankful that she hadn't been successful. No woman would be able to change him, damaged as he was. She was tired of worrying about him. But soon she would be dead and wouldn't have to care anymore. Probably she hadn't loved him enough. Or, had it been too much?

The truth was that he scared the hell out of her. The dead baby animals when he was a child, the bruised playmates, the weeping young girls. Their money had insulated him and would continue to do so for a long time after she was gone. But she didn't want to think about that. As he stood in front of her, pleading, she could see only the blue-eyed, towheaded boy who would fly into the kitchen, leaving the screen door to bang shut behind him, and run into her arms to tell her how far and how fast he'd ridden his pony, a smile lighting his eyes, his entire face. That was the boy who had brought out the best in her, putting a smile on her own lips and the warmth of a mother's love in her heart. *What had happened to that beautiful boy?*

Her thoughts softened her words.

"You're not the man that Francie needs, Paxton," she said. "You're too much for her. Francie needs someone less . . ." *What was the word she wanted?* "She needs someone less complicated than you are."

She didn't know Francie well, but knew enough to see that Francie didn't deserve to be saddled with a man like Paxton the rest of her life. She didn't know that Francie was strong enough, and it wasn't fair to either Francie or her son to put it to the test.

"So you don't think I'm good enough for Francie either?" Paxton said. "What the hell kind of thing is that for a mother to say?" He was confused. Nothing was as he thought it was. His mother was not like he had thought she was. Maybe she was insane after all.

"I suppose you think I had something to do with Lillian Cayley's death, too," he said, running his hand roughly through his hair.

"I can't talk about this anymore, Paxton," she said. Her shoulders sagged and she reached for the oxygen mask.

Paxton watched as she held it to her face. As the pure oxygen entered her body, her eyes lost their focus and she closed them so that she looked peaceful, like she was sleeping. If anyone had asked him at that moment what he was feeling, he probably could not have told them. All he knew was that he'd been close, so close, to realizing the one real dream he'd ever had in his life, only to be told—twice now—that he didn't deserve to have it come true.

34

Miles had decided long ago, before he'd lost his virginity to a fourteen-year-old slut on the floor of a vacant beach house, that he would never, ever pay for sex. So when he opened his eyes in his comfortable room at the Grand Hyatt Atlanta and saw the blonde he'd picked up in the hotel bar the night before rummaging in his wallet, he was peeved. She'd looked a class act to him, not overly made up, and wearing a sexy but not trashy low-cut sweater and boots. Even her tasteful jewelry had fooled him. In the thin strip of sunlight slicing through the blackout curtains, he could see that she had a bad case of cellulite on her behind and sloping shoulders that had been disguised by her long, full hair. He hated to be fooled.

"It would have been smarter to do that after you got dressed, don't you think?" he said, raising up on an elbow to see her better. "Maybe on your way out?"

The girl dropped the wallet onto the desk and sank down onto the chair, weeping histrionically.

Worse than being fooled, he really hated it when women cried. His Mary-Katie had been such a stoic over the past couple weeks and hadn't even cried at all that he'd seen. That moron Fitzgerald had gone overboard on her, getting her in the face and in the ribs—areas he'd told him to avoid. He'd had broken ribs himself before and knew that it hurt like hell. His only aim had been to get rid of the child, not for his Mary-Katie to be seriously injured.

"Just get the hell out," he told the girl, who was mumbling between sobs about flunking out of college and wrecking her car. When she got up, she

seemed to want to hide her body from him. Her clothes were spread over the floor and she stooped to get them rather than bend over. She hadn't been so shy the night before.

Miles reached for the television remote from the bedside table and pressed the On button. CNN came up on the screen, a presidential photo-op with some photogenic dictator.

As the girl hustled into the bathroom, he called after her.

"Hurry up. I've got to take a leak." As an afterthought he also told her to leave the soap and shampoo where they were.

Driving the six hours back home, it occurred to Miles that he should write a book. So many schmucks were making a killing telling losers how to buy real estate for cheap. He was a self-made guy. Bolstered by the check in his briefcase for half a million, he could see himself laying out his methods on paper and paying some hungry graduate student a couple hundred bucks to write it all down so that it made sense to the average Joe. Publishers, he figured, were always looking to make an easy buck, just like he was. There were CDs, too, to be made from those books. If he hit it big, he wouldn't even have to continue in real estate!

The idea kept him amused all the way home. Traffic was light once he got out of the Atlanta sprawl. October was a slow time for vacationers in the neighborhood.

When he was about an hour from home, he stopped to gas up the BMW and stretch his legs. He was hungry, but he wasn't even tempted by the sloppy pizzas and dried-out hot dogs the quick-stop had to offer. Since Mary-Katie had been laid up, he'd had to be extra careful about not sliding into thoughtless nutrition. Staying clean inside was as important to him as the pristine state of the Gucci and Brooks Brothers suits hanging in his closet and the shine on his shoes. As he paid for his gasoline, he took a slightly faded banana from a basket resting between a display of Mexican jumping beans and a selection of lighters that played "Dixie" and told the cashier to add it to his total. At least the inside of it was untouched by human hands.

"Sure," the man said. "Funny how many people buy fruit in here. Me, the only produce I want to see is between a burger and a bun. But my girlfriend, now, she's what you call macrobiotic." He indicated a plastic container on the *back counter.* "Brings her lunch to work every day, she does. All those vegetables make her skin glow like sunshine."

"No kidding," Miles said. His back was a little stiff from the drive. What he really wanted was to be at home, maybe taking a long soak in the hot tub before ordering up some sushi or Italian for dinner. It would be another week or two, he figured, before his Mary-Katie would be up to cooking. As it was, she wasn't a great cook, but she did make the effort on a regular basis, and that counted for something.

"Hey, you have a good day, man," the cashier said.

As Miles left the store, he noticed a chubby, pasty-skinned redhead squatting in an aisle, stocking a middle shelf with pop-top cans of ravioli and Vienna sausages. She gave him a lopsided smile and blushed as though she'd heard her loser boyfriend talking about her. Miles didn't like redheads, but he nodded to her all the same. His Mary-Katie had that cast of auburn to her hair that was subtle, classy, but this girl looked like she'd dipped her head into a bucket of strawberry-colored metallic paint. She was probably tattooed as well: he suspected that if she leaned forward, he'd see one of those giant bumper-sticker designs sticking out of her pants—hot pink roses or some vaguely satanic verse. Funny how those things never showed up on asses you wanted to see.

In the car, he ate the banana and chucked the skin into the garbage can by the pump. As he drove back onto the highway, he called his Mary-Katie by voice dial.

The phone rang four or five times before she answered.

"Were you asleep?" Miles said. "Did you take a pill, baby?"

"Yes," Mary-Katie said. "Are you coming home?"

"You sound great," Miles said. "I can't wait to see you. Atlanta sucked. You want me to pick up something to eat on the way in?"

"Sure," Mary-Katie said. "That's fine."

He loved that she was sounding more like her old self, despite the pills. He'd have to see about getting her off of them soon. Serious pills like the ones the doc had provided could be trouble, and he didn't want her turning into some slob of a drug addict.

"Let's eat on the deck. What do you think?"

"I want to stay inside," she said. "It's too cold outside. Do you mind?"

Miles put some pressure on the accelerator and slipped around a semi.

"Wherever you want," he said. "Call in to Grisanti's and tell them I'll get it in forty-five. Ciao, baby doll." When he hung up, he couldn't help but smile to himself. He put in a CD of Sills performing in Il Barbieri and thought about what a lucky bastard he was.

Carrying dinner and his suit bag in from the car, he decided it was better anyway that they weren't eating outside. No doubt it had been nearly eighty degrees that afternoon, but even in the garage the air had turned cool and a breeze came through the open door. There was no sense in his Mary-Katie picking up a chill, delicate as she was.

He took his time settling in. Mary-Katie had left his mail on the kitchen table, and he thumbed through it, finding nothing of interest. Nothing important came by mail anymore, but each day he looked forward to it with childlike anticipation.

By the time he was ready to go upstairs, darkness was falling quickly and he turned on every lamp he passed. They had the alarm system, which he'd rearmed as soon as he came inside, but he liked the criminal element to be aware that somebody was home. A few of these guys he occasionally employed could get squirrelly sometimes, or just plain greedy.

In the bedroom, he found his Mary-Katie sitting up in bed and tucked beneath one of the quilts the old woman had made. Coming home to his wife had been one of the main pleasures of his life. She kept the house immaculate, kept herself beautiful and slender (did she realize how bearing a child would have ruined her figure?), entertained the people he needed her to entertain. Seeing her still so pale dampened his mood some, but the smile with which she greeted him made him feel better.

"You took so long to get home," she said, holding her hand out to him. "I've done nothing but watch the stupid television all day."

Miles took her hand and sat beside her on the bed. But then she pulled him close to her and surprised him by kissing him hungrily, open-mouthed, as she hadn't in many weeks. He held her closer and felt the erection in his pants, a far stronger, more insistent one than he'd had for that slut in Atlanta. Sex with his Mary-Katie was always the best. Sometimes, even as he was chatting up a woman he'd chosen to sleep with, he asked himself why he was doing it when he had his Mary-Katie at home waiting for him.

"I've been waiting a hell of a long time for that," he said when they finally separated.

His Mary-Katie put her head on his shoulder. "I'm sorry," she said quietly. "I just couldn't. But it will be different now. We'll be different, Miles. Different people."

"Hey," he said, taking her by the arms and looking into her face. Her eyes had a feverish glaze. Was she really better? He couldn't tell for sure. But, sick or well, she wanted him again, which was what mattered. They were whole again.

"Let's put all that crap behind us," he said. "I've got a check for a new project right here." He patted the right breast of his sport coat. "We'll get away when it's done. What do you think? St. Croix? Palm Beach? You choose."

The idea of his Mary-Katie in one of her bikinis pleased him. She'd have to get back to the gym, of course, first. But she was so young. And it wasn't as though she'd gotten puffy lying in bed.

"Palm Beach," she said. "I think I want to learn to play golf."

Miles laughed. She was getting her sense of humor back. They'd tried golf lessons for her a few years back, but he hadn't liked the way the young pro put his hands on her hips as he stood behind her, guiding her swing. Maybe they would find somebody older down in Palm Beach.

"Why don't we talk about it over dinner," he said. "Paolo would be pissed to know I left our food in the warm oven for so long."

"Sure," Mary-Katie said. "I'm hungry."

As he prepared their dinner tray, Miles sang along with the Frank Sinatra CD on the stereo. When the bit about the man in Chicago who danced with his wife came on, it made him smile every time. He'd never been to Chicago, but had always imagined that he'd get along fine there. His reputation as enough of a tough guy to keep people from screwing him over pleased him. Sometimes he thought that his talents were wasted here down South. If he put his mind to it, he knew he could do some real damage in a place like Chicago.

Upstairs, it was quiet and dimly lighted. The television was off, and he wondered if his wife might be reading or, perhaps, asleep. Carting trays of food up and down the stairs was getting old. Even though she'd been coming downstairs more and more frequently—indeed, had handled things on her own the *past few nights—he could tell she wasn't a hundred percent yet. With a sigh, he realized now that they should have set her up in the guest room downstairs. It would have meant a lot less work for him.*

"Hey, babe," he said. "Can you get the light? I don't want to fall on my ass."

There was no answer.

"Babe? Are you asleep?"

As he came through the doorway, the overhead light threw the room into stark brilliance. He first looked for Mary-Katie on the bed, then realized that she was the figure standing in the bathroom doorway. Somehow she seemed taller than her five feet, five inches. She was wearing heeled boots, he saw. She was also pointing what looked to be a small-caliber pistol at him.

Miles laughed.

"What the hell? You can't be serious," he said.

In answer, his Mary-Katie pulled the trigger of her little gun four times in quick succession. He stumbled backward, dropping the tray, sending veal scallopini and pasta with marinara sauce and an entire bottle of a 1998 pinot noir bouncing across the carpet. And the sight of it might have been funny except for the spots of fuzzy activity in his side and his left leg. It wasn't until he'd been lying on his side, speechless, watching Mary-Katie move quickly around the room in her boots for what seemed like an eternity that the pain started in. He tried to tell her, to call her back from the deck doorway through which she'd disappeared, but couldn't come out with words, only low, pitiful moans.

The room was dark. She'd turned off the reading lamp as well as the overhead before she'd gone, the bitch. He knew that he'd eventually have to get up and do something about his wounds, but at just that moment he wanted to lie there and maybe sleep for a few minutes, then maybe think about what to do next.

35

SUNDAY BREAKFAST had been a sore disappointment to Bill. But he'd poured milk over his cold cereal and downed the glass of juice that Margaret put out for him without complaint. He had hopes that whoever was on duty at the jail would've brought in a box of doughnuts, but knew the chance was slim. If not, he might be able to persuade Margaret out for brunch at one of the inns in town. His talk with Delmar Johnston wouldn't take all day.

Delmar Johnston had been smart-alecky with Frank during his booking. He'd said that he had to think about a lawyer, that he'd just hang around the jail awhile and see what the food was like before he started making telephone calls. Bill fully expected that he would remember the lawyer about the time he got settled in the interrogation room, and that was okay. He'd made the unusual request that he wanted to make his statement directly to the sheriff, and that suited Bill as well. Nobody was in a rush except, perhaps, the parents of the Catlett boy, who had called a couple of times looking for answers. He was certain that they'd get them, eventually.

All bets were off when he pulled into his reserved space in front of the courthouse, where the jail was housed, and saw an ambulance speeding away, its siren off in deference—he hoped—to Sunday morning and all the churches in the neighborhood.

What the hell was happening now?

Daphne stood just outside the jailhouse doorway with Matthew John, the weekend jailer. They were laughing over something, but when they saw him, they straightened up.

"What'd I miss?" Bill said. "Who's in the wagon?"

Daphne said, "It's all under control now."

"What would that be?"

Matthew John spoke up, suddenly defensive. "I went to take the boy his breakfast, Sheriff, but he wouldn't wake up. I wasn't going to take any chances, so I called Daphne over here to help me check him out. He was so white. Looked dead as a hammer." He shook his head. "Sometimes they fake it, you know. But this boy definitely wasn't faking."

Daphne put a hand on Matthew John's arm. He was too old to hold the jailer job, but was never required to handle the inmates himself, except to deal with their food and just generally keep an eye on things. He'd had the job the better part of twenty years when Bill had arrived in Carystown, and there hadn't been any reason to let him go.

"I hope we're not talking about Delmar Johnston," Bill said, but he already knew the answer.

"They couldn't get him conscious," Daphne said. "He's critical."

"Of course he is," Bill said. "Shit." He was thinking that at least he wouldn't have to call Porter Jessup, the coroner, today. They were spending too much time together lately.

"Did he fall down? What?" Bill said. "Did anyone see anything?"

Matthew John shook his head. "It was just me since yesterday afternoon except for a couple of the deputies came in to do some paperwork. We got in one DUI around two this morning, but the Johnston kid looked to be asleep in his bunk. Didn't make any noise. Nothing."

Daphne shrugged. "Maybe he had some kind of seizure or something. Maybe nobody knew about it."

"Seems like a pretty strange damned coincidence," Bill said. "Seeing as he and I were going to have that chat this morning."

"What? Is he some kind of master criminal or something?" Daphne said with a sneer in her voice. "Anybody do a cavity search on him?"

Frank had searched him and was always thorough. But the kid was a dealer. Who knew what tricks he had?

"You got any ideas, Matthew John?" Bill said.

Matthew John glanced away, making Bill wonder if he wasn't hiding something.

Daphne spoke up. "Matthew John might have stepped outside for a smoke once or twice," she said. "No biggie."

"It wasn't but for five or ten minutes at a time, Sheriff," he said. "I've been trying to quit, but I'm just too damned old. If I quit, my lungs won't know what to do with themselves and I'll end up with pneumonia."

Bill took in Matthew John's sallow pallor and watery blue eyes, which seemed years younger than the wrinkled skin that surrounded them. If he were Matthew John, he probably wouldn't try very hard to quit either.

"We don't need to start casting blame about this minute," Bill said. "Let's see what the docs say." He turned to Daphne. "Get someone posted outside Mr. Johnston's hospital room, then you and Matthew John get the paperwork done on this mess. I expect there are one or two forms that need to be filled out." *So much for Delmar Johnston.*

Bill parked the cruiser at the edge of the church parking lot and got out to wait for Margaret. When she came out of the church, he watched her for a few minutes before she noticed he was there. She was wearing her hair differently this morning, the front of it pulled off her face and held back with a barrette at the crown of her head. She looked younger than her forty-nine years and he liked that. He also liked that she didn't go in for the large flowered dresses and stupid hats that some of her church contemporaries wore, as though they were dowdy seventy-five-year-olds instead of women in the prime of their lives. Her look was feminine, just at the edge of sexy. Her low-cut, rose-colored dress hugged the curved hips that he so loved to get a firm grip on.

They had made a cautious kind of love the night before, but, still, there was a distance between them, and he knew it was occupied mainly by the Russell girl. She was young enough to be his daughter, and probably crazy, but a man's desires didn't know any kind of logic. And having a loving wife didn't mean he couldn't think about another woman from time to time. It made him feel guilty as hell, but when he thought about the girl and her soft, clear skin and the firm lines that lay just beneath her clothes, he couldn't help but imagine laying her down in some open field somewhere, or even in the back of the cruiser—anywhere he could have her quickly, desperately. It would be over and done with, so he could regret it and go on.

Margaret waved him over. He blushed, as though she'd read his thoughts, so he took his time crossing the parking lot. It looked like he was going to have to pay for his breakfast with a chat with the busybody pastor and her husband. Fortunately, the newspeople who had come down when the body was found had worn themselves out and seemed to have gone away. With the prospect of a decent breakfast before him, he could handle a few Presbyterians.

"I can't imagine that Freida Birkenshaw had any idea about what's been going on," Margaret said. "She's just not the sort to put up with that kind of nonsense."

"It wasn't too long ago that boy of hers got popped for a DUI," Bill said. "Twice."

"More than ten years ago," Margaret said. "Not so much as a peep out of him since."

Bill nodded to the waitress to top off his coffee. "At least not around here," he said. "But there are plenty of stories about what he's up to out of Mama's earshot."

The crowd was light in the inn's dining room. Late spring and fall were its high seasons. Out in the lobby there was a poster for the town's annual May garden tour. Bill liked to say that flowers and dead leaves were the only things that brought tourists to Carystown.

"Don't, please," Margaret said.

"Don't tell me how to do my job," Bill said, bristling.

Margaret glanced around the dining room and lowered her voice.

"He wouldn't do anything *illegal*," she said. "Not on his own mother's farm. She's so sick, Bill. I don't believe it."

"I just said it was something I wanted to look into. I've got some state boys coming down on Tuesday. They're going to look around," he said. "That's all."

She had a blind spot sometimes when it came to the old families in town. She knew their dirty laundry—and some of it had involved, as a matter of course, her own family. There were limits, though, on what she was willing to believe.

With Delmar Johnston comatose, Bill was at a temporary impasse on the Catlett boy's case, and a good search of the farm seemed sensible. He could detour and check out Charlie Matter, but that would be touchy because of the freshness of the discovery of the little girl's body. He and Margaret still had to live in the town when both investigations were over, and he was having a hard enough time convincing people like the good pastor at church that he didn't believe in ghosts, only hunches. Though, in his own mind, he still didn't know *what* he believed. He only knew that he had come to believe Kate Russell. He decided to change the subject.

"You think you'll go to Lillian Cayley's funeral tomorrow?" he asked.

"I don't know," Margaret said, looking a little relieved. "I didn't know her all that well. Her daughter's sweet."

"I pretty much need to," Bill said. "Is my dress uniform clean?"

"In the closet," Margaret said.

Mostly, his relationship was cordial with the people in the East End. By tradition, it wasn't a very integrated area. In temperament it was a quiet, safe part of town where, unlike the trailer parks and low-income apartments on the northern edge of town, a person could go out for a midnight stroll and remain unmolested.

That Lillian Cayley had been brutally murdered had stunned the East End's residents. Even though many of them had been calling the station, worried about their safety, he still thought that the woman's murder seemed a personal one. Given that nothing appeared to be missing in the house, he suspected that it had to have been someone who knew her and wanted her dead. The daughter had been at work most of the evening, and, according to Mitch, with Paxton Birkenshaw for some time after that. That was another coincidence he didn't quite care for.

When they got back to the house, the answering machine was blinking. Before he could check the messages, the telephone rang.

"Delaney," he said.

"If it's not the ugliest sheriff in town," the voice on the other end said.

"You've got little enough room to talk, Jessup," Bill said. "Don't you zombies take any time off at all?"

"Hey, watch it with that zombie talk," Porter Jessup said. "That's professional insensitivity. I could sue the county over that."

"Go ahead," Bill said. "It ain't my money."

"You're going to feel all guilty about being mean to me when I tell you my news," Jessup said, pretending to be wounded.

"Well, you better spill it then if it'll make you feel better."

"Did you notice anything unusual about that little girl's bones when you got a look at them? By the way, the hair was hers. You definitely found yourself the Moon girl."

"Unusual?" Bill said. "Besides the fact that they were covered in dirt in a shallow grave? That was enough for me."

"Hah!" Jessup said. "See. You people need me after all. You didn't even notice that a femur, her pelvis, and one of her arms were fractured. Not to mention both of her cheeks and a couple of vertebrae."

"No shit," Bill said.

"That's not all. I took a look at her clothes. The only blood I came up with was on the front of the coat, like she'd spat it up. But there was something more interesting."

"What?" Bill said.

"Gravel," Porter Jessup said. "Tiny bits of gravel embedded in her clothes, some of it oily. We'll send it to the state lab to see for sure."

"Sounds like a plan," Bill said. "So you have any thoughts on the how of things?"

"You people really do want me to do everything for you," Jessup said. "Either she jumped off a tall building—which is unlikely because the ankles and the feet would be destroyed as well—or somebody crushed the hell out of her little bones with a couple good swift hammer blows. It's tough to bust up a pelvis that good with a hammer, though it *has* been done."

"I know you're going to tell me that the gravel gave it away," Bill said. "But it sounds like maybe she got herself run over by a vehicle."

"Bingo," Porter Jessup said. "And I wasn't even trying."

Bill wanted to tell Jessup that he was full of it, that he knew he had probably been working on the bones and the clothes day and night since the body came in. But it seemed a cruelty to shoot him down.

"I suppose you're going to want me to recommend you for a raise," Bill said.

"The county already can't afford me," Jessup said. "This one's out of the goodness of my heart." And although there was a joshing tone in his voice, Bill knew that he was partially serious. They had both wanted badly to know what happened to the girl, and now they were that much closer to finding out.

ꜰʀᴀɴᴄɪᴇ ᴋᴇᴘᴛ ʜᴇʀ ʜᴇᴀᴅ ᴅᴏᴡɴ as she walked behind her mother's white casket, her face covered by the pale green veil of one of the hats her mother had rarely worn. She knew that the two hundred people in the sanctuary would be watching her, wondering how she was holding up, waiting for her to break down. She felt like she'd done all the crying she was going to do, but the sounds of the mourners around her, the muffled sobs and throat-clearing, were starting to get to her. Feeling the presence of so many people who had loved or admired or feared Lillian reminded her that Lillian had never really belonged to her at all, that she'd been a surrogate mother to many of them, and a friend to the rest.

The stiff wool dress Francie wore abraded her skin, and in the back of her throat she could taste the last bit of cocaine she'd had more than forty-eight hours before. One phone call to Paxton was all it would have taken and she could have had all she wanted. She wouldn't have smiled through the service, but the fact that her mother's brutalized body lay in the box in front of her might not have felt so surreal and unbelievable if she'd been even a little bit high. While she craved the coke more than she had ever craved any kind of food, she was determined that she was through with it. She would have to keep Paxton away from her if she was going to keep her head clear. *Was she up to it?* Her desire for Paxton was so deep and visceral that she didn't know how she was going to fight it.

A woman leaned out from a pew and stretched her arms across the polished white surface of the casket so that the pallbearers had to halt the bier on which it rested. The woman's sharp cry struck at Francie's heart. For thirty-some years the woman had worked at school with Lillian, and in recent years Francie had often found them relaxing in her mother's backyard, talking over their school days. When the man who was standing beside her gently put his arms around her, the woman crumpled against his gray suit, sobbing.

As Francie waited with the pallbearers for the woman to get out of the way, she felt a flush of heat move through her body. Glancing to her left, she saw Paxton standing a row away from where they'd stopped.

Gone was the easy smile that seemed to come automatically to his lips whenever they saw each other. Fine lines of fatigue pulled at the corners of his bloodshot eyes. His dark suit and crisp white shirt were impeccably neat, as his clothes always were. He looked like a sad, dressed-up little boy, and she wanted to go to him and hold him in her arms.

But her mother was just eight inches away, her casket a final, harsh reminder of her existence and her opinions and her will. Lillian had known, somehow, that Paxton wasn't good for her. Now she was truly torn. A part of her wanted to try to save Paxton, to keep him so close to her that he would need nothing else and no one else to complete his life. But seeing how high he was—recklessly, publicly high—she knew that he was already on the edge of his self-control. And he wasn't holding on to it very tightly. It wasn't his fault, she knew. He was some kind of addict—addicted to sex, drugs, risk. He was sick. But she knew that she couldn't be the one to cure him.

All during the service, she could feel Paxton watching her from the back of the church. She tried to listen to the pastor as he eulogized her mother, staying noticeably away from the subject of her murder. He celebrated her life to frequent, ragged choruses of "Amen." But even as she rose to put the single white rose on the casket, she knew Paxton was watching her, and she silently cursed him for taking this moment from her and her mother.

Later, as she followed the casket out of the church, she knew right where Paxton was standing, but she avoided his eyes. If she looked at him she might relent and let him join her as she knew he wanted to. Or she might scream at him to stay the hell away from her. She knew she could go either way and didn't want to risk it.

The church was so full that she almost didn't see Kate and Caleb standing up against the back wall, a distinguishable space surrounding them. People didn't want to get too close to Kate, what with the discovery of the little girl's body. Francie hadn't talked to her in several days, and so hadn't heard the truth from Kate herself. The suspicion that Kate had been involved in her mother's death nagged at her. *But was she being truly honest with herself? Was it really Kate she suspected?* When she saw that Kate's face was wet with tears, she felt only pity for her.

As the casket was taken off its bier to be carried over the threshold, Francie stepped over to Kate and put her arms around her. When Kate only began to cry harder, she felt guilty. Kate was her friend and she knew she was hurting. Francie pulled away and rested her cheek against Kate's.

"I'll see you later," she whispered.

37

HIS MARY-KATIE looked damned good to him. Even from across the cemetery, Miles could see that she was in great shape. Her face was sad, but in a way that had always charmed him. There was something childlike about his Mary-Katie, an innocence in her aspect that thrilled him whenever he looked at her. The late morning sun mellowed the amber highlights in her hair, blowing softly around her face. He had missed her.

She stood close beside a man who held her arm proprietarily, but Miles wondered if he saw hesitation on his Mary-Katie's part. A reluctance to lean against the man even in her grief? Miles pegged him as one of those outdoorsy types, the kind who would drive a pickup truck, wear Patagonia anoraks, and carry a canvas messenger bag. He had never figured his Mary-Katie as someone who would go after such a schmuck, but she'd been gone a long time. In her desire to start her life over, she'd obviously slipped down a couple pegs on the style scale.

Miles was secure in the knowledge that he was the one who had lifted his Mary-Katie up to his level. Her grandmother had been a nice enough old bird, but not the kind to hobnob with social registry types. It was a wonder to him that his Mary-Katie had rejected him so brutally—violently!—along with all the advantages he had given her. Her ingratitude made him sad.

He wanted to call out to her across the tombstones to startle her. It was like a joke. Miles back from the dead!

She had indeed left him for dead, and part of him wanted her to be rotting away in some women's prison for attempted murder. His Mary-Katie should be the toy of some homely tattooed dyke instead of the Johnny Appleseed character standing beside her. It was only his mercy that had kept her from such a fate. The question was, did she even realize it?

How naive she had been, changing her name to her grandmother's, pretending it would make her invisible to him. Two weeks after she'd rented her little cottage in the country, the agency he'd hired reported back to him. She'd been living at his mercy for more than two years. She didn't know how blessed she had been. *No more. His patience had run out.* The call from the sheriff had merely prodded him out of inaction. If his Mary-Katie was in some kind of trouble, maybe he could help.

How, he wondered, could she have deluded herself for so long, imagining that she would never see him again?

The walking stick he carried now was his constant reminder of her perfidy, and when it had become clear that he would always need to have one with him, he started a collection. In honor of his trip to the land of moonshine and horses, he'd selected one carved from oak and topped with a redheaded serpent whose body twisted and curved so it appeared to be devouring itself.

While a walking stick gave him a kind of rakish air that he liked very much, the pain was less amusing. Dr. Narjal had kept him on morphine for weeks after the surgery. Now, it hurt only when he walked. There was no question that he would ever run again, or play tennis. He'd found it hard to stay in shape, but had managed. That inconvenience was something else for which he'd have to thank his Mary-Katie.

The burial was a brief affair, and the crowd diverse, as at so many southern funerals. He had a vague curiosity about who might be in the casket, mostly because he wondered what connection the person—whom he assumed to be female because of the white box—had to his wife.

When it was over, a number of the mourners surrounded the sheriff, but far more clustered around the stunning young black woman who, by her disposition and actions, seemed to Miles to be related to the dead woman. Prominent in the second group was a well-dressed young man with a shock of white-blond hair who tried to take the young woman's arm and pull her away from the rest of the crowd. She resisted. Miles couldn't hear what was said, but the woman was obviously distressed. The man tried again to get her to come with him, and this time Johnny Apple-seed stepped in and the two men exchanged words. As they argued back and forth, several of the other mourners, led by a woman whose protective movements caused her enormous breasts to sway alarmingly to and fro in her floral dress, engulfed the young woman.

Miles watched as his Mary-Katie hurried over to the sheriff to get him to take some action. But before he could get to the two men, the blond man punched Johnny Appleseed, causing him to stumble back, holding his hand against his jaw.

"Enough, Birkenshaw!" The sheriff's voice was sufficiently loud to carry to where Miles stood.

For a moment the blond man looked as though he would submit, but then he turned his back on the sheriff and the crowd and stalked away. When the sheriff started after him, the young woman called out for him to let him go.

In a move that surprised Miles, the sheriff halted, watching as the blond man hustled to a small Mercedes parked on the other side of the road. Then the sheriff turned and spoke briefly to Johnny Appleseed, who shook his head.

It seemed that the blond man was going to get away with socking Johnny Appleseed, and Miles liked the bastard for it. He thought that he wouldn't mind having a go at Johnny Appleseed himself.

His Mary-Katie went to Johnny Appleseed, who was looking a tad sheepish, and fussed over him. The other young woman, too, came over to see if he was all right. All heads turned when the Mercedes squealed off down the road.

Finally, the crowd began to melt away. Some walked to their cars, oth-ers to houses in close proximity to the cemetery. His Mary-Katie, her Johnny Appleseed in tow, went to link arms with the young woman. As they walked slowly down the path leading out of the cemetery and into the street, the women tilted their heads together like they were two girls in a shampoo commercial. It seemed that his Mary-Katie had made herself some friends in this hillbilly town. He watched as the three of them got into a small blue convertible parked near the cemetery's entrance.

Already he was jealous of both Johnny Appleseed and the black girl. He wasn't sure what would be the result of his reunion with his Mary-Katie, but he was damned sure that it wouldn't include anyone else besides the two of them.

The blue convertible was nowhere in sight, but, sure enough, a taupe-colored pickup truck sat in his Mary-Katie's driveway. That meant that she and Johnny Appleseed were much more than good friends. Miles could hardly blame the guy. His Mary-Katie was an excellent lay even on her worst day. Even half asleep she wasn't so bad.

Aside from the antiques mall, there were no other buildings close enough for him to draw anyone's interest, but Miles knocked anyway to make it look good, though he knew no one was home. After a decent interval, he tried the doorknob. Of course she would lock it. His Mary-Katie was careful that way. But it was an old knob with a single lock in the handle. No dead bolt. His Mary-Katie wasn't being *so* careful. He felt a twinge of disappointment. He had taught her better.

Miles slipped a small leather case from the inside pocket of his trench coat. He liked to have just the right tool for every job. He slid the thinnest picklock from its narrow slot in the case and fitted it into his palm. The lock was old, its tumblers likely nicked and bent. Two or three minutes passed, and he began to think that he would have to try again another day. But he finally finessed the thing. Opening locks was one of his talents, and it irritated him considerably if he came across one that wouldn't give in immediately.

His Mary-Katie's taste had regressed: the inside of the cottage reminded him of her grandmother's house in Beaufort. She'd taken nothing from that house that he knew of, but here were crocheted throws and large, colorful pillows and an overstuffed couch that looked as though one could disappear in its cushions. What a romantic his Mary-Katie was.

Miles walked around the living room touching the things that she had arranged, moving them subtly, needing to let her know in some small way that he'd been there. She wouldn't really know, of course. But he would.

He went over to the secretary and tugged gently on its door. Seeing it was locked, he started for the case, but reconsidered. He was not in any sort of hurry. He felt around the back of the desk and behind the shade, but found nothing. Running a hand along the desk's underside, he picked up a splinter in the pad of his middle finger. As he tried to suck it out, he glanced around. He spotted a vase on a whatnot shelf on the wall.

The splinter wouldn't come. He would have to deal with it later.

Taking the vase from the shelf, Miles shook it and heard something rattling inside. When he upended it into his palm, a small key fell out.

Regarding the key, he wondered what his Mary-Katie had been thinking, leaving it in such an obvious place. Why would she lock the desk at all? There was no evidence of children who might get into her things. Perhaps she was concerned about Johnny Appleseed prying into her life. It was true that she was masquerading as someone she wasn't. She definitely had things to hide. He smiled to think of how naive his Mary-Katie was, still so innocent.

In fact, there wasn't much of interest in the desk. There was a checkbook recording a modest sum and several bills, but nothing going further back than two years. Then he found the photo of himself, slipped in between a blank birthday card (had she been thinking to send it to him?) and a shoe catalog.

He put a self-conscious hand to the side of his head. Since the photo had been taken he'd lost a shameful amount of hair. Pride kept him from the hair weavers or the pills that promised new growth. But he wasn't above letting the stylist rinse a bit of color into it to hide the gray that had shown up since the accident. (Even though he wanted her punished, he preferred to think of his Mary-Katie's attack on him as a complicated kind of accident. She certainly wouldn't have done it if she'd been thinking more clearly. He knew that she loved him more than life itself.)

Looking at the photograph, he regretted the choice of the dove gray morning coat he'd worn for the ceremony. A darker gray would have been a better choice. His Mary-Katie had been young and inexperienced, and he'd had to tell her what would be appropriate.

It had been the sort of wedding that he knew young girls dreamed of, his gift to her to show his trust and devotion and intention to stay married to her forever. Why she never showed more gratitude than she had, he didn't know. He'd found the leather-bound album of their wedding pictures buried in her closet after she ran away, hidden as though she wanted to forget them. He'd given so much of himself to his Mary-Katie, and she had treated him shamefully.

Driven by his hunger, Miles went into the kitchen, to find that she'd returned to the spartan way of eating that he thought he'd educated her out of years before. There was nothing fresh in the refrigerator except a carton of eggs and a large bag of the Granny Smith apples that she liked so much. He grabbed a can from a six pack of diet soda and popped the lid, to drink it down standing before the open refrigerator. Looking around the kitchen, he found a milk crate with a few other recyclables in it and tossed it in. He liked to do his part.

After eating a few of the stale crackers he found in the cabinet, he replaced the box and took a nearly empty jar of peanut butter from its shelf. Taking a spoon from the silverware drawer, he ate some of the peanut butter, rinsing the spoon after each mouthful. Finally, the gnawing in his stomach appeased, he went to look around the rest of the cottage.

The bathroom held nothing of interest except a pair of worn toothbrushes, some men's boxer shorts, and some shaving gear. But when he went into the bedroom and opened the nightstand drawer, he found the .22 that had caused him so much trouble.

Where she'd gotten the gun, he didn't know. He'd surmised that it must have come from the Beaufort house. He couldn't see his Mary-Katie walking into a gun store asking for the best sort of gun to kill her beloved husband. And even the biggest sort of fool wouldn't have sold her a pop gun like the .22. He slipped the gun into his overcoat pocket.

There was little jewelry in the small box on the dresser: a few pairs of gold-plated earrings, a rather good cameo that he thought he remembered seeing on the grandmother, a gold bracelet with some sort of inscription inside (his eyes weren't the best for close-up work, and his reading glasses were in the car), and a couple of necklaces. All of her good jewelry, the jewelry he'd given her (including her wedding ring, he'd found to his dismay) was down at the island house. He'd caught Cammy—the woman who'd been living with him for the past few months and fancied herself his wife—trying it on one afternoon when she thought he was out of the house. He hadn't hesitated to backhand her because of it, though he suspected that she liked to be hit by surprise in that way. Cammy's baser tastes had initially repelled him, but she'd shown him some things in bed that his Mary-Katie could never imagine, let alone do.

When he opened his Mary-Katie's lingerie drawer, he was overcome by the scent of her. Grabbing a handful of her panties, he crushed them against his mouth and nose, inhaling the lavender air of them. Her taste for pretty underwear had grown in their time together, and it was something of which she obviously couldn't let go. The fine lacework caught on his beard, but he rubbed them over his skin anyway, from his lips to his ears to the underside of his chin. He remembered how he would use his teeth to remove panties like these from his Mary-Katie's body, pulling them down to expose the sweet puff of her pubic hair. The scent of the panties gave him an ache in his heart and in his groin. A soft moan came from his throat as he thought of all the nights of their being together that she had stolen from him.

38

FRANCIE STOOD a few feet away from the convertible as Kate said goodbye to Caleb. There was a coolness in the way Kate kept looking away from him, as though she didn't want to hear what he had to say. In the last year, Francie had come to think of Kate and Caleb as an inseparable entity, and the idea that anything was seriously wrong between them shook her a bit. But Caleb was an open, no-nonsense kind of guy. She wondered if their distance didn't have something to do with the discovery of the little Moon girl's body.

It hadn't been lost on Francie that it was found so close to where her mother had died. What connection there was between them, she couldn't imagine. Her mother had never even known the girl. But it seemed a bizarre coincidence.

After Caleb drove off, Francie led Kate into the house. As they crossed the threshold, Kate squeezed her arm.

"I know," Francie said. "It's still Mama's house. Every time I come in here now, I expect her to call out for me to make sure I've wiped my feet."

But today, at least, a breeze swept through the house, ruffling the curtains and cleansing it of the funk that had seemed to descend on it after her mother's murder. The couple from church who had watched the house during the funeral had left the windows open on purpose, she supposed, perhaps thinking to let Lillian's spirit out of the house. She didn't know, but was grateful all the same.

"It doesn't feel right," Kate said. "God, Francie, I feel so responsible."

Francie tensed. She'd been waiting for Kate to speak, to tell her what had gone on between her and her mother.

"I can listen now," Francie said. "I wasn't ready before. I don't know how to explain it, but I wasn't myself."

As they sat in Lillian's still-tidy living room, a rush of words poured forth from Kate, who apologized again and again for not telling Francie sooner, for not trusting her.

"Stop," Francie said. "Stop apologizing, Kate. I don't know if I would have believed you anyway."

"I almost didn't believe it myself," Kate said. "Until they found the girl's body. That night with your mother—I wish I could describe it better. It scared the hell out of the both of us." Her voice was a whisper that Francie could barely hear.

"If your mother hadn't come after me, I don't know what would have happened," she said. "I was losing my mind, Francie. Lillian was the only thing between me and I don't know what. If she hadn't pulled me out of there—I felt like I was going to be sucked into the ground. And I know that sounds insane, like I'm making it up."

"Maybe," Francie said. "But I'm trying to believe you, Kate. I just don't understand why you had to have Mama there."

"It wasn't like I *asked* her to come," Kate said. "I swear. You know how she was. She believed me when I told her about that night I followed— Okay, yes." Kate nodded emphatically. "I was following a ghost and I know how stupid that sounds. But Lillian told me that maybe Isabella was trying to tell me something and that I needed to listen. I needed to find out."

Of course, it sounded to Francie exactly like something her mother would have said. Lillian hadn't been superstitious, but she'd always been open-minded. *You never know how God's going to reveal Himself. You have to listen.*

And the idea of the little girl—the *dead* little girl, Francie reminded herself—asking for help, would appeal to her mother. Girls like Isabella Moon had been her mother's life's work.

"But how in the hell did my mother end up dead in our backyard, Kate?" she said, agonized. "How could someone do that to my mother? Do you think your ghost just up and stuck a *pitchfork* through her?"

She looked at Kate for the answer and wanted, really wanted, Kate to say something. Anything. At that moment, she would have gone along with it if Kate had told her that, yes, she thought it was the ghost. But Kate just sat there looking miserable. Kate had no more answers than she herself had.

Outside, a car door slammed and they looked toward the window. Francie got up.

"Kate," she said. "Do you think you could go in the kitchen and make us some tea?"

Paxton stood on the welcome mat looking even worse than he had at the funeral. And then the scene he'd made at the cemetery! But seeing him standing there, still looking so helpless, distressed her all the more. Should she put him off, or should she take him in and try to make him understand that they couldn't ever be together?

"Baby," he said tenderly. He started toward her, but Kate picked that moment to come back into the living room asking about the teakettle.

"What the hell is that bitch doing here?" Paxton asked. "We don't need her sniffing around."

"Be quiet," Francie said. "I'll call you later. Just go home, Pax." She laid her hand gently on his chest. If she could just get him to take his time and let her handle things, she knew they'd both be better off.

But instead of leaving, Paxton wrapped his arms around her, pulled her to him, and kissed her hard. Francie didn't pull away, but neither did she respond enthusiastically. This wasn't the way she wanted Kate to find out about her relationship with Paxton. But something had come loose in Paxton. He'd always been impulsive, but now she feared he'd completely lost his grip. He let her go.

"I guess you're coming in," Francie said. She stepped back into the living room. She gave Kate a weak smile and held her hand up to indicate that Kate should hold on a minute before she spoke.

Kate was having none of it.

"I don't know what to say to you, Paxton," she said. "Francie?"

"For starters, you can leave," Paxton said. "This isn't any of your business."

"Stop it," Francie said.

Paxton held on to her hand like an anxious child. She turned to Kate.

"There just didn't seem to be a good time to tell you. I kept meaning to, but I couldn't bring myself to do it." Suddenly, the enormity of her secret, her reluctance to tell even her closest friend about her relationship with the man standing beside her, came to rest on her heart. Had she been so ashamed of herself, of Paxton, that she thought she had to lie? Now that her mother was gone, she had to ask herself if it had been worth it. She knew now that she wasn't meant to stay with Paxton. It was already over.

Kate looked confused for a moment, but then Francie saw realization dawn slowly on her tired but still lovely face.

"Please understand, Kate," Francie begged. She wanted to tell her, too, that it didn't matter now anyway. But she knew that she owed it to Paxton to break it off with him when they were alone, even though the idea frightened her. There was no telling how Paxton would react in his current state. She no longer felt safe with this man who, for so long, had been her only lover.

"I don't think it was me you didn't want to tell," Kate said, her voice flat. She was staring at Paxton in a way that caused Francie to catch her breath.

"You'd better shut up," Paxton said, taking a step toward Kate. Francie pulled him back. Caleb and the sheriff weren't around to protect Kate, and she knew that Paxton meant to frighten her.

"Tell us, Paxton," Kate said, pushing him further. "What did Lillian have to say about the two of you? She knew, didn't she?"

"Mama didn't know anything," Francie said, defensive. *Was she so sure about that?* There had been hints from Lillian, but she hadn't wanted to listen. So much of her life in the past few months had been about pretending.

"You don't know shit," Paxton said. "You're just some loose piece of trash that blew into this town."

Francie saw that Paxton had begun to perspire, much as he had in church. He looked worn out, as though he'd been doing manual labor all day and threw on a jacket and tie when he'd finished up.

"Stop," Francie said. "Both of you. I want both of you to leave."

"What happened to Lillian, Paxton?" Kate said. Francie had never seen Kate look so determined, so certain and angry. Speaking up about the ghost seemed to unleash something in her. Francie was still having a hard time believing her story, but it was harder still to believe the direction in which Kate's accusations against Paxton were heading.

"I'm begging you, Kate," Francie said. "Just leave us alone. I'll deal with Paxton. I promise everything will be okay."

"You're a motherfucking freak is what you are!" Paxton screamed at Kate. "Making up all that bullshit about a ghost. You don't know anything about any of it."

Kate tried to speak over him, accusing him of knowing about the death of Isabella Moon, and Francie heard her say something about his being involved in both murders. She thought her head would explode from the noise the two of them were making. Kate's impossible accusations echoed in her mind. There was no way in the world that Paxton could have killed her mother. He wasn't capable of it and couldn't have hidden it from her even if he had done it.

Francie picked up a tall glass vase that Lillian had kept on the coffee table. Although she'd never liked its garish turquoise color, she said a frantic, silent apology to her mother as she threw the thing, to shatter against the wall.

Kate and Paxton were immediately quiet. They stared at her.

Francie could hardly speak, she was shaking so.

"Kate," she said. "You have to go. Take my car if you want. Whatever. Just leave."

"But I can't leave you here with him, Francie."

"Just go. Please, Kate," she said, her voice pleading.

Paxton was oddly silent as Kate looked from Francie to him and back to Francie again. Francie could see that she didn't want to go, but that she would because she trusted her. Francie didn't feel particularly trustworthy. She had no idea what she was going to do when the door shut behind Kate.

39

KATE KNEW she wasn't in any kind of shape to walk the mile and a half to the cottage. Her side and ankle ached from her run-in with Janet, and by the time she was out of the East End and reached Carystown proper, her feet were sore in the narrow black pumps she'd worn for the funeral.

She called the cottage on her cell phone, thinking Caleb might pick her up, but there was no answer. They had reached a tenuous sort of détente, one that didn't include any plans for even a few hours into the future. *Was he in Janet's bed at that moment? Could he be so callous?* She should have told Bill Delaney when he was standing in her living room that Janet had tried to kill her. By letting Janet off the hook—for the moment, anyway—she knew she had let Janet win in some way. But she had enough trouble in her life right now without adding the spectacle of weeks in court with Janet. The day might come when she would turn Janet in, but right now she had more important problems to deal with.

Her heart ached for Francie. Why had she taken up with that animal, Paxton? And why hadn't Francie trusted her enough to tell her? Lillian was the answer, of course. Now, in Kate's recollection, Lillian's genteel dislike for Paxton became palpable evidence of their enmity.

Kate had assumed that Paxton was just another spoiled playboy. But she'd obviously been wrong. Paxton was dangerous. Murderous. As she walked, she even looked over her shoulder from time to time, worried that he might have followed her.

When she reached the courthouse building, and the Sheriff's Department beside it, she almost passed by, anxious as she was to get home and off her feet. But concern for Francie propelled her through the Department's front door.

Today there were several people sitting in the waiting area who stared at her as she came in. A man in coveralls leaned to whisper something to the woman beside him. As Kate walked by, did she hear the words *cemetery* and *dead girl*? Maybe. Or perhaps she was just being paranoid.

When she saw that the young man from the newspaper was at the desk talking to the same female deputy who'd been there on her first visit, she knew that nothing those other people had said mattered. It was the reporter who was the problem. How he'd found out that she was even involved, she could only guess—he and the deputy looked pretty cozy to her eyes. She turned to hurry back out the door.

"Miss Russell!" the young man called out. He hustled away from the desk. "This is great," he said. "I've been trying to reach you."

"Please," Kate said as she stepped outside. "I just came in to talk to the sheriff."

"He's not here, ma'am. In fact, I'm waiting for him myself," he said, walking alongside her. "Did something else happen? Did you get any more messages from the little girl? I'm sure her mother would want to know. You should tell me the whole story. Help folks understand. Even if you want to talk to me off the record, I can help you."

"Leave me alone," Kate said. "There's nothing to understand. They found her, and that's all that matters."

"That's a good quote," the young man said. "See? We can work together. You can trust me."

When they reached Carystown's small bakery, Kate was momentarily slowed by the wonderful smells coming from its open door. She couldn't remember when she'd eaten last, and the smell of cinnamon made her feel faint with hunger. Without warning, she stopped and turned to face the reporter. Out of the corner of her eye she could see people watching them from inside.

"Here's a quote for you," she said.

When she leaned toward him as though she would speak confidentially, he stepped forward eagerly.

"Go fuck yourself!"

The crowd inside the bakery broke up in laughter, and Kate hurried away, her ankle screaming with pain. How dare the guy confront her on the street? She was no criminal, but he was making her look like one.

Astonishingly, he kept after her.

"What about Lillian Cayley?" he called, rushing to catch up. "I understand that you're part of that investigation as well."

Kate walked faster, pretending not to hear him.

"You deserve to tell your side of it," he said, bearing down on her.

Even though the afternoon was cool, Kate was perspiring as she passed the Bridge Street storefronts. Janet's office, her former workplace, wasn't far away. Everywhere she turned, she was faced with failure, with certain disaster. How she wished that she had been brave enough to leave town the week before! But the sight of Isabella Moon walking beside her mother—*had the child become such a normal sight to her?*—had paralyzed her, as though the dead girl had some sort of power over her. Worse, she had no energy left to run away.

Somewhere behind her a police siren stuttered on and off. Kate looked over her shoulder to see a sheriff's cruiser creeping along the other side of the road. Bill Delaney put down the cruiser's window. She could have wept with relief at the sight of him.

"Mr. Klein," he called. "You so hard up for stories that you're chasing people on the public streets now?"

"Just doing my job, Sheriff," he called back, not slowing.

"I suggest you cease and desist, Mr. Klein," he said. "Looks to me like you're bothering the lady."

"It *is* a public street, Sheriff," the young man said. "Nothing wrong here."

Kate slowed, wanting to know what the sheriff would do. When she glanced back, he waved her over to the car.

"Get on in," he called to her.

Kate didn't hesitate. She didn't care if he thought she was a murderer. Then again, would he be stopping for her if he didn't want to help her?

"Catch you later," the young man said as she brushed in front of him to step off the sidewalk. There was a note of malice in his voice that belied his saccharine smile.

The sheriff leaned across the cruiser's front seat and pushed open the passenger door for Kate, who slid inside, grateful.

"That guy's been a pain in my ass ever since he joined that rag of a newspaper," he said. "If you'll pardon my French."

"That's okay," Kate said. "Thanks."

"I don't know that you'll want to thank me when I put some questions to you."

Kate put her head back against the seat and closed her eyes. *So tired. Tired of running, tired of being pursued, tired of it all.*

"It doesn't matter," she said.

Gatchel's, on the outskirts of town, was more of a lunch counter than a place where people bothered to come for dinner. Kate had eaten there only a couple of times, and always with Caleb. Its peeling, concrete exterior and narrow windows gave it a closed-in, unwelcoming look. The sheriff held the fingerprint-smudged door for her and followed her inside.

"Hey, Bill." A suntanned woman in shorts that were three months ahead of the weather and a T-shirt that read BODACIOUS in glittering letters looked up from a magazine spread out on the counter. "Early dinner?"

She took in Kate with a look of blank curiosity. She smiled.

"Just coffee, Shelley," Bill said.

"Decaf for me, if you have it," Kate said.

"That'll take a minute," the woman said, getting off her stool. "I made some of those krispy rice thingies this afternoon. I'll get you all one of those, too."

Before Kate could demur, the sheriff told the woman that would be great.

The sheriff got his coffee first. Kate toyed with the napkin-wrapped fork and knife on the speckled tabletop.

"Maybe you want to tell me what's on your mind before I start flappin' my gums," the sheriff said.

"Am I really a suspect in Lillian's death?" she asked.

"I won't say you haven't been on the list," he said. "But you were never at the top of it."

"What if I told you I know who did kill Lillian?" she said.

She searched for corresponding interest in his eyes, but found nothing more than mild curiosity. She had hoped to shock him into trusting her more. She asked herself why it was so important that he trust her. He was nothing to her. Just a man with kind eyes.

"I wouldn't want to think you'd been withholding information," he said. "But I took a big flier on you a few days back and it paid off. I'm willing to be flexible."

The waitress served Kate's decaf and put a chipped plate containing two sticky squares of rice cereal and marshmallow cream on the table.

"My kids can't get enough of these," the waitress said.

Kate gave her a small smile of thanks and watched her go back to her magazine at the other end of the restaurant.

"Shelley's okay," the sheriff said. "Her husband took one in Afghanistan and never made it home, but she keeps the chip off her shoulder. Loves those kids to death."

Kate nodded. There were so many people in town that she hadn't bothered to get to know. Soon they would all know who she was, if they didn't already.

"So, who's the winner?" the sheriff said.

Kate saw no reason to hesitate. Francie's life might be at stake.

"Paxton Birkenshaw," she said.

"You don't say?"

The man was hard to read. But at least he hadn't laughed at her.

"You saw the way he was at the cemetery today," Kate said.

"People get emotional at funerals," the sheriff said,

"He came by Francie's earlier while I was there and it was pretty clear that they're together. At least I think they've been seeing each other."

"Free country," the sheriff said. "You got racial problems with that?"

Kate felt herself flush with irritation. "That's the stupidest thing I've ever heard," she said. "Francie is my best friend."

He took a sip of coffee and put the cup down. "My wife, Margaret, she had a best friend back in Louisville who she still talks to almost every day. That woman knows everything about me from what kind of toothpaste I use to what brand of underwear Margaret buys me. And if that woman were on the other side of the world and some guy looked at her sideways, she'd have Margaret on the phone in two minutes flat."

"Don't believe me, then," Kate said. "When he kills Francie, too, you can console yourself with the fact that your wife has a better best friend than I do. Unsolved murders seem to be your specialty anyway."

That stung him, and Kate was glad for a moment. She hadn't wanted to hurt him, but he'd put her on the defensive. The notion that Francie had hidden her relationship to Paxton from her had hurt *her* feelings badly.

The sheriff recovered quickly.

"Who are you?" he said, keeping his voice low. "And I don't mean, 'Who in the hell do you think you are?' Although that could certainly apply here. I mean that a woman named Katherine Russell with your Social Security number died down in Beaufort, South Carolina, a few years back, and you seem to have just appeared on the face of the earth just about two years ago. Add to that your recent association with two murder victims, and now an alleged murderer—not to mention the fact that someone was so desperate to run you down the other day that they broke through a fence and did a couple thousand dollars' damage to someone's land—and I'd say you've either got the damnedest luck of any human being on the planet or you're living a big fat lie."

This was the moment she'd been dreading since she fled the island. So many times she'd wondered how she would be exposed. She'd lived in fear of someone—Caleb, Francie, Janet—finding out, perhaps turning her in. But the anticipation had apparently been the worst of it. Now she just felt more tired than ever before, as though she'd come to the end of a long, long journey.

"Is someone looking for me?" she asked. "The police?"

"Should they be?"

"Not if there's any justice in the world," Kate said. They were silent for a moment. As she stared down into her coffee, she could feel him watching her. "What are you going to do?"

"Right now, I'm trying to decide if you might be a danger to the community," he said.

Nothing. He was going to do nothing. But what was it going to cost her?

She thought of Kyle Richardson. Would she do something so base to keep the world from finding out about what she'd done to Miles? *She knew she would. As many times as she had to.*

"What do you want from me?" she asked.

As though he'd read her mind, a brief, guilty shadow crossed the sheriff's face and he glanced away from her.

Yes, there was something between them. He had wanted her at some point, she knew. She also knew she'd be lying to herself if she said that she didn't find him attractive. Not so much physically, though he was in pretty good shape and had a rugged look that had been softened some by his fifty-some years. It was his solidity, his trustworthiness, that she found appealing, his way of commanding attention in every situation. He seemed safe, the kind of man who could wrap her in his arms and protect her from every bad thing in the world. Attraction had nothing to do with it.

"Does what you're running from have anything to do with anyone in this town?" he said, falling back into his professional, rather stern manner.

"No," Kate said. "No one here at all." *Just a guy a few states away that I pray to God is dead.*

"Frankly, I don't have time to deal with whatever you're hiding right now," he said. "As you so astutely observed, I've got more than one unsolved murder on my hands. You're more valuable to me here than you are locked up or in your car on your way out of town."

Kate was silent.

"Now. Did Birkenshaw say anything helpful? Did he implicate himself in any way?" he said. "Or did Lillian Cayley hint at anything before she died? Think. This is important."

Kate told him about Lillian's coolness toward Paxton, her concern that Francie needed looking after. She left out the part about seeing Lillian's spirit in Francie's apartment, that Lillian had appeared through Francie herself. She didn't want to push him any further than she already had.

"Nothing concrete? Did she say if he ever threatened her?"

"She never talked about Paxton specifically," Kate said.

"Not enough."

"When I accused him of killing Lillian, he got angry, violent—you saw how he was at the funeral. At Francie's, he acted like he wanted to kill *me*."

"That's it?"

"I'm sorry. I wish it were more," Kate said. "Francie needs to get away from him. I just wish I could help her."

"Maybe you have," he said. "It's a start anyway."

40

WHEN BILL DELANEY drove her home, the first thing Kate noticed was that Caleb's truck was gone from the driveway, her convertible parked in its place. The cottage was dark.

"I'll wait until you get inside," the sheriff said. "Unless you want me to come in and take a look around."

"That's all right," Kate said. "I'll be fine." She felt like they had gotten past the awkwardness she detected between them earlier, and there was a part of her—a weak, needful part—that *did* want him to come inside. But she didn't trust herself.

"I guess I don't need to remind you that you want to stay in Carystown for the foreseeable future," he said. "For your own safety."

"You think Paxton Birkenshaw doesn't know where I live?" she said. "I don't feel particularly safe, Sheriff."

"I'll take care of Mr. Birkenshaw in due time," he said.

"I just hope it's not too late for Francie. Or me," she said. She got out and shut the car door behind her.

Kate turned on every lamp in the living room and kitchen before heading back to the bedroom. She was hungry, but knew there was nothing in the house, as usual. If things had been better between them, Caleb might have picked up a bag of groceries after he left Francie's. But things were a long way from that sort of thoughtfulness. Her usual popcorn would have to suffice for dinner. At least it would be better than the cloyingly sweet block of crispy treat that she'd choked down at the diner because she didn't want to hurt the waitress's feelings.

Where was Caleb? Deep inside, she knew he wasn't lying when he told her again and again that he wasn't in love with Janet. Men didn't fall in love with Janet. Janet consumed men the way she consumed chocolate—greedily and for temporary effect. Kate just didn't know if she was ready or even *wanted* to forgive Caleb. Maybe it had all happened for the best.

When she reached to flip on the bedroom's overhead light, she found that it was burned out. With the dim light from the hallway, she started to make her way over to the bedside lamp, but caught the heel of her shoe on something on the floor, tripped, and almost fell.

"What?" she said. She turned on the lamp.

When she saw the shoes lying on the floor, her first reaction was puzzlement. She'd worn that particular pair only once, to the arts gala—the same one at which Caleb had told her he'd been unfaithful with Janet. Then she saw the dress laid out on the bed. But it wasn't just the dress. There were earrings, too, and several bracelets. Someone had laid everything out carefully, arranging the dress to look like the person wearing it lay down and just disappeared. The earrings were spaced evenly, just where they might have been; the bracelets had been slipped onto the wrist of the dress's transparent right sleeve.

Why would Caleb do such a thing? she wondered. But then she knew that it hadn't been Caleb. Whoever did it had chosen that dress, the one she'd worn to the gala. Caleb would not have been that cruel. Janet would.

Kate sat down on the bed, fingering an edge of the fine silk. The dress had cost her most of two weeks' salary, but she'd fallen in love with it the minute the saleswoman at Petals took it off of the rack. The sheer top with its crystal buttons and silky black shell underneath was elegant, but sexy. She'd bought it even though it reminded her strongly of many of the clothes she bought when she was with Miles. Caleb had whistled at her when he saw her in it.

"Now *that's* the kind of dress you should wear every day," he said.

Kate quickly drew her hand back from the dress as though it had bitten her.

Miles.

How like Miles! Not confronting her directly, but trying to frighten her.

One night, not long after they'd been married, they were sitting in the hot tub drinking wine when he began to talk about a girl he'd dated in college. Had Miles even finished college? She doubted it. The girl had "potential," Miles told her. She hadn't thought to ask him at the time what sort of potential he was talking about. Now she had a better idea.

He'd bought her things, Miles told her. Tasteful clothes, ladylike shoes. Even jewelry. And she had begun to wear them when they were out together.

"She wasn't as pretty as *you*," Miles said. "But, like I said, she had potential."

Then one of the girl's "stuck-up friends" told her that Miles had helped to steal a test for a psychology class, and they fought about it. (Even then, she knew better than to ask if he'd actually stolen the test.) The girl was drunk and had thrown a cup of beer at him where he sat behind the wheel of his car.

"I threw her out," Miles said. "Nobody pulls shit like that with me." He'd left her downtown and started to drive himself home, he said. But he had to pass by her house, which she rented with two other students. Finding the place dark, he parked his car down the street and waited. She came home in a cab about half an hour later.

"I could tell she was still drunk as hell," he said. "So I waited until she turned out her bedroom light and went to bed." Then Miles had started to laugh.

"She was lying right there on her cheap-ass futon in the middle of the room. Passed out. In five minutes, with just a key chain flashlight, I found every single thing I'd bought that bitch. Some of the stuff still had tags," he said. "I got cash back for almost all of it."

It wasn't so much the story that had shocked Kate, but the satisfied smile Miles wore when he finished telling it. She would think of the poor girl from time to time, lying there alone, miserable and disappointed and drunk, then passing out. She'd always wondered what the girl had felt when she awoke the next morning and realized Miles had been there while she was sleeping. Now she had her answer.

Panicked, she sprang to open the bedside drawer.

The .22 was gone.

Her little cottage, which had always seemed so remote from Miles, so safe, felt suddenly like a prison, a cage in which she was supposed to sit and wait for him to come and get her. She'd been such a fool, deluding herself for so long. If Miles had really been dead, the police would have found her years before. Miles, though—Miles was patient. He liked to savor his revenge.

Where could she go? The sheriff had told her not to leave, but did she have a choice? Then there was Francie to think of. She couldn't just abandon her to Paxton. *What could she do for Francie, really?* But the thought of Lillian's faith in her kept her from jumping into her car to run away from Carystown.

She picked up the telephone to call Caleb. He had to have gone to his own place. But she put the phone down again. She couldn't wait for him to come all the way there to pick her up. Miles could be sitting outside, not a hundred feet away from her. Watching. Waiting.

Kate threw her toothbrush into her purse and took the few hundred dollars of emergency cash from a canister in the kitchen. She opened the front door, half anticipating that Miles would step out of the darkness, but the porch was empty. After locking the door behind her, she rushed to the car. The car doors locked automatically when she turned the key in the ignition, but she locked them again with the button to reassure herself.

As she pulled out of the driveway and onto the street, she paused a moment to look at the home that had been hers and hers alone and wondered if she would ever see it again.

Caleb's house stood alone at the center of a hundred-acre piece of land that his parents had left him. As Kate pulled into the driveway, she heard Myrt and Earl, the two beagles that Caleb's father had kept for hunting, send up a howl. She parked beside Caleb's truck, close to the house.

Before she could get her purse out of the car, Caleb had the front door open and was calling her name.

"Kate, you've got to watch coming up that gravel so fast," he said as she ran toward the house. "You'll wreck your suspension."

When he saw her face, he stopped the lecture.

"What is it?" he said. "What's wrong?"

She looked back over her shoulder. There had been a couple of other cars behind her on the road. She was afraid that Miles might have been in one of them.

"Can we go in?" she said, looking up at Caleb.

In answer, he took her arm and brought her inside. He had a fire going in the great room and the television was on. All was normalcy here, contentment. A man's retreat.

"I know you already think I'm crazy," Kate said.

"I just want to understand, Kate," Caleb said. "I want this to work. I really do."

"I need you to listen to me," she said. "And I don't know what you're going to think when I'm finished. But I'm in trouble, Caleb." She paused, looking at his broad and honest face. *Not so honest, maybe. He's had his secrets.*

"You may not want to have anything to do with me when I tell you who I really am."

41

FRANCIE PUSHED the plate of noxious-smelling food a few inches away from her.

"Come on, baby," Paxton said. "You've got to eat more than that."

"I've had enough," Francie said. With Paxton here, she felt full inside, but it wasn't a feeling of satisfaction. It was a stolid, dead feeling that was so devoid of emotion that it could hardly be called a feeling at all.

"You didn't know I could cook, did you? One of the farm managers' wives taught me how to make it. It's white-trash food, for sure. Who knew your mother would keep that cheese in a box stuff around?"

"Don't talk about Mama," Francie said. "Please."

"Poor baby," Paxton said, coming around the table to comfort her. "It's this place. You shouldn't be here. Do you want to go back to your apartment, or maybe a hotel? We can stay wherever you want."

But Francie knew that she belonged in the house. She owed it to her mother. There was some kind of redemption here, some forgiveness that she knew she could receive from her mother. She could feel it.

"No," Francie said. "I want us to stay here." Paxton had to stay here, too. He was part of it all. She let him put his head against her shoulder as he knelt on the floor.

"Let me take care of you," Paxton said.

Francie touched his fine blond hair, which was so soft her fingers slipped through it as they would through water. She'd had a doll once whose long blond hair was almost as fine as Paxton's. She had played and played with the doll's hair, trying to work it into elaborate braids and twists, but it was impossible to get it to do anything but lie there, shining and golden. Even the clips and bows she put in it slid off, useless. The doll was probably still packed away in the attic, where her mother had stored so many of her discarded toys.

"Let's go in the other room," Francie said. The kitchen was the room that most reminded her of Lillian, and the smell of the tomato-soup-covered mess that Paxton had made was starting to get to her.

As they left the kitchen, Francie almost told Paxton that her mother had probably bought the boxed cheese for the food pantry at church, but she decided not to. Paxton didn't need to know everything about her mother.

"Not in here," Francie said, leading Paxton through the living room. They went down the hallway, past the closed door of her mother's bedroom and into her own room.

When she flicked on the overhead light, Paxton walked slowly, almost reverently, around the room, picking up pictures, reading the diplomas and award plaques on the wall.

"Hey, I remember reading about this," he said, tapping her high school valedictory certificate. "I wanted to call you or something."

"You should have," Francie said quietly. There had been nights, long ago, when she lay on the bed in this room, touching herself, imagining Paxton there with her. They were childish fantasies, focusing on intense kisses and a lot of rubbing against one another because she had been too young and inexperienced to imagine more.

"Of course I should have," Paxton said, taking her in his arms.

Francie closed her eyes, pretending she was a girl again and Paxton was the thin, muscular boy with deeply tanned skin and shining white teeth that she remembered, and not the dissipated, dangerous man she knew he had become. But if he had changed so much in that time, what, then, had she become? She felt tears slip from beneath her eyelids and onto her cheeks.

Paxton kissed her cheek where the tears had fallen.

"Poor Francie," he said.

"Why?" Francie whispered.

But Paxton covered her mouth with his own before she could say more, and she tasted him and the terrible dinner and a hint of tobacco and perhaps the mouthwash he'd used earlier in the day. After a moment it was just *him,* and she began to feel for the buttons of his shirt and the buckle of his belt, and before long she was tearing at his clothes with anger. If he was surprised, he didn't show it, but only answered her with equal violence, jerking down the tight panty hose that had bound her all day and unzipping her staid dress with enough force to break the zipper.

Before pushing her onto the bed, Paxton reached over and flicked out the stark overhead light.

It was right, Francie thought. They should be in the dark together, hidden from the light.

Francie opened her eyes to darkness. Paxton lay sleeping beside her, his arm thrown across her belly as though he would keep her from getting up.

Something, some sound, had wakened her. Before she was fully conscious, she thought it might be her mother moving around the kitchen, making herself a midnight snack as Lillian sometimes did when she was a girl. But Francie knew that wasn't right. Her mother was gone.

And yet.

She gently pushed Paxton's arm away. As she stood up from the bed, she felt semen run down the inside of her leg in a warm stream. She dabbed at it with the sheet, then slipped into her robe.

Out in the kitchen the sounds continued—a chair scraping its way across the floor, utensils being dropped in the sink. Strangely, she was unafraid as she crept silently down the hall on the thick carpet that Lillian had installed only a few months before.

"Mama?" Francie whispered as she approached the kitchen doorway.

The light was on in the kitchen. She'd expected it to be a mess, but nothing was out of place except the few dishes Paxton had used to make their supper and the plates and utensils on the table. But the room didn't smell of encrusted tomato sauce and cheese. It smelled thickly of honey. The smell was so strong and suffocating that Francie put a hand to her mouth.

"Mama?" she said.

There was a movement at the window in the back door. When she hurried to open it, she found that it was ajar the slightest bit. The fresh night air hit her with all its cold force, but even outside she could still smell the honey.

The night beyond the doorway seemed deep and unyielding; it might have been eleven o'clock or two in the morning. The neighbors' houses were dark.

Francie stepped out onto the patio, tripping the automatic security light.

"Are you out here, Mama?" she said.

There was an answering sound, the clatter of metal and wood, and she looked toward the garage.

Francie's breath caught in her throat when she saw her mother standing near the garage. She was struggling with an armful of gardening tools as though she were getting ready to put them away after her late-day gardening. Lillian's back was to her, but Francie knew it couldn't be anyone else.

Before she could call out to her, something stirred near the garbage cans at the edge of the patio.

"Pudding!" her mother said, turning around. "Scat!"

Francie wanted to weep at the sight of her mother's face. It didn't matter that the light was poor. Her mother looked much as she had the last time they were together. Her features seemed softer, but, as always, there was kindness in her face.

Francie put out her hand, wanting to touch her mother even though they were so far apart. It was then that she saw the little girl rise up from behind the garbage can, where she seemed to have been hiding from Lillian.

Lillian started toward the girl, a look of intense concern on her face.

"Child," Francie heard her say. Her mother held her hand out to her, but the girl turned away from Lillian and looked at Francie. She was a drawn and pale thing, clad in a yellow coat. Francie held the gaze of her dark, sad eyes for a moment.

"Mama!" she called out, aching for the touch of her mother's hand.

But Lillian was turning the other way, toward the yard, distracted by something Francie hadn't yet seen or heard.

Then Francie did see. Paxton, his golden blond hair shimmering in the dim light, rushed up behind Lillian. Raising his arms in the air, he swung some kind of tool at her. He swung it, hard, against her head. He hit her two, three times as Francie watched, a scream frozen in her throat.

Lillian fell to the ground. Finally, Francie found her voice and screamed, the sound of it rising into the sky so that she thought she could never stop, so filled she was with terror and longing and fear.

The scream seemed to twist and wind, and she closed her eyes to block out what she knew she would see next, and she couldn't stop the scream. It reached and grew until she heard another sound, a voice, calling her name. Someone was shaking her violently and she opened her eyes to see Paxton, begging her to stop screaming.

Francie threw herself backward, away from him, and the sleeve of her robe rent in two, the larger part of it remaining in Paxton's clenched fist. He moved off the edge of the bed and stood facing her.

"Get away from me!" Francie screamed. "I saw you! I saw you!"

"Calm down," Paxton said, trying to get his own breath. "Don't do this," he begged.

"How could you do that? You hit her with that—that thing! How could you do that? How could you kill her?"

"I tried to tell her, Francie," Paxton said. "She wouldn't listen to me. She hated me, Francie. She always hated me. You don't understand."

"Oh my God," Francie said. "You have to get away from me. You have to get away from me. Oh my God." Francie grabbed Paxton's abandoned pillow and held it to her stomach. She felt as though she would retch.

"Please, Francie, please," Paxton said. His voice now was full of tears. "Don't send me away. We're together now. It's a whole new start. We can go anywhere you want, do whatever you want to do. Please, please."

At that moment the only thing keeping Francie from leaping across the bed and strangling Paxton with her hands was the grip she had on the pillow. Even now it smelled of Paxton, of the shampoo he used.

"Baby, please. We'll go to Paris. Tomorrow," he said. He was pulling on his pants as he spoke. "You told me you love Paris. Anywhere. We'll get away from these memories. All this bad shit."

At that moment she knew that Paxton was insane. Did she pity him? *Yes, dear God forgive her, she did pity him!* But she wouldn't be moved.

"You have to leave, Paxton," she said, gaining some control of her voice. "You have to leave, now, and don't come back here. Do you understand? You cannot come back to me."

"You can't," Paxton said. "We have to be together. I know *you* understand, Francie. Please tell me you understand."

Every nerve in Francie's body demanded that she do her best to kill this man who stood, half naked and crying in front of her. But was he even a man? He'd always been a boy. He always would be. What had she done to herself, loving him? She already knew what she'd lost.

"Now, Paxton," she said, calmly. "You have to give me time. You have to give me this. You have to get away from me now."

He saw that it was something. His face brightened some and he wiped away the snot and tears with the sleeve of the shirt he'd put on.

"All the time you need," he said. "You don't think you'll forgive me, but you will, Francie. I swear you'll forgive me. And you'll even see . . . Well, we won't think about that right now. We have to concentrate on being together."

Francie didn't trust herself to say anything more. But she watched Paxton as he gathered up his shoes and belt and wallet and keys. When he passed near where she sat on the bed, she saw how he almost leaned close to kiss her but stopped himself. He gave her a small nervous smile.

"All the time you need," he said. "It'll come out all right. You'll see, Francie."

A minute later she heard the Mercedes start up in the driveway. The light from the car's headlights swept the wall above her as she sat there waiting, wondering what in the hell she would do, now that she was truly, horribly alone.

42

THE PICTURESQUE INN where Miles had a room hadn't been his first choice. There was a decent chain motel out near the highway, but it was closed for remodeling. He didn't like the eccentricities of the inn, its hundred-year-old floors that ran downhill in odd places, the peeling horse-hair plaster, the attitude of the staff that half measures were excusable because the inn was "historic." Its single amusing attraction was an oak-paneled pub room in which hung antique maps and large game heads, each wearing a look of surprise that seemed to indicate that it had no idea why it was indoors, stuck on a wall. Below the heads were homely wood-burned plaques bearing their names: Bocephus, Tom T. Bull, Mr. Sparky, Miss Trotters, Deer John.

His dinner in the restaurant had been unexceptional, a cassoulet of sorts that the waitress said contained buffalo meat and local farmers' beans and vegetables. Given that it was early spring and he wasn't completely stupid, he knew she was lying about the vegetables. But the bread had been good, a rye sourdough that seemed an appropriate accompaniment to the cassoulet. He washed the meal down with a cabernet that he sus-pected had been gathering dust for a long time, given the quality of the few diners that surrounded him.

Bored after dinner, he'd gone to the pub for a nightcap, though it was only about ten. He wanted to get a good night's sleep so he'd be fresh for his Mary-Katie.

From where he sat drinking his cognac, he had a particularly good view of the pub's single corner booth. The woman seated there commanded—

no, demanded—attention. She was definitely feeling no pain, but she was keeping it together. Her black hair looked like it had been hurriedly pulled back into a loose chignon, but the rest of her was crisp in a bright fuchsia blouse and slim black pantsuit. As she lifted her glass, Miles could see how beautifully manicured her nails were. Her substantial white gold jewelry and heavy diamond rings put off their own intense light. When she turned slightly to glance about the room (Was she looking for someone? Waiting for someone? In a town like this, a woman like her could hardly expect to remain alone for long), he saw that she had high cheekbones, but they were full and doll-like. As a baby, she would have been one of those round-faced darlings that people couldn't keep their hands off. Her lips were made up to look pouty, as was the fashion, but he could tell that she wasn't the sort to take any crap from anyone. But the most charming thing about her was that her stockinged feet had slipped out of her shoes, one tucked up beneath her on the banquette. He hadn't expected to run across a woman like this.

Miles told himself that he was here for his Mary-Katie, no one else. Another woman would be a distraction, and he needed to stay focused. But that didn't mean he couldn't look. Appreciate.

The waitress leaned against the bar, talking community college drivel with the older bartender, whose amused expression barely hid the fact that he would happily screw her with or without her consent if she let her shirt fall open any farther. After a few minutes she disappeared into the nearby restaurant.

"Crystal." The woman in the booth leaned forward a little to see where the waitress was.

"I think she stepped out for a smoke," Miles said. The innocuous jazz coming from the ceiling speakers was low enough that he didn't have to raise his voice much.

The woman nodded, obviously satisfied. She seemed the sort of woman who was used to getting her questions answered quickly and directly.

"This place gets quiet pretty quick," Miles said. "Folks must wake up early around here."

"We're not all farmers," the woman said.

"Thank God for that," Miles said.

"You're not one of the timber people," she said. "What? Are you here selling pharmaceuticals or something?" Her words were crisp; she was forming them carefully.

"You might call me a banker," Miles said. "But it's mostly pleasure."

The woman shook her head as though he were speaking nonsense. "I hope you brought your own," she said. "This place ran out of pleasure a long time ago."

"Too bad," Miles said.

Without another word, she slipped her shoes back on her feet and gathered her purse. She left two tens on the table.

"Good night," she said as she walked past his table. He saw her glance catch on the red head of the cane, and there was a flicker of consideration in her eyes.

"To pleasure," Miles said, raising his cognac glass to her.

When she was gone, the waitress reappeared and headed for the abandoned booth, slipping one of the tens into the pocket of her black apron.

"May I have my check?" Miles asked.

The waitress fumbled in her apron pocket for a moment, then pulled it out. She dropped it on the table.

Miles handed her a twenty without looking at the bill. This was strictly an all-cash trip. The woman at the front desk hadn't wanted to let him take the room without a credit card, but an extra hundred had changed her mind.

"Keep the change," he told the waitress.

There was no thank-you from her, just a perfunctory "Good night."

Out in the large, empty foyer that served as a lobby, Miles found the woman from the bar standing in front of the brochure rack. A bright orange folder that had HIDDEN CAVES emblazoned across its front dangled from her fingertips. Her eyes were reddened from whatever she'd been drinking and her lipstick was slightly smudged, but she looked damned good to him. The pantsuit was cut so it didn't hide any of her curves—in fact, its severity seemed to accentuate them.

She glanced again at his walking stick before she spoke.

"I live one street over," she said. "Second house on the right. If you want a nightcap."

Miles had no compunction about taking advantage of a drunk woman and he suspected that she would be an enthusiastic lay. But she wasn't what he wanted. He needed to stay focused on why he was in this stupid town, and getting involved with a woman like this one would only complicate things. In a town this small, she could even be a friend of his Mary-Katie's. (Though he doubted it. He suspected that this woman had very few female friends.)

Part of him hated to say it, and he tried to say it gently, so she wouldn't be offended. "Maybe some other time. Thanks."

It didn't please her. Her eyes narrowed and she peered at him from behind her heavily mascaraed lashes. Maybe she was seriously drunk, after all.

"No problem," she said. "Pity fucks bore me, anyway."

As Miles watched her rush out the door and down the inn's front stairs, he thought about chasing after her and beating the hell out of her with the stick. His heart was suddenly pounding in his chest and he knew he might have killed her. But he stood still until he was again under control. He looked around, wanting to make sure that no one had witnessed his humiliation.

Picking up a copy of the local newspaper that lay on the registration desk, he went up to his room. A few minutes later, as he reclined against the generous bank of pillows on his bed, he put the woman from the bar out of his mind. Reading the coverage surrounding the funeral he'd attended that morning, he learned just what sort of trouble his Mary-Katie was in.

43

"JUST WHEN I THINK you couldn't be more of a jerk, you do yourself one better," Janet said, pouring Paxton a glass of brandy. "Of course she threw your ass out. You're a sorry piece of shit, Pax."

"You always have that special turn of phrase, Janet. No wonder you're the popular girl," Paxton said with a self-assurance he didn't quite feel. The episode with Francie had shaken him. Janet knew that they'd had a fight—he'd told her only enough to get him the company he needed. He hadn't wanted to go home alone to lie in bed, waiting for dawn until, perhaps, the sheriff came and hauled him off.

"Screw you," Janet said, curling her feet beneath her as she sat on the leather sofa. Her silk robe fell open at the chest and he saw that she was naked underneath it.

Even though it was well after midnight, Paxton had seen a faint light from the television burning in Janet's bedroom, so he hadn't hesitated to ring the bell. Now they were in the library of her house, the only room she'd left untouched since her husband's death. The furniture was heavy-footed and covered in hand-tooled leather or burnished to a mellow shine. Row after row of books filled the floor-to-ceiling shelves, and the discreet wet bar tucked behind a games table contained a selection of rare scotches. The old man had had a man's good taste, or perhaps the room had been furnished by someone other than one of the town's chintz- and tassel-loving matrons who passed for professional decorators. Janet herself looked out of place here, polished and brittle even in her half-drunk dishabille.

He knew she hadn't been out much over the past few days. A small basket of mail sent over from her office sat just inside her front door, and he'd gotten a whiff of something rotten coming from the dishes piled in the kitchen sink when he'd gone looking for a glass of water. He could hardly blame her, though. Both of their lives had been weirder than hell lately.

"If you're not nicer to me, then I won't share my goodies with you," he said.

"How about I won't tell your mommy you're here, and you give me what you've got?" she said.

"I'm just messing with you," he said, sliding his stash across the massive glass-topped coffee table toward her.

She snatched the box before it stopped moving and expertly laid out some of its contents on the table, making four long and perfectly straight lines—two for each of them. She took her time, throwing her head back after doing each line to keep it going. Francie was always more tentative, as though each time were her first and she couldn't quite believe she was doing it.

There was a chance that Francie was suffering now that she knew about his killing Lillian. But he would make it up to her. Now, though, he knew she needed to be alone for a while.

"You really were in a hurry getting away from your nursey," Janet said, pointing at him. "Look at your shirt."

He looked down to see that he was missing a button and the plackets were misaligned, one button off.

Paxton sank his face into his hands for a moment. Just outside the room, Janet's grandmother clock struck one.

"I don't know if she'll take me back," he said, his voice breaking. "It's all so fucked up."

"Jesus, Paxton," Janet said. "She doesn't know what we did, does she? Tell me you didn't go confessing to her."

"What?" Paxton said, looking up at her. "No. Quit worrying about that. This isn't about that. Or you." Why had he come here, of all places, to the home of the most self-centered woman on the fucking planet? *Everything* was about Janet to her. But maybe that's what he needed right now, a diffusion of focus around the situation. Things had been way too intense at Francie's house. Something about the wild look in her eyes when she'd woken him up, like she'd just had the hell scared out of her. What had she said about *seeing* him kill her mother?

"The last thing we need is Nurse Goody Two-Shoes shooting her mouth off," Janet said.

Paxton took his turn at the table. He loved the immediacy of coke. It instantly put him in a good mood, even when things were going wrong like they were now.

"Don't be harsh," he said after a moment. "I come here for a little comfort and all you give me is a hard time."

Janet slipped off the couch, licked her finger, and ran it over the table-top to get the last crumbs of coke. She stuck her finger in her mouth and sucked at it lasciviously, making him laugh. Then she climbed onto his lap. Leaning close to him, she began to trace the outer rim of his ear with her tongue. By the time she was pressing her breasts against his chin, guiding one of her sweet nipples into his mouth, he knew that he was in danger of coming before she could unbutton his pants.

"When do you think they're going to have the funeral for the kid?" Janet said. They had ended up in her bedroom and were sharing the dregs of a pint of freezer-burned low-fat butter pecan ice cream. "It's just dumb luck that that cracker Charlie Matter never told the sheriff that I was out there that day."

"Enjoy it while it lasts," Paxton said. His buzz was slipping. The ice cream was good, but overly sweet. There was something unpleasant, too, about the smell of Janet's rumpled sheets, as though she'd had any number of men there before him. She was starting to annoy him. *Needy, needy Janet.* The sex with Janet was outfuckingstanding, but he was beginning to think that if he was going to keep Francie, he maybe needed to give her his full attention.

"What do you mean, 'while it lasts'?" Janet said. She grabbed his bare shoulder to try to turn him around to face her.

"I mean, the sheriff may be a loser, but he got lucky finding the body," he said, getting out of the stale bed. A shower sounded good to him right now. "You could be in some deep shit."

"*Me?* That's because *you* didn't bury the body well enough, asshole!"

Janet said, her voice raised. "You told me you'd help me, that you'd take care of it. *I* wanted to take her over the county line—anywhere but around here. But no, you bury her right under everyone's noses like it's some kind of joke."

Paxton sneered. "So you think the kid's ghost wouldn't have taken your buddy Kate Russell out of town?"

"It's still your fault," Janet said. "And don't bring up that bitch. That ghost stuff is a bunch of bullshit."

"I recall that it was you and not me who hit the poor kid with that monstrosity you call a car," Paxton said.

"It was a fucking accident!" she screamed. "It was a fucking accident and you said you'd help me!" Janet was suddenly up and flinging herself at him, trying to strike him on the arms, the chest—anywhere she could land her hands.

"Whoa, whoa," Paxton said, trying to fend her off. "Quit, damnit!"

He was finally able to wrestle her off him, and he pushed her onto the bed, where she crumpled tearfully and tried to gather the soiled top sheet around her naked body. He loved to play rough games with Francie and Janet or whomever, but he found actually manhandling a woman distasteful. Men he had no problem with, but women were a different story. There were things that a gentleman didn't do, and he despised Janet for driving him to it.

"I don't think they're going to figure out more than that someone ran her over," he said, trying to keep the anger and frustration out of his voice. "But if you keep acting like the town flake instead of the ball-breaking bitch you really are, honey, then they will start looking at what might be wrong with you. You'll say something to the wrong person, or you'll pass by the sheriff's office one day and decide you have to drop in and confess. If you think you feel bad now, imagine how you'll feel being locked up in the state women's facility." Actually, he suspected that Janet would do pretty well in prison. She was a survivor. But if she went, she would take him down with her, and he had enough to deal with now that Francie was falling apart as well.

She stared up at him. He could see that he was getting through to her.

"I'm the only one who can possibly connect you to the kid," he said. "I've still got that stupid scarf you left in your truck. But I can get rid of that, and Charlie doesn't even remember you were there that day or he would've said something by now."

"If he'd just sold me the place when I first asked him," she said, sitting up. She hurriedly wiped her tears away with the back of her hand. "It was his own damned fault. How many times did I go out there? I can't believe I begged that son of a bitch."

"You know he liked it," Paxton said. A pissed-off Janet was far better than a sulking, guilty one. "He just wanted to get close to that firm little ass of yours."

"What a creep," she said, reaching again for the sheet to pull it around herself as though Charlie Matter were there watching her, wanting to touch her. "I don't know why I even wasted my time. There's a place out in the west end of the county—the land's more level and there aren't twenty outbuildings to knock down. It's a great setup for a spa. Less traffic and close to the county airport. I could get celebrities in here."

Janet's eyes, though still shot with red from the tears and alcohol, were shining now. Whether it was from the coke or excitement, Paxton didn't much care.

"See," he said. "All you have to do is keep your head." Standing over her, he put his hand on her mussed and tangled hair, cognizant that his penis was within biting distance of her mouth. He squatted down beside her in case she flared up again.

"It'll be easy," he said. "Chances are it'll all just go away once the kid's buried and people move on to something else."

"No. I bet you were right the first time," she said. "Now that they know she's dead, they're going to want to know who did it."

"You watch," Paxton said. "They can't even figure out who killed Francie's mother. The answer's right in front of them, but they'll never get it."

The look on Janet's face slowly turned shrewd, considering. He'd seen her wear the same look when she was dealing with personal injury lawyers.

"Why?" she asked. "What do you know about Lillian Cayley?"

"I'm just an interested party is all," he said.

"Sure," she said. Her usually expressive face was suddenly unreadable to Paxton. He couldn't tell if she'd figured out that he'd killed Lillian and just didn't care or simply pushed the unpleasant thought away from her mind. Finally, she stood up from the bed without saying another word and went into the bathroom, shutting the door behind her.

When he heard the water in the shower come on, he knew he had nothing to fear from Janet. Pulling on his pants, he hurried downstairs to find the coke. He was feeling better, but a couple of lines would improve his mood even more. The idea of having sex with a clean Janet appealed to him, and he thought that he might even catch her before she got out of the shower.

Was everything just the result of dumb luck? *Janet let the water course over her face and chest, feeling it caress her skin. When Paxton had taken the girl to bury her behind the cemetery, she'd retreated to the shower, turning up the hot water until she could barely stand it. It had been the only thing that could stop her shaking.*

Charlie Matter was alone at the co-op. Because it was a slow time of year, some of the others who lived and worked there had part-time jobs in town or at the Buyer's Mart.

"Another year, six months," Charlie Matter said. He stood close enough to Janet that his sour smell nearly gagged her. But business was business and she stood unflinching. "What's the difference to you? Plus, you'd be putting all the good folks out here out of work. You've got to remember, it's not really up to me. We're a democracy, and not everyone here thinks money is that important."

"Who's to say I couldn't get them work?" she said. "A resort needs grounds-keepers. They could make this place something special."

"Right," Charlie said. "And the first fancy client you get in here who's come to get rubbed down with pig's fat or palm leaves or whatever and doesn't like Kyla's tattoos or Darrin's dreadlocks says she's too spooked to come back or even stay, and my people are standing on the sidewalk in front of the unemployment office."

"I never would've suspected you of being such an altruist," Janet said. The guy was full of shit and they both knew it. She also knew—about herself—that she didn't care so much about Chalybeate Springs (though she thought the name itself would sell the spa), but hated that Charlie Matter was being so stubborn about selling it. She'd started the negotiations well before Richard's death, and the prospect of developing the spa, along with the new house, was

just what she needed to keep herself going. Too many people in town thought she had no feelings, that what she'd had with Richard was not so much a marriage as it was a business arrangement: an old man's last fling with a vibrant young woman (who was, they were certain, after his money). But those fools were so wrong.

"Why six months?" Janet said. "You keep telling me that. Why not now?"

Charlie Matter smiled. "I've got to get back to work," he said. "Won't be long before the bees start waking up. Winter was hard on the hives this year."

Janet got into the Range Rover. Her cell phone buzzed with a message, but she ignored it. "Pig," she muttered as she watched Charlie Matter swagger his way toward the orchard where the co-op kept its beehives. There was a part of her, far down inside, that hated men. All men. Manipulative bastards, every one of them. Richard hadn't quite been the exception, but he'd been sympathetic to her needs. He had seemed to delight in letting her have her way, and she'd known instinctively when she shouldn't push him. Compared to Richard, other men were just plain small.

As Charlie Matter disappeared behind one of the greenhouses, she threw the Rover into reverse and backed up fast, coming within inches of one of the co-op's rusting vans. Still cursing Charlie Matter's obstinance, she put the Rover in drive and sped down the co-op's rutted road, the Rover taking the bumps as though they weren't even there.

In how many dreams would she relive that moment, that hideous, shuddering moment when she saw a flash of yellow appear and quickly disappear just at the front right corner of the Rover, and felt the silent (yes, it was silent), easy breaking of something beneath the Rover's right front tire? It might have been a long branch or a berm of gravel or even an unlucky fox. She slammed on the brakes, afraid to look behind her.

Pleaseohpleaseohpleaseohpleaseohplease let it have been a fox or a tree limb—but somehow she knew it hadn't been. Her life paused in that moment, suspended in the knowledge that she'd done something irreconcilable, irretrievable. The cell phone was ringing, but she didn't hear it. She was listening for something else, but there was only silence beyond the unconcerned rumble of the Rover's engine.

It is the nature of some people to immediately rush toward their mistakes, to confront them right away as though sudden action might erase them or dull the consequences. Such a thing wasn't at all in Janet. Despite her aggressive business reputation, she was a very careful person. A quick study, she always gathered all the information she could before she made a decision. Before she even approached what looked like a bright pile of rags in the road behind the idling Rover, she noted that she had rounded a curve and was well hidden from the co-op's buildings; neither was she in sight of the highway or the farm's entrance. She could also see that the thing in the road was a child, the dark-haired girl who had answered Charlie Matter's door on one of her visits.

"Little girl," she whispered. Was that her own voice that shook like a frightened old woman's? "Little girl."

She knelt beside the child, bits of gravel from the road digging into her knees. She touched the girl's shoulder, which seemed to be in the wrong place, just a couple of inches off. But the girl didn't move. Her dark eyes stared up at the naked branches of the trees above them and her mouth was open a bit.

Unable to look away from her soft, motionless face, Janet felt around for the girl's hand. "Please don't be dead," Janet said. "Please, God, don't be dead."

There was no pulse in the wrist, which seemed to Janet to be the size of a doll's. In her adult life, she'd never touched a child like this. There had been no time for children.

Janet saw, in her mind's eye, the events to come. In fewer than five seconds she saw the ambulance, the police cars, the television cameras, the courtroom, Charlie Matter accusing, accusing, accusing, the hours alone in her room, the stares of the people who had once been her friends, the horrid loneliness. No. She opened the Range Rover's rear door.

The child was light in her arms. She had to bend the girl's knees slightly to get her to fit in the width of the Rover's rear compartment. A faint, putrid odor of urine came from inside the girl's coat, making Janet gag. Glancing over her shoulder, she checked to see that no splash of blood or errant hair ribbon lay on the road to hint at what had just occurred. Still, though, the girl's eyes were open. Janet grabbed the wool picnic blanket she kept in the Rover for emergencies and hurriedly tucked it around the girl's body and over her face.

As she drove back toward town and to her house, her hands shaking so badly that she was afraid she might steer into the opposite lane, her mind raced to think what she would do next. It wasn't until she arrived home and was shutting the garage door behind the Rover that she knew she would call Pax-

ton, who was her friend, her confidant, her sometimes lover, whom she'd known and cared for (in her own way) since long before she'd married Richard. Paxton would understand.

Janet knew she'd made a mistake going after Kate when she came upon her walking south of town. *What if she'd succeeded in running her down? It would've happened all over again!* She simply hadn't been herself since the sheriff found the girl's bones where Paxton had buried them. She'd been blinded by hate and, worse, fear when she'd seen Kate. If Kate had never shown up in Carystown, no one would ever have known that the child was even dead.

But she might've driven right past Kate—maybe just easing toward her the slightest bit to scare her—if it hadn't been for their argument about Caleb. It wasn't her fault that he wouldn't stop bothering her, that he was so pussy-whipped by Little Miss Kate that he couldn't deal with his own guilt and had to pick at it, pick at *her,* until he felt better. Just as it hadn't been her fault that the Moon girl was walking almost in the middle of the road where anyone could've hit her. But if none of it was her fault, why couldn't she escape the weight of it all? Why couldn't she step out of the shower a clean and guiltless woman? It had been two years, *for God's sake,* since the girl's death. Why wouldn't it go away?

Above the sound of the water, she heard Paxton's knock on the bathroom door. When she didn't answer, he let himself in. She could see the outline of his body through the thick glass of the shower wall. What did it matter that he'd murdered Lillian? He was her only friend.

"Can I come in with you?" Paxton said, sounding like a boy pleading for a treat. "Or do you want to be alone?"

Alone. No, not ever again! When she had first heard about Kate's experience with the ghost of Isabella Moon, she was puzzled that it was Kate being haunted and not she. Then again, she knew that she didn't need some nighttime visitation to remind her of what she'd done. It was the silence she remembered that frightened her.

44

"BILL," MARGARET SAID, jostling him awake to take the telephone. "It's Daphne."

"I'm here," Bill said. He took the phone from Margaret and looked at the clock to see that it was after seven-thirty in the morning. It was a hell of a way to start the day, not even hearing the telephone.

"Hey, Sheriff," Daphne said. "The state called. They won't be able to get their guys down here until tomorrow. Some paperwork screwup."

"Not on our part, I hope," Bill said.

Daphne gave an irritated snort. "Not likely," she said. "I faxed it right up there like you told me."

"Don't get up on your dignity, Daphne. It's too early for attitude."

"That's not all," she said, ignoring him. "That Lucy from the mayor's office is all over the voice mail this morning because she read about Delmar Johnston in the paper. She wants you to call her."

"What do they say over at the hospital?" Bill asked.

"No change. Still comatose," Daphne said. "You won't guess what took him out."

"Quit with the games," Bill said.

"They think it might be rat poison," she said. "How weird is that? It's not like you can get high from it. And we sure don't keep it around the cells."

Bill wasn't happy to hear about the poison. He'd been hoping that Johnston's illness had been caused by food poisoning, or maybe smuggled-in drugs. The poison put a whole new complexion on things.

"Make sure that search warrant for the Birkenshaw place is handy, and double-check that it covers the main house. I'm going out there today. I'll be in the office in fifteen minutes," Bill said.

"But the troopers can't come until tomorrow."

"Step over to the prosecutor's office and make sure we've got a valid one for tomorrow as well. And where's Mitch?" he said.

"Right here," Daphne said. "You want to talk to him?"

"No," Bill said. "Just tell him to hang around until I get there."

"You don't think you're rushing this, going out to the Birkenshaws'?" Margaret said when Bill got down to the kitchen. "You've got half the state police coming tomorrow."

He was secretly relieved to get the state involved, though it made him look like a piker. There was just too damn much on his plate. And it was looking like he had that asshole Paxton Birkenshaw to thank for most of it.

"I don't choose the criminals," he said. "Mrs. Birkenshaw's no doubt a good woman, but her son needs to be locked up, and the sooner the better."

Margaret slid a banana and a glass of orange juice across the counter to him. But she pressed her lips together in a way that told Bill she wasn't finished.

"I just think—" she said.

"You've got to let go of this, Margaret," Bill told her. "This isn't 1968 and Millar P. Birkenshaw doesn't own the town or all the judges anymore. And his son doesn't get to do whatever the hell he wants just because he always has. Carystown isn't the same town you grew up in."

"You actually think that I want Paxton Birkenshaw to get away with breaking the law for sentimental reasons?" Margaret said. "What kind of person do you think I am?"

Bill was tired of the distance between them, and he hated to see the hurt, angry look in his wife's eyes.

"You know better than that," he said. "You just need to be realistic."

"And you just go ahead and dig that hole deeper," she said. She turned and went upstairs. Her footsteps quickly crossed the hallway above his head, and Bill heard the bedroom door shut. Margaret never slammed doors, but he could always tell the difference when she was irritated.

He wanted to follow her. He knew he'd been too hard on her. She loved Carystown and couldn't bear to see big-city troubles messing it up. But right now he needed to make a phone call to Frank that he wasn't looking forward to.

The news about Delmar Johnston only supported his suspicions about Mitch, who had been at the jail, cleaning up some paperwork, around the time Johnston was poisoned. Mitch was a show-off, always living way above his means, and while Bill had never imagined that he would stoop to attempted murder, he had a hunch and knew he had to follow it. The botched tire impression bugged him, too. Was it possible that Mitch was covering for Birkenshaw?

"Sure," Frank said when Bill told him what he wanted. "I can't say I'll be happy to do it, but if you're sure, we'll be there."

"I hope I'm wrong," Bill said. "Maybe we can all have a good laugh about it later. I'll give you a ring on your cell when I've got the time nailed down."

Bill took his time on the way out west of town. A misty rain fell on the windshield and put a shine on the asphalt. Whenever he was on the road and saw other officers driving, or even troopers, they seemed to be in a hurry, flashing lights or no. The truth be told, he wasn't anxious to get out to Bonterre. There would be trouble with the old lady if Birkenshaw himself were there.

Mitch sat in the passenger seat talking on his cell phone, trying to put off some young thing from up in Lexington. The girl shouldn't have had his department cell phone number, but there it was. Bill knew that he'd been too lax all along with Mitch and the other younger deputies. They acted like kids sometimes, not much better than the underage ones they occasionally busted for buying booze. Mitch was a particular disappointment, and Bill blamed himself.

"Sorry," Mitch said, flipping the phone shut. "What is it about a woman that makes her think because you're out of her sight, you're in somebody else's bed?"

Bill wanted to ask if that wasn't usually a pretty safe guess, but he didn't.

"What's up with the Cayley case?" he said instead. There was no sense in tipping Mitch to his suspicions about Birkenshaw, especially if he was involved.

"You saw the coroner's report," Mitch said. "Looks like maybe a tool got her first. Maybe a tire iron?"

"What about the daughter?"

"Francie?" Mitch said. "Her alibi's a little sloppy, but I'm trying to imagine what would make a nice girl like her want to stick her mother with a pitchfork after whacking her on the head. That's some nasty shit."

"Any sign that she has a substance problem? Or did you look into that?"

"No," Mitch said. "I just don't see it. She's got a steady job. The neighbors said she was pretty close to her mother."

"Just asking," Bill said.

"So, are you saying you want me to look at her harder?" Mitch said, defensive. "Is that what this is about?"

"Whoa," Bill said. "I'm only looking to find out who killed the woman. You handle the case how you see fit."

Mitch didn't reply, but Bill knew he'd gotten to him.

Bill showed the warrant to the Birkenshaws' housekeeper, who merely shook her head and let them inside.

Freida Birkenshaw kept them waiting in the two-story foyer. Once upon a time it would have overwhelmed Bill, with its marble floors, massive chandelier, and elaborately carved chairs that looked large enough to seat a race of giants. The only things in the room that appealed to him now were the sculpted bronze thoroughbreds displayed in lighted cases at either end of the room. He knew very little about art, but he could tell that they'd been done by a number of artists over a long period of time. One of the largest was a single, wild-eyed stallion who seemed poised to break through the glass and run through the foyer and out into the pastures beyond the house.

"Those will go to a museum when I'm gone," Freida Birkenshaw said, making her way slowly, carefully down the stairs. The housekeeper hovered near her elbow, looking worried.

Bill had heard that a small elevator had been installed somewhere in the house, but he suspected that Freida Birkenshaw wanted to make an entrance.

"Paxton won't know what to do with them, and Flora doesn't like to dust them. She has to do it only once a month, but she still complains, don't you, Flora?"

"Yes, ma'am," said the woman at her elbow. "But only because you stand over me like they're babies. If you'd leave me alone, it'd take me only five minutes."

When they finally made it downstairs, Freida looked over the search warrant. Bill waited without saying anything. There was nothing she could do about it, though he was surprised she didn't have a lawyer on the spot.

"So you want to rifle through our drawers, do you, Sheriff?"

"I don't like to do it, ma'am," Bill said. "But I might as well tell you that I'll be back tomorrow with a crew from the state police to search the rest of the farm."

"So I get the personal treatment here at the house? How thoughtful," Freida said.

"Is your son here?" Bill asked.

"I haven't seen him since yesterday," Freida said. "Why?"

Mitch cleared his throat. Freida looked to him and back to Bill.

"What does Paxton have to do with any of this?" she said.

"There are a few questions I'd like to ask him," Bill said. "As long as I'm here."

"Then it's just as well he's not here," she said.

Bill made sure that he and Mitch stayed close to each other. With Freida following close behind with the housekeeper, the search was long and cumbersome. The warrant hadn't been easy to get, given that no one, especially the judge, wanted to piss off the Birkenshaws.

They started downstairs in the more public areas of the house. Bill had never seen so many pantries filled with china and heavy silver. Mitch also seemed awed by all the drawers filled with knives, forks, spoons, julep cups, punch cups, and serving trays. They both were impressed with the late Mr. Birkenshaw's gun collection, and this time it was Freida's turn to clear her throat. Embarrassed, Bill elbowed Mitch and told him they needed to move on.

Out of deference to the old woman, Bill stayed out of her bedroom and sitting room, unwilling to believe that she would tolerate her son hiding anything in her private spaces.

They did a cursory search through the four guest rooms and the housekeeper's room behind the kitchen before they took on Paxton's suite.

"Does your son spend a lot of time at home, ma'am?" Bill asked, directing Mitch over to the nightstands on either side of the bed.

"Flora, I need a cup of tea," Freida said. "Will you bring it up?"

Flora left the room.

"I don't monitor my son's comings and goings, Sheriff," she said. "He's a grown man."

"Still, you must know who he spends his time with," Bill said.

"If you're asking me if he brings home a posse of homeboys to take drugs and play pool in the rumpus room on Saturday nights, no," she said. "Paxton doesn't bring his friends home. Women either."

"Is there a particular woman?" Bill said. "Maybe local?"

"Why don't you just come out and ask me if he's brought Francine Cayley here? Isn't that who you're talking about?" Freida said. "I don't know her very well, but Miss Cayley really doesn't seem to be the type to be involved in the drug trade."

"Do you like Miss Cayley?" Bill asked.

"My feelings about Miss Cayley are irrelevant, Sheriff. I'd appreciate it if you would get back to whatever it is you think you're doing in my house so you're out of here quickly. You've already noted that we don't have a methamphetamine laboratory in the basement, so I imagine you're close to being finished."

"Mitch. Find anything?" Bill said.

"Yes, sir," Mitch said. He held up a small glass vial. "Look's like coke to me."

"Bag it up," Bill said, glancing at Freida Birkenshaw, who for once had nothing to say.

As Mitch bagged and labeled the vial, Bill said, "I'm going to need to take a look in these dresser drawers. Do you mind if I just set them on the bed?"

"You're wasting your time and mine," Freida said.

While Bill was pawing through a drawer stuffed with white socks and cotton boxer shorts, Flora came back with a tea tray and set it on a table.

"Tea, Sheriff?" she asked.

"No, thanks," Bill said. Sitting down for a cup of tea and a chat with Freida Birkenshaw sounded like a special kind of hell.

The last drawer he had to deal with was a huge one at the bottom of a massive cherry armoire. It was the sort of thing Margaret loved, the kind of furniture she'd grown up with. They had a few of her mother's antiques in their house, but Margaret had felt burdened by so many of the things her mother left and hadn't wanted to move them to Louisville when she died. He wondered sometimes if Margaret missed living in a large house with people to wait on her. If so, she'd never said, and he was grateful.

Bill began to pull out piles of wool sweaters and regretted it immediately. There was nothing here. They *were* wasting their time.

"What's that?" Freida Birkenshaw said from her chair.

"What?" Bill asked.

"That purple thing," she said. "The one in your hand."

Bill looked down to see a purple wad of woolly acrylic. When he shook it out gently, it unfolded to reveal a pattern of black and white Scottie dogs down its length.

"I've never seen that before," Freida said. "It looks like a child's scarf."

"Yes," Bill said. "It does."

"Hey," Mitch said from the bathroom doorway. "That Moon girl. You asked me about a scarf a few days ago."

Freida stood up with the help of her walking stick. "It must belong to one of my great-nieces. Flora must have put it in there by mistake."

She looked at Flora.

"I guess I might have," she said doubtfully.

"Of course you did," Freida said, turning back to Bill. "Give it to me before you start accusing my son of more nonsense!"

She snapped her fingers at Bill. He was reminded of someone reprimanding a dog. He handed the scarf to her.

"Hey, Sheriff," Mitch said. "What are you doing?"

"We're not here to look for scarves, Mrs. Birkenshaw," he said. He turned back to the drawer and began refilling it with the clothes spread on the bed.

"Flora, take this," Freida said. "Get it out of here."

Flora took the scarf with both hands while looking nervously at Bill. She folded it and left the room.

Thus far there had been nothing to connect Charlie Matter and Paxton Birkenshaw except the comatose Delmar Johnston. The idea that Paxton Birkenshaw might have something to do with the death of Isabella Moon hadn't occurred to anyone—except, perhaps, Kate Russell. But he suspected that had more to do with her dislike of him than any fact. Still, Paxton Birkenshaw, whom he had always thought of as an extremely shallow man, was suddenly revealing heretofore unimaginable depths. There were a lot of questions that he apparently held the answers to. Now, it was just a question of tracking him down.

He put the drawer back into the armoire and stood up to brush the dust off. Margaret would be interested (eventually—the tension between them couldn't last forever, he hoped) to hear that the remarkable Birkenshaw house looked grand and imposing, but that when one got down to handling the things inside it, it was far dirtier than their own.

Freida Birkenshaw had retreated to her bedroom by the time Bill and Mitch reached the front hall. Before they were out the front door, Flora hurried into the hall after them, a look of worry on her face. Bill suspected it was a look she wore often, given the mercurial nature of her boss.

Bill stopped when she approached and leaned in close to him, her wrinkled mouth inches from his ear.

"I raised that boy from a pup," she said. "But I can't say he's no murderer."

"I appreciate your help, ma'am," Bill said. "Nobody's calling anyone names."

"That scarf is safe as houses," she said. "Don't wait too long, though. I got a granddaughter wants to start beauty college next year, and ain't no one else going to hire me for what Miz Birkenshaw pays me."

"No, ma'am," Bill said. "It'll be no time at all."

~

In the cruiser, Bill called Frank on the cell phone.

"Frank," he said. "You get that report done?"

"We're on our way," Frank said on the other end.

Bill wondered a moment if Mitch could hear Frank's voice, but a glance at Mitch told him that he was oblivious to everything but the intricacies of his own phone.

"Ten-four," Bill said, and hung up. There was a burning sensation in his stomach. He didn't like what he was about to do—it felt dishonest to him to set up Mitch. And now, with the complication of the Moon girl's murder, things felt completely screwed.

"Your kids coming down to stay with you this summer?" Bill asked. They had just passed into town. Charlie Matter's place was north of town, but they would have to go through town to get there.

"Hell," Mitch said. "I don't know what she's got the kids talked into. One wants to go to camp, the other one doesn't want to have shit to do with me. They're cute as anything when they're babies, but then they hang around their mothers for a while and damned if they'll listen to their old man. You and Margaret sure dodged that bullet."

How many times had he heard that kind of backhanded sympathy from people's mouths?

"We weren't exactly looking to dodge that particular bullet," he said. "It just didn't happen."

"Well, don't be too sorry," Mitch said. "They're sure more trouble than they're worth."

Bill decided to let it go. Mitch's rudeness put a kind of distance between them, and right now, distance maybe wasn't such a bad thing.

"Have you got anything on your mind you want to tell me?" he asked.

Mitch looked out the passenger window as the shop fronts of Carystown crept by. Traffic was heavy for a Tuesday.

"Can't think of a thing," Mitch said.

"You ever run into Birkenshaw on your travels? Maybe one of those disco bars in Lexington?"

"What kind of bars?" Mitch said with a laugh.

"You know what I mean," Bill said. "You get around enough."

"Sure. But you can bet your ass I'm not looking to hook up with rich white boys from Carystown," Mitch said. "What are you trying to get at?"

"It's a small world, is all," Bill said.

A heavy-duty pickup pulling a cattle hauler blocked the intersection at Main and First Avenue as it tried to negotiate the narrow turn, and traffic was backed up almost all the way to the station. There was almost certainly an amateur at the wheel. One of the drawbacks of living in a town smack in the middle of some of the state's best pastureland was the preponderance of farm boys who thought that if they could drive a tractor, they could drive anything. When they finally were able to make some progress, Bill passed the road to the station house without slowing down or stopping.

"I thought we were headed back in," Mitch said.

"There's something I need to take care of north of town," Bill said.

"Well, I need to get back into the office a-sap," Mitch said. "Will it take long?"

"We're almost there," Bill said.

45

WHEN PAXTON AND JANET awoke in one of the guest rooms—Janet's mood, too, had improved with their shower and the last of the coke, and she'd been more than happy to change their location—it was almost two in the afternoon. The bed was comfortable enough, but as soon as Janet saw how late it was, she was out of it.

"You can stay here if you want," she said. "*I'm* going into work."

Before Paxton could even raise his head from the pillow, she was on the bedroom's phone extension telling Edith, in an authoritative voice that belied the fact that she was stark naked, that she would be at the office in an hour and that Edith should be ready.

"You can't be serious," Paxton said. "The day's almost over."

"Listen," Janet said. "She's never going to take you back, you know. She's not even in your class."

"Why are you such a bitch?"

"I'm just trying to return the favor, lover. You should listen to me because you're certifiable," she said. "You need someone who understands."

"Francie understands me," he said. Such an early confrontation was going to ruin his whole day, or what was left of it anyway. And from Lillian's funeral to the late night romp with a newly invigorated Janet, the previous thirty-six hours had wrecked him. He was also out of coke.

"You just stick with that story," Janet said. "I'll be back tonight and I'll bring some dinner." She smiled gently, pityingly. He didn't think he liked Janet in a pitying mood. The incongruity of it frightened him.

As she left the room, she said over her shoulder, "I'm calling my house-cleaning girl, too. Stay out of her way, okay?"

Paxton made himself some coffee and retreated back into the guest room. Every so often Janet's nasty little dog came snuffling at the door, but he ignored it. He could hear the cleaning woman cursing quietly to herself as she made her way up and down the hallway. Janet must have told her someone was there because she didn't even bother rattling the doorknob.

He lay on the bed, flipping through cable channels. There was nothing on but late afternoon soap operas and Jerry Springer, then Oprah, on whose show some underwear model-cum-actress was hawking her new organic frozen food line. The boredom made him grateful for his own work. There were probably fifty things he needed to deal with in his own office. But the farm and breeding operation would do okay without him for a few days more. Francie needed his full attention.

He called her cell phone twice and got her voice mail. Each time it picked up, he was almost fooled that it was her and his stomach lurched. He knew her mother's number by heart as well. But he'd lost his nerve. He couldn't bear to call her there.

After a couple of hours he heard the back door slam behind the unseen cleaning lady. For the first time in a long time he was unbearably lonesome. Hunger gnawed at his stomach. Except for those few bites of ice cream, he couldn't remember the last time he had eaten. He knew that Janet would be back soon and that she would bring food. But he didn't want to see her again. At least not anytime soon. While he was no longer worried that she was going to fall apart, he did have some concern that she might start working on him again, making him some kind of project, like her house and her insurance company and her high-maintenance wardrobe.

In the end, after foraging for food in Janet's kitchen and finding nothing worth eating, he decided to call his mother and let her know he was on his way home, no matter what he might find there.

46

AS FAR AS Freida Birkenshaw knew, she had been the only one in her small group of friends who had married for love. Betsey Talbot and Mary George Watterson had been her closest friends, the ones with whom she'd grown up in the valley. Neither one had even ever met her other girlhood friends, the overbred Europeans she'd spent two stressful years with at finishing school in Montreaux. She hadn't known and hadn't cared what tatty royalty that bunch eventually sold themselves to. But she had walked down the aisle ahead of Mary George as she was delivered into the gnarled and liver-spotted hands of one of Saul Watterson's biggest creditors, and had wept with Betsey at the doctor's office up in Lexington when she found out she was pregnant by a feed salesman who made regular calls at her uncle's store.

The finishing school, with its classes in flower-arranging and French and party-hosting, was supposed to be (along with her family's money) Freida's ticket out of the valley. And her mother had almost convinced her that it was her duty to find herself some impoverished count or crusty diplomat who would whisk her out of their backward little valley and off to some damp, romantic county seat or town house on a crumbling European square. But Freida had been home for Easter break that second spring and helped a suntanned and grinning Millar Paxton Birkenshaw unload a temperamental roan stallion that her father had bought at auction. The next week, her mother had to threaten her with another year at the school to get her to stay through graduation.

Undistinguished but smart, Millar was making a name for himself in the horse breeding business. He wasn't interested in racing horses, just breeding and selling. Freida knew that he reminded her mother too much of the origins of her own family, and the smear of commercialism that had kept her out of the upper echelons of Carystown society all her life. She'd wanted Freida to overcome the prejudice that she couldn't. Of course, Freida eventually did, but it was on her own terms.

Freida and Millar had spent a childless twenty years together at Bonterre when she found herself pregnant. The night she passed a squalling, blanket-wrapped M. Paxton Birkenshaw, Junior, into his father's arms and saw the delight in his eyes, she was filled with a kind of happiness that she had never known she could experience. But it was the explosive and finite kind; somehow, she had recognized it as the last truly happy moment in her life.

Gone were the silent, lovely nights with Millar's body spooned tightly against hers. Gone were her solitary walks over the pastures and the week-long trips to the city. No longer was she the only one Millar sought out when he came in, dead-tired, from the work he loved to do on the farm.

All these years, she had tried to love the boy as much as she loved his father. And she had almost succeeded. Now, standing in her kitchen, dropping eggs and chicken livers into the mouth of the blender for the pâtélike custard that Paxton loved, her hips and lower back screaming with pain, she felt that her life had been filled with almosts: her son was *almost* normal, her husband had *almost* lived long enough to turn the troubled boy into a decent man, she and Millar had *almost* doubled her family's fortune, she had *almost* made the Birkenshaw name the most respected name in the valley, she had *almost* saved her beautiful boy.

She never cried anymore the way she had in that doctor's office with Betsey Talbot, whose baby had been a girl and was now in Maryland, married with two teenage children of her own. Freida never spoke of her shame at her son's failures. She had just thrown one more luncheon or spent more time around the stables, where she made the grooms nervous. Millar had never known how his son turned out. He hadn't been with her to hand over that ridiculous check to the family of the girl who claimed that Paxton had raped her, or held Paxton in his arms as he begged forgiveness for "the last time, I promise." She had been left to deal with the destruction all alone.

~

How long had it been since she had cooked a meal for herself or anyone else? Flora made her simple meals now—light custards and plain chicken and soups whose savors were lost on her useless taste buds and constantly sour stomach—but there had been years and years of dinner parties and picnics and incidental celebrations. She didn't miss the company, the men and women who came to the farm to cajole her to buy or sell horseflesh, and she had little desire to see friends from town or state politicians who came to eat her food and attempt to curry her favor and thus fill their pockets with her money. But she did miss the thrill of composing a meal as though it were her own precious symphony. Her two years in Europe had given her a taste for real food, and she had been a careful student. Millar had joshed her about showing off her "fancy French ways," but of course he had eaten every bite that was put in front of him, and more. The doctor had been too obsequious to warn him away from Freida's béchamel sauces and custards and thick, butter-sautéed beefsteaks sawn from the several local steers they had slaughtered each year. Between the truck farmers and her own gardens, she had surrounded herself with an abundance of food. Now, many of those farmers were long dead and she was dying of not only emphysema, but a pernicious, painful cancer that should have finished her off long ago.

As she hobbled about the kitchen assembling the meal, she felt a surge of new purpose, or old purpose, really. It seemed to her as though she'd been on a long, long trip and had only just returned to find everything where she'd left it: the ramekins on a high upper shelf of the dish pantry, the shaky stepping stool she'd meant to replace five years ago (how had Flora put up with it for so long?), the drawer filled only with whisks and spatulas of every size, the sturdy KitchenAid mixer that Millar had bought for her sitting beneath its quilted hood, the bank of cabinets filled with cast-iron and porcelain cookware that she'd ordered from France back when it first became fashionable in the sixties. It was all there, waiting for her.

Flora had had no objections to being sent off for the rest of the day. She had taken the grocery list to the store, brought back the things Freida requested, and gone out again, mumbling about her niece needing some looking after. Freida waited to see if she would say anything about the sheriff's search of the house, but Flora had remained her stubborn, reticent self. The subject of Paxton had become like a wall between them. Flora had never criticized her for the way she'd raised Paxton, probably because she was just as responsible, and they both knew it. Freida knew that Flora had probably hidden the scarf, but it didn't matter.

After three agonizing hours, Freida's work was done. It went slowly because she had to stop several times for oxygen and hadn't taken any of the Oxycodone drops she usually took in the afternoon, because she wanted to be sharp for the cooking of Paxton's supper. It wasn't an evening for mistakes. The peppered beef tenderloin section rested beneath a towel beside the oven, the mashed potatoes sat waiting to be refreshed with garlic sauce just before she served them, the ingredients for the spinach soufflé were ready to be assembled, and the chicken liver timbales had begun to bake. The only shortcut she'd taken was with the bread. Her hands—her poor, lovely hands that Millar had often lifted to his lips and kissed so passionately, so teasingly—no longer had the strength to knead and form bread dough, so she'd used the vile Japanese bread machine that Paxton bought her two Christmases previous. And dessert? Peaches (alas, canned) with raspberry puree. Though she didn't know if they would get to dessert.

When she was finished, she took the elevator upstairs, anxious as always that the thing would stop mysteriously and she would suffocate and die without anyone knowing where she was. The contractor had assured her many times that the tiny elevator was well-ventilated, so suffocation was impossible, but, still, the claustrophobic space unnerved her.

She lay down on her bed and closed her eyes, meaning only to take a brief nap to calm the frantic beating of her heart. She slept deeply, dreaming of her mother, who looked achingly young and lovely in a pale blue frock that Freida remembered from her mother's wardrobe. But her mother was angry, her olive skin flushed with heat so that she seemed to Freida to glisten and sparkle in the spreading moonlight. The very sky seemed to be filled with her mother's shouts, and Freida could see her father, looking like a shadow in the moonlight, walking across the hill behind the house. Freida called to him, but he didn't turn their way. In frustration, she lay on the ground, inching her body in her father's direction. Finally, she was able to push off with her toes and leave her mother shouting after her as she sped along the ground feeling every undulation of the land, every pebble and rock and mole depression beneath her. As she picked up speed, her hair flew behind her like a tattered flag and her cheeks burned. When she crested the second hill, she saw her father again in the distance. Now there was another little girl at his side, and Freida felt a stab of jealousy. There should be no other little girls in her father's life, no other small hand in his! And it was here that the sleeping Freida began to be afraid and the dream-Freida stopped just over the hill's crest. She didn't want to get any closer to her father, but especially not the little girl, whose bright yellow coat was like a patch of sunshine against the murky sky. Above the two of them, the moon began to rise quickly. Now the moon sagged above her, so heavy with light that it was like a pure clear liquid over everything it touched. The light was cold on her skin, and she curled herself into a ball for warmth, and when the sleeping Freida awoke, her body was stiff and the room, so warmed by sunlight in the afternoon, had grown cold with the dropping of the sun behind the hills.

Freida stretched out her limbs one at a time and rose from the bed with some difficulty. But before she could make her way over to the closet to find something suitable to wear for dinner, the telephone rang.

"Mama," Paxton said.

What she heard in his voice broke her heart for the thousandth time.

"Come home, Paxton," she said. Her hand shook as she hung up the phone.

47

"YOU THINK WE'VE GOT ENOUGH to pick up Birkenshaw?" Mitch asked in between bites of the burger they'd picked up at a drive-through.

Bill wasn't hungry. His own stomach was nervous, but he hadn't minded getting Mitch some food. In fact, he considered the restaurant stop a kind of charity.

"I expect that it won't be too difficult. The judge won't be too happy to see us again, though."

"That's what money will do for you," Mitch said.

"It's not the be-all and end-all," Bill said. "There are other things a man needs."

Mitch shrugged. Most things did seem to come easily to Mitch, Bill thought. The job wasn't too tough or routinely dangerous, he had decent kids that he didn't have to spend much time or thought on, and he was like candy to women. But, of course, there was that whole bit about walking in another man's shoes.

He slowed the cruiser at the curve just before Chalybeate Springs. Was it his imagination, or did Mitch flinch as he put on the turn signal?

"I want to have a chat with Mr. Matter," Bill said.

"You think he knows anything about Birkenshaw being involved in the kid's death?" Mitch said. "He wouldn't have kept that back, do you think?"

Mitch's words took Bill by surprise. He'd been so focused on Mitch's connection to the case that he hadn't given much thought to the fact that Matter and Birkenshaw might be caught up in the girl's murder together.

The ugliness of the notion stunned him. The little girl's death had obviously been painful. Had she found out something she wasn't supposed to about their drug dealing? The mother would have had to know about it, wouldn't she? Although, she was such a piece of work, it was possible that Matter had never brought her far into the business. They hadn't been able to discover any sort of motive two years before, but this, maybe, was a motive.

"No, you wouldn't think so," Bill said. "But if Matter himself is involved, he might have had reason to."

"No shit," Mitch said. "I don't like coming out here. These hippies give me the creeps."

"I can see that," Bill said. Noting the Closed sign on the door of the shop, he parked the cruiser near the house.

"You want me to wait here?" Mitch asked.

"No, I don't want you to wait here," Bill said, getting out. He leaned down to address Mitch face-to-face. "I would've dropped you by the station if I didn't want you along. I've just got some questions, but a little show of strength wouldn't hurt."

"It's awfully windy out there," Mitch said.

"Yeah, well I figure you've got enough hair spray on that you'll stand it."

A shadow of irritation crossed Mitch's face. He was vain about his hair.

"It's not hair spray," he said defensively. "It's gel."

"Whatever," Bill said, shutting the cruiser door firmly behind him. In any other circumstance, he would have laughed, but he wasn't in the mood.

As they approached the porch, Mitch stayed at the bottom of the step while Bill went on up. Before he could knock, Hanna Moon opened the door.

"Are you bringing my girl back to me, Sheriff?" she asked. Her voice was fretful. "Charlie says we'll have to have an undertaker, but I want her here with us. There's a nice place up on the hill way in the back. She liked it up there."

"No, ma'am," Bill said. He didn't bother to mention that it wasn't exactly legal to bury people wherever one chose to put them. Hanna Moon's eyes were clear today. She wore a purple velvet dress whose nap was flat and shiny in places, and black Chinese peasant shoes with brightly patterned socks on her feet. She was not a young woman and her weathered face was heavy with grief. There was none of her usual loopiness about her, and Bill wondered if it wasn't an act that she put on and off at her convenience. His confidence was shaken—people he thought he knew, he didn't. He was tired of being surprised.

"It may be a couple of weeks more," he said. "The coroner wants to be thorough."

"Those newspeople went away fast this time," she said. "Two years ago, they couldn't get enough of my Isabella. Isn't that funny? Hey, you want to come in?"

Bill didn't have an answer about the newspeople, so he was glad enough to dodge the question. As far as he was concerned, the farther away the press was, the better. The next election was another eighteen months off, but already he was seriously concerned about his chances. With the Moon girl's murder not yet solved, and the two other, more recent deaths, he wasn't counting on anything. He had more than a decade until retirement and hated to think they would have to depend on Margaret's money for the rest of their lives.

"We don't need to come in, thanks," he said. "What I'd like is to have a word with Mr. Matter if he's in."

"Sure," she said. "I think he's in his office." She turned and shuffled off down the dim hallway. Bill could hear her calling.

"Charlie, company."

After a minute or so he heard a door slam somewhere back in the house. Hanna Moon hurried toward the front door.

"I forgot," she said, giggling nervously. "He's not here."

"Really?" Bill said. "We'll just hang around until he shows up, if you don't mind." He turned and headed down the steps.

"He might be a while," Hanna said after him.

Two more cruisers rolled up the gravel lane and parked—one was Frank's, the other bore a state trooper's insignia.

"There he is, Sheriff," Mitch said, pointing in the direction of the property's run-down barn.

Charlie Matter was headed across the stretch of worn gravel and weeds separating the house and the barn. "Hey, Sheriff!" he called, waving. "I'll be with you guys in a minute." He hustled through the barn's yawning doors.

"I'm thinking that Mr. Matter doesn't really want to chat," Bill said. He gestured to Frank, who had gotten out of his cruiser and was standing by. Frank nodded and headed in the direction of the barn. He stayed close to trees along the road and disappeared behind the springhouse.

"Go ahead and turn back anyone who tries to come up this road," Bill said to the trooper. "And make sure whoever else is in the house stays inside."

"Sure thing, Sheriff," the trooper said. He was a strak, serious-looking guy with MORGEIWICZ on his name tag and reminded Bill of a younger version of Frank.

"We probably ought to go and see what Mr. Matter's up to," Bill said. His mind was mostly on what Charlie might be doing in the barn, but he couldn't help but wonder how Mitch was taking all this. A glance told him that Mitch appeared not so much worried as focused on the job at hand.

They had almost reached a long row of compost bins when they heard the first shot. The bins were lousy cover, but they ran over and ducked behind them.

"Where the hell did that come from?" Bill said.

"Sounded close to the barn, but I don't know," Mitch said. "Shit. I'm going to look."

"Maybe he's after you," Bill said.

"I think Matter's a scared son of a bitch. I bet he's off to the next county by now."

"Just stay down," Bill told him. He readied his weapon, rose up on one knee, and took aim at the barn. Charlie leaned out cautiously.

"Matter!" Bill yelled. "Drop your weapon!"

But Charlie took a shot in Bill's direction, and before Bill even realized that it had hit the dust about ten feet to his left, he had one off back at the barn. Mitch, too, began to fire. The shots were deafening.

As they ducked down again, another shot fired, but even with the ringing in his ears, Bill could tell that this one hadn't been headed in their direction.

"Frank," he said.

"What?" Mitch said.

"I really don't want Matter dead," he said.

This time, as they aimed, Charlie Matter hurled his gun out the barn door and onto the gravel.

"No gun, man!" he yelled. He stepped cautiously out of the barn with his hands in the air. "See, I got no gun!"

But before the last word was out of his mouth, there was another shot and he fell to the ground with an agonizing scream.

"Holy shit!" Mitch said.

"Hold your fire!" Bill shouted toward the barn. He fumbled for his radio, hoping Frank's was on as well. "Frank, hold your fire!"

He turned to Mitch. "Get an ambulance here." Over Mitch's shoulder he saw gray wisps of smoke working their way around the edge of the barn's opening. *Shit, what the hell else could go wrong?* "Better get the fire department out here, too."

Hanna Moon had thrown herself over Charlie Matter. When Bill reached them, he saw that Charlie was on his side, holding his bleeding leg. Either Frank had intentionally missed with that last shot or it hadn't been a clear one.

"You need to get back," Bill told Hanna Moon. "You, Matter, don't you move!"

He holstered his weapon and pulled the handcuffs off his belt.

"Ma'am, now!" he repeated.

Hanna Moon made low keening noises over Charlie as she slowly moved away. Bill rolled him over and snapped the handcuffs on his wrists.

"He tried to fucking *kill* me, man," Charlie said. "That son of a bitch is fucking crazy! I'm going to bleed to death, man. You're going to let me bleed to death, aren't you?"

"Your ride's on its way," Bill said. "And you're lucky you're such a piss-poor shot, because if you'd hit one of us, you'd be in a bigger world of hurt."

Charlie put his head down, and Bill could see that he was trying to hold back tears. In the distance there were sirens.

Mitch and the trooper reached them at the same time. Frank was trying to lead Hanna back to the house.

"Why'd you run, Matter?" Mitch said.

"I don't have to answer any of your questions until I get a lawyer," he answered. Then he gave a howl. The pain was settling in.

Bill watched Mitch and Charlie, waiting to see what would pass between them, but nothing happened.

"You want me to read him his rights, or do you want the deputy here to?" the trooper asked.

"Go ahead. And keep an eye on him, if you would," Bill said. He knew that if anything transpired between Charlie and Mitch, he'd hear about it from the trooper. He had that look of enthusiastic sincerity about him.

As he approached Hanna, she broke away from Frank to beg him to let her go to Charlie. "I can't lose both of them," she said. "Please, please."

Bill nodded and told her to stay at least five feet back, and she ran off. He turned to Frank. "You want to tell me what happened?"

Frank shrugged. "I thought the bastard was going to run. I didn't see him pitch the weapon. End of story."

"You didn't hear him?"

"You think I had ear protection out there?" Frank said. "I couldn't hear squat."

"That was pretty damned careless of you, Frank."

"You forgetting what you wanted me out here for?" Frank asked. "What's up with Mitch and our drug dealer friend having a quiet moment? Shouldn't we take Mitch in now?"

"Have you noticed the barn? Besides the smoke, it smells like someone dumped a few hundred gallons of cat piss in it," Bill said. "If there's not a meth lab in there or under it, then my mother was a redheaded whore."

Frank looked toward the ruined building. "There won't be much left. I hope there's enough equipment left to prosecute."

"As soon as we get this mess cleaned up, consider yourself on administrative leave," Bill said. "Here they come." The fire trucks had cut their sirens as they left the gravel road and were approaching the barn. The ambulance came behind them, and Bill waved the driver in the direction of Charlie Matter.

The EMTs worked quickly, and within five minutes had Charlie on a stretcher headed for the ambulance. Hanna Moon hovered over the stretcher telling him that she would bring lots of crystals to the hospital so he would heal quickly, but he turned his face away from her. The barn continued to burn behind them. The firefighters had gotten started, but from the building's age and state of disrepair, it looked to Bill like it was going fast.

"Hey, Mitch," Bill said. "I'm going to have Frank accompany Mr. Matter here and the trooper to the hospital. Would you—"

"Frank! Where is he?" Charlie screamed, trying to twist around to see Frank. But his restraints kept him firmly in place. "Where is he? Don't you let that bastard near me! He tried to kill me just like he did Delmar! Don't you let that bastard near me!"

"Shut up," Frank said. "You're delirious, Matter."

"Ask him," Charlie said, looking at Bill. "You ask him why nobody messed with us. You ask my buddy Frank, here. My buddy Frank who tried to shoot me in the fucking back!"

Bill looked at Frank. Good, solid Frank. Frank had been the one to take Delmar Johnston to the jail in the first place. Did it make any sense? Frank?

"He doesn't know what he's talking about," Frank said. "You know these hippies are half stoned most of the time."

Hanna Moon spoke. "I saw him go out to the barn," she said, pointing to Frank.

A brief look of worry flickered across his face.

"Just the once." Then she was quiet again, looking nervously away from him.

"Frank," Mitch said. "Aw, man."

"Bill," Frank said. "You're not going to believe this crap, are you?"

"You think I don't have cameras, old man? Security?" Charlie said.

"Bill?" Frank said again.

It made Bill sick to do what he had to do, but he was looking at a potentially dirty cop, one who had already tried to kill at least two people. And Frank was still armed.

"I'm going to take your gun, Frank," he said.

"Oh, hell, Bill," Frank said. "This is going to kill Rose." He raised his arms. "Go on," he said. "Do what you have to do. But I'm telling you this is a mistake."

"I pray to God it is," Bill said. "But when Officer Morgeiwicz gets you back to the office, you'd better call yourself a lawyer."

48

KATE STOOD at the back window watching Myrt and Earl tumble over each other as they chased last year's leaves blowing across their dog run. Heavy clouds, dark and gray, crowded the sky, making the day wintry and dull. All winter she'd looked forward to spring with its bright skies and fragrant, budding trees. Now she wondered if that sort of day would ever come for her again. She pulled Caleb's sweater tight around her, trying to get warm even though the air in the house wasn't at all chilled. She was cold from the inside, and she knew that no blanket or sweater or blaze in the fireplace could warm her.

They'd spent most of the previous night talking in front of the fire. She, curled in the capacious mahogany and leather chair that had belonged to Caleb's father, and he, leaning forward and listening intently from the couch. Of course, she had done most of the talking; she still felt raw and emotionally stripped from all that she had confessed. Caleb had waited to speak until she finished.

"That bastard will never hurt you again," was all he said.

She knew that it was only bravado talking, but she was reassured enough to finally fall asleep there on the couch an hour or so before dawn. He hadn't pressured her to come to his bed, and she was grateful. When she'd awakened, she found a note signed *Love, C.,* telling her that he had to go into work for a while but would bring her some clothes from the cottage.

Everything was out in the open between them. All their secrets were told. The only thing that truly stood between them and a future together—if she decided they had a future—was Miles. There was still Caleb's skepticism about Isabella Moon, but that was just going to have to run its course.

The child had picked her and not someone else. Why? She would probably never know. As Kate stared across the grass, she almost felt lonesome for the child. Perhaps her absence left room for Caleb, or maybe for the rest of her own life. She just prayed that Miles would disappear as well, leaving her in peace. But she knew Miles well enough to know that it was damned unlikely.

After a lunch of soup and crackers and cheese from Caleb's well-stocked refrigerator, Kate tried to call Francie at her mother's house. But when she heard Lillian's cultured voice tell her to "please, leave a message," she dropped the phone's handset back onto its cradle, unnerved. It was as though Lillian were keeping track of her, reminding her of her charge—to watch out for Francie.

"I'm so sorry, Lillian," Kate whispered to the Heavens. Lillian, wherever she was, would have to understand. Francie was going to have to look out for herself for a while. How could they both have fallen for such dangerous men? It was hard to believe that Paxton and Miles could exist in the same universe.

Kate had once thought that there was a vast gray gulf between good and evil. It was obvious to her now that that divide was not a gulf, but a single sharp line. There *was* no gray area. She'd lived in evil the whole time she'd been in Miles's shadow, including the years in which she thought she'd escaped him. She was desperate, so desperate to make her life good. What it would take, she didn't know. She hoped that coming clean with Caleb had been the start.

"You need some real food," Caleb said, pulling out a package of thick steaks from the grocery bag on the counter. "I bet you had popcorn for lunch. Did you even get any breakfast?"

"I ate just fine, thank you very much," Kate said. She felt better wearing her own clothes, more at home. "I even shared with Myrt and Earl."

"You've got to quit spoiling those dogs," he said. "Nothing's worse than a fat beagle."

Even as he spoke, he was opening the steak package to trim the fat off of the meat and put it in the dogs' bowls.

"I don't think *I'm* the one the dogs have to worry about," Kate said. As Caleb trimmed the meat, she opened the bottle of cabernet sauvignon he'd bought to go with dinner. He'd also bought some prestuffed potatoes, a bag of salad, and ice cream for dessert—*her* favorite, mocha chip, not the butter pecan he preferred. He was trying so hard to take care of her. Standing there in the warm kitchen with him, it was almost as though the past two weeks had never happened. She could almost believe that life could go back to the way it was. But then she chanced to glance at the front door, where Caleb's twelve-gauge leaned, loaded, against the wall.

Her hand shook a little as she poured wine into two of the stemless wineglasses she'd bought for him for Christmas at the gourmet shop in town.

She held out a glass to Caleb. "Should we drink to something?" she said.

He took the glass and leaned to kiss her gently on the cheek. He smelled of wood smoke and soap. The shadow of his beard was rough against her face.

"Us?" he said.

Kate tried a smile, but it felt false to her. She sipped the bittersweet wine, almost wishing it were something stronger. She'd never enjoyed being drunk, nor had she ever liked any sort of mind-altering medication. But now she recalled the morphine-induced stupor into which Miles and the fake doctor had put her after she lost the baby, and knew she wouldn't mind living again in that kind of fog for a week or two. Wouldn't have to think in that state, wouldn't be afraid, no matter what happened to her.

They went to the couch, where Caleb had set down her bag. She'd changed her clothes there in the living room and the bag's contents were spread across the cushions.

"I'm sorry," she said. "What a mess." She gathered up the clothes and shoes and underwear scattered about and tried to stuff them into the bag.

"It might all be kind of random," Caleb said. "I did the best I could."

Kate moved the bag and its overflowing contents to a nearby chair. "I can't believe you went there," she said. "Miles could have shown up any time. He's like that. He likes to surprise people. Scare them, really."

"Listen," Caleb said, pulling her down to sit beside him. "We could be wrong. That clothes stunt could've been Janet."

Kate shook her head vigorously. "No way."

"Listen, Kate. Please."

"He won't give up," Kate said. "He's come back for me. I shouldn't have come out here. Now you're in danger, too."

"We don't know that."

"The picture at the cottage," she said. "I know you don't believe me, but Isabella was warning me."

"Coincidence," Caleb said. "And maybe the picture just fell out of some papers."

"He'll kill us both," Kate said, looking into his eyes. There was no ignoring the doubt she saw in them. She knew she couldn't expect him to believe her. It didn't matter that she'd finally told him the truth. Their whole relationship had been based on lies.

"Come here," he said.

She let him wrap his arms around her and they sat together for a time. She tried to relax, but it was no use. If Miles didn't come today, he would come tomorrow or the next day or the next.

When the fire died down and the room began to cool, Caleb said he needed to take a few minutes and chop some wood. They'd spent so many pleasant nights in front of his fireplace over the winter that they used up all that he'd bought in the fall.

"I meant to do that today," Kate said. It had been a lost afternoon.

"Do you think you could eat?" Caleb said, stroking her hair. "I know it's early."

"More wine," she said. "I think I want a lot more wine."

Caleb kissed her hair. "Get on up," he said. "I got two bottles."

Kate followed behind him in the kitchen, putting together the salad and turning on the oven for the potatoes. The wine had mellowed her somewhat. She wasn't terribly hungry, but Caleb was trying so hard, she couldn't bear to disappoint him.

Outside, one of the dogs set to barking and the other began to howl, its voice straining. Kate froze.

"Relax," Caleb said. "It's probably a groundhog."

"Sure," Kate said. The dogs were always barking at something: a deer grazing near the woods, skunks, the rumble of faraway cars.

Caleb took kibble from a container beneath the sink and put it in the dogs' bowls with the steak fat.

"Let's just put the potatoes in the microwave," he said as he headed toward the door. "I'm hungry."

Kate turned off the oven, put the potatoes in the microwave, and set it to cook for twelve minutes. As she worked, she realized that she was also counting in her head. It wasn't evening yet, but outside the windows the afternoon was grayer still, as though it might snow. *Forty, forty-one, forty-two, forty-three . . .*

She refilled her wineglass.

Fifty-six, fifty-seven, fifty-eight . . .

Outside, the beagles were yapping furiously, as they often did when Caleb brought their dinner out. She told herself that looking out the window would be giving in to her paranoia. Turning the pages of a magazine sitting on the table, she didn't even notice that it was a sports magazine she didn't care for.

Seventy-two, seventy-three . . .

Now there was no sound from the yard.

Seventy-six, seventy-seven, seventy-eight . . .

When the back door opened, Kate jumped.

"You'd think I never feed those dogs," Caleb said. "I think it's about to turn cold again. They'll be sleeping in the doghouse tonight." He stopped and looked at Kate. "What's wrong?"

She laughed, letting go of the tension that had filled her chest. "Just being a scaredy-cat," she said.

"You really do need some more wine," he said.

He took her hand and led her back to the kitchen.

"Shit. I forgot to do the wood," he said.

"Let's just eat," Kate said. "Now you've got me hungry."

He left her in the kitchen to get the wood basket from beside the fireplace. "We can't eat in front of a cold fire," he said. When he opened the back door, the dogs began to bark once more.

Kate busied herself clearing the coffee table of its magazines and whatnots. She set out silverware and salt and pepper and sour cream for their potatoes. Keeping herself together, keeping things as normal as possible, was going to be important to her sanity. Miles might confront her at any time: on the street, in some parking lot, at the cottage. He might even draw out his game, stalking her over months, maybe years. Just to let her know that he was watching. She hadn't completely given up the thought of leaving town. Maybe she could convince Caleb to go with her, to get out of town and start over somewhere, perhaps out on the West Coast. *Maybe, just maybe, it was like Caleb said. Coincidence.*

She went to the stereo and turned it to the light jazz satellite station they liked. Seeing what a mess she made when she'd dressed, she stuffed her clothes into the duffel bag, leaving only a long silk scarf trailing across the back of the couch. She smiled to imagine Caleb trying to pick out what clothes she might want.

In the kitchen, the timer *dinged* and she went to get the potatoes from the microwave.

When the back door opened, a blast of chill air swept through the kitchen. The sound of the dogs was louder, more furious.

"I hope you got a lot of wood," Kate said. "Now it really is cold in here."

"Johnny Appleseed says maybe you can put *this* on the fire."

Kate stiffened at the sound of Miles's voice. She didn't want to turn around. She wanted Caleb to come up behind her and put his arms around her waist, laughing and teasing her about being such a scaredy-cat. She wouldn't shy away, or hesitate, but would let him touch her and hold her and they would figure out how to get past everything that had happened. But that wasn't the way things would go, she knew. From the direction of Miles's voice, there was the sound of something heavy dropping to the floor.

Kate turned to see Miles standing in the open doorway. He looked much as he had the day she'd left him, down to the splattered blood on his clothes.

Miles kicked at the ragged mound at his feet.

"What do you think?" he said, sounding winded.

It was the boots that she noticed first, or perhaps that was where, in her stunned state, her mind told her it was safest to look. She and Caleb had picked them out together at an outfitter's in Lexington, and she remembered how she had liked their bright green and yellow laces because they reminded her of a child's shoelaces, though the boots themselves were sturdy hikers and quite expensive. Now, both the laces and the boots were almost unrecognizable. They, along with Caleb's blue jeans, and the saddle-brown field coat she'd always looked out for as he walked the dogs out in the fields and woods, were covered with amorphous blossoms of blood. But it was the raw mess that began at the coat's ruined collar that made Kate turn away and vomit on the floor. Miles had tried to remove Caleb's head from his body with some kind of tool—perhaps even the axe that Caleb had planned to use to chop the firewood—but hadn't gotten very far.

"Aw, Mary-Katie," Miles said.

Kate retched more. *She couldn't have seen what she had seen! The idea of it was impossible. Was she dreaming? Would she wake up and find Caleb watching over her, ready to comfort her from her nightmare?* She had forgotten the sound of Miles's voice, the subdued drawl that intensified theatrically when he was dealing with good ol' boys. But he was here with her now, and the years that she'd been away from him suddenly melted away as though she had never lived them.

With her hair hanging down over her face she couldn't see the thing on the floor, but she knew that it was still there. Maybe Miles had made a mistake and killed someone else, someone dressed like Caleb. Maybe Miles had Caleb tied up outside. But another part of her, the part that knew what evil Miles was capable of, told her to *stop it*. Caleb wasn't tied up outside and he hadn't gone for help. Caleb was dead.

Without looking at Miles, she started for the front door and the shotgun. But before she could get out of the kitchen, she slipped on some blood that had pooled on the floor. Miles, the runner, caught her before she fell.

"Whoa," he said, laughing.

She thrashed in his arms, desperate to be free of him. Or, better, to kill him once and for all. This was nothing like the slow, agonized despair that had driven her to shoot him the first time. She'd been deep in pain then, a pain that had festered over time. These feelings were as fresh as Caleb's blood, which was now on her shoes, her hands.

"Let's get you settled down," Miles said, breathless with the effort of re-straining her.

As he dragged her across the room, he seemed to be even stronger than when she had left him. Only now, Caleb had died for her. It didn't matter what Miles did. She had nothing to lose.

Kate threw all of her weight against him and they hit the stone fire-place. She heard a muffled *crack* but didn't know if it was Miles or she who had been hurt. Trying again for the gun by the door, she realized that the sound had been nothing more than the pot of artificial flowers falling from the mantel to the floor.

Miles was too fast for her and tackled her before she could get her hand on the gun.

"Oh, my Mary-Katie," he said, still breathing hard, "you're so pretty. Even when you're mad."

Then Miles rolled her over on the braided rug she'd helped Caleb buy that winter after the dogs had chewed up the old one after bringing them inside on a single frigid night. She saw regret in his eyes.

"Don't look," Miles said.

But she wouldn't look away, and when his soiled fist came close to her face, she could see the black hairs on his knuckles before they smashed against her cheek and she was thrust into oblivion.

49

IT WORRIED PAXTON SOME that he didn't know what he'd find when he got out to the farm. His mother had sounded bad. Wrecked, in fact. The old woman was going to die and that was going to leave him all alone.

No longer could he imagine Francie moving into the house, making love with him on every available surface—the many beds, the marble tables, the diminutive Victorian couch in his mother's morning room, in the vast Jacuzzi tub his mother installed in her suite when she began having trouble walking. She was fighting their being together and he didn't understand why. It was so obvious that they were each other's fate. *Why couldn't she see it?* With her mother out of the way, and soon his mother as well, there was no one left to stand between them.

Part of him, that ugly, self-destructive part of him, urged him just to turn the Mercedes around and drive and drive east until he ran into the mountains, to drive up the nearest one and take a curve just that much too fast and end it. But maybe, he thought, it would be better to take Francie with him.

It occurred to him that if he were going to attempt something that ambitious, he would have to be in a state of absolutely no pain—Francie, too—and that meant plenty of coke. Janet had sucked up the last he had with him (he'd helped, but Janet was really greedy about it). He would need to get more from Charlie Matter.

But Charlie Matter was on his shit list. He'd come to suspect that he'd been lied to, that there was no one in the Sheriff's Department who was protecting them, and that Charlie Matter was keeping all the cash for himself.

Damn, the cool evening air felt good on his face. He was hungry, too. Janet had had crap for food. She was covered up in M&Ms and anchovies and expensive crackers and, of all things, cans and cans of that white-trash deviled ham junk. But who could live on that?

Several hundred yards short of the farm's main gate, he slowed the Mercedes and turned onto an unmarked gravel road. The car idled as he fished the east gate key from the glove box and got out to unlock it. There was no telling what kind of bullshit was going on with the cops because of Delmar Johnston. They'd already scared his mother, and she didn't scare easily. He didn't know if that lame-ass sheriff had the balls to stake out the house—he wasn't even sure that anyone was looking for him. It seemed sensible to him to come in the back way just in case. As he drove slowly down the gravel lane, he kept the headlights off even though dusk was falling quickly. There was a smell of wood smoke in the air, probably from the manager's house. The aroma made his mouth water. But, hungry as he was, it was the half-gram emergency stash in his bedside table that he was craving, much more than the food his mother would have waiting.

"Hey, something smells good in here," Paxton said. He paused in the library where his mother sat reading a book. "Give me a minute, Mother."

She didn't reply, but nodded. He dashed up the front stairs, anxious to get to the stash. A light snort or two would make cocktails that much more pleasant.

Upstairs, he emptied his pockets, putting his phone and keys and wallet on the dresser, and went into the bathroom to splash some water on his face. In the mirror, he saw that he was looking more tired than usual. It had been a hell of a couple three days: Francie freaking out, that bitch Kate Russell on his back, Delmar Johnston. The list seemed endless. Maybe he should try getting a massage or something. Take some more time off. It couldn't hurt.

When he opened the drawer in the bedside table and didn't see the stash right away, he slid his hand to the back, feeling around for it. Had he misplaced it? Maybe taken it out without thinking? He felt a momentary pang of worry, thinking that his mother had perhaps found it, or Flora. But what would *they* do anyway? They probably wouldn't have even known what it was. And neither of them was in the habit of going through his things. That had stopped about the time he left for prep school.

Paxton went back downstairs, deep in thought about what he might have done with the stash. If he *had* lost it, he would have to start thinking seriously about where to get more right away. There were a couple of people who hung out at The Right Note who he'd heard could get coke, but more likely he would have to go out of town or deal with Charlie. And that was just damned *un*-likely.

His mother was still sitting and reading when he came into the room. When she saw him, she closed the book and gave him one of her rare smiles. "I'm glad you've come home," she said.

"What's the occasion?" Paxton said. Tonight, his mother wore black pants and a black silk blouse that he hadn't seen before, with a double necklace of chunky pearls and a simple gold bracelet on one wrist. On her feet she wore black velvet slippers, a distinct change from the sturdy shoes she'd taken to wearing since the cancer surgery had slowed her. Her pale hair was pulled back with a simple black bow. He loved his mother's steely grace. He had to hand it to her. Even half dead she looked like some kind of queen.

"You're looking quite the lady of the manor," he said.

He'd always thought she was the most beautiful woman in the valley— at least the most beautiful *older* woman. Francie, of course, was the most stunning woman he knew.

"I've made you dinner, darling," she said as he bent to kiss her cheek. "Surprises and surprises."

"I remember you said that the first time you made me eat beets," he said. "Do you want your scotch?"

"I've made us something special," she said. "I may be dead this spring, Paxton, long before rum season. So I've made us frozen daiquiris. Are you surprised?"

"What surprises me is that you've started without me," he said.

A frozen daiquiri was not exactly what he'd been looking forward to. He didn't much care for rum. How could she have forgotten? But he went to the bar and poured the rest of the daiquiris there into the waiting glass. Without the coke, it was looking like any port in a storm. He was starting to feel pissed off, but he still stepped over and clinked his mother's glass. He took a brief sip of the sweet frozen mush, then another. The glass contained a serious amount of rum. Perhaps he would enjoy the evening after all.

Tonight, his mother certainly *was* full of surprises. By the time they made their way into the small dining room, the intimate one that they used just for family meals, Paxton had a serious buzz on. All the worries he'd had at Janet's had flown from his mind, and he was left with a hopeful feeling about the future. Screw his mother—the dear old thing—if she didn't think that Francie would have him in the end. By her own admission, she didn't really know Francie.

He knew his Francie. And what she needed was to be spoiled like she'd never been spoiled before. The first thing he would do was make her quit that stupid job at the hospital, and they would get a place together. Maybe, if his mother hung on much longer, they would build something splendid on the farm, perhaps just at the edge of the woods. It would be cozy, but he'd let her decorate it however she wanted. They'd go to London or Ireland together and pick out antiques and stay in quaint inns whose ancient rafters would shake with the sounds of their lovemaking. He grinned to himself at the wonderful notion of how happy they would be together.

"I need you to help me bring dinner in, Paxton," his mother said. "Flora's off with her niece tonight."

"That niece of hers looks like she was hit with an ugly stick," Paxton said, following her into the kitchen. The notion of an ugly stick struck him as wildly funny, and he gave his mother his best devilish grin, but she wouldn't laugh.

"Don't be so grim, Mother," he said. "I didn't say it about you. *You're* my lovely and very wise mother." He kissed her on the cheek, too high to notice that her body slumped just a bit as he touched his lips to her papery skin.

"We'll start with the timbales," she said, pulling herself together. "But bring in the beef and potatoes and the soufflé as well."

"It's your party," he said.

Paxton played the butler as he brought the food in, putting the dishes on the table where she indicated. The soufflé was still hot, despite the fact that it was sagging dangerously in its mold. When he went to put the dish down, a potholder slipped, but it took him several seconds to realize that he'd burned himself. Raising his fingers to his face, he looked studiously at their bright red tips.

"Have you hurt yourself?" his mother said. "Let me see."

Paxton held out his hand to her and for a moment he thought she would kiss them, as she might have when he was a boy. When she didn't, but told him to put his fingers in his water glass, he felt a vague sense of disappointment.

"My water glass? Come on. Where's my real mother?" he said.

"Just do it, Paxton," she said. "And sit down."

Paxton did as he was told, although, despite their violent red color, his fingers didn't seem to hurt much at all.

"Better?" she said.

They settled down to the chicken liver custard, which was one of his childhood favorites. She had topped it with the *sauce madère,* which he preferred to the béarnaise she'd often made for his father.

"I wonder if you could teach Francie how to cook," he said offhandedly as his spoon scraped against the bottom of the ramekin.

Freida was surprised but tried not to show it. To her, it was as though they were engaged in some elaborate game. She thought she'd set the rules, but given her son's increasingly incoherent state, she could see that she was just going to have to play along.

"Of course," she said. "I'm sure she'd be a very able student."

"She's amazing, Mother," he said. "There's nothing that Francie can't do."

Despite the slight lack of focus in his eyes, Freida saw that he was sincere. She knew that he'd long ago learned to imitate sincerity—that he had no real conscience or capability for empathy had been evident to her since he was a young child. But now, looking at him, she saw a flicker of real emotion in them. It pricked at her heart. Was she acting now just out of selfishness? The things he'd done—she wouldn't have to live much longer with them. And there was no chance for him and Francie. Ever. Even if she could bear to see Francie put herself at risk by marrying him, he had already made their future together impossible. That he'd killed Lillian, she had no doubt. The other things? She didn't need to think any further about them. It would do neither of them any good.

"She's lovely, Paxton," she said. "Your father would be very proud."

Paxton grinned like a small, satisfied boy.

They started on the rest of the meal in silence. She ate small bites of food. She rarely had much of an appetite these days, but tonight she had none. Across the table her son's movements slowed and became more careless.

She watched as Paxton quickly downed the water in the glass in which he'd soaked his fingers. She was about to object, but stopped herself. Did it really matter? The question shocked her. Was she thinking of him as dead already? She took a large draught of her wine.

"I'm so thirsty," Paxton said. "Let me have your water, Mother."

She held out her glass. Both of their hands were unsteady, and some of the water sloshed on the table.

He drank half of the water and put down the glass. Fine beads of sweat had broken out across his forehead. She had put four times as many drops of Oxycodone in his daiquiri and the timbale as she would have used on a bad day, before her pain became so persistent and deep that the doctor had given her Fentanyl patches as well.

"What is it?" she said.

"I have to go to Francie," Paxton said, trying to stand.

"No," Freida said, holding onto his arm.

"I have to tell Francie that it's going to be okay," he said. "She has to be here." He was sounding breathless, afraid.

"Wait until you're feeling better," Freida said. She didn't want him to collapse in his chair. She wouldn't be able to move him, and there was something wholly undignified about dying in the dining room.

She rose. "Let's get you up to bed, Paxton. You can call Francie when you feel better."

"I feel like shit," he said, holding his arm across his stomach.

~

In the close quarters of the elevator, Freida could smell her son's sour sweat as he leaned against her. It took all her strength to support his six-foot-plus frame.

The elevator had a manual door switch, and she felt something in her shoulder tear as she reached for it with the same arm against which Paxton leaned. She cried out, but Paxton was too far gone to notice. It was her own fault, but now she just wanted to get him into his own bed. What she was feeling, physically or emotionally, didn't matter.

They made slow progress toward his bedroom, with Paxton mumbling incoherently against her. But it soon became apparent that they weren't going to make it all the way to his suite.

"This way, darling," she said, steering him toward the celadon guest room, which was nearest the stairs. "This is a good place to rest."

"No," Paxton said, suddenly sounding wide-awake.

The deepened timbre of his voice frightened her. But his eyes closed as he slumped onto the tall mattress, his legs still hanging at an angle off the side of the bed.

Freida sighed and sank into a nearby chair, putting her head back and closing her own eyes. Here they were. It was too late to turn back. Her decision had been so sudden—only today. Or *had* it been only today? Hadn't she always known that she was, ultimately, the one responsible for her son? Something inside her had made him the way he was. She had thought that she'd feel philosophical, or guilty, or sinful at this moment. But she just felt tired. Her shoulder screamed with pain, her chest felt as though it would cave in. Her oxygen was far away, in the living room. She hadn't thought so far ahead as to bring it, and now she was trapped without it.

Paxton's breathing became shallower as she sat listening. She remembered how Millar would stand over his crib at night, waving her out of the room so he could hear his son breathing as he slept. They had never stood there together. It was always Millar, alone.

Eventually she was able to get up and lift Paxton's legs onto the bed. A thin line of drool ran from the side of his open mouth. His body was still.

Freida closed his mouth gently and brushed his blond hair from his brow. So much like his father, and his father's father. All Birkenshaw. He'd never looked like her or anyone in her family. It was as though she'd given birth to someone else's child. But he *was* hers, and always had been, even if she hadn't really wanted it to be so. She kissed his damp forehead, her lips lingering just a moment.

In the light from the hallway she carefully opened three of the Fentanyl patches from her generous prescription. Hers was a compassionate, old-fashioned doctor, and they were both realistic about her pain.

Freida rolled up the sleeve of her son's shirt and stuck the patches, one by one, on the soft, pale skin of the inside of his arm, running her fingers over them to make sure they were smooth. Then she rolled the shirtsleeve down and arranged the coverlet over her son's sleeping form. Tucking the coverlet against his chin, she again kissed her son and left the room.

Freida made her way down the hall to her own room and sat on the bed with a labored sigh. Her chest was tight. She slipped off the velvet slippers—she had loved wearing them, but her feet hurt badly and she missed the sensible clunkers that sat waiting in her shoe closet—and lay against the bank of pillows that Flora kept fluffed for her on the bed. Her cane fell to the floor. Fumbling in her pants pocket, she found the other three Fentanyl patches. Her hands trembled as she opened them, and by the time she was finished, bits of wrapper lay about the bed. She quickly gathered them up and dropped them onto the bedside table. There was no need to leave a mess for Flora.

When the patches were safely stuck onto her arm, she lay back beneath a quilt that the farm manager's mother had made just for her. Its slightly ridiculous pattern of fences and steeples appealed to her less than its peaceful green and blue background, which reminded her of hills beyond the Quair rising up to meet the sky.

Freida panicked a moment when she remembered that she had forgotten to decline a party invitation from the priest's wife. It lay open on her morning room desk, waiting to be answered. She thought briefly that she would get up and scrawl a quick response, but she decided against it. The woman would just have to understand.

Somewhere in another part of the house she heard a cell phone ringing and knew it must be Paxton's. He was beyond hearing it. After five or six rings it stopped.

All she had to do was lie there and wait and hope that she didn't suffocate before the drug killed her. She was a little afraid of dying. It occurred to her that she had probably better pray. She knew that her suicide might be excused, given that she was already dying a slow and painful death. But murder was another matter. And she was murdering her own son; there was no question of that. Could He forgive her that, the way she had forgiven Paxton everything that he had done? Finally, the tears came. If God was, indeed, waiting for her, she prayed that He would be merciful.

50

"I THOUGHT WE'D TAKE the scenic route home," Miles said.

His Mary-Katie sat beside him in the passenger seat, her head resting against the window. It had saddened him to hit her, but she just wasn't seeing reason.

"Hey," he said, pushing her hair behind her ear with one hand while keeping the other on the steering wheel. Ten minutes out of town and the landscape was already getting hilly.

He would've preferred some enthusiasm, perhaps some gratitude for getting her away from Podunkville. Few things annoyed him more than ingratitude. A purple bruise had bloomed on his Mary-Katie's cheek, but he expected that it wouldn't last more than a couple of days. They would be holed up in the house for a while anyway, getting reacquainted. After that, a few days relaxing on the beach—it would be temperate enough for another month or two at least—would bring her around. He hated to see her so pale, as though she'd been hiding out in a cave for two years. Perhaps he would order a tanning bed for the house so she could get some color back.

"Listen," Miles said. "There may be someone at the house when we get there, but I don't want you to worry about her. I told her to get out before we get home. She's stubborn, though. Thinks she's my new wife." He laughed.

When his Mary-Katie didn't respond, he worried that she had decided the silent treatment was what he deserved. He didn't want to get their reunion off on the wrong foot, and it had already presented a number of challenges.

"Don't worry," he said. "Cammy is out of there. I knew from the day I caught her trying on your jewelry that she had the wrong idea about our relationship. I mean, hers and mine. *You* are my wife. Till death do us part, Mary-Katie. I've always been serious about that. I hope you've never questioned that about us."

It was a big change for her, he knew. She'd left all her belongings behind her. Attachments. He should probably try to be kind. Since he had decided to forgive her and take her back, he was going to make a conscious effort to be nice to her. Forgiveness was important.

The road was quiet. They had about fifty miles to go before they'd even get to a four-lane highway. He didn't care much for the back roads, but they needed the time alone together.

"What was with that loser, Mary-Katie?" he said. "I've got to say that I'm disappointed in your recent taste in men. Was he a lumberjack, or what?"

This time he got a response. His Mary-Katie blinked several times, as though she were keeping back tears.

"A man's got a right to defend his wife and property, babe," he said. "He was definitely trying to appropriate you. Very uncool, taking another man's wife."

He was about to tell her that she needed to concentrate on being *his* wife once again, when she suddenly made a fist of her two hands and swung at him, hitting him on the chest so hard that the car swerved violently into the opposite lane and they just missed ending up in the ditch on the other side of the road. His Mary-Katie was thrown back against her door and she began screaming, calling him an animal and other unpleasant names. She was ugly when she screamed.

"Shut the fuck up!" he screamed back at her. He put the car in Park, even though it was facing the wrong way, half on the shoulder, half in the opposite lane. Then he grabbed her by the shoulders and shook her until she stopped.

She cried then, blubbering on about how *Caleb* had been the only man to be truly nice to her in her life. He shoved her harder toward the door and told her he'd heard enough, that Johnny Appleseed was part of the past and she needed to realize that her future was with him.

"I'm thinking that you weren't stupid enough to tell anyone in that piss-ant town about me. The way you left the island, you can't have," he said. "My guess is they'll think that *you* killed the lumberjack."

She just stared at him, her skin puffy and her eyes an unbecoming red. He did seriously doubt that she'd opened her mouth. If she had, chances were that she hadn't been too specific.

"I'm going to kill you," she said. Her voice was still shaky, but he could tell that she thought she meant it.

Miles put the car in Drive and pulled out into the road. "You tried it once," he said. "How'd that work out for you?"

Dusk was coming fast into the already gray sky. It was still early spring up here, and the cold made Miles all the more anxious to get home. There, the azaleas were nearly finished blooming, but here the trees were only budding and their jagged branches cast long, faint shadows across the road.

"Hey," he said. He was willing to try again, to really put himself out for her. "Remember that license plate game we played when we drove over to Dallas? You thought I cheated, I was so good at it."

She wouldn't look at him. When she tried fumbling in the glove box, he assumed she was looking for a tissue because there was a thin stream of snot running from her nose. Disgusted, he took his own handkerchief from his pocket and offered it to her, but she ignored him, choosing to wipe her nose on the shoulder of her own jacket.

"Nice," he said. "Looks like you've really learned something from your new friends."

"Fuck you," she said.

"That's pretty, too," he said. "We'll talk about that later."

Suddenly, she sat up straight and looked past the steering wheel to the left shoulder of the road. Miles saw a look of fear, maybe shock, on her face. She was fixated on something, but he couldn't tell what it was. They were passing a run-down farm operation with a number of busted-up trac-tors and a crumpled-up silo, but there wasn't anything remarkable about it.

"What is it?" Miles said. "What's the problem? Are you sick?"

As they sped on, his Mary-Katie turned her head, straining to look behind them.

"What?" Miles said.

After a moment she turned back around and settled onto the seat. She seemed to go all introspective on him, not realizing that he was talking to her. It was a habit of hers he hadn't missed.

"However you want to play it," Miles said. "It's going to be a long drive. Suit yourself."

"Are you sorry?" she said.

"I don't spend a lot of time worrying about the past, Mary-Katie," Miles said. "You know me better than that."

"Because if you want to tell me you're sorry, you'd probably better do it soon," she said.

"We're going to have a lifetime together, Mary-Katie," Miles said. "We need to look forward. I've got two new projects. One's over in Louisiana. A big one. We'll go check out the land together. It's a sweet, sweet deal."

"What I don't understand is why you married me, Miles," she said. "It's not like you couldn't get someone else, someone who was dumb enough to put up with you even if you almost had her killed. Even if you were selfish enough to murder your own child. There are women like that."

Miles was starting to feel uncomfortable. He hadn't wanted to get into things that had happened so long ago.

"So, if it was my kid, then I get equal say in what happens to it. Right? Isn't that the way it is?" He shifted in his seat. "And that's a big fucking *if.* Don't you think?"

"You're not sorry, then." She said it as though it were some kind of fact. Like she was saying, *The sun is yellow.*

Miles was about to turn his head to look at her, but the road curved abruptly to the left and there was a little girl ahead, in the middle of his lane. He got a quick impression of long, dark braids and a bright yellow coat and red boots. It occurred to him in the moment before he cried out and swerved across the road that she looked ready to go out and play in the snow. Then the sedan was headed down the hillside, breaking the scrub trees as it plunged, airborne, toward the Quair. Finally, it bounced down hard and Miles's head and shoulders burst from the windshield and he was free of the car, shooting through the air like a man fired from a cannon. A thousand thoughts flooded his head—*Where was the pain? Shouldn't he be in pain? Had he left his toothbrush at the inn? What had his brother been hiding in his gym bag that afternoon before he died? Who is watching?*—but a single thought tore itself away from the rest: *Why had he only heard his own scream and not his Mary-Katie's?*

Then Miles closed his eyes because he couldn't bear the anticipation of plunging into the chestnut tree ahead of him, a tree whose thousand twisted limbs beckoned in the failing light like those of some freakish and dangerous mother.

51

MORGEIWICZ, THE YOUNG TROOPER, had acceded to Bill's request to transfer Frank away from the Carystown jail to the regional lockup in Bolton County with an attitude of solemn efficiency. It wasn't lost on Bill that, twenty-five years before, Frank had probably been just as sincere and just as serious about being a Marine as this young man was about the law.

As soon as the paperwork was done, Bill drove out to Frank's house. He knew it would only have been a matter of time before Frank's arrangement with Charlie Matter went bad of its own accord. Would Frank have run from his wife, leaving her to deal with the shame of the meth business all alone? He doubted it. Frank had been desperate, but Bill knew he loved Rose more than anything. In fact, maybe he loved her too much if he had let it drive him to attempted murder.

Rose's sister, Julie, had been there to help handle the tears, the disbelief. It was the disbelief that had remained in Rose's eyes when he'd gotten up to leave. There would be the call from Frank, soon enough, to bring her around.

It was only later, with Mitch and Daphne, that Bill shared his theory that Frank had intentionally avoided killing Charlie Matter.

"I don't think he could do it," he said as the three of them sat in his office drinking cups of the strong coffee that Mitch had made as soon as they got back from Frank's house. Mitch had waited in the cruiser, but he'd seen the regretful look on Bill's face when he came out of the door.

"You don't think he *wanted* to get caught?" Daphne said. "I just don't see Frank in this at all. It's like finding out my dad was dealing."

"Well, if you had a disease that was killing you slowly and your husband made the kind of salary this county pays its deputies, I expect he would do some moonlighting," Bill said.

"Pumping gas or working at the quick-stop, maybe," Daphne said.

"We don't know how deep he was in," Mitch said.

"I'm sure Mr. Matter has all the details," Bill said. "Not that we don't need to hear Frank's side of it." He was feeling a little guilty about having suspected Mitch of being Charlie Matter's inside man.

"That bastard Matter," Mitch said. "Between him and Birkenshaw, they've made this town some kind of sewer."

"Paxton Birkenshaw?" Daphne said. "What about him?"

They filled her in on the details of the search at the Birkenshaw house. Bill told them both once again to keep mum on the details and absolutely to stay away from the press. When he mentioned the press, he gave Daphne a severe look. This time, she had the decency to look a little chagrined.

"Things are going to get ugly," Bill said. "We've got to bring in a big name and his mama's not going to like it. And it's more than the drugs and his possible involvement with the death of the Moon girl." He turned to Mitch. "I want you to continue with the Cayley case with an eye toward Birkenshaw. He's been seeing Francie Cayley and I'm thinking that her mother objected."

"No kidding," Mitch said. "I knew she was too good-looking not to have some guy on the line."

"Wow. Great police work," Daphne said sarcastically.

Mitch gave her chair a kick. "I don't see you out there investigating anything," he said.

"At least I wouldn't be stonewalled by a suspect just because she's pretty," Daphne said.

"Quit it," Bill said. Who needed children when he had these two?

"If you'd been paying attention to my reports, you'd have known she wasn't a suspect," Mitch said. "You want me to bring her in?" he asked Bill.

"Birkenshaw is the one we need to bring in, but it seems we're suddenly short-handed. I need you to get a couple of hours' sleep and then relieve Clayton at the hospital. I'm thinking we'll be questioning our friend Charlie Matter in the morning if his wound is as insignificant as I think it is. We'll pick up Birkenshaw tomorrow when the troopers get down here."

"What about Delmar Johnston?" Daphne said.

"For Frank's sake we'd better start praying he makes a full recovery," Bill said.

A few minutes after eight, Margaret came into the station, which was empty except for Bill. With a sympathetic smile, she set a small cooler on his desk.

"I hate for you to miss a lunch *and* supper," she said.

Bill pushed away from his laptop, on which he was writing out the details of Frank's arrest, and sighed.

"I'm sure glad to see you," he said. "This is a goddamn dog's dinner of a mess, Margaret."

As she unpacked the cold sandwiches and fruit salad, he brought her up to speed on the situation with Frank and Paxton Birkenshaw.

"It sounds like you should go out there tonight," she said. "Freida Birkenshaw isn't going to sit by and watch while you haul her only son off to jail. She'd spend every penny she has to protect him. You know that."

"I've got two prisoners in the hospital. Fortunately, or unfortunately as the case may be, one is unconscious. But the other one's meaner than a snake. The troopers will be down here at seven in the morning. Nothing's going to happen in the next eleven hours except me writing reports and going over Frank's. Who knows what he left out when I had him doing interviews around the Catlett boy's death?"

"You know best," Margaret said.

This was all going to come down on him, whether Birkenshaw got away or was hanged on the green in front of the courthouse. It just didn't matter. It was damned embarrassing, was what it was. He looked incompetent as hell, and not just in front of the whole world, but in front of Margaret. That's the thing that really galled him.

"I just wanted you to know that you were right about Paxton in the first place," she said. "I shouldn't have pressured you one way or the other."

Damn. It was just like her to take the wind out of his sails with an apology when *he* was the one who had been a jerk.

"Don't apologize," he said. "I don't know that my moving any faster would've helped anyway. It wouldn't have made a difference for Lillian

Cayley. But maybe I could've gotten Birkenshaw talking about Charlie Matter. And Frank."

They didn't linger over the food. He found himself feeling better after the sandwich. The calories had helped, but Margaret's company had made more of a difference.

As she repacked the cooler, the front door opened. Francie Cayley stood in the doorway, a dark blue raincoat pulled tight around her, looking uncertainly into the dimly lit lobby area. Although he hadn't locked the front door, Bill hadn't wanted to invite any curiosity seekers to drop in for a chat.

He stood up and went out to meet her.

When she saw Margaret following behind him, Francie shrank back.

"I don't want to bother you," she said. "I wasn't sure what else to do. Who I should call."

"You want to come sit down?" Bill asked her.

"What is it, honey?" Margaret said.

Francie spoke, her voice just barely controlled. "I can't get hold of either Kate or Paxton," she said. "I've tried his cell phone and at his house. And someone is *always* supposed to answer at the house. He hates Kate. I'm afraid he's done something to her."

Margaret led her over to a chair. "Sit," she said, easing her onto the seat.

Francie nodded to Margaret and sat, but took a breath and continued to address Bill, who stood over her.

"He killed my mother," she said. "Don't ask me how I know, because you won't believe me. All day I've been trying to figure out what to do. But when I couldn't reach Kate, and then Paxton—I don't know. I just think something is wrong."

Margaret shared a glance with Bill. Not an I-told-you-so look, but a mutual agreement.

"Where did you last see Paxton? When?" Bill asked, already mentally preparing to call the state police post to get someone out to help bring Birkenshaw in. With Kate Russell in imminent danger, he wouldn't have to bother a magistrate until the morning. It was the excuse he needed to do what he should have done earlier.

"He left my house late last night," she said. "You have to help me find

Kate, please. She's not at the cottage, and I've tried to reach Caleb, her boyfriend, but all I get is a busy signal. For hours. Please."

Bill knew it was the wrong time to mention that her friend Kate had her own secrets. It was entirely possible that Kate Russell had left town.

"If we can pick up Birkenshaw, she'll be fine," Bill said.

"Do you know what he'll do to her?" Francie said. "Do you want her dead, too? She doesn't deserve this. She only wanted to help me."

"Bill," Margaret said. "I'll go with her."

"I didn't go in, but I've got a key to the cottage," Francie said.

There was no way he was going to send Margaret out to look for a murderer or potential victim. But he also knew that he was going to have to give in.

"Let me make some calls," he said. "I'll get someone out to the Birkenshaw farm to see if he's there and bring him in. Then we'll go find your friend."

Darkness engulfed the cottage. The lights from the antiques mall illuminated the edge of the yard, but that was all. Bill pulled the cruiser into the empty driveway.

"Does she have any other friends she might be staying with?" Bill asked.

"No," Francie said. "I would have told you. Can we please go in?"

"I'd rather you stay here," Bill said.

But after she handed him the key, she followed him up to the front porch. When he had trouble with the lock, Francie said, "Here, let me do it." She opened the door, but Bill went in ahead of her to turn on the lights.

The cottage was empty. The neatly straightened living room looked as though it were ready for company. Bill checked the kitchen, noting the refrigerator's pitiful contents.

Where are you, Kate? He wanted to believe that she hadn't left town. Sometime after their conversation at the diner he'd come to terms with his feelings for her and had promised himself that he would never pursue her. Leaving Margaret was out of the question, but he still felt a desperate need to find her and make sure she was safe.

In the bedroom, Francie noted the open drawers and gaping closet.

The room didn't look ransacked, only carelessly abandoned. A single out-fit, including jewelry, lay on the bed.

"That's weird," Francie said. "She wasn't getting ready for anything special that I know of. And she wouldn't wear that to work."

Bill, who was clueless about what any woman besides Margaret would wear, made a mental note of her observation.

"Looks to me like maybe she was packing," he said.

"She might have gone out to Caleb's," Francie said. "Sometimes she spends weekends out there."

On the way out to Caleb Boyd's place, the young woman beside him was quiet except for the occasional direction. Boyd's father had been one of the barbershop regulars, but not a loafer, and a well-known turkey hunter. When others would spend day after day in the woods and come home with nothing, Trace Boyd would drive up with six or seven good-sized males. When his wife died, though, he'd stopped showing up at the barbershop. He died in his sleep six months later.

Unlike the cottage, Caleb Boyd's house was ablaze with light. Bill was glad to see it.

"Her car's here," Francie said. "Caleb's truck, too. Look." She pointed to the small convertible in front of the house. Boyd's pickup truck was parked just outside the garage.

Before Bill could park and shut off the engine, Daphne radioed in that she and two state troopers were set to meet at the station in half an hour.

"Are you coming back? Or do you want me to take them on out when they get here?" she asked.

"We've just arrived at Boyd's house," he answered. "It might be an hour before I get back to the office, so you'd better take them on out. I'll be in touch when I'm done here and find out where you are."

"Ten-four, Boss," Daphne said.

When Francie started out of the cruiser, Bill held her back.

"I know I can't make you stay in the car," he said. "But we need to go up *together*."

He was sorry to see the look of hope on her lovely face change to one of fear.

"Of course," she said.

On the porch, Bill rang the bell several times. Behind the house they heard the distinct barking of beagles. They were so noisy, their yelps frantic and wild, that Bill wasn't certain how many of them there were.

"Let's head around back," he said. "The dogs must be locked up."

"They've got a run," Francie said.

Bill didn't like that she was with him. The area was exposed and Birkenshaw could have been hiding anywhere.

"Stay behind me," he said. "Please."

Around the back of the house security lights flipped on as they approached, throwing the yard into a pool of bright white light. He saw the beagles now, a good-looking pair that crowded the fence as they barked furiously.

He and Francie headed for the back door, which he noticed was standing wide open. He was about to tell her to stay close when she started to scream.

She grabbed his arm and tried to pull him back from the doorway where the mangled body of a man, presumably Caleb Boyd, lay blocking their path.

52

THE SOUND OF THE RIVER sloshing against its bank lifted Kate to consciousness. An icy breeze stirred her hair. She was confused at first, knowing she was inside the car, but she opened her eyes to find the windshield gone and the driver's side jammed with tree branches.

"Miles?" Her voice sounded unfamiliar to her, quiet and raspy.

There was no answer from within the branches.

When she tried to shift in her seat to get a closer look, she found that one of her legs was trapped in the crush of the dashboard. The deflated air bag lay like a giant balloon over her lap. Panic rose in her chest and she pushed at the air bag frantically with her bound hands as though she were battling some animal trying to trap her. Finally, it was off of her, and she wriggled her foot out of her shoe and inched her leg out, crying aloud with pain.

The pain made her want to curl into a ball and close her eyes and check out again. Maybe if she did, she would eventually awake to find herself in her own bed back at the cottage, Caleb breathing evenly beside her as he slept.

She called Miles's name again, but the only answer was the constant *slap slap* of water against the riverbank.

Miles was gone, somewhere out in the falling dark. Dead or alive, she didn't know. *Did she really care? Yes.* She surprised herself with the sudden hope that Miles was horribly, brutally dead. If he weren't dead, if he'd awakened—she looked at the tree branches and asked herself how that might be possible—and had gone for help, she would never be free of him.

She saw her life through the insane scenario that he'd been babbling about before the accident, living in the island house like the last few years had never happened, like they had been some extended hallucination. She felt the panic rise again. If there was anything that living with Miles had taught her, it was that there were worse things than death.

Outside the absent windshield there wasn't much to see except the tangle of branches. Neither could she see the top of the hillside from the passenger window. The sedan had turned over several times on the way down, and she vaguely recalled the sensation of feeling afloat in her seat belt. What a bizarre favor Miles had done her by strapping her in so carefully after he'd forced her into the car. If he'd been less concerned about her safety (or, really, her ability to jump out of the car) and more about his, he might still be in the driver's seat, pinned to it or gored by the intruding branches. Miles had always considered mandatory seat belt laws an unnecessary limit on his personal freedom.

Kate took a mental inventory of her body. When she twisted to the right, she felt some small pain, as though one of her ribs were bruised. But other than a dull ache behind her eyes and a sore arm, her leg was the only thing that seemed to be seriously injured.

It was getting darker. And colder. Accustomed as she was now to the country, she didn't want to be in this abandoned place alone. As the last daylight faded away, she noticed a small bright circle just outside the front of the sedan: one of the headlights had stayed on. She imagined the headlight like a lazy eye, dangling from its socket.

She struggled with the scarf binding her wrists, chewing on its rolled edge. The taste of the silk was bitter on her tongue, and she had to stop frequently to gather saliva to lessen it. As she worked the scarf she soon realized that one of her upper molars was loose in her mouth. It had almost certainly happened when Miles hit her back at the cottage. She cursed him out loud, screaming his name, half hoping he could hear her.

An hour passed. Small, urgent rustling noises came from outside the sedan, and she saw the bulbous form of some kind of rodent run through the tree's branches. Whatever it was, it didn't come inside the window, and she was grateful. Caleb had told her that the river rats could grow to be as big as cats and had been known to try to hide themselves in the clothes people were wearing. Packs of dogs, too, roamed the countryside at night, and it had been a long, cold winter. In her life, she had been used to protecting herself from other humans, not animals, and she felt a new kind of fear. Although she was cold, tiny beads of sweat formed a line across her forehead. She felt feverish.

The night was so quiet that she could have cried. Every five or ten minutes she heard vehicles passing by on the road far above her. Was anyone looking for her? Francie was too bound up with Paxton. Eventually, the sheriff would want to talk to her again; he had been concerned about her going into her house alone the night before. Now she wished she had asked him inside. If there was anybody who was qualified to rescue her the way she needed rescuing now, it was Bill Delaney. But he didn't even know she was missing.

Miles had obviously not flagged anyone down, or he would have been back for her by now. That meant he was out there somewhere, perhaps only a few feet from the car. The thought filled her with dread, but she knew that she wasn't safe where she was. She decided that she had no other choice but to try to make it out of the car even with her hands tied.

Then she laughed, realizing what an idiot she'd been. She twisted around to the console box between the seats, feeling her way for the latch with her fingertips. It took her several minutes of breaking off small pieces of the branch that was wedged against it, but eventually she was able to raise it. She felt around the compartment until her hand recognized the hard rectangle of Miles's favorite chrome Zippo lighter. She'd given it to him as a stocking stuffer on their second Christmas together so he could use it to light the cigars that he always, thoughtfully, took out to the patio to smoke. She had hated the cigars, but now she kissed the cool metal of the lighter's case, knowing it would be her salvation.

As Kate climbed out of the sedan, the headlamp blinked out, leaving her temporarily blind in the darkness. The acrid smell of burned silk followed behind her as she felt her way, hesitating. The moon hadn't yet risen, and she could hear the river better than she could see it. When her eyes finally adjusted, she saw that she was closer to the water than she'd first thought.

Her side was sore, but her leg didn't trouble her much and she knew that she'd been lucky to be able to walk away, even if it had taken her several hours. She wasn't wearing a watch, but guessed that it was somewhere around 9:00 P.M. *If* she'd been back at the cottage, *if* it had been two weeks ago, *if* Isabella Moon hadn't come into her life, *if* Miles hadn't been such an animal, perhaps she would be lying on her sofa now in her chenille bathrobe, reading a novel or making plans with Caleb on the telephone. *If.* As Miles had said, *That's a big fucking if.*

Caleb. She squeezed her eyes closed, trying to get the picture of his bloodied body out of her mind. *It was her fault. She'd killed him just as surely as if she'd pointed a gun at him and pulled the trigger.*

What would she tell Bill Delaney when she got back to town? The truth would have to come out about who she really was and where she'd come from. And what if Miles had been right about everyone thinking that she killed Caleb?

The weak light from the Zippo showed the hillside to be a maze of brush and broken trees and twisted pieces of the sedan. But she kept the lighter on too long, and the metal burned against her skin so that she dropped it.

"Please, please, please," she whispered as she felt around the ground. She couldn't imagine going on in the dark without it.

At last she felt a spot of warmth against her bare foot and bent down to find the lighter among some fallen leaves. As she tried to rise from the ground, her side exploded with pain and she cried out. Crouching in the darkness, she doubled over. Sweat dripped down her neck, soaking the collar of her blouse. When the pain subsided some and she was finally able to stand, she struck the Zippo again and held it aloft, briefly this time. She was relieved to see that her best chance of getting up the bank would be to go sideways for several yards before heading to the road above.

She moved slowly. After a minute she found walking with one bare foot too difficult and slipped off her remaining shoe. She had loved to go barefoot as a child, to the despair of her grandmother, but now she just tried not to think about the snakes or bits of glass or used condoms or beer tabs she might be stepping on.

When the growth on the bank thinned some, she started up the hillside. As she climbed, using pliable saplings and rope-thick vines as handholds, she could hear the passing traffic and her heart lightened despite the stabbing pain in her side.

Yes, she'd had to tell a few lies to get away from Miles, and, of course, the whole Isabella Moon affair was bizarre beyond words. But what harm had Isabella Moon really done her? Hadn't it been Isabella Moon she had seen by the side of the road, staring after them as they passed by in the sedan? Hadn't it been Isabella Moon standing in the middle of the road so that Miles saw her and veered off the road and down the embankment? If anything, she was grateful to Isabella Moon. If Miles were indeed gone— *please let him be dead please let him be dead* (her very heart cried for him to be dead)—she had nothing left to fear.

Something touched her hair. When she waved her hand to brush it away, she felt something rough and wet, something alive against her skin. She cried out.

"Mary-Katie." Miles's voice was a choked whisper.

"No," Kate said, looking up. "Miles."

She backed away, pressing a hand to her mouth. The moon had risen and the light was better on the hillside. After a moment she could make out one side of Miles's face. It was torn at the cheek so that she could see most of his upper teeth. The rest was a mass of bloody tissue. One arm hung down at a broken angle, the other she couldn't see. His inverted body swung slowly, like a horrific pendulum.

In those first seconds, she wanted to run away, to leave Miles there and pretend that she hadn't seen him. But she felt something down inside herself respond to the scene in front of her. There had been a time when she'd tried to kill Miles herself. She still wanted him dead, and all she had to do was walk away and not look back. But she couldn't make herself run away this time.

Miles's eyes opened and closed slowly, as though they would blink away the blood that had run into them. When she got closer, his eyes didn't focus. Perhaps he couldn't even see her. Kate put her hand up to his face and wiped some of the blood away with her fingertips. Still, he did not look at her. She began to suspect she had imagined that he'd spoken at all.

"Miles," she said. Her hand stroked the undamaged side of his face. But, strangely, she was not repulsed by the carnage on the other side. "Miles. Does it hurt?"

Miles made a sound in his throat, but she couldn't tell what it meant.

"Do you want me to go for help?"

This time she fancied his eyes looked toward her for the briefest of moments. He blinked with agonizing slowness. Droplets of blood, like tears, dripped onto her bare feet.

How many times had she imagined Miles helpless before her? Her daydreams, though, had been less than creative back in those days after he'd had her beaten and the child inside her killed. Torching him in his bed had been one of her favorites. Poisoning him with drain cleaner had been another. A hundred simple deaths. But *this* she couldn't have planned in a million years.

"I could help you, Miles," she whispered, getting close to his untorn ear. "I could help you down, if you want."

There was no response from Miles. He might have been a deer carcass strung up into the tree to let the blood flow out.

She stood regarding him a moment, a little unsure how to proceed. It was bad enough that she was once again faced with Miles, even in his present state. But she was also now dizzy with exhaustion and pain. What she really wanted to do was to curl up on the bank and sleep, even though it wasn't much farther to the top. Every so often there was the tempting growl of a passing truck or music from a car. She told herself that it would be easy to keep going, that she could flag someone down, call for help, get Miles an ambulance. But a thick sort of lethargy was settling over her, and her enthusiasm for the climb up the hillside was becoming weaker and weaker. And there was something else. *She didn't want to save Miles.*

Never had she seen Miles so helpless. He had never told her what it was, but he'd hinted at some failure in his past, some incident in which he'd been caught unawares and sworn it would never happen again. And it hadn't for a very long time. But now here he was.

"I could help you down," she said again. "Let me." She put the Zippo in her pocket. Her eyes had adjusted to the night and she didn't need anything to help her see.

Kate lifted her hands to Miles. As she gripped his shoulders, she could feel the odd gap at his shoulder that meant the arm was completely disengaged from its socket. But Miles didn't cry out or make any sort of sound as she tugged at him, gently at first, then more forcefully.

She swung Miles back and forth in the shadows, trying to get him loose from the low-growing tree that held him captive, its branches creaking in protest at her efforts to steal its gruesome prize. Every so often a limb would break and fall somewhere nearby or she would snap one beneath her feet as she moved. As she and Miles engaged in their strange and bloody dance, his inverted head resting against hers, his breath burbled against her ear, a shallow, watery sound. The memory of all the nights she had spent sleeping close to him, his body cradling hers and his breath damp against her neck, came back to her. Even with all that had passed between them, she couldn't forget.

With a loud *crack,* the tree gave up and turned Miles loose. His weight dropped onto her, casting her to the ground, and she found herself on her back and out of breath, Miles spread across her like some grisly, awkward blanket. She lay there a moment, paralyzed, with Miles crushing her.

Lying there, she realized that sometime in the night she had ceased to be afraid. It was almost a comfort to have Miles there with her, his blood still warm on her face. Below them, the river coursed quietly, ignoring them. Even the animals seemed to be staying away. Her own body was numb, but she still shivered, despite the heavy cover of Miles. She knew she had some sort of fever. It occurred to her that she might be dying. But even that did not frighten her.

She worked her way from beneath Miles so that only his head lay in her lap, and she sat up to rest against a fallen log. The scent of the wood's moldering leaves reminded her of the night in the cemetery with Lillian, and she was filled with the same sense of peace she'd felt lying on the ground, sheltering Isabella Moon's grave. It was the smell of home—not the one she'd made for so many years with her grandmother, but a different kind of home. All her life she'd heard how all living things went back to the earth: ashes to ashes and dust to dust. That Miles should die here, so close to the thing he would eventually become, seemed to imbue him with more honor and dignity than she thought he actually deserved. He was not nearly noble enough. Surely not as noble as Isabella Moon, she thought. No one had more dignity than an innocent child.

As she watched, Miles's eyes still blinked slowly, but they never looked left or right that she could tell. Their gaze was decidedly internal. Miles wasn't looking at anything outside himself. She smiled to think how typical *that* was.

She wondered that he did not look at his own body, particularly the shaft of tree limb extending a foot or so out of his lower abdomen. The limb's cruel shape stood outlined in moonlight. Did she imagine it, or was there a sort of shimmering aura surrounding it? Indeed, there was something magical about the night, in the calm of the air, the nearness of the river, and the moonlight glistening on its surface. She thought of the stories of elves and sprites in her grandmother's leather-bound books, the ones her grandmother had also read to her father when he was a child. Perhaps her father had died, and was there with them now, wondering himself at what she was doing. She shook the thought away, knowing it was a little crazy. Her head, though, felt fuzzy inside, and her thoughts couldn't fully form themselves. Fatigue overwhelmed her and she closed her eyes to rest for a few moments.

Mary-Katie.

She woke to see Miles still resting on her lap. Now his eyes were closed. *Had he spoken her name? How she'd come to hate that name, but now she knew that she was forever Mary-Katie, that she'd never really been anything else and never could be.*

Please, she heard him say. She wasn't certain that his lips had moved, but she believed that, were he to speak, it would be exactly what he would say.

She felt a kind of pity for Miles. He was more animal-like to her than ever at that moment, helpless as he was and smelling of blood and urine and feces. Dapper, polished Miles who had never had a chest hair out of place around her unless he planned it to be so. She stroked his sodden brow. *Poor Miles.*

Realizing she was thirsty, Mary-Katie turned her gaze to the river below them. But she knew that Miles had so many things to tell her that she couldn't go yet. So, she listened as the words poured forth into the night air: recriminations, promises, dreams he'd had, jokes that she hadn't heard in several years. He was suddenly the Miles she knew when they first met, the one who charmed her grandmother with his clever stories and good manners. Where had this Miles been? Tears filled her eyes as she listened, the words breaking and catching on the trees around them, settling down only to disappear like flakes from a spring snowfall.

He had one last request of her, and she couldn't refuse him. They would never be the same people again, the two of them, but something between them had been tenuously healed.

She took Miles's head in her hands and lifted it so she could slide away and let it gently down again to rest on the leaves. *Why wouldn't he open his eyes? Surely he would want to watch.*

"Wait," she said.

Mary-Katie bent over Miles's twisted body and grasped the ragged shaft of limb buried in his gut as though it were some primitive Excalibur. At the first pull, his back arched a couple of inches from the ground, but the limb's outer covering of bark crumbled in her hands and he fell back with a grunt of escaping air.

"Sorry," Mary-Katie said. She giggled.

She tried again, this time bracing her foot against Miles's thigh. She twisted the limb to the right a bit as she pulled, ignoring the pain that blossomed in her own abdomen.

As the limb came free, she stumbled backward, her hands still wrapped around it. Even in the scarce moonlight, she could see the gore that had come out with it, and she tossed the limb into the darkness.

"There," she said.

She'd done the last thing that she could for him, the last thing he'd asked her to do. She didn't need or want thanks for it.

Without looking down at him, Mary-Katie stepped over Miles and headed down to the river to get a drink. Her fingers were cold and sticky; she thought that she might wash them in the water as well. Her progress down the hillside was slow, but she had no conscious measure of time.

When she got to the river, she found that she could not reach the water because of the broken logs and silt that crowded the bank, and so she crouched beside it, watching. It wasn't such a wide river. She thought that she might even be able to walk across it if she wanted to find out what was on the other side. She was about to try again to get to the water when she became aware that someone was behind her, watching her.

"Who is it?" Mary-Katie said. She stood up and turned around to see a little girl standing on the bank just a few feet away.

It was Isabella Moon, yet it was not. This child had long, straight auburn hair and a happier mien than Isabella Moon. Her nose turned up at its end and the girl tilted her head fetchingly as she watched her. But she had the same ethereal grace that the other child had had, the same quality of light about her. The girl held out her hand to Mary-Katie and waited for her to decide if she would take it. There was no urgency about her, only a sense of calm and pleasant expectation.

The fatigue that had plagued Mary-Katie finally seemed to be gone, and her head cleared so that everything around her seemed etched in the same pure light that surrounded the child. She took the child's hand, following her as they walked along the river's edge, the water rippling beside them like the sweetest of music.

53

MARGARET CLIPPED a hand's width of asparagus from its bed and dropped the spears into a basket. They would have asparagus for about another month. In the garden there had been the usual battles with the local wildlife—chipmunks, rabbits, and the occasional groundhog. It seemed they had won this year, sacrificing only a half row of lettuce before they were able to trap two rabbits and transport them to a pasture outside town. At her parents' house those many years ago, her father would've just shot them as vermin and pitched them into the woods or the sinkhole, but there were laws about discharging firearms within the town proper. And the vengeful crew that had replaced Bill and all his deputies after the last election would certainly throw Bill into jail if he so much as took a single shot at a squirrel.

Bill looked up from his book and smiled as Margaret came in the back door.

"You coming into the shop this morning?" he asked.

"I want to clean this, then get a start planting the second round of green beans," she said. "Maybe around eleven? I'll bring us lunch."

"Sure thing," he said, going back to his book.

He was dressed with careful precision down to his pleated khakis, which he'd ironed himself, and a bright green polo shirt. When she ran her fingers lightly, affectionately, over his head as she walked by, she found that his skin was smooth and knew that he had shaved it that morning in the shower. She was proud of him for so many reasons, but she was also grateful that he'd kept his dignity despite the many coroner's inquests and Charlie Matter's trial. It had been a stupid thing for him to run for reelection, but she had known better than to try to talk him out of it. His pride had kept him from just letting his term run out and leaving town, and she had thought that she should at least safeguard some of that pride, even though it meant he would be hurt.

Margaret walked to work, just as she had when she'd been director of the museum on the other side of town. This morning a trace of humidity hung in the late morning air from an unusual, after-midnight rain shower that had dampened the grass and streets. With the antiques shop just six blocks away, it was an easy walk. Best of all, she would be spending the day with the man she loved instead of a crumbling house full of scandal-loving blue-blooded gossips whose snide comments had caused her more than a moment's pain.

She and Bill had discovered a whole new strata of friends in Carystown, the shopkeepers and real-estate people whose work kept Carystown going and whose interests had more to do with putting food on their families' tables and paying their kids' college tuition than what cocktail party they had or hadn't been invited to.

When she reached Bridge Street, she crossed at the light and kept her head down as she passed the single empty storefront on the block, a shotgun space whose trim had been painted as bright a yellow as the city's historical code would allow and whose front window sported an unbroken line of black-and-white Scottie dogs across its bottom.

Someone had, thankfully, smeared a wide swath of white paint over the lettering on the window, so that only a portion of a single letter *S* was visible. The interior of the shop was empty, but not quite swept clean, and much had been made about the scattering of boxes, broken pottery, incense sticks, and damaged pieces of clothing that lay on the floor.

It seemed the shop had opened almost overnight after Charlie Matter's trial was over and he was sent to prison for thirty-five years for drug manufacturing and trafficking. (In a fit of conscience, Frank had waived his right to a trial and was given ten years for conspiracy and ten for poisoning Delmar Johnston. His attempted murder of Charlie Matter had never been pursued. It struck Margaret that no one, not even the prosecutor, had given enough of a damn about Charlie Matter to make any kind of issue out of it.) It was rumored that the mentally broken Hanna Moon had been paid a couple thousand dollars by someone from out of town for the use of her daughter's name on the shop: Isabella Moon's Fantastical Notions.

There were plenty of moneyed tourists, who had never heard of the dead child, to purchase enough of the shop's tarot cards and crystals and copper bracelets, Ouija boards, and cheaply made Indian clothing to keep the shop open for a few months at a time, but in order for a business to survive in Carystown year-round, it had to draw at least some locals. But not even the most crass and curious of town residents could bear to cross its threshold.

Eight months it had lasted, and there were those in town—chief among them Carmella Pulliam, who had a fondness for old embroidered table linens and liked to come into Delaney & Lowe's to browse—who believed that the place might have stayed open if Janet Rourke hadn't made it her personal mission to get it shut down.

It was Carmella's opinion that Janet Rourke had been involved with Paxton Birkenshaw and felt responsible in some way for the girl's death. Bill also thought that Janet had known more than she'd told when she was questioned about her relationship with Paxton. But she had insisted that they were no more than friends, and social friends at that.

Janet, for whom Margaret had never much cared, had indeed seemed an unlikely champion for the dead child, and was certainly no arbiter of good taste with her expensive but sexy clothing, heavy jewelry, and heavier makeup. She wondered if perhaps Janet's objection to the shop didn't have more to do with the baby that she had borne in the midst of all the town's troubles after an unashamed and very public pregnancy. Old-fashioned as Carystown could sometimes be, no one had condemned her, and her insurance business was thriving despite the fact that she wouldn't name the baby's father. She was just another aging professional who had wanted a baby more than a husband. There was also talk that she was planning to buy the Chalybeate Springs Co-op property and make its ancient sulfur spring the centerpiece of a luxury spa. That would happen only if she could keep the place from being declared a permanent toxic waste site. But Margaret suspected that if anyone could keep that from happening, it would be Janet.

Inside Janet's agency, a different young woman sat at the desk that Kate Russell had once occupied. Margaret knew that Kate Russell's disappearance had been one of the great disappointments of Bill's life. It was a disappointment Margaret didn't share, except for the fact that she'd left him without any serious, public confirmation about her supposed contact with the dead girl, which didn't help his credibility with the voters. She knew that Bill felt guilty, too, because if Francie Cayley was correct, Kate Russell—or whatever her name had really been—was probably as dead as her boyfriend, Caleb.

Paxton Birkenshaw and his mother were gone as well. Bonterre was up for sale. Margaret was only one of a handful of people, including the coroner, who knew that Freida Birkenshaw had killed her son, that it wasn't the other way around. It had been Bill's last concession to the collective dignity of the old families.

But it was Francie Cayley for whom Margaret felt the most sorrow. Things were better for her now. She was making a new life for herself in Texas, where no one had ever heard the name Isabella Moon. Francie's Christmas card to Bill and Margaret had mentioned that she was engaged to be married, but she hadn't given any details. Margaret could hardly blame her.

Delaney & Lowe's was surprisingly busy for a Tuesday. Margaret had to set their sandwiches in the tiny office refrigerator as soon as she came in so she could help with customers.

Bill had surprised her with his willingness to learn about all things antique. They specialized in fine linens and mid-nineteenth-century American furniture, which was getting harder and more expensive to come by. But, as he had said, you couldn't swing a dead cat in Carystown without hitting an antiques store that sold early twentieth-century tchotchkes and Depression glass, so they might as well go for it.

The morning ended with the sale of an enormous walnut dresser that Bill had picked up at auction down in Tennessee. The thing was incredibly heavy and just this side of primitive, but he'd bought it on a hunch and today it had paid off.

"Let's celebrate," he said, when the couple who had bought it left the shop. There were no other customers and the scheduled tour bus wasn't due in town for another hour.

"I have apple juice in the back," Margaret said.

"Good enough," Bill said.

She brought the juice and two plastic cups from the office.

"I don't think so," Bill said. "I just made us a thousand bucks profit. This calls for the real thing."

He plucked two crystal glasses from the place-setting display on a dining table and wiped them out with a paper towel.

Part of her knew that it was for her that he had stayed in Carystown. She would've gladly left if he'd asked. But he hadn't. When the occasional clueless out-of-towner would ask what he knew about that dead little girl *what's her name?* and what he knew about the rich guy who'd gone crazy and killed himself and those other people, Bill would tell them that it was a shame, all that had happened, and that they might go by the library to read about it in the old newspapers.

"To us," Bill said, raising his glass. "And my damned good judgment."

Margaret laughed.

"Wait, I haven't finished," Bill said. "And my damned good judgment in marrying you, Margaret Lowe Delaney."

They clinked their glasses and drank, happy in each other's company. Margaret brought out the sandwiches and they ate quickly at the desk, talking about their next buying trip. Bill was in favor of a trip to Virginia, but Margaret insisted that the market was already overpriced there, that they would do better to go west, or maybe to Indiana or Ohio for some primitive pieces. Before they could settle on a choice, a pair of well-dressed women in their sixties came in wearing looks of wary eagerness. Margaret knew they imagined that they'd find incredible bargains in this hick town they'd just discovered.

She greeted them, then tactfully went to work on some paperwork at the desk while Bill cleared up their lunch things and took them out to the Dumpster in the rear alley.

One of the women called her friend over to look at the walnut dresser that Bill had sold only an hour before.

"Look at this, Jenny," she said. "Have you ever seen anything like this? Look how deep the drawers are."

"I'm so sorry," Margaret said. "That piece has already been sold, but I have several other walnut dressers along this back wall."

The woman either didn't hear or pointedly ignored her.

"And look," the woman said. "There's a penny in this drawer. It looks brand new."

Her friend took the penny from her hand and examined it. "You know, my mother used to say—she'd be a hundred years old this week if she were still alive—she used to tell me that when you come across a penny on the ground, or even hidden away, it means that someone dead is thinking of you."

Someone dead.

Margaret pressed her mouth together in a hard line. She never knew when it was going to happen, when she would be plunged into the hell that had been the past few years. For all the pretended normalcy of their almost-new life, she knew they were never going to be free of it. Someone, something would always call them back. If it wasn't some prying or ignorant tourist, it was a look in Bill's eyes, a fleeting look of deep hurt that he couldn't hide from her. She glanced to the rear of the store where the back door still stood open. It was a small mercy that he hadn't heard the woman, but a mercy all the same.

"I bet these people that own the store put it there," the first woman said. "Like you do when you give someone a new pocketbook for a gift."

Margaret gave her a bright, professional smile that signified nothing.

When Bill came in a few minutes later, he found her alone. He went to where she stood looking out the front window of the shop.

"That was quick," he said. He touched her lightly on the shoulder.

"They weren't serious," Margaret said, sliding an arm around his now-slender waist. She kissed him on the cheek.

"What was that for?" he asked.

"Nothing," she said. "You should probably call the trucking company about that dresser. That couple sounded pretty anxious to get it shipped."

"Yeah. I wonder why?" Bill said.

Margaret shrugged as if to say it didn't much matter why. That it would soon be out of the store was the only thing that was important to her.

Later that night, as she lay in bed with her husband sleeping at her side, she said a silent prayer of gratitude for his love and strength and tenderness. But, along with the gratitude there was, for the first time in their life together, a nascent fear of the day when he would no longer be there.

Read on for an excerpt of
Laura Benedict's newest novel

CALLING MR. LONELY HEARTS

a dark and provocative novel
about three friends whose lives are coming unraveled
by a lie they told years ago.

Published by Ballantine Books

CHAPTER 1

She was just plain Alice, and they never let her forget.

Roxanne and Delilah, who was called Del, knelt close to Alice by the light of a candle, the skirts of their stiff blue school uniforms crumpling against her. Del rested a hand on Alice's shoulder as though she might try to get up from the leaf-strewn ground and run away. But they all knew she wouldn't. Roxanne used a twig to stir some pungent concoction in a shell-thin African bowl she had brought from home. The odor suffused the copse like the fug from an ancient outhouse. To Alice, it smelled suspiciously like a baby's dirty diaper. There was something else, though. Something caustic and chemical-smelling that made her eyes water.

"I don't have to eat it, do I?" Alice said.

"Oh God," Del said. She hadn't wanted to go along with this whole thing in the first place. She was nervous enough about being in the park after dark. And there was something deeply wrong with what they were doing, she knew. Witchcraft on television was fine, but this was something else.

"Of course not," Roxanne said, her voice patient. The bowl was heavy in her hands, though it hardly contained anything at all. If she were a few years older than thirteen, she would know it was heavy with her own desire—a desire that she could, at that moment, identify only as dimly sexual.

"Get her coat off," she told Del.

"Come on," Del said. "Don't be a baby, Alice."

She reached for the buttons on the front of Alice's pea coat, which was exactly like the ones she and Roxanne were wearing, though Roxanne's had a black velvet scarf with elaborate roses etched into its nap tucked beneath the collar. Alice didn't help with the coat, but she didn't resist, either. Del flung the coat and the blue cardigan sweater with its Our Lady of the Hills crest onto the dormant grass.

Alice shivered in her blouse, hoping that she would be able to leave on at least her skirt and socks.

Roxanne nodded. Del's cold-numbed fingers tugged at the buttons of Alice's blouse.

"For pity's sake," Roxanne said. "Alice, you need to unbutton your blouse. You don't have to undo it all the way. Then you need to lie down."

Alice did as she was told. Roxanne put down the bowl and tucked the discarded coat beneath Alice's head. She brushed her fingertips over Alice's brow and smiled. Sweet, tender Alice. Though perhaps not so sweet, she whined sometimes. But at least she was Pure Alice, who had never been kissed—a virgin, as they all were.

"Now. Everyone be quiet," she said, picking up the bowl. Her hands shook a bit with the excitement of it all. She closed her eyes.

The words she spoke—seemingly to the sky, or the air in front of her— were unintelligible to the others. Her tone was one of supplication: a petition or a prayer, not so different from the prayers the priests said at mass. She tried for the same singsong in her voice, the same careful cadence. She's added a few thoughts and words of her own to the spell she took from the satanic witchcraft book she stole from the public library, thinking that they would make it more effective.

The herbs in the mash were ones she remembered being used in a joyful Santeria rite that her mother had taken her to, when her mother was on one of her "spiritual quests." It was this blending of dark magic and the divine that she believed would give them what they wanted.

Alice squeezed her eyes shut, trying to ignore the cold, but she had to clench her jaw to keep her teeth from chattering. Del picked up the flickering candle in its fragile hurricane and curved over it as much for warmth as to protect it from the unpredictable air around them. Roxanne pressed her fingertips against Alice's shoulder. She dipped the fingers of her other hand into the bowl, then touched them to Alice's bare chest.

Alice turned her face away from the hideous smell. Whatever was now on her chest felt like frozen sand. But she held still. She was doing this for all of them. Roxanne didn't recognize the depth of Alice's faith in her. Alice would die for her.

Del watched, wondering how Alice could let something so strange, so horrible, be done to her. Alice's face was as plain as her name, not homely, but fair and unfreckled, with high, broad cheekbones and too-thin lips. Alice's was not a threatening or even very expressive face. She smiled often, but her smiles were tentative, as though someone were always watching her and she didn't know if she should be smiling or not.

Alice reminded Del of a stray dog that had hung around their house for several months. She hadn't liked the way the dog flung itself at her feet, its belly exposed. It was a sneaky dog, pushing their elderly spaniel away from her kibble when it thought no one was watching, peeing on the rug when her mother let it inside, shivering, on snowy days. She knew she would probably go to hell for thinking so, but she wasn't sorry when a speeding pizza delivery car knocked it to the side of the road, its neck twisted.

She had never known Alice to be sneaky, or to do anything that would hurt or betray any of them. But there would be a first time, she was certain.

She watched as a woolly caterpillar inched its way into Alice's dull blond hair, its body curving gracefully as it moved. As it crawled toward Alice's cheek, Alice's lips and forehead contorted. Was she in pain? Del held her breath, thinking Alice might cry out.

"Roxanne!" Del said, stopping Roxanne in mid-chant.

Alice's eyes opened in a bald stare before rolling back to show two half-moons of white below their trembling lids. Even by the light of the candle, her lips looked blue; her body stiffened and began to spasm, lifting itself from the ground.

Before Roxanne could move away, Alice's left arm hit outward, catching Roxanne mid-stomach so that she gave a loud gasp. The bowl flew from her hand.

Del began to scream, then—remembering that they were in the park and anyone could hear—covered her mouth to stifle it.

Alice jerked her teeth clapping together with each violent throw of her head, her small, flat breasts shuddering. Now it was Roxanne who stared. Alice was like a mechanical doll, broken, frantic and wild in its malfunction. She was fascinated. Everything about Alice was always so predictable, so studied. But she had become interesting.

With a final upward thrust of her torso, Alice's body was calm, but her face was tinged blue, her eyes slitted, still with just their whites showing.

As Del scuttled away to crouch beneath a tree, the candle dropped to the ground, shattering its glass globe.

"We killed her!" Del said. "Shit, Roxanne. We killed her!"

Roxanne tilted her head, watchful. A slow curl of breath escaped Alice's mouth and dissipated.

"She's breathing," she said. "Quit freaking out. There wasn't anything in there that could hurt her." She twisted around to find the bowl, but could see nothing in the gathering dark. "And now it's all gone." They would have to start over again because she hadn't finished. Just another few minutes.

"We have to get someone," Del said. "What's wrong with her?"

Roxanne was in motion now, stuffing things into her book bag.

"The only place anyone is going is home," she said. "Just don't tell anyone you saw her tonight. She probably won't remember anything anyway—damn it, Del, the candle!" She pointed to the ragged circle of burning leaves surrounding the still-lighted candle. The flames were small and tentative, etching black stripes into the palms of the leaves around it.

Del found herself looking stupidly at the fire for several beats, knowing what was going to come next, imagining Alice's frozen body being consumed by the flames.

"Del!" Roxanne shouted.

Del swept handfuls of leaves on top of the burning ones, patting them with her hands. Were the leaves stoking the fire or stopping it? She couldn't tell.

"Help me," Del said. But Roxanne didn't move. Del buried the flames until just a few whispers of smoke rose from the pile.

"We have to go," Roxanne said. "Are you coming?" In the distance, they heard a shrill whistle, someone calling a dog or a child indoors.

"How can you be so hateful?" Del said. But Roxanne was moving away, confident that Alice would come to herself. She had homework to get to, and she was already thinking of the sketch she would do of Alice's face, that look of emptiness, of complete abandon.

Del ran, her book bag thumping against her back. At the edge of the park, she crossed Arthur Street without bothering to go down to the crosswalk at the corner. When a passing car blew its horn at her, she stumbled onto the opposite sidewalk. She made her way up the hill toward her house, breathing hard in the cold night air, hardly believing what she was doing.

Every lamp in every house she passed seemed to be burning as though to expose her. A dog she didn't know emerged from one of the yards and jogged along beside her for a few moments. Glancing down, she saw that it was short-haired, light brown with large splotches of black—a shepherd, maybe, or some mix.

"Go home," she said, but it didn't even look up at her. She wondered if her fear had attracted it. She was afraid for herself. Afraid for Alice. A dog like this—maybe even this very dog—might find Alice in the park. Her mind couldn't form the next horrible thought.

At the next corner, the dog stopped while she walked on. She looked back to see it staring after her, its breath lifting in misty bursts beneath the streetlamp.

Her father's car was in the driveway. It was after seven and she had missed dinner. When she tried to decide what she would do next, she could think only of Alice. How could she go into the house as though nothing had happened and eat the food that her mother left warming in the oven for her? How could she sit down and do her homework, watch Seinfeld or Saved by the Bell or some stupid movie and wait for the phone call from Alice's father, who would want to know why Alice hadn't come home?

She thought of how she'd let that caterpillar crawl into Alice's hair. She would go to Hell for what she had done, even though it wasn't her fault Roxanne was so mean.

As she slipped into the garage, she dropped her book bag gently inside. The smell of cooked sauerkraut came to her through the kitchen door, but she wasn't hungry. She tripped over her father's toolbox—the single-car space was stuffed full with boxes and bikes and workshop equipment— and felt something sharp graze her leg. Groping around the shelves by the door, she finally laid her hands on the flashlight they used for camping.

Del hurried toward the back of the empty park, praying that the pale glow she saw was some trick of the streetlamps or someone using one of the barbeque grills for a winter picnic. But she knew better.

"Alice," she whispered.

The flames clung to the ground in the copse like a brilliant orange blanket. Alice stood in the opening, silhouetted against the light. She cried out, holding her forearm to her eyes against the beam from Del's flashlight. In the moment before Del jerked the beam from Alice's face, she saw that Alice's skin and clothes were streaked with dirt and ash. Bits of leaves poked from her hair. Del thought of the caterpillar, but knew it was the least of Alice's problems. It was the wild look in Alice's eyes—a look of fear and anger and confusion—that caused her stomach to clench.

"Stay away from me," Alice said. "Go away."

"But it's me," Del said, slowing her step. She was more afraid of Alice than she was of the dog that had followed her up the road. But it wasn't actually Alice that she was afraid of. It was whatever had happened to Alice, whatever had changed her. The flashlight's beam caught one of Alice's legs, which were covered with dark streaks: blood, maybe, or feces?

"I saw you," Alice said. "I saw you run away."

"I'm here," Del said, trying not to look at Alice's exposed breasts, which were sharply divided by the stripe of noxious salve Roxanne had applied. "We have to leave."

The fire didn't seem to be spreading beyond the copse, but, still, she knew it wouldn't be long before someone saw it. There would be questions.

Alice wouldn't move.

"You just passed out for a few minutes," Del said. "It wasn't even that long."

"I was dead," Alice said her voice flat.

"Let's go home," Del said. She didn't like this Alice at all. This Alice frightened her.

"You both left me here," Alice said. "And I was dead, but he told me to come back."

"Don't be stupid," Del said. "Just come on. We'll all be in trouble if you don't come." She was on the verge of leaving Alice alone again, now that she knew Alice was alive. It didn't matter anymore that Alice was the purest of them or that Roxanne had promised that the so-called spell would attract a guy for them, and only for them. She told herself that it was a bunch of bullshit that Roxanne had made up. If only Alice would be quiet about it.

"He came for us, but you didn't even wait to see him," Alice said. "Don't you want to know what he looks like?"

"Get your stuff," Del said. The fire had not yet reached Alice's coat and sweater and book bag. But it was Del, not Alice, who gathered them. She buttoned Alice's blouse and stuffed her into the coat as though Alice were an idiot child. Then Del shoved the book bag and sweater into her arms, causing Alice to stumble backward.

As they left, Del almost tripped over the lost bowl. She kicked at it, driving it several feet away.

"Stop! Roxanne will be mad if you lose her bowl," Alice said.

Roxanne, who was the one who said they should leave Alice in the park, the one who ran away first. Del has known Roxanne since they were both four years old, but she still didn't completely understand why Roxanne did some of the things she did. Her mother had told her that Roxanne "acts out" because she didn't know her father, and that she thought she was special because she was "artistic." But those seemed like lame explanations to Del.

"I wouldn't worry about Roxanne, if I were you," Del said.

Ignoring her, Alice ran to the bowl and tucked it into her book bag.

They walked in silence until they reached Alice's house, one of the grand old mansions overlooking Victoria Park's duck pond.

"Fix your hair," Del said. "You've got leaves and stuff in it."

Alice bent over and quickly brushed her hands through her hair. When she came back up again, she smiled at Del. There was a smear of dirt across her left cheek, but Del didn't mention it.

"Thanks," Alice said.

Del didn't respond, but turned away to walk home. She couldn't wait to get away from Alice, whose eyes had at last lost their wild look. It was seven-thirty and Del was finally hungry. She didn't ever want to see Alice again.

After she'd gone only a few steps, Alice called to her.

"He looks like an angel," Alice said. "A perfect angel."

CHAPTER 2

Week 16 4/7

Dillon got out of the steaming Escort and eyed the expensive-looking car crumpled against its front bumper. He prepared himself to give the asshole who was driving it the scare of his life. Scaring people was one of his chief pleasures, and he had decorated himself accordingly: even the tattoo artist (a nice piece of ass out in San Francisco) had been skeptical about inking the row of blood-dripping fangs across his forehead. He himself was particularly fond of the scrollwork goatee on his chin, but the righteous row of studs on his upper lip, along with the ones over each eyebrow, were, as they say, the icing on the fucking cake.

He'd been coasting down Gravois Street, a single finger on the wheel, enjoying the raw pleasure of the night wind through the Escort's open windows. The few hours before dawn were the best, the coolest of the day in what had been a hot Cincinnati summer. In his pocket were a fresh thirty bucks and a couple of hits of Ecstasy he'd picked up playing roadie for The Toasted Bobs. They'd sat around the club drinking a few after-hours beers, but he was hardly even buzzed. Certainly not buzzed enough to miss seeing a car right in front of him. There was a stop sign at the bottom of the hill, which he'd intended to ignore, but no streetlight, and the car had seemed to appear out of the darkness from nowhere.

Now they were both in the middle of the intersection and his chest hurt like hell because the stupid airbag hadn't gone off.

He got out and tapped on the glass to get the attention of the guy inside the other car.

"Man, where are your fucking lights, man?" he shouted. There were no witnesses, no other cars around except the ones parked curbside. The houses around them were dark.

At first he thought the man inside the car was dead or something, the way he was leaning into the car's steering wheel. Then he sat back, and, without waiting for Dillon to move, pushed the door open.

"What the fuck?" Dillon said, jumping back.

He didn't look to Dillon like someone who'd just been in a car accident. He looked calm, and was, from what he could see from the interior light of the car, dressed in the kind of clothes guys only wore in magazines. Probably a faggot. Probably a fucking lawyer, too, driving a car like this. He could smell the leather from four or five feet away.

"Are you all right?" the man said.

"Where'd you come from?" Dillon said. "Where are your fucking lights? You could've killed us both!"

"Did you break something?" the man said, reaching out to touch his arm, which was crossed over his chest. "Maybe you should sit down."

Now Dillon was getting aggravated. The guy was acting like he was in charge, just like every other asshole in a suit. He jerked away.

"Shit," Dillon said. "This was your fault. And my car's fucking totaled."

"That's a shame about your car," the man said.

He couldn't bear to stand in front of this smug asshole who didn't seem to get that his only form of transportation, his only freedom, was gone and that it was *his* fault. Proving it would probably be a pain in the ass. People like this guy almost never had to pay for their fuckups. There would have to be police. He wanted to climb back into the Escort to see if there was a joint rolling around. *Calm.* He needed to keep his shit together and make this suit understand.

"I'll tell you right now that my insurance is no good," Dillon said. "So you're screwed right off the fucking bat. And they always blame the guy who does the rear-ending, even if it's the other guy's fault." At this, he gave the man a look that said he wasn't going to take the blame, that he wasn't somebody to be messed with. "You're not going to stick me with this bullshit."

"So, I take it that you don't want me to call the police?" the man said.

Dillon didn't like that he couldn't see the man's eyes in the dark, couldn't read him. He didn't like to get violent unless he was pushed, but he was ready.

"That would make your life easier? More pleasant?" the man said.

He couldn't tell if the guy was serious or was just taking his time, mocking him with his Eurotrash TV accent.

"I'm saying that if this shit gets all complicated, you're not going to get squat out of me anyway," he said. "So I wouldn't even bother."

"Hm." The man put his hand to his chin, thoughtful.

Dillon waited, breathing hard. It bugged him how quiet it was. Nobody on the street had turned on so much as a porch light to see what was going on. But it wasn't the kind of neighborhood in which people spent a hell of a lot of time outside. The house nearest to them was covered in graffiti and the only car in its driveway was up on blocks. Still, not even a random gangbanger had bothered to check out what was going on. It felt to him like a movie set where the crew was all out of sight, like one of those fake towns where the buildings were just fronts held up by wooden frames. He'd seen enough episodes of *The Twilight Zone* on the Sci-Fi channel to be a little freaked out. He didn't like the feeling.

He watched as the man walked to the back of the car (which he later learned was called an Aston Martin) and stroked its rear end like it was some kind of pet. It looked like the kind of car that would get carried away in a padded truck, rather than hauled up behind a tow. Following him, Dillon saw that maybe the damage wasn't so bad. The Escort was definitely totaled. There would be no fixing it and it had probably only been worth about five hundred bucks ten minutes earlier.

But the worst part was that the car didn't actually belong to him— it was registered in his sister's name. She was always doing nice things for him like that, covering for him, lending him a little cash when he needed it. This was one more thing he was going to owe her for. She was patient, though. Always patient, even when he really fucked up.

"I'll tell you what," the man said. In the glow of the Escort's remaining headlight Dillon could see that he was the kind of guy that chicks really went for, with expensive shoes and a hundred-dollar haircut that looked messy.

"I agree with you that we shouldn't trouble the police," he said. "What things of a personal nature do you have in the car? Do you have a screwdriver?"

"I don't know," Dillon said. "The usual shit. Why?"

In five minutes the Escort was cleaned out and he had the license plates off. It was a beautiful plan, and he wished he'd thought of it himself. Maybe the guy was some kind of mobster who did shit like this all the time. He didn't like messing with those kinds of guys, but he wasn't looking to argue. And it occurred to him that his sister's asshole boyfriend had probably come up with the money for the car, so maybe it wasn't such a loss. His sister would be sad, but he would make it up to her. She always forgave him in the end.

The Aston Martin fired up with the kind of muted rumble that those fancy European cars always made. He wasn't sure yet what the guy wanted from him, why he wanted to help him out. *Probably wanted him to suck his dick, and no fucking way was that going to happen!* After this was done, he planned to just take off, leaving the guy and the car behind. He was about ten blocks away from the apartment of a keyboard player named Beefheart that he knew well enough. He'd walked farther.

As the man drove the Aston Martin over to one of the opposite corners, it made a scraping noise against the pavement that lasted a few seconds, then stopped. He could see now that the Escort really had gotten the worst of it. The man left the Aston Martin idling and came back to where Dillon waited. He carried a container of lighter fluid in his hand.

"Let's not linger here," the man said. "You have a cigarette lighter?"

Dillon dug in his front pocket and held it out.

"No, you should have the pleasure," the man said. "But let's hurry, shall we?"

It had seemed like a hell of an idea when the guy suggested it: to burn up the car and report it stolen. The man handed Dillon the lighter fluid.

Dillon gave him a questioning look—what the hell was a guy like this doing with lighter fluid in his fucking expensive car?

"It's an excellent spot and stain remover," the man said.

"Right," Dillon said, taking the can.

He leaned into the Escort and squirted the fluid over the cloth interior and onto the soiled floor mats. He'd always liked the smell of lighter fluid. Once upon a time it had been a cheap kind of high, but that was baby stuff, and besides, it gave him a bitch of a headache.

He flicked the lighter at the edge of the driver's seat. It took a moment to catch, and he thought maybe it wasn't going to work and the guy was playing some kind of trick on him, and maybe this whole thing was a stupid idea. Then it caught, and there was a rush of heat in his face and he felt himself being jerked away from the car.

He and the man stood a good ten feet back, watching the interior of the car fill with smoke and yellow light. The sight of the burning car gave him an intense feeling of pleasure. In fact, he could feel an erection coming on in his jeans. Fire had never gotten to him like this before. He felt warmth on his face, and liked it. It made him feel alive, this fire. But he knew that if he stood there much longer, it would heat the studs on his lip and dry his eyes out so they felt like sandpaper.

Across the street, a light came on in one of the houses.

"Time to go," the man said, turning his back on Dillon. He moved toward the still-running Aston Martin.

Forgetting all about his earlier decision to get away from the guy, Dillon followed. He sank into the car's soft leather passenger seat. It was the kind of car he'd never imagined owning, but now that he was inside he could see the appeal of it. The seat seemed to mold itself to him, and the touch of the leather reminded him of his grandfather's pigskin bomber jacket that hung far back in the coat closet at his sister's place. He hadn't oiled the jacket down in a while—if he didn't get to it soon, it would begin to crack and eventually tear. Someday he would have a motorcycle, and he would want it then.

"I could use a drink," the man said. "You?"

"Nothing open now," Dillon said.

The man backed the car a few feet, and pulled out into the road. Dillon looked back through the rear window at the Escort, which now had smoke billowing out the open door and passenger window.

"That's going to be one fucking mess," Dillon said. But it wasn't going to be his mess.

"I was thinking about driving out to one of the casinos," the man said. "Twenty, thirty minutes."

"Yeah," Dillon said. "But if you try to put a hand on my dick, I'll fucking cut it off."

The man didn't move in his seat, but kept looking at the road. Dillon didn't like his smile.

"That won't be a problem," the man said.

Dillon was drunk, but not drunk enough to miss that the building through which Varick led him sometime after ten o'clock the next morning was a pile of shit. A collage of peeling paint and faded work-safety posters covered the walls; the windowless steel doors they passed were dented, some almost scratched bare of paint. The hallways smelled of chemicals and rubber and mold. He didn't like the rustling noises he heard from the building's recesses. He hated rats—truth was, he was scared as hell of rats—and this place looked like Rat Paradise. While he had definitely crashed in worse places, this didn't look like somewhere a guy in a thousanddollar suit would live. He tripped over a piece of PVC on the floor and fell into Varick, who pushed back at him, hard, like he didn't like it. Still, Varick smiled, his teeth—teeth that weren't so pretty as the rest of him—bright in the dusty light of the hallway.

"Steady there, my friend," he said.

"I still feel like I'm on the fucking ship," Dillon said, as they stepped into a freight elevator. The casino they'd gone to, The Golden Galleon, had a dance floor that spontaneously tipped every few minutes, causing the dancers to suddenly get close to each other. The band was crap but he had danced, while Varick sat by looking bored, because the women in the place had been fucking hotter than he could stand. When one sweetheart with a skirt like a cheerleader's and a halter-top that barely covered what Varick had called her "assets" came over to the table, he couldn't refuse her. He remembered guiding her to the edge of the stage and kissing her; her lip gloss was sticky and tasted like a strawberry Popsicle. Then one of her girlfriends had come over and laughingly pushed him away and the girl he'd kissed started dancing with her, ignoring him. He remembered feeling embarrassed and a little confused, but Varick waved him back over and bought him another drink.

Now, Varick closed the gate on the elevator and took Dillon's arm to lead him to the back. "Can't have you falling out," he said. "Safety first."

It freaked him out the way the guy was treating him like some kind of kid brother. Maybe he was a fag after all, and he was just moving slow.

"No fucking way," he said.

"Is there a problem?" Varick said.

Had he spoken aloud? Shit. He was too fucking drunk. He rubbed at the row of studs over his right eyebrow—one of the piercings was getting infected, he could tell. Fucking cheap-ass piercing parlor over in some bum-fucked Kentucky town. He should've gone to his regular place.

Varick was looking at him. Again, that smile, a smile that wasn't quite friendly, but might be mistaken for friendly at first glance.

Dillon didn't see any sense in answering. He was pretty sure the guy wasn't a fag. If he was, there was a four-inch pigsticker in his boot to let the guy know his true feelings about the matter.

When the elevator clanked to a stop, Varick opened the gate and gestured for Dillon to step out. A giant number 7 was painted on the opposite wall.

The institutional green paint job in the hallway was recent enough that Dillon could smell the fumes. Stopping in front of a door near the end of the hall, Varick flipped up the cover on the keypad beside it and pressed some numbers. When he was finished, he pushed open the door and stood aside.

"Make yourself comfortable, my friend," he said.

ABOUT THE AUTHOR

LAURA BENEDICT's short fiction has appeared in *Ellery Queen Mystery Magazine* and a number of anthologies. For the past decade she has worked as a freelance book reviewer for *The Grand Rapids Press* in Michigan and other newspapers. She lives in southern Illinois with her husband, Pinckney Benedict, and their two children. *Isabella Moon* is her first novel.